HUNTERS & GATHERERS

ROCK SAVAGE

STEM CELL PRESS

New York City

STEM CELL PRESS
A division of Stem Cell Duplicators
New York City

Copyright © 2025 by Rock Savage

Contact: rocksavage.ny@gmail.com

All rights reserved. No part of this publication may be reproduced, distributed, or transmitted in any form or by any means, including photocopying, recording, or other electronic or mechanical methods, without the prior written permission of the publisher, except as permitted by U.S. copyright law. For permission requests, contact rocksavage@armbreaker.com.

The story, names, characters, and incidents portrayed in this work are fictitious. No identification with actual persons (living or dead) is intended or should be inferred.

Library of Congress Catalog Card Number: 2025921647

ISBN: 979-8-218-82128-9

First Printing, December, 2025

Cover art & interior illustrations by Reece-Alexander Norris-Paterson

HUNTERS
&
GATHERERS

PART ONE: FRIDAY

CHAPTER ONE

LOSERS

BLEEDING AND STINGING from the hanging vines that lashed his arms and face, Trask hurtled after the dark shape scurrying over the jungle floor. Dark, glossy green foliage blurred past.

He was gaining on it. He heard the soft grunt of fear beneath the rustle of leaves and caught a glimpse of his quarry scrambling down the narrow animal trail before it disappeared again into the undergrowth. Spitting out a mouthful of leaves, the outcome of a glancing collision with a low branch, Trask cursed and threw himself into a reckless high gear. From behind him, the shouts of his teammates filtered through the deadening baffle of trees.

The elimination round was devised to test each team's ability to provide themselves with nourishment. Sustenance. Meat. If Trask failed to make the kill, it would all end here and now.

Little of the day's light made it down this far even in the mid-afternoon. The jungle was shrouded in a perpetual netherworld of semi-dark, through which layered rays made only scattered contact with the leaf-choked floor. But now, ahead, patchy streaks of bright color indicated a break in the overhanging canopy. Trask drew his weapon from his belt— a length of bamboo whittled to a razor-sharp point—and stuck it between his teeth.

He spied his prey again, now only yards ahead.

An instant later they burst into a clearing.

His feet sank into thick sludge. His quarry slipped and rolled, losing precious inches as its short legs churned to regain a footing.

Halfway through the glade, Trask pounced.

The pig squealed. He threw his arms around its middle, and they tumbled over each other, plowing a path through splattering mud. It squirmed in his grip, long snout twisting, short tusks seeking to rip his flesh.

He crushed it beneath him, immobilizing it, and they skidded to a stop.

Throwing an arm under the pig's throat, Trask jerked its head up and back. The pig, as if sensing its time had come, ceased its struggles. Its terrified gaze strained towards him, the whites of its eyes glistening, the dark irises red-rimmed with fear.

With his free hand, Trask plucked the sharpened stake from between his teeth, pressed the tip against his captive's throat—and looked into its eyes.

Hal charged into the clearing well ahead of the pack, his FX9 cinema camera's viewfinder sweeping over the muddy trail before pulling the action into frame and locking onto it with a jolt.

He moved in expertly, bringing the lens close to his subject's faces to capture the drama of the moment to the fullest: Man and beast, locked in the final deadly embrace; a scene played and replayed endlessly throughout time immemorial, spanning humanity's grim, scraping ascent over misty millennia from naked savagery upward, to scale the exalted summit of civilization and attain mastery over technological wonders beyond the dim imagining of their primitive ancestors.

The money shot.

But it was not to be. Beneath Trask's grip, the pig snuffled. It exhaled with a soft sigh—almost a sob.

It was too much for Trask.

He relaxed his hold, cast a furtive glance over his shoulder, then breathed into the animal's ear. "You owe me one, pal."

Trask's teammates stormed into the clearing, shouting in triumph at the sight of their prize in his clutches. But their jubilation changed to cries of dismay when it slipped from his embrace and scrambled for the trees.

"No!" Erika screeched. "Trask!"

Brad hurled his makeshift spear like a javelin. From behind him, Rashad and Dudley released theirs. Dudley's windmilled into Rashad's, knocking it askew. Brad's flew straight toward its target, but fell short, burying its tip in the soft earth just as the pig's hindquarters slipped out of reach. The spear's shaft pivoted upward to stand erect and quivering— then slowly toppled and collapsed into the weeds.

Brad watched the pig disappear into the brush, then clenched his fists and spun on Trask.

"Dude, what is your problem?"

Trask dragged himself to a sitting position. His army surplus fatigues and t-shirt were smeared with grime. He scraped a handful of viscous gunk from his hair and flicked it away.

"Sorry, man. Maybe we can still—"

A gunshot. All eyes turned upward to gaze through the overhanging foliage. A bright red flare arced lazily overhead. It reminded Trask of seeing the Challenger explosion on the History Channel as a kid.

"That's it," Dudley announced with bitter finality.

Brad glared. "Great. Nice going, Trask."

Trask's whole body ached. He got up, swatting rotten detritus from his clothes and trying without success to evade Hal's intrusive, in-your-face style camerawork. Exasperated, he snarled into the lens.

"Do you fucking mind?"

Hal didn't fucking mind, but he kept rolling. Trask shoved past him to thread his way through the accusing gauntlet of his team, their cold stares burning into him—except for Paula and Rashad, who fell in companionably to either side of him as he passed.

"There's still hope," Rashad said. "The others might've choked too."

"It's my fault," Paula said. "If we'd kept the tortoise—it was way bigger than that little pig."

"No, you were right. I'm pretty sure you were right."

"Anyway, we're not completely empty-handed. We still have the onions," Rashad said. He held up a handful of withered and unrecognizable vegetation.

Brad scowled.

They trudged out of the clearing and back down the trail the way they'd come, with Brad silent and fuming in front of them.

It was all over. They hadn't even made it through the qualifying round. And Trask had no illusions about who'd be the first to get the axe. Michelle's team would win, no question. And he'd already gotten into it with her before things had even got started.

"You better get on Michelle's good side fast," Rashad said, as if reading his mind.

"Why? What did I do to her?" As if he didn't know.

Rashad snorted. "Um, you called her a bitch, remember?"

"I did?"

"Yeah, and you were right," Paula said. "She is."

No argument there. But being right about that sure wasn't going to change anything.

And it wasn't just Trask that would be getting the boot. The winning team would choose three members each from both of the others for immediate banishment. That was how it worked. He hoped Rashad and Paula would survive the axe. He felt bad enough for whoever was going to pay for his screw up, but they were his friends. Even though they'd barely had time to get to know each other.

The ratings were in. The first episode was a disaster.

Bentley grimaced and shook his head, his dreams of a mansion in Beverly Hills dashed and swept under by the waves breaking outside.

He'd believed in the show. Oh, not in the creative sense—I mean, come on!—Hunters & Gatherers was a *reality* show for God's sake, and not a startlingly original one either—but commercially, financially, he'd believed. Others had succeeded before him with the same basic raw materials.

Where had he gone wrong? Had the whole reality business run its course? He should have picked up on that, if that was it. Reality was out of favor again, just like in the sixties. Overdone. Too much of a good thing. But that didn't make sense. What's ever been good about reality? People liked it anyway. Or at least, if they didn't, they still got their jollies watching other people suffer through it.

He threw the sheaf of printouts at the conference table and massaged his brow between thumb and fingers, then dropped his hands and pulled himself together at the click of the door handle.

Barry.

"Rob, the network—" Barry stopped to stare in puzzlement. "You doing something to your eyebrows now?"

"What?" Bentley reached for his brow, and in so doing, caught sight of his fingers—smeared black with ink.

"Goddamn printer." Pulling out a handkerchief, he rubbed at his face and demanded, "The network what?"

"People," Barry said. "Jean."

"She's coming?" A ray of hope. "When are we expecting her?"

Barry shrugged. "On the way. Oughta be here in ten minutes or so."

Bentley stood up from the table. "Who knows, it might actually help."

"Why not?" Barry said, following him down the hall to the front door. "People watch the news at least."

Bentley turned a sour look on him and studied him for a few seconds before stepping outside.

The combination of cool ocean breeze ruffling his unnaturally black hair and blazing hot sand under his bare feet instantly lifted Bentley's spirits. Things weren't all bad. The island was a paradise. He imagined himself the lord of his own private corner of the world, like Marlon Brando, savoring the tingling sensation of finely packed sand splaying his toes as he strolled across the wide white expanse, and suddenly felt fat. He pushed the thought away. The clean air was bracing, the view breathtaking.

And after fourteen dismal years of Bioforce and Nizoral, just a few days of walking barefoot in the scorching sand had wiped out all traces of the most infuriatingly tenacious case of athlete's foot ever to evolve on the microcosm of a man's sole. If nothing else…

Bentley expanded his chest, sucking in the oxygen-rich air. Beside him, Barry picked up the vibe, and Bentley put an arm around the younger man's shoulders.

"We'll show them. We won't be defeated. You'll see."

La Naufragée was one of the countless uninhabited volcanic islets that dotted the Indian Ocean seven hundred miles northeast of Madagascar, loosely administered by Victoria, the Seychelles capital on Mahé. Twelve hours, and half a world ahead of Los Angeles.

Behind them, the beach gave way to luxuriantly tropical triple canopy rainforest. It marched across the sloping terrain, crisscrossing ravines and lagoons, to turn steeply upward and climb the volcanic central peak almost to the summit. At the other end, rocky mountainsides dropped down to the sea in jagged basalt cliffs.

Ahead, shimmering in the afternoon sun, the blue waves rolled in to break on the glistening sand and dance away, leaving a rich scattering of sand dollars and clumps of deep green seaweed.

A short distance off, Michelle's party dragged driftwood and dry jungle undergrowth onto a growing pile that would soon become a crackling bonfire—a beacon for the other two parties yet to return.

Bentley frowned as Michelle's shouted orders drifted to his ears.

Having spent most of his professional career pretending to like people in the hope that they would pretend to like him in return—and that the masquerade, propped up by the network of mutual acquaintanceships and social interdependencies thus generated, would blossom into a status quo obligation to support his undertakings—Bentley was mystified by the uncanny skill displayed by those who took the opposite approach. These, like Michelle, antagonized those around them in the most galling way, yet in doing so managed to force them under a yoke of servitude against astonishingly little protest. He almost admired the ability—while reserving a measure of disdain for those who succumbed to such bullying.

And of course not all of them had. Trask certainly hadn't. There was another interesting character. A rebel. Bentley had been too in his younger days. It hadn't gotten him anywhere.

But it had gotten Trask somewhere, he remembered. Trask was a computer gamer. Or had been. A serious computer gamer. A whole different world. They had online tournaments that had become major, worldwide events. Trask had won a bunch of championship titles. And he'd been involved in some kind of hush-hush live-action game development project for a while too, before it mysteriously went dark, or claimed to have been.

He'd given it all up, though. And now here he was.

Just audible over the soft roll of the surf, the faint thump of distant rotor blades met Bentley's ears. He squinted up at the sky.

"Here they come," Barry said.

The helicopter sailed toward them, banked and angled across the shore to skim over the beach. Emblazoned on its side, the logo of the local network affiliate, *NEWS 5 SEYCHELLES,* stood out in crisp blue italics. They trotted forward to meet it as it settled into its own shadow in the sand.

Bentley ushered Jean into the bungalow's brightly lit office-slash-conference room and Barry closed the door behind them.

A long desk against one wall held a server, the printer, and a short-wave radio telephone setup—their only means of communication with the mainland. It was connected by some arrangement to a transceiver on Ste. Catherine that relayed calls to Mahé over the still primitive but functional cellular network between the outer islands.

Bentley was jovial. "Glad to have the extra push," he said. "Not that we need it. Just the first episode, after all."

"Yeah, and it sucked," Jean countered, looking about the room with disapproval. "You saw the ratings."

"Things'll pick up. Right, Barry?"

"You bet they will," Barry said, gratified to be called upon. "It's an exciting concept. The first episode is just backstory. Now that we got the expository material out of the way, we're ready to get to the meat of the story. Hunters and Gather—"

Jean cut him off. "You mean 'Punters and Blatherers'? That's what USA Today called it. Funny, huh?" Nobody laughed. "You tanked bigtime."

"We got a rough start," Bentley conceded. He could see Jean rankled at the assignment. It was a time-honored practice, bolstering a non-starter's ratings by planting a teaser thinly disguised as a news item. Surprisingly, the incongruousness of it didn't seem to register much with audiences—and what did that tell you about the news in general? But as a creative executive, Jean clearly regarded this kind of salvage operation as beneath her.

"Where's Grant?" she said. "We'll do some staged coverage, see if we can pump some life into this crowbait. Network's promising something huge for next week. Any idea what that might be?"

Flustered, Bentley looked to his writer for help. "Barry'll come up with something, he's a great writer, one of the best. It's his concept," he added, demonstrating his esteem with a warm pat on Barry's shoulder.

Jean turned on Barry. "Well?"

"Offhand, I'm thinking more run and jump situations," Barry began. "It's a natural given the setting and, you know, attire."

Bentley took the inspiration and ran with it. "Great! Maybe even a little partial nudity. Here and there, a dropped—something or other, in the water—good, clean, tasteful, but—"

"When I said 'huge', I wasn't talking about your little coeds' anatomy. The network wants action."

Bentley was recovering his steam. "We'll come up with something.

You want huge, you'll get it. We'll brainstorm, do a few interviews. It'll be fun. Glad you're here to help out."

"Well I'm not. They throw me one more bullshit fluff piece I'm jumping to cable. Can I have a drink? Where the hell is Grant?"

Bentley turned to Barry. "Go get Grant." He winked at Jean as Barry hurried out. "What'll you have?"

"Martini. And where's Trask?"

"Trask?" Surprised.

"They liked *him*. Don't ask me why."

"Look at her," Paula said.

Michelle stood up, slapping the sand from her long, smooth, bare legs and strolled towards them, one hand behind her back, obviously hiding something. They tried to brush past, but Michelle was on them like wet leaves.

"Were you *lost?*" she taunted. "Oh, wait, I think that's another show."

Trask stopped in front of her, his face still smeared with pale gunk, now dried and cracking like the Mona Lisa. Michelle's smile broadened.

"Doing a little solo mud wrestling?"

"Lay off, Michelle," Paula said. Michelle ignored her.

The others around the campfire watched with amused interest. Noticing Rashad clutching his wild onions self-consciously, a few laughed.

Michelle's brow furrowed in mock pity. "Aww, is that all you got?" Adopting an air of innocent curiosity, she added, "What is it?"

"Rashad thinks they're onions," Dudley muttered. "Nobody else does."

Michelle laughed out loud. "You poor things. You must be starving!" Swinging her hand around from behind her back, she said, "How 'bout some—pork!"

She thrust the severed head of a wild pig under Paula's nose, the coarse black fur matted with blood. Paula gasped and shrank away.

"Screw you," she breathed.

Even Michelle's own party looked embarrassed. Nils, the other Team Captain, waved the newcomers over. "Hey guys, don't take it so hard. Have a seat. We don't have any s'mores, but we got plenty of fish."

And pork chops. Michelle continued to gloat. When they walked past her, Trask murmured, "Don't be a bitch, Michelle."

Rashad heard him. "See?" he said.

"You're right! Now I remember," Trask said. He slapped his forehead, jarring loose a few flakes of crusted muck. They sprinkled into Michelle's cleavage.

She followed him with her eyes, glowering. "Pack your bags, Trask."

"We'll see."

The relaxed, party atmosphere that preceded the latecomers' arrival had dissipated. The bonfire died down to a heap of crackling embers. A few contestants got up to fetch more kindling before it went out altogether.

Looking around for somebody else to pick on, Michelle spotted a couple under a blanket a little ways off.

"Hey, Janet," Michelle said, "Isn't this like the third guy you've made out with today? Who is it this time? Tony?"

The blanket fell away, exposing the pair. They pried their lips off each other and sat up.

"Yo," Tony replied.

Janet smirked. "How do I know who to vote off if I don't know who I like?"

Trask looked around for Jeremy, expecting trouble, and spotted him up by the mess hall, only now making his way toward the beach, drying his hair with a bath towel.

Trask and Paula shared a look. Paula didn't like Janet much either. Bimbo starlet type. Gorgeous, shameless, reeking of the obnoxious self-confidence of the beautiful but dumb.

Janet saw Jeremy coming and stood up, and Tony released her with an exaggerated show of disappointment. She threw a mischievous smile at him over her shoulder and moved to the fire to sit beside Paula.

"Slut," Paula said.

"Prude." Janet's vacant smile challenged her to escalate, but Paula didn't take the bait.

The campfire was more for the sake of atmosphere than any practical considerations. They didn't need to cook their own food. Meals were still served in the mess hall, prepared by Catering in a kitchen supplied by a walk-in pantry and freezer. In fact, Trask wouldn't have been surprised if they *did* have s'mores. It was all pretty fake. Everyone knew they weren't really expected to survive on seaweed, fish and the tiny crabs that skittered sideways over the beach—supplemented by the occasional scrawny rat or wild pig. Everyone on the show, that is. The home audience was a different matter. They must believe, in the interests of that most basic of human necessities, their own entertainment. The roaring fire helped make that possible while augmenting the experience both aesthetically and symbolically. In other words, it was an inexpensive mood-establishing gimmick for this afternoon's shoot. Either way, it was Trask's big sendoff, he had no doubt, despite his pointless show of defiance to Michelle.

There were twenty-four contestants in all. All twenty-something, most scantily clad, the men in shorts and t-shirts or Waikiki-style buttondowns—unbuttoned to reveal tanned and glistening bare chests; the women also in shorts, also in t-shirts and/or bikini tops. All generically handsome or superficially beautiful—unexcitingly attractive in the way you'd expect considering they'd all been chosen to attract a general audience. Not Trask's usual kind of crowd. But it wasn't that he particularly disliked them (except maybe for Michelle). Surprisingly, a lot of them seemed okay. They were stereotypes mostly, but then he had to assume they—and the show's producers—thought he was too. It was just hard, he finally had to admit to himself, facing them now—looking like shit, covered in shit and—why mince words?—disgrace—as a loser. A shit-faced loser.

Kind of a new experience.

But he was up for it and getting the hang of it.

CHAPTER TWO

SHOOT

AS THE WRITER it shouldn't have been Barry's job, but on paper he was Assistant Director, so he'd coached everyone for the segment. Acknowledging that you had writers involved in a "reality" show would be a break with tradition amounting to betrayal, seized upon by the viewers as evidence that the integrity of the show was compromised. Never mind that integrity wasn't part of the synopsis, and that someone had to come up with the various scenarios and the host's patter (though Grant insisted he was just as capable as Barry, and in fact was).

After comparing the lists of the day's spoils, Barry had assembled the Team Captains. They'd all caught some fish and crabs, Nils's team had brought down a few small birds. There were coconuts, and what one of Trask's teammates insisted were onions, which everyone doubted, but it didn't make any difference. Michelle's team was the clear winner, the pig clinched it.

Earlier, Jean had communicated to Barry her strong hope that Trask would survive the elimination, making it clear he was expected to pass on this hope to Michelle. So Barry held her back after telling the guys to take their places around the fire. Like everyone else, Barry was intimidated by Michelle, and wasn't as forceful as he might have been otherwise. He just said, "Rob and Jean really like Trask. He went over really well last night."

Michelle didn't reply, only stared at him, waiting.

"They liked you, too. We consider both of you invaluable, if you know what I mean."

"I understand," Michelle said, and stalked away.

Having performed his duties as he saw them, Barry glanced at his watch. It was almost time. Hal and Fred were performing final operational checks on their camera rigs. Howard, the production's Best Boy, doubled as a camera operator against union regulations. He lacked the expertise to operate a professional handheld camera, but as a lighting tech he knew how to turn things on and off. He'd be going for coverage with a tripod-mounted Canon that Hal had positioned off to the side.

Barry trudged through the sand to fetch Bentley from his bungalow.

The campfire segment was the standard "banishment" scene, in which a number of aspiring actors' and actresses' hopes would be utterly dashed by their being declared unworthy to continue in their respective roles of gritty he-man and alluring ball-breaker. There was some consolation, though. By being banished, they were essentially given an opportunity to audition indirectly for bit parts as pathetic losers and vindictive harpies by their reactions; characters which, if played well, could open up possibilities for future careers in front of a camera.

With Barry and Jean beside him, Bentley stood behind the stationary camera. The viewfinder showed a line of faces stretching away from the camera, and a wealth of human interest—for anyone who could be persuaded to care.

"Roll camera," he directed.

Hal said, "Rolling," and was echoed by Fred and Howard.

"Action."

Into the bonfire's light stepped a dashing, beachwear-clad media personality—Grant. The host. Blond, Nordic, athletically fortyish, his grave demeanor offset by an eager charm, he confronted Trask and his teammates, flashed a rueful smile, then turned to the victors.

"Michelle. Nils." Solemn pause. "Trask." A longer pause. Then, seemingly off the top of his head:

"The time has come. Without enmity or malice, but with fairness and firmness, the die has been cast, the choices made. We await the verdict."

Grant had hoped for some reaction from Trask, but there was none. Concealing his disappointment expertly, he went on. "Trask, the First Team has won the right to select three of your members for expulsion from the island. Do you accept their decision as final and irrevocable?"

Trask sighed. He shook his head. "Yeah."

Yeah. Grant paused, hoping for more, but it looked like that was the extent of Trask's feelings on the subject. What in the world did the audience see in this guy? He'd heard Trask had been a hit with the first episode's handful of viewers, but couldn't for the life of him figure out why. It sure as hell couldn't be his vocabulary.

He turned back to Michelle. "Captain."

He extended his open palm toward her. In it were six small blue flowers.

"These blossoms are native to the island. Their pistils are ripe with nectar—" The line was a little ponderous in Grant's opinion, and he wondered if the average viewer even knew what a pistil was (*he* hadn't, until Barry had told him). So he pointed at it. And with sudden inspiration, he ad-libbed, "—glistening with the sweet dew of life." He brushed a fingertip across the soft, spiny arrangement, then lifted it to his mouth. His lips parted, he brought his finger to his tongue, then stopped, and held it upraised before him instead. As if in warning.

"Yet for us, its nectar is deadly poison."

It seemed to go over. There were a few gasps. One from off-camera. Barry, undoubtedly miffed at the departure from his scripted lines.

"Take them," Grant continued, handing them to Michelle, "and give one to each of those destined for banishment." Michelle nodded. Grant stepped back, his turn before the cameras over for now.

Keeping his lens trained on Michelle's face, Hal took a step back to take up a position behind Trask. From there, his movements paralleled hers in a series of two-shots as she moved down the line.

Her eyes played over the losers. She advanced on Paula, frowning with just a touch of unconcealed dislike.

Paula visibly steeled herself for the coming blow—but Michelle suddenly turned and thrust the flower instead at the stunning blonde to Paula's right. Amber.

Amber's eyes instantly brimmed with tears. She stared at the poisonous offering with a stricken expression, then closed her eyes.

Michelle watched with forced patience as twin teardrops squeezed from between Amber's closed lids and rolled down her reddening cheeks. Nobody spoke or moved.

The tears hung quivering from her chin. She sniffed, suppressing a whimper, and they dropped away.

She took a deep breath through her mouth and let it out.

She opened her eyes wide.

Wider.

And screamed like a score of white-hot needles had just been shoved into her fingertips.

Michelle practically jumped out of her skin. Everyone else gasped and recoiled.

It wasn't just a scream—it was one of those bloodcurdling, hands-flying-up-to-claw-at-her-temples-in-an-ecstasy-of-terror screams. And she wasn't screaming at Michelle—she was looking at the treeline behind her.

And then Hal said, "What the…!" and jostled Amber aside to shove past both of them. "Get down!" he yelled. Contestants scattered. The nearest ducked. Hal hurdled them, landed in a braced kneeling position in the sand, camera trained on—

Nothing. There was nothing there.

But there *had* been, they could all see that. Because where it had been, the tall mangroves trembled in the wake of something big fleeing into the jungle. Hal held on them for twenty seconds. Just as he lowered his camera, there was a flash in the middle distance—as if someone out in the jungle had taken a picture with a flashbulb. With a muttered curse, he raised the camera again, but it was too late.

When Amber finally calmed down enough to give a semi-coherent account of what she'd seen, she still wasn't much help. Something had stepped out of the trees. Her screaming had caused it to dive back into them. She hadn't caught a lot of detail. Under repeated questioning it became clear that, intellectually, Amber just wasn't up to the task of putting into words what she'd seen. It became a guessing game, with leading questions compromising the reliability of the whole account.

According to Amber, whatever it was was almost as tall as the trees at the jungle's edge. That would make it maybe twelve feet. It walked on two legs. Its hands had "lots and lots of fingers." Big, round, red eyes. No hair—instead it had whiskery thingies. Tendrils, someone suggested. Uh-huh.

Everyone was shaken. But some were skeptical. They knew the network had sent Jean to try to pump up the show. They'd picked up on the fact that the ratings had been lousy.

Could this be some kind of gimmick? Did they put Amber up to it?—or was she in on it from the beginning? She seemed like she was a pretty good actress. That scream was pro-quality Jamie Lee Curtis stuff.

"You saw the trees," Rashad said. "There was something there." But suspicion had set in. Easy enough to fake that part.

Bentley was talking to the shoot's two-man security team. After they trotted away he announced it was probably a bear or something, and Security was checking the area. He didn't want to lose his light, and asked for everyone's cooperation in getting back to work.

Grant decided as the host it was time to set a brave example. He looked around. Fred and Hal were still shooting. They'd transitioned smoothly to documentary mode with the fluidity gained in the last few days' experience working a reality shoot.

Yes, it was time for people to see what Grant was capable of in a crunch. He strode forward and took his place beside Bentley.

"Expect the unexpected." Grant's rich tenor commanded attention. Taking his cue, Bentley stepped aside.

"Isn't that what a show like ours is all about?" Grant asked. His audience understood it was a rhetorical question and held their silence.

"In the unexpected lies truth. It's through our unguarded, spontaneous response to the unexpected that we reveal our true selves. Our true courage, our true desires, our strengths and fears, all those things that make us what we are. Some may say a show like Hunters and Gatherers is a mere mindless entertainment, no more. But, my friends, it is much, much more. It is a journey of discovery in which we hope to uncover our true nature, the very essence of what it is that makes you you and me me—"

Grant balked, thrown by the unexpectedly awkward phrasing. No matter—he'd come up with something and cut it in later.

"We welcome the unexpected. We invite it, as the natural complement to the trials we have come here voluntarily to undergo—in the ultimate quest, though it be gained at great cost, for the triumph of the human spirit."

Grant looked to Bentley, respectfully relinquishing command to his superior officer.

Bentley shook himself out of his Grant-induced trance. "Uh, yeah, let's—okay, let's back up to where Grant says whatever it was, before Amber screams. Get some overlap."

He stopped to ponder, then, after a whispered conference with Jean and Barry, turned to Hal. "We're keeping all that, though, the scream and the whatever." He gave Amber an appreciative nod. "Very nice. Excellent performance."

A few contestants exchanged knowing glances at that.

Everyone got back in their places. Grant ran over his lines in fast forward. " '…native to the…ripe with nectar…'—whatever I said about 'deadly', okay, got it."

"Roll camera," Bentley said.

Grant handed Michelle the now somewhat bruised-looking flowers. "Um, here, give one to each of the…uh, those destined for banishment."

Dispensing with the previous take's strivings for suspense, Michelle plopped a flower without ceremony into Amber's already outstretched palm. Amber didn't bother to conceal her relief.

Michelle moved over to stand before Brad—then jabbed the flower at Dudley instead.

Dudley was caught completely off-guard. "Awww…" he whined. Accepting his banishment like the high school nerd accepts his ritual after-school beating by the class bullies, he hung his head as Michelle moved on down the line.

To stop before Trask.

Off-camera, Jean nudged Bentley. Bentley made a helpless gesture and kept silent.

The flower in Michelle's hand floated toward Trask. His eyes were locked on hers as he reached for it, and when she dropped it, he missed. Hal's camera followed its descent. It landed on Michelle's bare foot. She grimaced and stooped to retrieve it, and when she straightened back up Trask was smiling.

"Sorry. Guess I'm not good at catching stuff," he said. He took the flower, pinched off the pistil, stuck it in his mouth and sucked out the nectar with a loud slurp.

"Yum."

The other contestants were horrified.

"Are you crazy?" Michelle yelled.

Rashad caught Paula's eye and she grinned back.

"I've been munching on these little fuckers all day," Trask said. "Must be a real slow-acting poison. Try one, maybe it'll work better for you," he offered.

"Cut," Bentley said. Jean tittered.

Fuming, Grant looked to Bentley for support, but Bentley was chuckling along with Jean.

"Rob. Come on!" Grant protested. "He screwed up my whole thing about—"

"Don't worry about it, Grant, it was a great take."

"I love it!" Jean said. "It's real. It's offbeat. Just what the show needs." Leaving Grant to seethe in silence at the betrayal, she drew Bentley out of earshot of the contestants.

"You can't let him go," she said.

"What can I do? Rules are rules, he got voted off."

"So re-shoot it tomorrow. Who's gonna know?"

"It's—I'm worried about a lot of improvising. We have a plan."

"Rob, I'm right and you know it."

"But Michelle…"

Jean was almost amused. "You're hopeless," she said. "I'll deal with Michelle, whose show is it anyway?"

They made it through the shoot without further incident. After banishing three members of each of the other teams, Michelle was obliged to give up two of her own to bring the others up to fighting strength. They were now three groups of six.

They lingered around the fire, welcoming new teammates, saying their goodbyes to those who would be leaving. The latter still had work to do before their final dismissal. Reaction interviews, to be edited into montages with the audio serving as sentimental voiceover to shots sifted from earlier triumphs and failures. Following dinner, they'd be transported to Mahé and hotel rooms in Victoria. After a night's reflection on their fates they'd catch the Air Seychelles flight to Frankfurt, followed by a six-hour red-eye to New York.

They'd be home in two days.

Bentley waved Trask over and put an arm around his shoulder as they headed for the bungalow. Grant and Michelle stared after them.

"Let's pack it up," Hal said. He cast an uneasy glance at the treeline as the crew began winding cables and packing up the equipment. It was getting dark.

~~~~~~~~~~~~~~~~~~~~~~~~~~~~~~~~

Trask was pretty uncomfortable with the whole idea, and it didn't go well. Jean hovered in the background smoking through most of it, leaving Bentley to do the dirty work.

"It's only television. We'll re-shoot the scene, who's gonna know?" Bentley said. "Me and Jean'll handle Michelle, she'll play along. We have ways." He winked.

Trask forced a half-smile, but cast a longing glance at the door. "I'd feel like a fraud," he said. "I couldn't be myself."

"Trask! You're thinking of it all wrong. Forget how you feel. You gotta be a performer. Look at all the rest of them. You're practically the only one that's not an actor."

"Who's an actor?" Trask was genuinely surprised.

"Well, Lance for one. Heather, for another."

"Really? She said she was a librarian."

"That's right, she did. Beverly, Janet. Well, some of them are models, like Jeremy and Tony. But let's see, Fredo, even Brad's an actor, if you can believe it."

"Jeremy's not an advertising guy?"

"Only when the cameras are rolling."

"So the whole thing really is fake."

"Fake! Of course it is," Bentley said, with cheerful enthusiasm, as if seeing it in this new light was going to change Trask's mind. "It's just entertainment. Like we'd really bring all of you out here to the middle of nowhere just to watch you starve! Where's the fun in that?"

He frowned, glanced at Jean.

Jean stared back at him, pondering. "No," she said.

"Starving's no fun. It's boring," Bentley agreed. "People are fun. Personalities, relationships. Who can resist that? And you've got personality, my friend."

"I don't know," Trask said, feeling the smallness of his personality with a dull acuteness. He wasn't about to go along with it, but he hated being a refusenik. He'd rather try to talk them out of it. "I mean, how would everybody else take it? I'd be like the teacher's pet. It'd be unnatural, my teachers always hated me."
~~~~~~~~~~~~~~~~~~~~~~~~~~~~~~~~

"The teachers aren't grading your work," Bentley said. "The folks at home are, and they're giving you straight A's. You can't flunk out."

"But I did. The rules were pretty clear."

"But Michelle didn't have to choose you. In fact she was told not to."

Oh, that made it better. God, they'd tried to rig the whole thing already. "You told her that?"

"Well, Barry did..." Bentley said, like maybe he'd had nothing to do with it.

It was getting easier to say no. Trask shook his head.

Bentley looked at Jean. She shook her head too.

It was pretty stupid of him that he hadn't figured out what was going on. Actors. It was no more real than what he'd thought he was getting away from. Another virtual competition with virtual opponents.

Bentley looked like he might cry. It was probably just an act, but Trask really had to get out of there just in case. He stuck out his hand.

"I better get my stuff together."

Bentley shook his hand limply. Jean gave him a tight smile without extending her hand. Trask paused at the door.

"What about Paula?"

"Paula?" Bentley said, his mind already elsewhere.

"The one with the red hair. She an actress too?"

"Paula... No. Works in a hospital or something."

Jean wasn't as upset as Bentley'd been afraid she would be. "Don't take it too hard, Rob," she said. "It's a blow, but it's survivable. The stuff from earlier looked great, especially with Michelle and the pig. The struggling, the squealing—both of them!—dirt flying everywhere. Nice camerawork too. Hal's good." She opened the door, paused and smiled.

"God! Who would have thought one of those skinny things could hold that much blood. But I think we can get away with it. After all, they show that kind of shit on PBS day in and day out. Violence, killing. Blood is good. They know it. We know it. And now we've got our own." She took Bentley's arm. "Your punters came through this time."

They stepped outside. Bentley again felt his spirits rise. Jean was really something, a true creative executive, not one of those imagination-impaired bean-counting suits. A fellow traveler. He felt like they'd really hit it off. Nothing wrong with having another powerful network executive in your corner. Good for now, good for future enterprises too.

They strolled arm in arm out onto the beach.

CHAPTER THREE

BORING

SNORLOK'S EYES CAUGHT a glint of small movement and sharpened.

A spinning, disk-shaped object hit the floor and flattened against it with an accelerating whirr. A fastener of some sort. With a metallic plunk, its counterpart skipped out from under the engine and rolled away.

A grunt of annoyance told Snorlok he had found his father.

He was about to retrieve the lug, but then wondered if, after all, he wasn't supposed to be here. He kept still.

The engine room was vast. He felt dwarfed by its immensity, awed by the harsh beauty and power of the machinery, its throbbing hiss and hum. But the engine was silent now, its intricate network of cables, hoses and gauges seeming to sag with a forlorn realization of their own inertness.

The enormous chassis spanned the length of the chamber, its furthermost portion lost in darkness far down at the other end. An array of pneumatic braces and twisted cable held it suspended above the gray resin floor.

Accompanied by groans of exertion, metal squeaked and scraped against metal. With a dull clunk, a large mechanical brace slid out from under the engine on a slick trail of lubricant.

A cluster of sinuous tentacles snaked out from beneath the chassis—thick loops of tough-skinned flesh, unraveling from a sinewy, grease-covered limb. Coiling around the first small connector, they dragged it under the engine.

After more squeaking and a final grunt, a deep voice rumbled an order.

Snorlok flinched. His presence was already discovered.

Obediently, he padded toward the wall to fetch the second fastener. After a few moments' hunting, feeling Strindlak's glowering impatience boring into him, Snorlok located it and scooped it up in a fist-like cluster of tentacles similar to his father's.

Returning, he dropped it into Strindlak's waiting tentacles. They disappeared beneath the engine. After much huffing and scraping, Strindlak emitted a grunt of satisfaction.

Stooping to peer beneath the machine, Snorlok glimpsed Strindlak's mammoth pods, tentacles splayed out like tree roots, shuffling away into the dark deeps of the chamber.

As he watched, a glob of clotted fluid dropped from the just-installed brace into a glossy puddle on the floor beneath.

Snorlok wondered how much longer the repairs would take. He knew his father well enough to know Strindlak lacked the required temperament and concentrational abilities for lengthy consultation of the ship's manuals. In fact, Snorlok guessed he hadn't even looked at them. In the worst case, it could become a trial and error business with ultimate success depending on simple common-sense winning out against all odds over genuine knowledge.

They could find themselves stranded here until help arrived. If it ever did.

From down the chamber came a light click.

Father was powering up the engine.

Snorlok straightened up and stepped back. His usual apprehension in the presence of the mighty engine seeped back at the sound of its coming again to life—a deep thrumming that resonated throughout the chamber, charging the air itself with bristling electricity.

From beneath the chassis came a sharp report, followed by an angry hiss of expanding vapor. Snorlok stooped again to peer along the underside of the carriage—just in time to see a fireball erupt from the belly of the engine and slam the defective brace to the metal floor. Jets of igniting gases pinned it there.

Snorlok jumped back up, poised to flee. Strindlak came running from the far end of the chamber, cursing. The engine ground to a halt. The deep thrumming died with a low, choking moan. Black smoke rolled over the floor.

Bellowing in frustration, Strindlak ordered Snorlok from the room. As if the misfiring had been his doing.

Out in the dimly lit corridor, his pod tentacles scuffing over the soft-composition flooring, Snorlok plodded in the direction of the quarters he shared with his siblings.

Once there, of course, he'd just end up complaining to Ropsnag and the twins. What else was there to do? They'd pass the time grumbling, go to sleep, and wake up to grumble away another interminable cycle.

It was boring.

Snorlok sighed. It wouldn't be so bad if only—

He stopped and turned.

The red gleam of the light strips struck a rose-hued spackling of iridescence over the section of corridor in which he stood. The portal he'd only just passed reflected a deep crimson from its glossy black surface.

There was no one around. And there wouldn't be anytime soon. Strindlak's repairs had suffered another major setback. And Mother was where she always was.

He stood gazing at the portal. Weighing the risks.

Father would be furious, which was not something to be taken lightly. It was forbidden. In no uncertain terms, and especially now. But it was tempting.

Just to see. Just once.

They'd never find out.

Meals were prepared by the show's caterer, Evans, and served buffet style in the mess hall next door to Bentley's bungalow. It was simple chuckwagon fare—tonight they had barbecued beef patties with onions and pickles, beans, cornbread and potato salad.

Contestants straggled in. Rashad loaded up a plate and took his place one seat away from Paula.

The mess hall offered a measure of relief from the prying lenses of the cameras. There wasn't supposed to be a mess hall, after all, so there was no point shooting in it.

Everyone glanced up at Trask's entrance. They'd all seen Bentley and the network executive walking him over to the bungalow after the shoot. Trask grabbed some cornbread and took the seat Rashad had saved for him next to Paula.

"So, what happened with Bentley?" Rashad said.

Michelle's eyes bored into Trask. He shifted uncomfortably.

"Nah, it wasn't anything," he said. It wasn't enough. He went on, before anyone else could pick up the line of questioning, "I guess, you know, since I was the team leader. He just wanted to—for me to tell you, Dudley—" he looked at Dudley, then Amber, "and Amber, you know, you did a great job, both of you. It was a pleasure having you on the show. That kind of thing." He added quietly, "I'm really sorry, Dudley."

Dudley was touched. "Aww, that's okay, Trask."

"No hard feelings, Dudley," Michelle said. Maybe she didn't mean it that way, but it came off as sneering. Unable to face her, Dudley picked up his knife and fork and took out his frustrations on his beef patty instead.

Last in line, Lance and Vince found a couple of empty chairs. One by one, they'd all been filled.

All but three.

Everyone looked around, checking each other off. Michelle frowned. "Janet."

After a moment, Paula said, "Tony."

Sound of a toilet flushing. The bathroom door opened.

"Tony, wash your hands," Michelle ordered.

Tony returned to the bathroom. Raising her voice over the sound of the running faucet, Michelle said, "Tony, where's Janet?"

"What? I don't know," came his annoyed reply.

"Jeremy's gone," Rashad said.

The faucet shut off abruptly. Tony charged out of the bathroom, shaking water from his hands. "Janet's with Jeremy? That asshole, I knew it!" He stormed outside.

Michelle grimaced. "Paula's right, she is a slut."

Lance had barely started on his supper. He slapped his napkin down on the table, shoved his chair back as he rose, and stomped out after Tony, slamming the door behind him.

"I wouldn't worry about it," Nils said.

"Who's worried?" Michelle replied. "She's a big girl." But she glanced over at Amber when she said it, and everyone else did too. It seemed like Amber was losing it in some weird way. Sitting there staring at nothing with a glassy, faraway look. Suddenly no one doubted that Amber had seen something out there. What kind of large animal could there be on an island this small? Bentley had mentioned bears. What a joke.

Trask stood up. Rashad followed his lead, then Brad, smacking his lips and grumbling at the same time around a mouthful of cornbread.

Fredo groaned. "Oh, man. Come on. They're grown-ups. They don't need no chaperones, man."

"Yeah, right?" Brad said. He sat back down.

Outside, Tony was shouting Janet's name. He must have checked the dormitory. That didn't leave too many other possibilities aside from the jungle. In a huskier, threatening voice, he yelled, "Jerrrremy!"

They heard Lance, trying to talk Tony down. And then someone else.

"What's going on?"

"Oh, hey, Grant. Nothing, just, looking for Janet and Jeremy. Thought maybe they're out here somewhere."

"In the jungle? Doesn't seem like a good idea."

Grant opened the door. "Why don't you come back inside and finish your dinner? If they don't show up soon, we'll sic Security on them. Have them arrested," he joked. Esha and Beverly were with him, fresh from their post-banishment debriefings. Lance followed them in. A second later Tony returned, looking pissed. He crossed the room and slumped into the sofa, where he proceeded to pout with all the magnetic appeal a young menswear model could muster. A couple of the girls gazed at him, mesmerized.

"Hey, gang," Grant said as Lance took his seat and began eating. "Sorry to interrupt. We still need a couple of interviews. Amber, you, and you, Trask. Only take about ten minutes each. Who wants to go first?"

Trask was already standing anyway. "I'll go first."

Grant nodded. "Stan'll be taking you guys over to Saint Katy at eight. Should give you plenty of time to get everything together. No rush."

Trask followed him to the door.

Grant stopped and turned. "Oh. I forgot, Jean said there's room for two on the chopper if any of you want to."

Amber looked up hopefully, and Esha jumped up and raised her hands. "Okay," Grant said, "you two can fly. Ten minutes, Amber, all right?"

She nodded. Grant closed the door.

"Aww," Dudley said, pouting. "What a gyp."

Michelle gazed at him with undisguised contempt.

Tony, unable to restrain himself, jumped up from the sofa and stomped back outside.

<center>~~~~~~~~~~~~~~~~~~~~~~~~~~~~~~</center>

Something rustled in the undergrowth—a scattering of decayed vegetation, the snap of a breaking twig. The crunch of leaves crushed beneath some shifting weight.

Animal grunts. A soft moan.

"Oh, Janet…"

They lay grappling at each other on the loamy bed of the jungle floor. Janet guided Jeremy's hand upward with her own to grope under her shirt. Their lips locked in a wet kiss. Her fingers played over the hard curve of his buttocks, squeezed, and slid across his hips toward the front of his jeans.

He kissed her harder and she moaned again, thrusting her hips against his with a rhythmic, pumping motion.

Things were definitely getting into high gear.

Panting in her ear in short, shallow breaths, he rolled over on top of her and tugged at her shirt. She wriggled out of it and pulled him close again. With his open palm he caressed her full, round breast in a smooth circular motion, lightly brushing and teasing her distended—

She stiffened at a low fluttering sound—followed by a drawn-out baritone blat, like pressurized gas escaping through a moist orifice.

She pushed away from him, squinted at his face, silvery and one-dimensional in the darkness.

"Let's not get that intimate, okay?"

"It wasn't me," Jeremy said with wounded honor. "I thought it was you."

She peered at him. "You sure?"

"Honest, babe."

After a moment's hesitation she said, "Okay," and drew him close again. They quickly began to recapture the magic. Then just as quickly broke off again and sat up.

"Oh—my—God," she said, covering her nose and mouth.

Jeremy blew out through pursed lips. "Holy—!"

Janet shoved him away. "You liar!"

"I swear." He sounded worried. "It wasn't me," he added, lowering his voice.

They froze.

Something had moved in the trees up ahead.

"What was that?" Janet said, her voice fearful. Gesturing for quiet, Jeremy cocked his head to listen. Another movement. A creaking sound, like someone shifting their weight to one leg—preparing to take another step.

Janet's eyes were bright with rising panic.

Jeremy seemed to relax, and then he gave Janet a bad start by saying out loud, "Some asshole's fooling around."

Janet shushed him, but he clambered to his feet. Crouching, he crept in the direction the sound had come from. Janet rose and tiptoed after him.

They stopped to listen. Nothing.

"Who's there?" Jeremy said.

There was no answer, but a furtive rustling just ahead betrayed a presence. Jeremy turned to Janet with a sardonic smile. "Tony. It's—"

"Jerrrrremy!"

It was Tony, but his voice was faint, coming from far away. From down at the camp.

In the few steps they'd taken, the jungle seemed to have closed in around them, blotting out what little was left of the day's light. It was dark as the depths of the sea under all the trees. Jeremy started forward again, hyperalert. Janet followed, clinging to his waist.

"Jeremy, let's just go," she pleaded, but Jeremy was afraid of turning his back on whatever it was that was there, maybe just a few yards or feet in front of them.

It was quiet up ahead now, but the brooding silence seemed to conceal a shadowy massiveness. Jeremy ducked hanging vines and eased branches aside as he advanced, slow step by slow step, feeling the pull of Janet's reluctance at his back.

They moved ahead another inch and hit some obstruction. A knot of vines, choking low-hanging branches.

Jeremy peered at the tangle of dusky growth. Behind it loomed a deeper darkness his eyes couldn't penetrate. He reached out, trying to feel his way through inky blackness.

Arm outstretched before him, fingers spread wide, his fingertips stole forward.

He recoiled and stopped dead in his tracks with a gasp. Janet's trembling fingers gnawed at his upper arm like chattering teeth.

He'd touched something solid. It felt moist. Clammy.

He stared hard, squinting. He could make out a hint of mottled coloration. It had to be some kind of tree—what else could it be? Not like all the others around them, but still, just a tree. The jungle was full of trees. That's what jungles were. A bunch of trees.

He gave it another tentative poke.

Its bark had a fleshy, spongy feel. He jerked his fingers away again.

He wasn't sure, but it seemed like when he had touched it, something higher up above their heads had made a sound. Like a sigh.

Almost against his will, he lifted his gaze toward the source of the sound—just to be sure he hadn't really heard it.

He looked up. Way up. A good three feet above his head.

It was no tree.

Not unless trees in this part of the world had big, round, glowing red eyes.

The eyes blinked. Sideways.

Jeremy screamed as if his lungs were on fire.

All the feeling poured out of Janet's legs like molten cellulite. She dropped to her knees in ululating terror.

The thing before them jumped straight up, crashed back down amid a great snapping of branches, and trumpeted in Jeremy's face like a blood-maddened rogue elephant, huge eyes goggling, wildly flapping facial organs emitting a continuous farting blast of rancid gas. Jeremy's hair stood on end as if from the force of a blow dryer.

He bolted.

He kicked Janet as she tried to get up, knocking her flat on her face, and without a backward glance tore shrieking through the jungle as if the night itself had come alive and was coiling after him to swallow him whole.

Trask's post-banishment interview wasn't going anywhere. Grant decided to wrap it up.

"I think we've got all we need, Trask. Thanks for being on the show."

Trask just nodded. Through the whole thing he'd hardly showed any emotion. He didn't blame anyone else for his team's loss, so there was nothing there to play to. No display of anger, resentment, any of the emotions a normal person ought to feel under the circumstances. God knows Dudley had. But Trask just wouldn't open up.

They'd caught a tortoise. They'd let it go. That was at Paula's instigation—she'd been pretty sure it was an endangered species. Did Trask feel any bitterness about it? No, he figured she was probably right. He made some half-assed joke about his team being too civilized to cut it as survivalists.

And it didn't help much that Trask obviously didn't like Grant, and though Grant was professional enough to hide it, the feeling was mutual. Grant knew a troublemaker when he saw one. He couldn't say he was sorry to see him go.

He nodded at Howard. Howard hit the spacer bar on the keyboard behind him to stop the recording.

"That it?" Trask said.

"Yes, that's it."

Trask stood up and handed his clip-on mic to Howard. "Good. I don't know how much longer I could have gone on without saying what I really think."

"What's that supposed to mean?"

"Just that, aside from my team losing the first round—that was by the rules—the whole thing is rigged or just completely fake. Nobody's what they say they are. We're not camping out in the jungle, we're sleeping in a dormitory and eating pigs in blankets, which puts us at least a level beneath the Cub Scouts. Barry coaches people on what to say, Bentley tries to manipulate everything to suit what he thinks the audience wants. I mean, you'd expect a certain amount of that, but—and then! Jean shows up and the next thing you know the Swamp Thing pops out of the jungle. But only Amber sees it. And Hal, who doesn't count, since he's part of the whole setup."

Grant wasn't all that surprised by the outburst. He'd seen Trask's audition video, with Trask talking about testing his fitness for survival as an "actual human being" against other "actual human beings". He had a hang-up about things being "real". His vision of the show had been naive and overly idealistic from the start.

It wasn't hard to figure out. Trask had wasted his life playing computer games, and now he was trying to make up for it. He'd gone on and on about taking up martial arts and all kinds of other stuff. Freerunning, whatever that was. He was probably just bitter that none of it had paid off. He'd still lost.

"But you know what? I don't even care," Trask was saying. "It's all bullshit. Whoever wins in the end, I'm pretty sure it's going to be whoever you guys choose."

Grant took it all complacently. Let him have his little tirade. Trask would soon be out of his hair forever. So he just smiled and said, "I'm sorry you feel that way, Trask. The show's producers are doing everything in their power to make it authentic—without, however, unduly endangering the lives of the punters and the crew."

Trask frowned. "The what?"

"The lives of the cast and—" Grant reiterated, but then broke off, listening. "What is that, is that screaming?"

Yes it was.

One of the girls, somewhere in the distance, screaming her head off. Grant wondered if they should—

"It's Janet," Trask said. He threw open the door and was outside racing across the sand before Grant had even managed to struggle out of his chair. Howard stared, slack-jawed while Grant fumbled for his clip-on mic.

"Help me with this thing," Grant said.

The screaming was closer now. Most of the cast and crew had gathered in the glare of the mess hall's wall-mounted exterior floodlights to gawk at the jungle. Hal's camera-mounted spotlight lit up a circular section of the wall of trees that rose up thirty feet away across the stretch of sandy turf.

From off to the east, someone else called out.

Security had been out combing the area earlier. Roger had come back. He unclipped his two-way radio.

"Jim," he said. "It's Janet and Jeremy."

"Okay, Roger," Jim radioed back. "Roger."

A second later they heard him calling Janet and Jeremy by name.

Janet was getting closer. She sounded hysterical. Hal's bash light roved over the trees, trying to anticipate the exact spot where she would emerge from the jungle.

The screaming stopped, and now they heard a thrashing through the underbrush. Hal's light picked up movement. Branches shook, leaves trembled. She'd burst through any second now. Any—

There!

Only it wasn't Janet.

It was Jeremy.

He broke from the trees straight into Hal's spotlight. After the deep darkness of the jungle it dazzled him. He threw up an arm to shield his eyes and stumbled toward the gaping onlookers.

Michelle grabbed him by the arms and shook him. "What happened?"

"Where's Janet?" Tony said from behind her.

"Fuck if I know!"

They heard her again. A high-pitched wailing now, punctuated by sobs.

Everyone looked at Jeremy. No way was he going back in there. Tony and Brad started for the trees—just as Janet burst through.

Streaming tears carved runnels through the grime covering her cheeks. Her hair was full of twigs. Arms scraped and bruised, shorts slick with mud.

But the thing you couldn't help noticing right off was that she was naked from the waist up. Her breasts stood out starkly in the harsh light. They bounced hypnotically—superbly—from side to side as she ran towards Tony.

But she didn't run straight into Tony's outstretched arms as expected. Instead, she flew past him, straight at Jeremy. Jeremy shrank away, but Janet, not even slowing, plowed into him, fists flying, and beat him to his knees. He curled up into a fetal position on the ground, groaning while she kicked him. Hal was all over them with his Sony.

Ducking a low branch, Jim stepped out of the jungle. He took in the scene and slung his shotgun over his shoulder.

Nobody had yet made a move to pull Janet off Jeremy. Jim caught her by the wrists and gently drew her away, and Tony took control of the situation from there. Murmuring in her ear, he led her into the mess hall.

The crowd began to dissipate. Bentley stood staring at Hal's camera with a wistful expression. "Guess we can't use that," he said.

"Are you kidding?" Jean said. "We'll just smudge out her tits."

Bentley was shocked. "Breasts," he corrected.

"Yeah, breasts. Isn't that what I said?"

"Fred, go find out what happened."

"I better get going," Jean said. "Tell Amber and what's her name, would you?"

Bentley nodded. "Nice offer, taking the girls."

"No problem. We're all at the same hotel. We'll have a slumber party. I could use a drink." She winked at him.

CHAPTER FOUR

DISCLAIMERS

"CONGRATULATIONS, STRINDLAK GRATCHNORR," the voice chirped, as the personalized message scrolled across the display, "on your choice of the Flardnux 12000, the finest family recreational vehicle available anywhere, at any price. We think you'll agree—"

Strindlak swatted at the keypad. The voice was cut off, the onscreen message instantly replaced by another.

"At Flardnux Corporation, the comfort and safety of you and your loved ones always come first. Therefore, we strongly advise that all systems be thoroughly inspected by qualified service technicians prior to embarkation on any extended outing. That we may better assist you—"

Growling, Strindlak slapped the keypad, entered a command and swatted it again.

The animated Flardnux logo dazzled him momentarily, then fractured to race offscreen in all different directions, leaving a boldface legend:

FLARDNUX 12000
ELECTRONICS SUBSYSTEMS and MECHANICAL COMPONENTS
Troubleshooting Guide and Repair Manual

Girding himself for a marathon session of befuddlement and frustration immeasurably compounded by his own ignorance, Strindlak advanced to the next screen.

ACTIVATE DIAGNOSTIC PROCEDURES

Green button. Tap.

A sequence of numbers and symbols streamed past at staggering speed, then was abruptly replaced by a three-dimensional schematic of the ship's engine. At the top of the screen, the words *Mechanical Failure Detected* flashed once, paused, then began to strobe. Glowing cursors ricocheted over the diagram, pinpointing malfunctions. A discordant beep sounded. A section of the schematic glowed red, enlarged with dizzying abruptness. Strindlak recognized the refurbished brace he'd failed to properly install earlier. Cursors hovered over it, blinking accusingly.

But apparently that was the least of his problems.

WARNING WARNING WARNING

the screen blazed at him. The voice was back. It was inappropriately feminine. *"In the event of serious mechanical failure, Interstellar Travel Regulatory Commission Guidelines require that the manufacturer direct the operator to the following Governmental Advisory Notice.*

"Do not attempt to bypass this Notice. Your controls will not respond, and you will be prevented from accessing further instructions, until it has been read aloud in its entirety and you have signified verbally at the prompt that you have understood its message.

"Please speak into the microphone."

Suddenly things had gotten serious.

"Liar," Brad snarled. "You didn't see anything."

He held Jeremy's shirtfront wound tight in both huge fists, pinning him against the wall.

"Brad, put him down," Esha said. "You're choking him."

Brad dropped his captive and turned on Janet.

"You didn't see anything. We only have his word."

"I heard it," Janet said. "And smelled it," she added.

"He farted."

"Oh, come on, Brad," Lance said. "You think he made up the whole story as a coverup for cutting the cheese?"

Brad thought so. "Did you?"

"No, Brad." Jeremy, his face still red from the strangling he'd gotten, was nearly in tears. "Honest, Lance, there's something out there."

"It was something big, like what Amber saw," Janet said.

"Yeah, we only got her word for that too," Brad said.

Tony'd been sitting silent through the whole thing, trying to keep from snickering at Jeremy's disgrace. But now Brad was calling Janet's veracity into question.

"Hey, Brad, Janet wouldn't lie," he said.

Michelle turned to Fred—the second cameraman. The only crew member present. "Do *you* know anything about this? Is there somebody here we don't know about? Maybe someone whose job is to make things interesting by scaring the shit out of us?"

Fred shook his head. "No. There's nothing like that going on."

Nils finally spoke up. "So what do we do?"

There was a long silence. Then Fredo said, "Why don't we ask Trask, man? He's a smart dude, maybe he's got some ideas."

"Where is Trask, anyway?" Zach said. "And speaking of Amber, where the hell is she?"

Michelle glared at him.

Brad glared at *her*. "*She* voted them off, remember?"

"Your stupid team lost because of him, remember?" Michelle said. "And what makes everybody think Trask is so smart? If he's such a genius, why's he on his way home?"

Nils put a hand on her arm and said to Zach, "Trask's outside with Rashad and Paula. Amber and Esha are over at the bunkhouse getting ready to go."

The intercom buzzed behind him. He turned around.

Dudley got up from the sofa where he'd been sitting by himself and picked up his bag.

"I guess I better too." Head down, he trudged for the door.

Nils hung up the receiver.

"Come on, everybody. It's time."

They sat in the sand, listening to the sound of the waves washing up onto the shore, staring out over the ocean, all but invisible save for the shimmering reflections of an infinity of stars. Trask had never seen so many. Growing up in the city, it had never occurred to him that from places like this you could actually see the Milky Way. It stretched overhead, so thick with stars it looked fingerpainted across the sky in white luminescence.

No one talked, and right now that felt okay. There was something about the still-warm sand, the sound of the waves, the night, the jungle at their backs, that gave it a feeling of timelessness that none of them wanted to disturb.

In only a little over a week, they'd become best friends. Now it was over. After tonight, chances were they'd never see each other again. That was what happened. But these last few moments would last forever. In spite of everything, Hunters & Gatherers had given them this.

He smiled. Punters.

They heard voices. Jean and her pilot emerged from the bungalow, followed by Bentley and Barry. As if on cue, cast and crew members began to fall out onto the beach. The air filled with excited chattering as the group swept past. Their little patch of sand suddenly felt crowded.

Trask reached for his duffel bag and stood.

Jean's voice pierced the hubbub: "Girls? Zero hour." Esha and Amber, dragging their bags, hurried to her side.

Fear clouding his mind, Strindlak hurried to the transporter chamber. After all the dire warnings in the government Notice, there was little question he had to act fast, and hope it wasn't already too late.

He wasn't even sure if he knew how to activate the thing. It was built into the transporter controls, he remembered that much—along with the protection it offered, it greatly enhanced the transporter's capabilities, facilitating the plotting of coordinates and remote visual surveying operations.

The Notice had included an overview of the sort of disasters that might befall a hapless traveler in just this situation. He'd had no inkling of the potential danger.

Unfortunately, little was known of the early history of this particular planet, whose service as a transport hub dated back to a much earlier era. But surviving records alluded to resistance encountered during construction of the below-ground docking facilities as "ferocious". Beyond that, details were sketchy to non-existent, and subsequently little to no data had been collected.

Strindlak couldn't be certain what kind of lasting impression he'd left on the things, but the evidence wasn't encouraging. He'd been seen by at least one of them, and it had let out an eerie, keening wail that had sent him scurrying back to the dense thickets of concealing vegetation he'd stumbled from.

The wailing had been replaced by a gabbling pandemonium, audible even over the din of his violent retreat, and in which he'd recognized the articulated vocalizations characteristic of speech. Not good.

And thinking back on it, it did seem the creatures had been engaged in some sort of organized activity that could indicate an at least nominal level of intelligence. Even worse.

Nightmare scenarios flashing through his mind, he skidded to a halt at the transporter chamber, slapped the control panel and shoved his way through the opening door.

He experienced a brief attack of confusion at finding the transporter already powered up. In his agitation he must have left it on. He could imagine the scolding he'd have been in for if Glumrok had found out.

At least he'd managed to escape that.

He hurried down the chamber toward the platform.

A loud coughing filled the air, modulating to a putter, followed by an accelerating whup-whup-whup as the chopper's rotors began to turn. The beach was awash in the glare of foleys. Grant took up a well-lighted position from which to figure prominently in the spectacle of emotional leave-taking. Another engine fired. The mob carried Trask, Rashad and Paula down the beach to the small pier where the motorboat was moored.

Time ratcheted up to a jerky series of jump cuts. Amidst a flurry of goodbyes, Clayton and Beverly stepped into the idling motorboat. Dudley was already aboard.

Trask tossed in his bag. Quick hug from Paula, a warm kiss on the cheek. A manly hug and a handshake from Rashad.

"Let's go, Trask," Dudley said, as if there was some urgency about it.

Stan, The boat's pilot, held out a hand. Trask took it and hopped aboard. Stan cast off and stowed the mooring lines, climbed into the captain's seat and looked over his passengers. Everyone was settled.

At Stan's nod, Nils and Brad gave the boat a heave that sent it drifting sideways from the pier. When it was safely cleared, Stan engaged the clutch and gently opened the throttle. Picking up speed, the boat curved away from the pier to a final chorus of goodbyes.

They were off.

Trask looked back. A cluster of figures, anonymous in the dark, sur-rounded Grant—waving like a madman in a blaze of light, shrinking into the distance. Trask turned to face the gloomy expanse of ocean ahead and settled back into his seat. The cone of light cast by the boat's headlamp seemed to illuminate the sum total of all matter in the universe. It might have been all that stood between them and nothingness.

It was all over.

Beside Trask, Dudley sighed.

They'd reach their immediate destination in under fifteen minutes. Though tiny Ste. Catherine was always kept carefully off-camera, in day-light it was clearly visible from La Naufragée.

Trask's limbs felt weighted down by the familiar feelings of depression and loss seeping back into him.

Back to mundane reality.

CHAPTER FIVE

DEPARTURES

STRINDLAK GAZED UPON THE SCENE depicted with such striking realism and detail within the imager.

Even with the shield unactivated the imager was a technological wonder. He didn't even pretend to understand the combination of motion sensors, heat and light detectors and external transmitter/receivers that enabled the depiction in three-dimensional full-motion view of faraway objects and life forms with such faithful detail.

He'd completed a full inspection of the perimeter and been relieved to learn the island was well isolated from others in the vicinity by a wide expanse of ocean.

He was still puzzled by the changed settings, though. Fortunately, the *Return to Previous Transport Coordinates* command had saved him the trouble of having to manually navigate back to the same strip of shoreline. He must have jarred the control knob upon his earlier return—not improbable considering his flustered state.

His fears dispelled, he fell to studying the planet's curious inhabitants, marveling that such seemingly harmless creatures could be capable of the kind of murderous aggression described in the Notice.

Perhaps the earlier form had been supplanted. Innumerable studies supported the view that the self-annihilation of aggressive forms was a common route to dominance by milder types, as had been the case on his own planet.

They were intelligent, though. Now, watching them, he found himself fascinated by the complexity and cooperative nature of their actions. There was something irresistible about the things' behavior. They were charming, in their way. And they'd attained to a level of technology beyond the building of simple shelters, he noted. A large piece of equipment he'd glimpsed earlier on the strip of land fronting the sea was undoubt-edly some form of rudimentary machine. Probably a crude digging or drilling device judging by the revolving segment at the top. And nearby, another, smaller object lay at the land's edge. An adjunct to the larger per-haps. Several of the creatures gathered around it as he watched.

Strindlak found himself touched in an almost profound way. Here they were, the dominant but still primitive species of a world inconceiva-bly distant from the planet of his birth, taking the first tentative steps to-ward mastering the basic building blocks of advanced technology that might someday put them on a par with the grand achievements of his own species. It was almost like witnessing a re-enactment of the forgotten flowering time of the fully-evolved society of which he himself was but a humble representative.

His heart went out to them.

He shook his head, chortling. There was no threat here. Perhaps other creatures, in earlier times. But not these. Especially so *few* as these.

Still, further contact would be avoided conscientiously. Prudence as well as the law dictated it.

Wrapped in his musings, Strindlak took absent note that a number of the creatures had disappeared into the larger machine, while some of those surrounding the smaller now stepped onto it.

And besides, cut off as they were from others of their kind, how could they hope to mount a campaign of terror against—

He stared, his train of thought abruptly derailed.

The smaller object was being pushed off from the land.

Strindlak's brow tendrils fluttered.

The object was buoyant.

To his consternation, it glided forward, then left the land altogether. In no time it was speeding away under its own power across the open sea.

He let out a yelp.

Fool! These things have mastered mechanized travel!

They're not marooned here. They're going for help.

Brow tendrils writhing in horror, Strindlak tore his gaze from the im-ager to scan the display menu in rising panic. Like an idiot, he had allowed himself to be lulled into complacency, captivated by the things' curious behavior—and now he had but moments left in which to act.

~~~~~~~~~~~~~~~~~~~~~~~~~~~~~~~~

They were two hundred yards out when it happened.

It started as a diffuse glow deep beneath the waves, growing brighter as it rose toward the surface, sharpening to a blazing blue line that curved clear around the island.

Dudley jumped up and scrambled backwards, knocking Beverly off her seat. Lying sprawled in the stern, they gaped upward when the glow burst through the surface and shot into the sky, trailing a glittering curtain of blue-green streamers.

Trask turned to trace the thing's unbroken circle, and saw it rising in the distance beyond the central peak. It seemed to climb up the sides of an invisible dome, its circumference narrowing as it accelerated toward the apex.

From the shore drifted screams of dismay.

At the wheel, Stan stared in wonder, hypnotized by the sight. The boat plowed through the water.

Trask glanced at Stan, then back at the sky in time to see the ring close to a point far overhead and blink out. The streamers followed, spiraling inward like water swirling around the sides of an upside-down sink to disappear through a pinpoint drain at the top.

The whole thing had lasted only seconds.

The motorboat surged onward, now mere yards from where the light had sliced through the waves.

Trask yelled. "Turn! Turn!"

Stan jerked to life, spun the wheel, the boat veered to port—and slammed into an invisible wall.

Its nose splintering, the motorboat pivoted and leapt from the water up the side of the unseen barrier. It overturned in mid-air, hurling its passengers into the sea. Trask hit the water hard and went under. He twisted, kicking toward the surface just as the boat crashed back down.

He broke from the water to the sound of screams as the boat came roaring back up. Its aft section rose up from the waves and swung hard around, slamming into the barrier with a bang. The impact tore the motor free. As Trask watched through stinging sheets of seawater, it flew straight
~~~~~~~~~~~~~~~~~~~~~~~~~~~~~~~~

up, end over end, clanging against the curving wall—until gravity brought it plunging back.

Dudley surfaced at the foot of its arc. The still-spinning propeller caught him in the thigh. He shrieked as it churned through his flesh and plummeted past in a spray of blood.

Trask kicked towards him and lunged, catching him under one armpit. Dudley flailed and screamed. Heads bobbed in the water a short way off. Nearby, the capsized boat pitched and rocked, then settled onto the now eerily still waters. Dragging Dudley, Trask kicked toward it and latched onto the side with his free hand, shouting for help.

Stan and Beverly's voices echoed back.

"Trask!"

"Dudley's hurt. Where's Clayton?"

The others swam over. There was no trace of Clayton.

"My leg," Dudley moaned, his face gray.

Trask tried to reassure him. "You're okay. It's the salt water."

Dudley wasn't okay. His legs drifted up toward the surface. Even in the dark, relieved only by the light of the stars and the thin wedge of moon climbing over the horizon, the gushing blood was visible as a dark smudge clouding the water. Chewed half through by the propeller, Dudley's leg bobbed at an unnatural angle, held together by thick strands of mangled muscle and tendons. Stan grabbed hold of his other arm to help Trask keep him up. Beverly yelled for Clayton.

Her shouting was drowned out by a throbbing roar.

In the terror of the boatwreck they hadn't noticed it until now: the unmistakable chopping sound of the helicopter's rotors, steadily gaining in volume.

They looked toward the shore. It was headed straight for them.

From its undercarriage, a searchlight's beam flashed over a head and shoulders. Clayton, making for the shore. Without slowing, the helicopter flew on.

"No! Shit!" Trask let go of the boat and waved his arm. "Stop them."

Beverly stared at him, then said, "Omigod!" as the nature of the new emergency dawned on her. She waved with both arms, legs pedaling beneath the surface. Dudley was losing consciousness. Trask handed him over to Stan and joined Beverly to try to wave the chopper back. Its searchlight found them and locked on as it glided forward.

"It's no use," Stan shouted. "They think we're waving them in." He cursed. "They're coming to rescue us." The chopper was nearly on top of them now.

"Under the boat! Get under the boat," Trask yelled. Beverly dove, and Stan ducked under the overturned hull, dragging Dudley.

Grabbing a cleat, Trask hung on to the side, ready to swing underneath in an instant, unable to peel his eyes away from the doomed chopper. They were slowing. There was a chance—

It happened so fast, at first he thought they'd made it through.

Then the cockpit exploded. Trask had a glimpse of shattered glass spraying over the barrier's curved surface before he dove under the hull.

The crash of impact was followed almost instantly by a deafening blast when the fuel tank blew. The flash lit up the sea beneath the overturned boat. Shockwaves pounded the water. Flaming debris rained down, hammering the hull over the survivors' heads as they huddled gasping in the air bubble. The fiberglass shell cracked under the battering, spitting out sharp spikes of splintered planking that stabbed at them from above. Huge chunks of twisted metal steeped in burning fuel plunged into the ocean around them, boiling water into steaming geysers.

Dudley's eyes were rolling back in his head. His maimed leg drifted out from under the sheltering hull as a meteorite of white hot metal roared past. It grazed his heel. With a scream that turned hideously into a bubbling gurgle, he was torn from Stan's grasp and swept away. A blazing rudder slammed into the water to follow him downward with a butterfly motion—bathing his terrified face in lurid light for a final, brief instant before he disappeared into the depths.

Back on the beach the cast and crew stood in uncomprehending horror. The weird lights had frightened everyone, but they knew nothing of the barrier. It looked to them like the news chopper had simply exploded. They'd seen the capsized boat in its searchlight moments before, and now gaped at the destruction raining down on it from above.

Hal had caught the whole thing. He was always on. Bash light still mounted on his FX9, he panned over the beach to follow Paula and Rashad to the edge of the shore.

Paula fell to her knees in the surf. "Trask." It was a cry of mourning, not of hope.

Bentley shook himself out of his daze. "Train those lights on the water for survivors," he yelled.

Techs scurried back up the beach for the equipment.

With his hand on Paula's shoulder, Rashad peered into the darkness. There was enough moonlight to make out the white crests of the nearest waves tossed up by the hail of destruction, breaking as they neared the shoreline.

Jim, the big security guard, waded into them.

Crew members dragged lights and their trailing cables to the shore, aimed fresnels out over the water. There was no sign of life in the vicinity of the wreckage.

Rashad gave Paula's shoulder a squeeze and waded out.

Grant shouted. "There!"

A fresnel swung up, roved over the surface.

"Where? Where?"

"To the left. Come down. A little more… There!"

Two heads bobbed in the water a hundred yards out.

Trask. And Stan.

Jim and Rashad swam toward them.

"Where're the others?" Jim said.

Trask shook his head. "Clayton should have made shore by now. Beverly's behind us." He stopped to catch his breath, then turned. "I'll get her," he said, but just then Rashad called out from the darkness off to their right.

"I've got Beverly. She's okay."

Trask stared across the darkened ocean at their backs, toward Ste. Catherine, then turned back to Jim. "Dudley didn't make it. There's nobody else."

Jim nodded. They made for the beacons on the shore.

Paula ran out into the surf to meet them. Trask saw tears in her eyes, and was suddenly grateful to Michelle. If she'd banished Paula. Or Rashad…

All around him people were crying and talking in hushed voices. Trask only half listened, his teeth chattering. He looked around. Jim and Stan stood nearby, talking to Bentley. Down the beach, others had found Clayton. He'd gotten disoriented in the dark and ended up far to the east before the lights had come up.

Bentley came over. "Trask, what happened?" he said.

Trask suddenly realized they had no idea. "That blue flash," he said. "It left behind some kind of invisible barrier. They crashed right into it, right after we did."

Beside Bentley, Grant said, "Nobody could've survived that, Rob."

Bentley shook his head in disbelief. "Jean. She was our champion."

CHAPTER SIX

ADAPTATION

BENTLEY HUNG UP the receiver. He'd managed to get through to Ste. Catherine using the field set in his office, and had been fielding calls with it non-stop for the past forty-five minutes. Fielding but not necessarily receiving. The goddamn barrier was playing havoc with the reception.

"They can't see us. We can see out, but they can't see in. That thing out there, they're saying it's like a giant mirror ball."

The production crew had gravitated to the bungalow after the accident—that was how everyone referred to it—and now sat around like grunts in a foxhole, wondering where the next 500-lb. bomb was going to drop.

"At least we can communicate," Barry said.

"You call that communication? I've had twenty-five dropped calls in the last fifteen minutes."

"Well, if we were on land lines we'd be completely out of touch."

"What about our footage? The show's sunk."

"I've been thinking about that." Hal turned to their electrician.

"Dylan, can we feed video over the radio? If we had someone to receive it?"

Dylan, in addition to being an experienced and talented gaffer, held a degree in computer science and had a thorough working knowledge of electronics and digital systems technology. He was the youngest member of the crew, about the same age as the youngest of the punters.

He thought it over. "Sure, we could do that. We'll have to compress the hell out of it, and it'll still take forever. Won't look like much, either, you're going to get a big drop in resolution. Not to mention all the noise and distortion using shortwave."

"So it won't be broadcast quality, but it'll work."

"Yeah. It's a good idea."

Bentley wasn't happy. It was going to look like shit.

"Rob," Hal said, "we're not talking about the show, right? We're talking about the accident. It's big news. And it's ours. The network's not going to give a shit whether it's broadcast quality or not."

There was a good chance this stuff was going to be Pulitzer quality, though, and it would have Hal's name all over it.

Bentley saw the light.

"But how do we do that? It's all digital files."

"It's no different from analog," Dylan said. "Just like digital TV. It's still radio, just takes up a lot more bandwidth. Like I said, it won't look great, but you'll have a picture." He grew thoughtful.

Bentley recognized the look—Dylan was already considering technical issues, logistics.

"What do you need?" Bentley said.

"We'll transfer the files to your laptop. Jack into the radio with an ethernet adapter. I'll have to fool around with the electronics a little."

"Dylan, the network's sending a boat over," Hal said. "When they get here, we can transmit to them directly, to their shipboard radio, right? Without going over the network through Ste. Katy?"

"Sure. Still up for grabs though, line of sight, if that's what you're thinking."

"We can scramble it, though."

"Of course. But—"

Hal nodded. That wasn't going to be a real problem to the professionals probably already scanning the airwaves.

"Do what we can."

"I'll see if I can figure something out."

Bentley pushed his laptop across the table to Dylan, and stood up.

"Get to work on it."

There were two quick raps on the door, it opened, and Jim walked in. He casually acknowledged the roomful of people staring at him with a nod. He was six foot six. Used to being stared at, Bentley guessed.

"Rob," Jim said, "I'm going to go out and have a look around."

From their first meeting, Jim had always called Bentley "Rob". Barry, who'd been there, had called him on it, and Bentley still remembered Jim's patient explanation that, because he was from Texas, and had been brought up right, he called his mom "ma'am" and his dad "sir". But beyond that, he didn't much go in for a lot of titles and honorifics. As he'd said, it just wouldn't've come out natural-sounding for him to be calling Bentley "Mr Bentley". And since it would've been ill-mannered calling him just "Bentley", Jim would just call him "Rob". He'd added that "Rob" didn't act as if he minded, and Barry had just blinked a couple of times and sat back down.

"Roger'll stick around here to look after the fort," Jim added.

Feeling the upward tilt of his head to meet Jim's gaze, Bentley just said, "Thank you, Jim."

Hal perked up. "Look around where?"

"Thought I'd retrace Jeremy and Janet's tracks, see if I can find whatever spot they met up with their critter. Could be there's something up there can give us a clue to what we're dealing with. Never know."

Hal jumped to his feet, grinning. "Give me two seconds to get the rest of my gear."

Jim looked at Hal, as if measuring him up for the first time. "Probably nothing to see. But on the other hand, it's dark and we'll be heading into the jungle, so there might could be some risk involved. I'll want you to keep behind me and do as I say."

"You're the boss, Jim," Hal said. He hurried out.

Jim turned back to Bentley.

"Anybody talk to those kids? I imagine they'll be a little shook up after what happened to that boy Dudley and the girls." Jim was forty. A little older than Barry, a lot younger then Hal, and twenty-five years younger than Bentley. But he was the only one who referred to the contestants as kids.

"Probably could use a little pep talk."

Bentley was surprised, and a little ashamed that he hadn't thought of it himself. Of course Jim was right. Jesus, it was a hell of a thing for anyone. What the hell was he going to say to them?

"Just a suggestion," Jim added, seeing what he must have taken for hesitation on Bentley's part.

"Want me to talk to them?" Grant was always ready to put on any kind of a performance.

"No, no, I'll—I suppose it's my job. As producer," Bentley replied—

dreading the grim task, with all its potential for distressing displays. Tears. Displaced anger.

Over in the cast dormitory, their shared fate had cast a deep gloom over the contestants' collective mood. A few had seen friends killed before, but most hadn't. It wasn't an easy thing to get over, and a certain amount of shame comes with the realization that hits you when someone close to you dies suddenly—that your immediate concern is for your own safety. The dead are beyond the meager solace of sympathy.

"We have to do something," Lance said.

"Yeah? Like what?" Brad asked him.

"We already tried crashing a boat and a helicopter into it," Michelle said. "That didn't work. Maybe we could try throwing rocks at it."

"Okay, so maybe we can't do anything about the—force field, or whatever it is," Lance said. "But what about everything else? In case you haven't noticed, we've got company. And now we're trapped in here with them. I kind of doubt it's all a coincidence."

Trask sighed. "What do you suggest, Lance?"

Lance took it as a challenge, and his temper flared.

"Well I don't know about you, Trask, but I'd sure like to get our hands on one of these things creeping around and ask it real politely what the fucking deal is. Just call it idle curiosity."

"Yeah, well, politeness is definitely key. According to Amber, her monster was about the size of a fucking rhinoceros standing on its hind legs."

"Who the hell asked you?" Michelle snapped. "What you think doesn't count. You shouldn't even be here."

That brought the discussion to a halt.

Paula said, "God, Michelle."

"I didn't mean it like that." Michelle was suddenly on the defensive, virgin territory for her. "He was voted off. He doesn't have a say, he's not part of the group—"

"It doesn't matter how you meant it," Beverly said, her voicing rising. "Forget the stupid show. He's here. We're here. And Trask and me and Clayton are just as stuck here as you are."

"Okay, guys. Let's not fight with each other," Nils said. "Whatever it is we're in, we're all in it together. But it's dark outside and we don't have any weapons. Better to wait till morning."

Lance tried a different approach. "What do we need weapons for? We don't know they're hostile. They haven't hurt anybody. The helicopter was an accident."

The others mulled this over. It was true. Sort of.

"I'm with Lance," Rashad said.

Paula agreed. "Me too. I want to know what's going on."

Trask shook his head, but didn't say anything.

Lance stood up. "Let's have a show of hands." He raised his own. "Those in favor?"

Rashad and Paula raised their hands. Brad grumbled, but raised his too. Vince, Zach, Fredo. Sondra. Clayton.

Jeremy had worked his way unnoticed to Janet's side, and stood with his hands in his pockets. Tony crossed his arms over his chest.

Beverly's hand came up. Nils finally put his up too.

Michelle jumped when the door opened.

It was just Bentley. With Barry behind him.

Bentley registered surprise. "What's going on?"

"We're organizing a search party," Lance told him.

Bentley was caught off guard. Maybe they didn't need a pep talk after all. But it was out of the question.

"That's not necessary," he said. "Jim's going out with Hal. We'll find out whatever there is to find out soon enough." He felt a tug at his sleeve, shot an annoyed frown at Barry, then turned back to Lance. "Get some sleep."

Another tug. Urgent. "What is it?" Bentley said.

Barry cleared his throat. "Rob, can I have a word?"

Exasperated, Bentley gestured for him to take the floor if he had something to say.

"With *you,* Rob," Barry said.

Bentley sighed heavily. "Excuse me," he told the company, then allowed Barry to drag him back out the door.

"What?" Bentley demanded once Barry had closed the door and they were out of earshot.

"Rob. It's a made-for-TV moment. We should have been taping this already. We should be taping everything." He was insistent. "You gotta agree to the search. Think about it. Night. The jungle. Fear of the unknown, the perception of danger. Drama, excitement. It's all there. We have to adapt, Rob. Make the most of the circumstances."

Bentley pondered, partially swayed but indecisive.

"I'm sure there's no real danger," Barry added.

"What about the legal issues?" Bentley said. "It's an uncontrolled situation."

"Draw up a new release. They can sign as a group. Like the Declaration of Independence."

Jim and Hal—the latter hauling his shoulder-mounted camera with floodlamps and external stereo mic attached—appeared at the steps.

"We're ready," Hal announced.

"Rob?" Barry said.

Jim looked at Barry. Barry avoided his gaze.

Bentley hesitated, then nodded. To the others he said, "Come inside."

"I don't much like it, to be honest, but I can't stop anybody that wants to," Jim said. "I'll take three only, plus Hal. And Roger still stays back here at the camp just in case."

"I'm going with Jim or I'm not going," Fred said. "This wasn't in my contract."

"Go ahead. Lance can head another party," Hal said, looking over at Jim. "I'll go with them."

Jim just shrugged.

"I'm going with Jim too," Michelle said.

Trask got to his feet. He was still opposed, but clearly uncomfortable with the idea of staying behind while his friends and erstwhile teammates went ahead without him.

"We're going to stay together," Rashad said. "Just like old times." He and Trask, Paula and Brad—half of their original team—plus Vince. Filling in for Dudley.

Three search parties. Jim had already given his rifle to Roger, but still had his revolver and shotgun.

"One of you better take my pistol," he said. "Trask?"

Trask seemed surprised to be singled out. He thought about it, but shook his head. "We'll be okay."

Jim looked at Lance, studied him for a few seconds, then handed him his Colt .44, saying, "This here's the safety. It's on."

Lance took the weapon with an easy familiarity and thumbed off the switch.

"Not anymore."

In Jim's opinion it was kind of a melodramatic, overly macho and reckless move, but the kid obviously knew his guns.

"Be careful," he said.

CHAPTER SEVEN

PUNTERS

TRASK LED THE WAY with a 9-volt lantern. Its unfocused beam splashed over a haphazard network of vine-draped branches. Shadows loomed and wheeled as the small party tunneled onward through night-hallowed rainforest.

The other parties headed by Lance and Jim should be far away by now. They'd taken the eastern and western flanks, while Trask's party moved straight up the middle, in a line that would eventually take them to the foot of the central peak. But they didn't intend to go that far. That could wait until tomorrow, and daylight.

Trask didn't regret his decision to accompany his teammates, or even the fact that he'd agreed to take point. But he still thought it was foolhardy. For all they knew, whatever was out here could well have the advantage over their night-blindness, and the lantern was almost certain to alert it to their presence long before they were aware of its own. And then what? Exactly what were they planning to do if they found the thing? Get it to sign one of Barry's releases?

From somewhere up ahead came a faint crackling, like static electricity.

Trask motioned for a halt. He hadn't noticed it until now, but the jungle soundtrack that had accompanied their movements earlier—the occasional rustle of dry leaves, the soft chirps and croaks, the whirr of the wings of nocturnal insects—had stopped. The silence was absolute. Crystalline.

He clicked off the lantern, arms prickling with goosebumps. It took a few seconds for his eyes to adjust. The moonlight filtering down through the dense canopy gave their faces a faint greenish cast, compliments of the barrier. Everything else was varying shades of gray.

They crept forward. Up ahead, water gurgled over a pebble-covered streambed.

They were nearing a creek.

It must be connected to the lagoon they'd crossed earlier in the day, Trask realized. Inside the barrier, the ocean's waves were stilled. But the tide would still exert its pull, causing the waters of the lagoon to flow gently in and out.

Trask picked his way between the trees with care, guided by the sounds. And then he heard it again. Just audible over the stream's drumming murmur: the zzzzt! of electrical discharge. It was cut off by a sucking pop—loud enough to reverberate up the shallow ravine they were nearing and echo faintly back.

There was something down there.

They weren't alone.

Looking down through a dark maze of tree trunks and tangled branches, Trask saw the moon's reflection trembling on the surface of the water.

He slipped out of the trees and moved down the steep slope of the ravine, the others following in single file. At the bottom, they continued downstream along the banks, alert for anything strange or out-of-place.

Any unhuman presence.

Behind Trask, Paula caught her breath. He glanced around, she pointed and everyone froze.

Ahead, water swirled around a large granite boulder standing in midstream. Behind it, something was moving. A light played over the boulder, casting a soft halo around its edges and reflecting off the rocks beyond. And its hidden source was moving toward the banks on which they stood.

They ducked behind a thick stand of tall ferns higher up the banks. The air around them turned sour with the smell of fear.

Feeling woefully exposed, Trask stared hard. Paula gripped his hand, her palm clammy with dread.

They heard shuffling steps. The glow lengthened, spreading around the boulder's edge like moonrise.

But even though they could see it coming, they were totally unprepared for what stepped out into the open with a snapping of twigs and crunch of dry leaves. Paula let go of Trask's hand and clapped hers over her mouth to stifle a cry of surprise.

Whatever it was, it sure as hell wasn't human.

It had a face like one of those weird deep-sea fishes that you only saw in pictures. Big, round, unblinking eyes peered out above a jagged red gash for a mouth. Antenna-like spines sprouted from its cheeks, brows and chin. There was no discernible nose.

Its torso was thick and barrel-chested. Long slender arms ending in heavy club-like paws hung to its shins. The massive, elongated head was sunken between hunched shoulders, giving it a stooped, simian posture.

At first glance, you naturally took it to be some form of living creature. But on the next, you weren't so sure. There was no underlying musculature beneath the sleek and featureless skin. Everything was fish-belly smooth. It looked too stylized, like something designed. Manufactured.

But what really made it impossible to accept it as real was the pulsating light wrapped around it like a halo. The thing glowed like a television screen in a darkened living room. Instead of flesh and blood, it looked like it was made up of millions of gleaming pixels.

Computer graphics. CGI. Special effects.

It was good, but not quite convincing. Its outline blurred when it moved, leaving behind tiny, sparkling motes that strayed for a brief instant before swimming back to catch up and lock back into place.

It wasn't real. It couldn't be.

Brad couldn't restrain himself. "It's some kind of—" he began, but Rashad silenced him with a punch on the shoulder.

The creature stopped to stare at the stream in what looked like confusion or astonishment. Then it turned toward the trees. There was a halting tentativeness to its motions.

It couldn't have been much more than five feet tall. Now that they'd gotten over the initial shock, it didn't really look all that dangerous.

The thing tried a few more steps, walking with unusual care, as if unused to the feel of its own legs.

One step. Then another. And another.

It walked right into a tree.

It hit with a solid whack and staggered backwards, flapping its arms in a comical attempt to retain its balance.

The punters forgot their fear. One after another, they stood up. It still hadn't noticed them.

"Is it sick?" Paula said.

It finally lost its balance altogether and stumbled toward the stream, arms windmilling. Its pod-like feet skated over the slippery, moss-covered boulders at the water's edge. It plunged in head first.

Brad scowled. "This is bullshit," he said in a loud voice.

"Quiet, Brad!" Trask hissed, but Brad wasn't playing along anymore. "Come on, look at it! You believe that?"

The thing was floundering now, slapping at the slow-moving waters in obvious distress. At last gaining a foothold in the shallow stream, it flexed its knees and made a leap for freedom—straight at the punters.

It landed at their feet in a heap, giving everyone a bad start except Brad, who was busy scanning their surroundings through narrowed eyes for hidden cameras. "Bentley! Grant! Okay, wise guys."

The creature finally realized it had company. It peered up into Paula's frightened face, let out an odd yelp, and scuttled downslope, jerking to a stop with its back up against a boulder.

"It's afraid of us," Paula said. She took a step toward it.

"Don't get too close," Rashad said.

Undissuaded, she crept closer, cooing at it like it was a lost kitten. "Are you okay? Do you need help? It's all right, we won't hurt you."

Adding his protestations to Rashad's, Trask got as far as "Paula, I wouldn't—" when the thing snapped its jaws open, exhibiting rows of glistening teeth, and screeched like a braking subway car.

Paula gasped and threw herself backwards, skittering away face up on hands and feet.

It was rough going. She lost her footing and skidded back down, pelting the creature with dirt and loose pebbles thrown up in the process.

The thing was now baring its needle-like teeth in a warning grimace and emitting alarming hooting sounds. Trask made a grab for Paula, but her momentum only dragged him along with her. Together, they slid helplessly down.

Paula's outstretched palms thudded into the creature's chest, stopping her cold. It snarled once and everybody stopped breathing.

With Trask's hands on her waist, Paula sat facing the thing in silent terror, afraid to make a wrong move, her own heartbeat thumping in her ears.

Seconds ticked by. Only the creek's soft, gurgling murmur broke the stillness.

Whatever it looked like, it was definitely solid, and it sure felt like flesh and blood. Even though it wasn't warm like normal flesh and blood would be.

Paula let out a slow, deep breath. Willing herself to stay calm, she carefully leaned back to ease up on the pressure of her hands against the thing's heavy torso.

"Okay, little guy. It's okay."

It wasn't cold either, though. Room temperature.

The thing goggled at her. A tremor passed over its chest, but it remained still.

Her touch was light as a feather. Almost there.

Slowly, she lifted her hands free.

The attack came without warning. A clubbed fist raveled open to expose razor-sharp talons and lashed out with stunning ferocity, tearing the skin from her arm in ribbons. Paula screamed and thrashed. It struck again and again. Trask's face was splattered with blood. He threw his arms around her waist, Rashad reached for her from behind him, and the two of them dragged her uphill, feet skidding in the loose dirt.

The thing clubbed a fist and with one last terrific swipe landed a blow on Paula's temple. Her head pitched sideways, twisting out of its reach. Trask wrenched her away and they tumbled down the bank.

Rashad scrambled up. Behind him, Vince was yelling, waving his arms to try to scare the thing off while Brad heaved rocks at it. Where they struck, its skin rippled in waves of distortion.

Paula was swooning, covered in blood, but free.

The creature, hissing with fury, thumped its wrists together. With a sudden loud crack, it was swallowed up in a flash of white fire.

It was like an exploding galaxy in miniature. The fireball swelled spectacularly, then disintegrated in a burst of glittering pixels. They drifted lazily toward the ground on little trails of exhaust like Macy's Fourth of July fireworks.

Brad and Vince stared in amazement.

The punters were alone. There was nothing left of the thing. It had been blown to bits.

~~~~~~~~~~~~~~~~~~~~~~~~~~~~~~~~~~~~~~~

From his favorite recliner in the bungalow's living room, Bentley heard Trask yelling, and all the commotion as everyone piled out of the buildings.

Well, here we go again. He threw down his pencil.

How the hell was he supposed to get any work done?

He'd been trying to take advantage of the time he had to himself to re-think the changed format. The show was going forward, but in a radically new direction. He was having enough trouble just keeping abreast of things, let alone trying to jot down his ideas for a new treatment.

To tell the truth, he couldn't help feeling a little conflicted. Yes, yes, big things were happening and the weird goings-on were, he supposed, a shot in the arm after the tepid reception of the Thursday night premiere. He'd seen the footage. It was all very compelling, very watchable, if you liked that sort of thing. He just didn't appreciate the creative elements of his show being usurped by outsiders. It really galled him, if you wanted to know the truth, that his newest project was showing every sign of turning into some kind of grade B sci-fi/horror crap—a genre he particularly des-pised, and one of the few he still at this point in his career had the confi-dence to disdain. The only reason he'd gotten involved in a "reality" show in the first place—the only reason—he was a filmmaker after all—was that he had a little time on his hands between other projects. Big projects. He had big projects in development. That is, he would, if his blockhead of an agent would get off his fat ass and scrounge up a decent script.

Bentley stared at his notes with unseeing eyes, despairing and suffer-ing. It was that old existential dread of losing one's self—sinking down into some nameless black hole of disreputable oblivion, never to regain the standing he'd—well, never actually had, so "regain" maybe wasn't en-tirely accurate, but aspired to at least.

He tried to cast off the feeling. After all, Trask was still out there yelling. He'd probably better go out and see what was going on.

His eyes focused on his notes. Scribbles, really. A quick jotting down of whatever came to mind. Here and there a rough sketch. Just prompt-ings to get the old creative juices flowing.

His sketches had a naïve quality, he recognized that. Nothing wrong
~~~~~~~~~~~~~~~~~~~~~~~~~~~~~~~~~~~~~~~

with it. Some artists had that too, some very talented ones. Here you had what might be an offhand likeness, just a quick gestural thing. Bardot, maybe, or Raquel. He could never quite get the breasts right. They seemed to just float there, not anatomically connected. He tried to visualize. How were they attached? Where did they start, where did they end? Well, it was pretty clear where they ended. He'd covered that part with a black rectangle.

He'd have to finish his work some other time. Trask was practically right outside now, probably over at the cast dormitory. Yelling at someone to call off the search.

With a sigh, Bentley stood up from his chair.

Brad laid Paula on a bunk with surprising gentleness. He'd run all the way back from the stream carrying her cradled in his arms. She'd been unconscious through most of it, but was awake now and hurting.

Trask went to the bathroom to fill a pan at the sink. There was a small cabinet above it he'd never noticed before, and he opened it with a surge of hope. It was empty. Snatching up soap and towels, he hurried back to Paula's side, barely acknowledging Bentley and Barry's breathless entrance. They were obviously dying to know what happened, but knew enough to keep their curiosity to themselves for now.

Brushing away leaves and bits of bark stuck to Paula's arms and face, he began to cleanse her wounds, starting with the deep cut that ran down her cheek from beside her left eye almost to her chin.

Brad stood looking at Bentley with all the vague suspicions he felt written all over his face.

Outside, Howard was calling out through a director's megaphone. "Call off the search. Repeat, call off the search. Everyone back to camp."

It was all a bit surreal.

"We need hydrogen peroxide. Or alcohol or something," Trask said to Bentley. "Where's the first aid?"

It was at the top of one of the lockers against the back wall. Bentley found it in the fourth one he tried, a small metal case bearing a cross emblem. One of those little kits designed for minor cuts and scratches you might bring along on something as fraught with peril as a picnic lunch on your front lawn.

Trask scowled when he looked inside. There was some hydrogen peroxide at least, and some kind of generic antiseptic ointment. Tweezers, a small safety scissors, some gauze bandages. A 12-tablet bottle of Tylenol. Not much else.

"Next time, cast a fake paramedic," he said.

Bentley took offense at his tone. "As you were all informed, the staff physician was held up in transit. He'll be here on Monday."

"Nobody's going to be here on Monday," Trask said, and immediately regretted the way that sounded. "No one can get in and we can't get out, remember? It's bad enough even without getting attacked by—"

Paula moaned, and he left the thought hanging while he wiped her wounds with gauze soaked in peroxide. It could have been a lot worse—it had sure looked like it with all the blood. But thankfully most of the cuts weren't too deep. It was the blow to the head that worried him most. Using his fingers, he combed Paula's red hair away from her temple to look at it. It was swelling and turning all kinds of colors. She was kind of drifting in and out of consciousness now, and he worried that that might be a sign of concussion. He didn't know much about that kind of stuff, and had a heavy sinking feeling that no one else here did either.

"We need some ice," he said. Barry went out.

"By what, Trask?" Grant asked.

Brad started in. "I'll tell you by what, dirtbags."

"It wasn't them, Brad," Trask said without taking his eyes off Paula. He covered the cut on her face with a long strip of gauze and began taping it down.

"I know computer shit when I see it," Brad said. "That thing wasn't real. It's some kind of special effects bullshit."

"I know what it looked like, Brad, but it wasn't. It's not possible." Trask wasn't all that inclined to defend the show's producers at this point, but they sure as hell weren't behind this. It was way out of their league. Or anybody else's. "I need something to bind up her arm."

Vince shook a pillow out of its case and tore the case into strips, handing them to Trask one at a time.

Paula winced when he raised her arm.

"Yeah, I know," Trask said. "It's going to be okay."

She lay still while he bandaged her forearm. Trask thought she looked woozy, near fainting again. Her skin felt cold. He wondered about shock. He thought maybe he was supposed to raise her legs. He stuffed some pillows under her ankles and pulled a blanket over her. She looked at him a little dreamily, another probably bad sign.

Barry returned with Evans, the caterer, who'd crushed some ice in a baggie and wrapped a towel around it. Trask took it and pressed it against Paula's temple. She flinched, bit her lip and looked away—toward the window opposite her, and the jungle outside across the wide stretch of sand.

"Is she okay?" Bentley said.

"Yeah, she's fine."

Bentley ignored Trask's sarcasm and murmured something sympathetic-sounding. Then he turned to Brad and said, "What are you two talking about?"

Trask heaved a heavy sigh. "The thing that—whatever it was that did this… It looked like CGI."

Paula was aware that people were talking, that Trask was beside her, and Brad and Bentley and Grant and Rashad and Vince were gathered around them, but it was all kind of a haze. She hurt all over, she was pretty sure, but it didn't hurt, if that made any sense. She felt like she was watching it from somewhere, like it was a movie, and they were all in it, but it wasn't real, they were just saying lines. The words must have made sense, but she couldn't follow the conversation because she could only remember a few of them at a time. She guessed maybe she was in shock. She wasn't afraid anymore. She felt sort of detached. Was that shock? She didn't think she was going to die. That was good.

Watching the movie of her, Paula, on the bunk in the room full of people talking was calming in a way.

And now she realized there was another movie playing and she was watching it too. Only, *really* watching it. From where she was, with her eyes. It was a movie of the view outside the window. There were other people in this movie.

They were coming this way.

She remembered then that there were other search parties, not just hers. Someone had yelled for them to all come back. So now they must be coming back.

The person in front was a man, and he was carrying a woman in his arms like Brad had carried her. The woman was unconscious, like Paula herself had been off and on for the past few minutes or hours, whichever it had been. Or maybe asleep.

It was hard to make out who was who. The glass was streaked with dirt. And of course it was still dark out there.

Bentley said something that sounded like an answer to something someone else had said, but she couldn't remember what that was, even though it must have been just a second ago.

"CGI did that?" He sounded skeptical. Paula smiled at the sound of surprise in his voice.

"You bastards, you know what—" Brad started to say, but then Trask said, "They don't know anything, Brad. They don't have the technology. Nobody does."

Paula couldn't follow that, it was too many words.

Funny how when people talked to Brad they always said his name, like it might make him pay attention better. She liked Brad. He had brought her back. She liked Trask too. She just couldn't figure out what they were talking about, so she watched the movie instead.

The people in the movie were closer to the light around the dormitory now, and she could see even through the smudgy window that they were covered with mud, and their clothes were torn like hers. Even though the movie seemed to be in slow motion, they moved like they were in a big hurry. It wasn't just mud, Paula saw now. That was when she realized she'd been smiling, because she stopped smiling then.

She wasn't headachy, it was too numb up there still. She was drowsy is what her mom would have said. But her eyes opening up really wide made the drowsiness go away a little.

"The technology…" Bentley's voice said.

"It doesn't exist." Trask. "Not now. Not here."

"Then where?" Grant. "What are you talking about?"

Paula wondered too, but the people outside were really close now and there was something else not quite right. Something about them looked funny.

It was the woman.

They came right into the circle of light outside the dormitory as they passed the corner of the building.

She wasn't unconscious.

Paula rose up on her elbows.

It was her head.

Someone was screaming and it wasn't a movie anymore. It was Paula herself, and she couldn't stop. She just screamed and screamed and screamed.

The woman outside the window had no head.

The bandage on Paula's face tore loose. Fresh blood gushed from her cheek and down her chin. She was shaking her head, violently, blood flying off of her face and all over everybody, covering her ears with her hands to shut out the sound of screaming, only it didn't shut it out, it just made it sound different. And the people in the room were shouting, and Trask was beside her again, trying to hold her, while she pounded against his chest with her fists. She didn't mean to. She just couldn't help it.

CHAPTER EIGHT

OPERATIONS

LEAVING TRASK to try to calm Paula, Bentley hurried outside with everyone else, catching up with Hal at the tail end of the arriving party as the others disappeared into the mess hall.

"My God, Hal," was all Bentley could say.

Hal told them to wait outside while they covered her up.

"It's not something anyone would want to see if they don't have to." He went inside, leaving them standing around in confusion when the door closed behind him.

Hands in his pockets, Bentley waited patiently, almost serenely. He looked from one to the other of his colleagues, then at Brad, at Rashad and then Vince. The punters were looking to him for direction, he guessed. The excitement was wearing off, and with the feeling of inertness that ensued came a sense of awkwardness. It was hard to say what would be a decent amount of time to wait before entering, or what sort of demeanor would be expected of them when they did. Would someone be calling them in? And why was he, the Director, standing out here like an idiot waiting to be invited?

"This is ridiculous," Grant said. "I'm going in."

Without waiting, he opened the door and strode through, leaving Bentley no choice but to follow. Bentley felt his blood pressure rise again as they all crowded inside.

The punters had laid Sondra on one of the long dining tables. In this context, the brushed aluminum top made it look like an operating table.

The operation had, of course, been a failure.

A white tablecloth someone had pulled over the body sprouted glistening crimson flowers. It *was* hard to look at. Where Sondra's head should have been there was just a void. Zach must have felt that too, because he pushed another wadded up sheet under the covering and pressed it up against Sondra's neck. There wasn't much need to stanch the bleeding, which was sluggish at this point, but it did help to alleviate the cosmetic shortcomings.

The proceedings were shrouded in a respectful silence. Dazed punters stared with vacant expressions. Roger, the second half of the camp's security, stood by the door. He'd been taking a nap on the control room couch when the shit hit the fan. Bentley'd passed right by the control room on the way outside, but hadn't even thought to alert him.

Barry cleared his throat. Bentley wasn't sure if that was a sign Barry was about to speak or a signal that he, Bentley, ought to utter some carefully chosen words. He mulled over the question, but was given a reprieve when the door creaked open again and Janet, along with two of the other girls came in. Bentley tried to remember their names. Rhymes with "hell". Gabrielle? That was it. One of them.

The girls tiptoed over to the couch opposite Fredo and Clayton, and sat identically with their hands tucked between their knees, staring wide-eyed at the white tablecloth with the flowers in what—if it hadn't been so horrible—would have been almost comic solemnity. The other one was May or Mei something, Bentley remembered.

Tony arrived next, with Jeremy close on his heels.

Bentley cleared his throat.

"Lance," Grant said. "What happened?"

Lance didn't seem to hear him. He stood over Sondra's corpse with his back to them. Bentley wondered where her head was. Probably best to let that come out in the normal course of conversation. Still—

"Lance. What was it?" Grant prodded.

Rashad moved over to the table and put a hand on Lance's arm. "Did it glow? Like a TV?"

The question seemed to register. Lance frowned.

"A TV?"

"Like a computer screen," Brad said. "with big red eyes and things coming out of its face…"

"Things…?" Lance sounded confused.

"Antennas," Rashad said. "A big glowing monkey with antennas."

"But like in a movie," Brad said. Lance was becoming agitated, but Brad kept after him. "Like some kind of special effects monster in a movie."

Lance exploded. "Like in a *movie?* Are you kidding? Have you all gone nuts? Sondra's dead! She's *dead!*"

Brad and Rashad glanced at Bentley. They all felt chastened, but they weren't sure why.

"We can see that, Lance," Bentley said.

"It was an alligator, man! A fucking alligator," Lance shouted. The tears finally came. He bowed his head, fighting to control himself, then looked back up, straight at Bentley. "The lagoon was crawling with them. How the hell would I know? I'm from West fucking Hollywood, I don't know anything about alligators. We waded right into them." He choked back a sob and stopped to catch his breath before continuing in a low, rasping monotone. "They were probably all around us. We didn't know.

"She lost her shoe. She was laughing, because her shoe got stuck in the mud under the water. She reached down to get it. She said, 'It's really stuck,' and started tugging on it.

"We were laughing, and Sondra was fooling around, like it was a joke, and then everything just—water just started flying all over the place." He paused again for another breath, but they all knew where it was going.

"Her shoe was in its mouth. It was mad from her tugging on it. It was so fast. She was still laughing when it…"

It was enough. He broke down. Rashad helped him into a chair.

Everyone was horrified. Somehow it was even more shocking than the otherworldly alternative. Alligators were real.

Barry fidgeted. "That would…those would be…crocodiles, actually," he said. "Alligators are native to…"

Not appropriate. Barry's words trailed off under Bentley's glare. A long silence followed.

Finally somebody said, "Poor Sondra."

Bentley looked around. It was Janet. Everyone bowed their heads in sympathetic communion.

"I just keep thinking," Janet continued. "I just…"

"Yes? What?" Bentley prompted.

"It could—" and now *her* tears began to flow "—it could have been me."

With a little cry, Tony leapt to his feet and rushed to her side to console her, murmuring reassurances slathered with cringingly embarrassing endearments. Jeremy watched with tight-lipped resentment. The other punters all stared at Janet with something resembling hatred.

Bentley looked at Brad, then Rashad, and frowned.

"Alligator, huh?"

"No," Rashad said.

Barry picked up the lost thread of his part of the conversation, left dangling and unresolved. "…Florida, Louisiana. The—"

"Quiet, Barry," Bentley snapped.

"Not the thing we saw. No way," Rashad said.

"It's understandable. No one's holding it against you. You got Paula out alive. It was dark—"

"Aren't you forgetting something?"

Everyone turned around. Trask was standing in the doorway.

"How is she?" Rashad asked.

Trask nodded.

"No. What?" Grant asked him.

"Our monster wasn't the first one. What about whatever it was that scared the hell out of Jeremy and Janet? Was that an alligator?" He turned on Jeremy. "Was it?" he demanded.

Tony held Janet and glared at Jeremy. Jeremy made no answer, but his fear was apparent. Brad was ready for a fight. "Listen, Grant—" he began.

But Trask wasn't finished. "And what about the thing Amber saw this afternoon? Alligator? Hal saw it too."

"I didn't see it," Grant said.

"Good for you," Trask said. "But a lot of us have seen them now. They're all the same, but they're all different too. Ours was some kind of radioactive Hello Kitty that blew itself up after Brad punched it in the nose with a rock. Only it didn't have a nose. Just lots of teeth and claws.

"Face it, man, something really fucked up is going on and we better figure out what it is and how to deal with it fast."

"Let's not let our imaginations—" Grant began.

"Yeah, let's not," Trask said. "Let's just stick to the facts. Okay. Listen, Grant, the thing we saw was like something out of a cut-rate Industrial Light and Magic. Brad's right, it was good, but George Lucas is better. The only problem is, our monsters are real. Take another look at Paula if you don't think so.

"And they don't seem to be here for our entertainment. More like we're here for theirs."

Bentley could see Grant was irritated by Trask's manner, and couldn't help sympathizing. Hell, it wasn't Grant's fault. Or his own either for that matter. This could have happened to anyone. At the same time, though, he was—beneath the deep sorrow he felt for their loss—secretly thrilled by the charged atmosphere. He checked to make sure Hal was on. Yes, he was.

"We understand the seriousness," Bentley said. "There's something— unusual going on, I know that. I can figure that out. But we have…we…" He was flustered by the petulance he heard in his own voice.

"What we have" Grant said, "is a once-in-a-lifetime opportunity."

Here was something. Bentley turned to Grant, only too happy to let him handle the situation as long as the cameras were rolling. Better for the Director to stay behind the scenes, holding the reins so to speak, but with the wisdom to give the cast the creative freedom to make the most of the performance aspects. Despite what Barry said, Grant did have a certain something. He had everyone's attention now, Bentley noted. Even Barry's.

Grant stepped forward onto center stage.

"We'd be fools to deny there's something remarkable taking place. Something fantastic, unexpected. And yes, terrible. We—none of us—will ever forget the horror, the tragedy. We've shared a great loss. People we knew only briefly, but came to love as family in that short time, thrown together as we were to endure hardship and struggle, to test ourselves to the fullest. Determined to meet any occasion with fortitude and honor. And in honor of their memory, we have no other course but to rise to the occasion."

Nearly overcome, Grant paused to fill his lungs, confident that none would venture to intrude upon the moment with an ill-timed word.

They were just kids after all, like Jim said. They weren't soldiers. Marines. They weren't battle-scarred, hardened and tempered steel-nerved veterans of hand-to-hand trench warfare, and they weren't used to seeing their friends coming back from patrol with their heads missing. But he was. He'd seen plenty of action as a Marine Lieutenant in the First Gulf

War. He knew the kind of devastation a relentless series of murderous surprise attacks could wreak on troop morale.

And he knew how to rebuild it.

"The challenge now has become greater than any of us could have foreseen," he said. "The stakes are high. But the rewards too are high. Yes, we face a grave and unknown danger. But one that we will conquer as surely as freedom must triumph over evil and oppression in whatever part of the world good and strong men and women may be found to defend against it. We've been caught off guard and dealt a heavy blow. But have faith, my friends. Have faith.

"Together, as the whole world shall soon see, we will prove ourselves able to overcome any obstacle, any hardship, any threat, however terrible. We will not be defeated.

"You came to this island mere contestants in a simple game of skill. As hunters and gatherers.

"You will leave it—as heroes."

Everyone stood gaping, transfixed. They had never seen this side of him, Grant knew, but they would be seeing more of it from now on. He was a leader. There was no mistaking it now. If not for the distressing presence of a corpse on the table behind him, Grant was certain the room would have burst into spontaneous applause.

"You fucking assholes," Trask said. His manner abruptly changed. "We need guns. What do we have?"

Noticing that all eyes were on him now, Bentley stopped scraping at the scab in his ear and put his hand in his pocket.

"Jim's shotgun," Roger said. "And high-powered rifle." He hefted it.

"Pistols," added Barry.

"*My* pistols," Bentley said.

"Me and Jim have one each," Roger said.

Lance looked up at Trask. "I lost Jim's. I put it in my belt to go in after…" He hung his head. "It must have fallen in the water."

Trask nodded. "Anything else? Knives? Anything we can use."

Barry snapped his fingers. "Rob, there's a barrel full of machetes in the storage shed."

"Get them," Trask said.

Barry looked to Bentley for confirmation. Bentley gave him the nod, and Roger followed him out the door.

"Anything else?"

"That's it," Hal answered. "Jim and Roger have all the heavy firepower. Jim's not back yet."

"They keep the big guns," Bentley said. "Know how to use them."

Trask nodded again. Bentley was gratified that Trask could see the sense in that. He was reasonable. It was always good to be reasonable, especially now.

The door opened.

Barry was back. He stood with his hand on the doorknob.

"Rob..." Barry turned his head to direct their attention outside. Toward the jungle.

From far away came a faint boom.

The distant report of a shotgun.

Then another.

All eyes were on Bentley again. He glanced around the circle of faces, looking to him for direction as another faraway boom sounded.

"For their sake I hope you're right," Trask said. "Where are those machetes?" he said to Barry as they piled outside.

The thing howled and Jim's shotgun roared.

Before he could chamber another round, it was gone.

He threw a glance over his shoulder. The light from Fred's camera bounced over the trees in the rear, seeking some way of escape up the steep sides of the dell. There was no sign of the thing.

Jim faced forward again. His gaze skipped over the marshy vegetation, narrowed eyes searching.

Michelle's voice drifted down from the ridge above.

"Michelle!" Jim shouted, keeping his eyes trained on the terrain ahead. "Can you see it? Where's Erika?"

Fred called back, "She's here with me."

With Michelle's help, they were looking for a way up out of the dell.

"Jim, I see it!" It was Nils, far off to Jim's right.

Jim whirled.

"It's coming your way!"

They could all hear it, trampling reeds as it slogged through the muck forty yards away.

And then they saw it—not the thing, but its glow, playing over the undersides of the tree branches, moving towards them. Only for a second—then it was gone, and the dell was quiet again.

A wave of swamp water sloshed over Jim's ankles. More seconds ticked by.

He took a single step forward. Light exploded over the ferns ten yards to his front, and the thing reared up under a splashing mountain of bilge water.

It had the face of a dead catfish, with dull gray eyes and slender stalks of tendrils jutting from a sloping forehead. Thick tentacles for arms, ending in stinger-like talons. The huge mouth hung open, jaws quivering. Bogwater drained from it like swill through a scupper.

It lowered its head and bore down on him, parting the tall fronds like a charging rhino.

Jim threw up his shotgun and fired. The thing veered to his right and hurtled past. He swung around and ran after it, unable to shoot without risking hitting Fred and Erika. It was headed straight for them. Captured in its unearthly glow, they scrambled up the side of the dell. Guided by Michelle, they'd found a way out.

But they hadn't seen the thing coming for them.

"Fred, it's right behind—"

Jim's words were drowned out by a bellowing roar.

Erika screamed. Before Jim had covered even half the distance, it had her by one leg and was dragging her down into the ferns.

And here came Nils, splashing towards it from their left.

The yard bristled with cast and crew. Those who had weapons held them at the ready.

Jim's shotgun had boomed, five times, then there'd been a long pause, then another boom. Twenty seconds later, two more. Since then, nothing.

The minutes stretched past the quarter-hour mark.

People were growing restless. Hal moved through the crowd, capturing reaction shots, logging coverage. His bash light found Bentley, talking to Barry. Barry shrugged. Hal swung the light toward the jungle.

Another ten minutes passed. Some of the cast had begun talking about "going in after them" when from deep within came the sound of running feet. Hal's light steadied on the wall of trees.

Groans, whimpering. Movement. A splash of color.

The search party burst from the jungle. Jim, at their head, half-carried Nils. Behind them, Erika hobbled on one leg, supported on either side by Michelle and Fred, her other leg gashed and bloody.

Nils pressed one hand against his lower abdomen. Something pink and red, streaked with black, bulged between his fingers.

Fred stumbled, his camera fell to the dirt, and Erika went down. Michelle struggled to help her back up.

Nils dropped to his knees. Jim left him there and whirled to face the jungle.

"Take them!" he said.

Punters dashed forward, lifted Nils by his arms and legs. Others picked up the girls and carried them away at a run.

Jim raised his shotgun. Roger stepped up beside him and lifted the high-powered rifle. It trembled in his hands.

Weapons at the ready, they braced themselves for the onslaught of whatever horror came.

And they waited.

And waited.

And only silence met them from the darkness of the trees.

Bentley walked up to Fred's camera lying in the dirt, and stooped over it.

The lens was cracked. The housing mangled.

He looked up to see Grant beside him, shaking his head.

"They've damaged the camera," Bentley said.

Sound of distant thunder. Raindrops splattering against the barrier high above their heads.

Whatever was out there, it was a no-show. Jim lowered his shotgun. Roger followed suit, and they turned and trotted for the cast's quarters.

The dormitory was crowded with punters, most standing around Nils. They'd laid him on a bunk against the long windowless wall.

It didn't take Dr Kildare to see that Nils was in serious trouble. He lay on his back, face gray, breathing labored. He'd quickly lost consciousness after they'd gotten him inside, and stayed that way.

The punters looked up at Jim.

"How's the bleeding?"

"Stopped," Rashad said. "Mostly."

Jim nodded. "Don't touch anything," he said, and motioned Hal and Roger over to the side. By "anything", it was generally understood that Jim meant the steaming and blood-streaked intestines bulging from Nils's torn abdomen. After a few words with Jim, Hal and Roger hurried out.

Trask was in the bathroom washing his hands. He came out, shaking them dry and Jim said, "Good," and asked him if he thought he was up to doing some emergency surgery.

Up to it or not, Trask was ready.

The punters moved out of the way. With Jim standing next to him, talking quietly to help keep his courage up, Trask started pushing Nils's insides back through the ragged horizontal wound.

Nils's torso was slick with blood. More squirted out when Trask squeezed a swollen length of intestines back through the gash. It made a slurping sound when it passed through. Bubbles seeped out around it, releasing a fine spray of mist when they popped. Clotting blood caked Trask's fingers. When he took his hand away, it stretched into thin dark strings like hot caramel. The sheets and mattress on which Nils lay were soaked black.

Jim's two-way burbled and he plucked it from his belt.

"Give me some good news, Hal."

Hal's voice came back. *"I've got the hospital on Mahé. Can you hear him, Doctor?"* He was over in the bungalow's conference room, holding Roger's two-way up to the field radio's headset. An emergency room doctor at Victoria Hospital was on the other end.

Jim said, "Est-ce okay en Anglaise?"

"Yes, yes. This is Jim?"

"Doc, you're going to work with Trask while I hold the radio."

"Very good. Mr Trask?"

"Yes." Trask's voice was trembling, but so far his hands were steady.

"Explain to me please the nature of the patient's injuries."

The doctor had been shocked and frustrated by the lack of provisions, and at something of a loss over how to tend to the kind of traumatic injuries Nils had sustained without medical supplies.

They did have needles and thread, and there was still some hydrogen peroxide, but that was next to useless in Nils's case. Between the two of them, Trask and the doctor had done what they could.

Jim had handed the radio over to Rashad to help stretch the skin closed over the wound while Trask sewed it shut. Afterwards, they'd tied strips made from cotton sheets around it and taped it all up with duct tape.

Then—after Trask got done puking in the toilet—they took shifts watching over Nils, calling in periodically with updates on his status.

His condition steadily worsened.

CHAPTER NINE

BAND-AIDS

STRINDLAK BENT OVER the worktable, muttering.

Behind him, cradled in its rigging of struts and suspension cables like some monstrous termite queen, loomed the immense bulk of the ship's engine.

He paused in his work to refer to a diagram in the wall-mounted display, then fell back to muttering as he made a series of minute adjustments to the workpieces.

Satisfied, he reached for the welding torch. It looked like a hatchling's plaything in Strindlak's big fist. He had far too many tentacles for such a simple device, and kept most of them coiled out of the way. Doubtless it was designed for use by the appropriate utility drone, but Strindlak hadn't the patience to go through the necessary transformation using the ship's transporter. It didn't matter. He was getting results.

The workpieces glowed red, then orange. Metal flowed. Strindlak jerked the torch away and the metal alloy solidified instantly in a secure bond.

He shut off and set down the torch, loosened the clamps and snatched up his still piping-hot creation. His bare flesh responded with an angry hiss. Blisters erupted and burst in a barrage of dull pops. Several tentacle-tips caught fire.

Unmoved, Strindlak hefted his handiwork with grim delight, snatched up a heavy fastening tool, and turned toward the waiting rotor mechanism.

From a throne-like structure on a raised dais in a mammoth chamber adjacent to the engine room, Strindlak's mate presided over a quivering multitude.

Glumrok was similar in form to Strindlak, but with some striking differences. Her hide was an iridescent copper with emerald highlights.

Down her back ran an elegant, horny crest. One tentacled fist gripped a long baton. From its headpiece sprouted a colorful fountain of softly undulating tendrils.

At Glumrok's feet sat young Churlo and Pirnod—proud halflings in their second mutation. And stretched out before them lay a shag carpet of bobbing mushrooms. The hatchlings. Mere infants, with the primary mutation still years ahead of them, they goggled in rapt attention as Glumrok wove a tale.

Her words, unfathomable to most of the assembly, were uttered in deep, bell-like tones that resonated throughout the chamber.

A portal opened. Ropsnag entered quietly, careful not to disturb the proceedings. Glumrok nodded a greeting without pausing in her discourse.

Ropsnag was older than the twins, but like them had not yet undergone his third mutation—as had Snorlok.

There was a fifth, female sibling, still in her first, on whom Glumrok and her brothers lavished much affection. Little Zillior was already tucked away in her sleeping pod on the second level.

Ropsnag threw a guarded look at Churlo and Pirnod. Careful to conceal the gesture from their mother, Pirnod responded with a muted flapping of foretentacles. Much relieved, Ropsnag came forward to join his siblings at the foot of the dais.

Ropsnag and the twins were too grown-up for such bedtime stories, but their mother's voice washing over them instilled in them a profound sensation of warmth and well-being.

Pirnod looked over at Churlo. Churlo opened sleepy eyes to gaze back. He smiled a tranquil, secret smile, and Pirnod and Ropsnag smiled back.

All was peace. Contentment.

Tentacles smeared with grease from the installation of his handiwork, Strindlak stood at the control console.

He flipped a switch.

Readouts flickered to life. Dials and knobs glowed. He seized the ignition lever and thrust it home. The engine responded instantly, with a musical hum, smoothly increasing in volume. Power.

Strindlak looked up to watch the rotor and was rewarded at once when it began to turn.

With a stuttering cough, it jerked to a stop.

He looked down. The meters were still functioning. In fact, they were peaking wildly.

The hum modulated to a discordant scraping, underscored by an ominous rumble.

Eerily, the rotor began again to turn. It picked up speed. A blue nimbus formed around it. It began casting off sparks. The scraping and rumbling were joined by a high-pitched whine. The entire huge apparatus began to shake in its moorings.

Strindlak lunged for the override lever and slammed down hard with his fist, flattening it against the panel.

He was too late.

The engine was responding to its own impulses now.

The evening dragged past.

Lance had apologized to Jim for losing his pistol, with an uncharacteristic shame that made everyone feel even worse for him than they already did. Jim told him he figured he'd have lost it too, given the same circumstances.

At Jim's suggestion—which he'd phrased with a gentleness that reflected a surprising sensitivity—Lance had gone out with Brad and Vince to dig a hole. They had no idea how long they were going to be trapped on the island, and couldn't just leave Sondra on the mess hall table indefinitely.

Jim had meant to go with them, but his arms were clawed up as badly as Erika's leg (even though he insisted it was "no big thing"), and Vince had told him they could handle it. So he sat on a bunk and tried to relax. But he kept getting up to check on Nils, and then sitting back down until he got mad at himself for not making himself useful and went out to help anyway.

After Jim left, Zach took his place at the sickbed, wiping Nils's forehead with a water-soaked towel. None of them could say if that was the right thing to do, but it was hard to not do anything at all.

Janet and her clique had left a little later without saying where they were going. Nobody asked or cared. The rest had gone over to the mess hall to help Evans get the place cleaned up.

It was well past midnight. Paula had drifted into the mess hall in the middle of Nils's operation. It was probably pure adrenaline that had lifted her out of her dazed condition and now it was ebbing away, leaving her groggy. She'd helped Beverly wash and bandage Erika's leg and brought her a couple of Tylenols for the pain, feeling guilty about the two she'd taken herself.

With Erika bandaged up and asleep now, Paula and Beverly tried to check Michelle for injuries, but Michelle wasn't having any. "Get away from me," she snapped. "I don't need a nurse. I'm fine." She got up and dropped into a nearby plush chair.

Trask was already slumped in another. He'd stopped shaking, but was in no condition for any new emergencies.

Thankfully, things seemed to have quieted down.

Glumrok glanced at the wall in irritation.

An incessant clattering from the engine room had interrupted her story in mid-verse. It would be impossible for her to continue until the din abated.

Ropsnag and the twins found comfort in her annoyance, taking it as a sign that the sounds were no cause for alarm.

They jumped when the ship resounded with a spluttering belch. A prolonged rattling shook the chamber. The sea of hatchlings chopped and skittered, smacking into each other like miniature bumper cars.

Glumrok half-rose from her throne just as the tremors stopped and a final lurch tossed her back into her seat.

She glanced once more at the wall with displeasure before shifting her large frame to a more seemly position, and issued a calming announcement to the hatchlings, with further words of reassurance to the halflings. Churlo and Pirnod looked up at her with the trust of innocence.

She smiled—it was somewhat forced—and resumed her narrative. She'd barely picked up the thread when she was cut off again. This time by a keening wail.

Wracked by convulsions, the engine snorted and groaned. A spray of igniting fuel blew off a hose cap. Overloaded generators spat black smoke downward to roll across the floor.

From deep within the engine came a chaotic pounding. With an explosive bang, a massive piston burst through the metal cowling like a crossbow bolt, knocking Strindlak to the floor when it took him in the eye. It rebounded down the chamber toward the vaned rotor mechanism. The rotor was spinning with a vengeance now. Individual vanes merged in a silvery blur of metal.

The piston slammed into them, knocking the entire mechanism off-kilter. A deep rumbling filled the engine room as the wobbling rotor worked itself free of its axle.

Frantic hatchlings milled and nittered in fear.

The nursery shook with seismic ferocity. The keening wail coming from the engine room built to a piercing screech, then a grinding roar of protesting metal, and finally an ear-splitting pounding and crunching that ended with a horrific BANG!

Glumrok stood immobile, paralyzed by uncertainty. Time seemed to stand still.

But only for an instant.

With a howl, the colossal rotor sliced through the wall like a chop saw wheel through a slab of butter.

Spinning like a windmill, it bounded across the floor, mincing hatchlings, banked on its side and clove through Pirnod at a forty-five degree angle, heaving his severed upper body ceilingward, arms flapping like chicken wings. Its fury unabated, the rotor sailed on like a frisbee and punched cleanly through the opposite wall to carve a clattering path of destruction through the ship.

Glumrok gaped in stunned astonishment.

From the engine room, alarms whooped and clanged. Through the first smoking hole in the wall, Strindlak's horrified countenance peered out. He clambered through and raced across the nursery, trampling squealing hatchlings underfoot.

The outrage was too much for Glumrok. She snatched up the baton topped with waving tendrils and gave chase, using it to shower blows upon Strindlak's head and back as he sprinted after the rogue machinery.

The burial party, minus Jim, had returned. Physically and emotionally exhausted by their labors, they sprawled in chairs and bunks, too tired to move or talk.

Still at Nils's bedside, Zach dipped the cloth in the pan of water and wrung it out. He looked over at Trask, his expression helpless.

"I don't know what I'm supposed to be doing."

Trask shook his head. He'd just gotten back from calling the hospital again fifteen minutes ago and all they'd told him was to "keep monitoring" Nils's condition.

There wasn't much to monitor.

He got up and went over to the bunk where Paula sat beside Erika and pulled up a chair. "How is she?" he asked.

"She'll live," Paula said, without a trace of irony. Normal had suddenly become strange. Trask looked her over.

"How are you?" he said.

She looked at him for a long time before replying. He tried not to read her thoughts. He was having a hard enough time trying to figure out his own.

Finally she just said, "Nils..."

They looked over at his bunk. A tremor shook Nils's body, rattling the bunk beneath him. It lasted only a few seconds, then he relaxed and lay even more still than before. He hadn't made a sound.

Zach leaned closer to him and watched his face for a few seconds, then looked around to see Trask and Paula watching. He looked away, suddenly self-conscious, like he'd been caught doing something forbidden.

Michelle watched Nils too, then turned her unreadable gaze on Paula. "Why don't you just say it?" she said. "He can't hear you."

Trask shouldn't have been surprised that this was hard even for her. "Michelle—"

"Nils is going to die," she said. "They didn't bring anything except aspirin and Band-Aids. Those things out there—"

Paula cut her off. "What things? What was it?"

Michelle seemed lost in her own private nightmare.

"We're all as good as dead," she said.

Trask wasn't sure if she was talking to them or herself.

"Michelle." Brad pulled his chair closer. "Was yours an alligator too?"

Michelle looked up at him and stared, then shook her head. "You really are an idiot," she said, and started to laugh. Brad was more surprised than angry.

"An alligator." Michelle laughed so hard it hurt. She bent forward in her chair, gasping for breath, then covered her eyes with her hands to try to hide the tears when her laughter gave way to sobs.

Paula came over and knelt beside Michelle's chair, pulling her close to nuzzle her head against her shoulder. Michelle didn't resist. She reached out and Paula held her tight—smoothing her bangs away from her face with her free hand as Michelle's tears ran down her own neck, looking at Trask with a stricken expression.

The thunder outside rumbled.

Trask stood up, confused. From Nils's bedside, Zach was looking at him too, with that same pleading look. "I don't know what to do for him."

"None of us do," Trask said quietly.

Why were they all looking at him? What could *he* do?

Without looking up, her voice muffled in Paula's arms and wet with tears, Michelle said, "What did we do to it? Why's it doing this to us?"

Trask shook his head again and looked away, grimacing. Was that going to be his answer to everything from now on? A shrug? Shaking his head?

When Michelle was able to talk, she told them what had happened. She'd seen it all from the ridge, looking down through the trees. She'd seen the thing that attacked Erika. And then Nils. Except for the same surreal glow, it hadn't looked anything like theirs.

Strindlak tugged another strip of patching material from its packaging and stuffed it into the jagged opening, spraying it over with foam sealant. The huge gash made by the runaway rotor stretched almost from floor to ceiling, centered on a ragged-edged hole where its spindle had punched through. He'd already repaired the other hole in the far wall of the nursery and was gaining some facility with the materials and technique.

The real difficulty had been getting Glumrok to put aside her trumpeting rage and allow him to get back to work. Her overreaction was typically female, out of all proportion with the damage. A couple of scratches in the walls, a few dozen hatchlings, most of which were doomed anyway, muscled back toward the rear of the chamber by their stronger brood-mates and headed for the chute. Hardly cause for such a dramatic display. He shook his head in disapproval, then smiled and shook it again with wry fondness—a deep affection that was sometimes difficult to feel when Glumrok was anywhere in the immediate vicinity.

He hummed as he directed the spray of foam over the prepared surface. His thoughts turned to the damaged rotor.

He'd managed without much trouble to straighten the three bent vanes. The fourth, unfortunately, had been mangled beyond repair when the rotor had at last collided with one of the ship's main support beams.

It would have to be replaced.

He puzzled over the problem. There was really nothing suitable on the ship.

And then it hit him: There was, though, something *outside* the ship. One or two of the primitive shelters employed by the planet's inhabitants were covered with metallic sheeting very similar to that from which the rotor vanes were constructed.

He shut off the spray, weighing the risks of foraging for supplies from amongst the natives' resources. "Property" might be a more apt choice of words.

It would be stealing, he was forced to admit.

The idea was tempting, though, and easy to rationalize. After all, if he couldn't get the engine up and running, they could be marooned here forever.

He'd have to use the transporter. As a rule, he shunned the device, deeming it not only undependable, but hazardous. For all its advanced technology and impressive capabilities, it wasn't without the usual assortment of crackbrained design flaws.

He set aside the patching material and considered.

Anything large enough to be adapted to his purpose would present a problem. Its edges would extend beyond the transporter platform's boundaries, resulting in a disruption of the energy field that could short out the system. He'd have to physically lug it to the ship and enter through the hatch.

If he was going to do it, he'd have his chance soon.

And with that thought, Strindlak realized he'd already made up his mind.

Everything slept, it was established fact. His own observations indicated the things were diurnal, and the planet's parent star had long since slipped past the horizon, plunging the hemisphere into its long period of night. If he knew anything at all, the natives would now be tucked into their pods and it would take nothing short of a cataclysmic event to shake them from sleep's paralyzing stupor.

He picked the sprayer up off the table and resumed his work, finishing the job quickly.

CHAPTER TEN

PLAYBACK

THE WATCHERS in the darkened control room gripped the arms of their chairs as the image in the playback window careened over glowing fronds. Jim's face loomed into view and was gone. From the studio monitors came his shout—"Go!"—over a horrible cackling. A brightness offscreen swung into frame, overloading the white level in fiery smears of video distortion.

Jim's shotgun boomed again. Dark shapes blurred past, the image yawed and swirled, fronds slapping it, jerking away.

"Michelle! Can you see it? Where's Erika?" Jim's voice was far off now.

The camera-mounted flood flicked back on, and there was Erika, up ahead, tearing through the ferns.

"She's here with me!" Fred's voice yelled from behind the camera.

And then came Nils's shout. "Jim, I see it!"

The floodlight's beam stroked the dell's sheer walls, searching for the way out, and finding it. Erika made for it.

"It's coming your way!" Nils said.

The picture angled down at the ground and spun, suspended over a pair of legs and feet—Fred's—struggling to clear the base of a sharp rise. The image bounced and whirled as the ground receded. He was climbing.

The next instant a pulsing glow added its brightness to the flood's beam, and another boom sent echoes rumbling over the cliff face.

Jim yelled. "Fred, it's right behind you!"

Something growled and snapped, and Erika screamed.

Legs flashed into view, dissolved into streaks of light. The ground blurred, whirled, and with a final jolt and a crack, the picture froze. Erika was shrieking now, whooping in pain and terror. There was a crunch, and everything went black.

Illuminated by a small worklight, the faces of the control room's inhabitants were reflected in the blank playback window. Red power lights and glowing LEDs dotted the background behind them.

Hal sat before the display, fingers poised over the keyboard. Behind and to either side of him sat Bentley and Grant. Watching their reflections in the screen, Hal saw Grant shoot Bentley a look of frustration.

He swiveled his chair toward them. Barry's eyes were still glued to the monitor—proving the inherent raw and magical power of television: Even when there's nothing on, you can't help sitting there transfixed by it.

Fred was backed up against the wall behind Bentley—reliving the horror.

It wasn't over yet.

The video signal was dead, but the terrifying soundtrack of pummeling sounds over Erika's screams still blared from the speakers.

A savage snarling erupted, and Nils roared like a berserker. There was a smack of something hard striking leathery hide, and a chunk! like a meat cleaver sinking into tenderloin.

Jim yelled, "Nils!" but Nils's roar had changed to a howl of pain.

"Go, Fred," Jim shouted. Another shotgun blast, followed by a furious pounding, like someone clubbing a shark with a baseball bat. Jim's curses were drowned out by a wild slavering, and he yelled again.

"Go! Go!"

From somewhere, Michelle screamed, "Jim, where's Nils?" and Jim yelled back:

"I have him! Run!"

There was another crack, and a pop, and the audio track went dead.

Hal depressed the keyboard's spacer bar, stopping playback, and pushed his chair away from the console. He turned toward the others.

Grant's disappointment showed. "Is that it?"

Bentley's too. "Shit, Fred, couldn't you've...?"

He caught himself, and looked around.

Fred was shaking uncontrollably. "Hey, sorry, man!" he practically shouted. "I'm not a goddamn war correspondent, okay? If it hadn't been for Jim—and Nils—!"

He groped for the door handle behind him, found it, and yanked it open. Bentley held up a placating hand.

"Sorry, Fred, my bad. You did a good job."

Fred stared at him, shook his head, then turned and went out the door.

They listened to his footsteps crunching away across the sand. Grant got up to close the door. He flicked on the overhead lights.

"Not much there we can use," he said.

Barry still stared slack-jawed at the screen. He roused himself. "What do you mean?"

"He ran," Bentley said. "We got nothing,"

Barry looked from one to the other in disbelief.

"Are you guys nuts? It's fantastic. I couldn't have scripted it better my-self."

Bentley shot him a glance. "Really? You think?"

"Shit! I *wish* I'd written it. For pure, in-your-face, gut-wrenching real-ism, you could never beat that. And the performances! I'm telling you, this is the shit. This is what it's all about. It's awesome, Rob."

"He's right," Hal said. No question, this was great stuff. "Came at a high cost, though."

"You're telling me," Bentley said, only partially mollified. "Those cam-eras cost a fortune. I can't risk any more of 'em. And even if we had the budget, where the hell are we going to find a replacement stuck in this goddamn terrarium?"

He weighed the priorities and announced his decision. "We'll keep Fred on the interiors from now on, for the human interest sequences."

"I'll go out," Hal volunteered. "I was in Vietnam."

"This isn't Vietnam," Grant said.

"You're right," Hal shot back. "It's worse."

All was finally quiet in the cast sleeping quarters. The last of the ex-hausted punters had scaled down the slender thread of jittery wakeful-ness to crash into their waiting bunks. Trask slept fitfully, his dreams haunted by a succession of gruesome replayings of his surgery on Nils. In the last, after Trask finished stitching him up, Nils jumped up and smiled and thanked him, then vomited his insides all over the room.

With a soft creak, Trask's bunk sagged under a sudden weight near his knees, and he came half-awake, opening unseeing eyes to the darkness.

"Trask," someone whispered.

He bolted upright, electrified with sudden fear, then caught his breath and lay back down. "Shit. Jim…"

The big man sat beside him, his face ghostly in the pale light cast by the floods outside the windows. The room filled with faint rustlings as other sleepers began to stir awake. Fred, having opted to spend the night with the cast, sat up and groped for his camera.

"What is it?" Trask said.

Paula lay in the next bunk over, her head close to Trask's. "Is something wrong?" she whispered. Jim looked at her, then over toward the windowless opposite wall.

"Nils."

Somewhere, someone began crying.

"I was going to wake you up for your watch," he said to Trask. "I just thought I'd check on him first."

Trask followed Jim over to the opposite wall. Like fearful, nightgowned wraiths, Paula and Michelle drifted over to join them at Nils's bedside.

Nils's form was a weightless emptiness hovering over the upper berth. Someone turned on a lamp. One by one, the rest of the room's occupants sat up to stare at the ghastly stranger in their midst who only yesterday had been one of them.

"Rest in peace, Nils," Rashad muttered. Everyone bowed their heads. Trask pulled the sheet up from the foot of Nils's bunk to cover him.

"Go back to sleep," Jim said softly to the others, then asked Trask if he was ready for his shift.

"What time is it?" Trask felt like he'd barely slept.

Jim looked at his watch, then said, "You know, I'm still good for a while. Why don't you get another couple hours." He kept his voice low to keep from waking the others up any more than they'd already been. But they were all wide-awake now, listening from their bunks. From a dark corner came Janet's querulous voice.

"Will they come after us here?"

"No reason to think so," Jim said. He added in a whisper to Trask, "No reason to think not, either."

"Look, Jim, I'm fine. We'd probably all feel better if you got some rest."

Jim gave Trask his appraising look, then nodded.

"Know how to use a shotgun?"

Trask hesitated. His first impression of Jim, showing up for the shoot loaded down with firepower, had been that he must be some kind of a gun nut. Maybe he was.

Maybe that wasn't such a bad thing.

"I guess so," he answered without conviction.

Jim lifted the shotgun and stood, holding it upright. "It's a slide action, real simple. Just pump it once—like so—" he demonstrated, sliding the pump back, then home with a solid clack, "—to feed a shell into the chamber." He handed it to Trask. "We're a little low on shells. Didn't think I'd be needing many."

After another moment's hesitation, Trask accepted it. He hefted it uncertainly.

"Careful now, it's loaded."

Trask adopted a shooting stance, raised the barrel to aim at a spot on the wall above Nils's bunk.

"There's seven rounds left in the magazine," Jim went on. "It's a twelve-gauge. Got a kick, so brace yourself."

Trask tucked the heel into his shoulder, choked up on the stock and rocked his elbow, finger on the trigger, getting the feel of it. He spread his feet wide, held the stance for a few seconds, then lowered the gun.

"Think you can handle it?" Jim said, reaching for it from behind.

A metallic screech shattered the night.

Trask jumped back, smacking into Jim, and Jim tripped over a stool and went down. Men and women leapt from their bunks, roaring in unison like a choir of the damned.

Squealing in protest, the aluminum siding buckled. With a sharp crack, a seam at the far corner split open. A slender vertical wedge of light poured through the gap to play over the terrified punters inside. They plowed screaming into each other as they all tried to run in different directions at once.

Jim was kicked back down and trampled when he tried to rise, while outside, something growled and slavered, then groaned in awful exertion. In the corner, a glowing device resembling a giant needlenose plier worked its way into the crack. It snapped shut and began tugging violently at the edge of the siding. The aluminum warped and rattled like a thundersheet in the jaws of some monstrous doberman.

The building rocked on its foundations, sending punters fleeing to the opposite wall. Rivets popping like firecrackers, the aluminum panel peeled away from its supporting studs. Torn half free of the twisted uprights, it billowed like a sail, and with a tremendous jerk broke away altogether.

It tipped outward. Rays of light crowned its jagged upper edge, radiating from a hidden source. It tipped still further, then sagged toward the ground, and the light outside exploded in a sunburst around a monstrous glowing head.

Two gleaming red eyes peered over the aluminum siding's upper edge at the pandemonium inside.

Stunned punters' screams died in their throats. Everyone froze.

The gleaming eyes stared. Massive shoulders hefted the needlenose pliers. They protruded as an extremity from the end of one mighty arm, surrounded by a clutch of thick, clawed spines and pincers, along with something that looked like a dual-bladed reciprocating saw.

The thing hesitated, then lifted and waggled its spines in a hideous caricature of a wave. Greetings! I come in—

BOOM! A shotgun blast crumpled its face, staggering it and blowing a stream of glittering motes out of the back of its head.

BOOM! Silhouetted before the creature's pulsating glow, Trask pumped the shotgun.

BOOM! Recovering, the creature spun around,—

BOOM! clutching its prize,—

BOOM! and hauled ass

BOOM! toward the jungle.

BOOM! BOOM!

Click…click…

Trask lowered the barrel. The thing was gone.

The punters gaped between the naked struts of the demolished wall, open to the now still night. Then at Trask.

Breathing hard, shaking, features strained with a fury no one knew he had in him, he shouted, "What the *fuck* is going on?"

Feet pounded on the sand outside. Bentley, Grant and Hal flew into view and skidded to a stop like cartoon characters to gawk at the damage.

From the frayed top edge of the gaping breach in the wall, loose shards of aluminum swung like delicate pendulums. A twisted stud teetered, then dropped to the floorboards with a dull clunk.

Bentley, Grant and Hal gazed in wonder through the break—past Trask and Jim, who turned slowly toward the back wall to follow their gazes.

There stood the others, bunched together, backs pressed up hard against the wall as if facing a firing squad. At one end, Janet slid, fainting, toward the floor.

And in the middle stood Fred, face twitching, his whole body tremoring as he lowered his handheld from the shooting position.

Fred had gotten the take.

Dragging its metal prize, the creature tore through the enveloping rainforest like a photon torpedo in a bowling alley, uprooting saplings and sweeping them aside like ninepins. The aluminum siding wobbled in its grasp, throwing off reflected light in strobing rays, splattering the creeping undergrowth and ceiling of branches overhead with cold blue fire.

In two enormous strides, it leapt over a rotten stump and hurdled a boulder the size of a Lexus. The sheet grazed it and twisted sideways, its corner bulldozed through earth, scattering rocks and sending them tumbling down an incline to the banks of a stream. Kicking up clouds of pebbles that skipped over the water ahead of it, the creature plunged in to splash toward the opposite shore. Startled crocodiles glided narrowly out of its path, snapping at its legs.

Unfazed, the thing won through to the opposite banks without incident save for crushing one huge reptile's skull like a clam in a final flying leap onto solid ground.

Behind it, bereaved survivors swarmed over the carcass. Taking no notice, the fugitive dove back into the jungle to crash away through the trees, making for the sloping foot of the central peak beyond.

"Yes… Yes…" Bentley scowled, covered the intercom's mouthpiece, and threw up a hand at his chattering associates crowding the editing console in a sharp gesture for silence. The air of quivering excitement ramped down a notch as Hal hit the spacer bar on his keyboard, pausing playback.

On the widescreen main display, the image froze:

Trask, backlit by the glowing monster, its outlandish features momentarily shattered, punched back through its head and inverted by the initial shotgun blast.

Bentley gazed at the astonishing sight and shook his head as he half listened. His manner was gravely sober.

"Of course," he said, in response to some earnest demand from the speaker—Michelle, calling over the mess hall's intercom.

"Yes, we're going to keep studying the take, see if there's anything you might've missed in the excitement—in the… Yes, thank God no one was hurt… Thank God…"

With care, he hung the receiver back in its hook. A wide grin split his face. The aura of solemnity evaporated into babbling ecstasy.

"Sensational!" Grant enthused.

"The network—!" Bentley began.

"Hah!" Barry crowed. "You want huge?"

"They're gonna die," Hal said with deep conviction. "They're gonna fucking die."

Grant chuckled. The others shot him eager, questioning smiles. Relishing the attention, he answered, "Could you believe the look on Fred's face?"

"Priceless!" Bentley shouted. He lifted a glass. "To Fred!"

The others chimed in. "To Fred! Hip hip—" The cheer died on their lips as Bentley put a finger to his own, injecting a note of caution.

"Sssh. They'll hear you."

Framed by mangled struts, lit by the external floodlights shining in through the demolished wall, Nils's corpse still lay on its bunk, covered by the sheet Trask had pulled over it. But Nils slept alone in the dormitory this night. The living had long since fled.

To the mess hall.

There, on couches and mattresses and blankets spread over the floor, they rested in fits, marking time in shallow sleep until the morning.

It was still Trask's watch. He sat slouched in a chair, the shotgun across his lap, his clenched nerves jerking to taut alertness at every muffled cry or moan from the sleepers, listening intently for any hint of motion outside.

PART TWO: **SATURDAY**

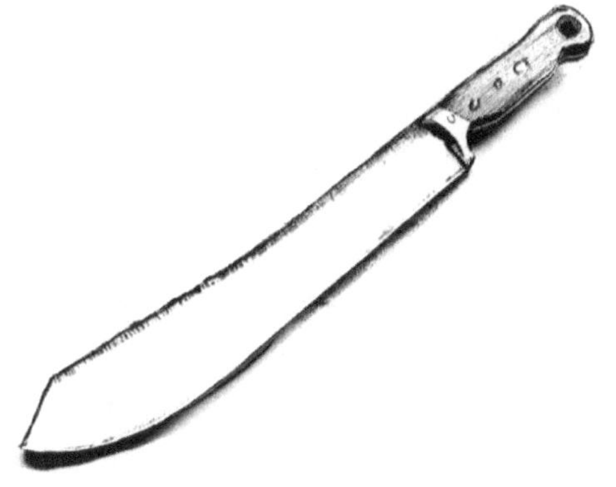

CHAPTER ELEVEN

SMASH

BEFORE DAYBREAK there were a half-dozen boats assembled beyond the barrier with more coming by the hour.

Bentley had already seen them. He'd been up all night. At first, when it was still dark, he could only guess at what they were by their lights. But now the sky had lightened to a deep greenish-blue and he could make out their general outlines and colors.

Mostly police, coast guard and whatever. The local media. But there were others too. Even a couple of sailboats—the yachts of rubbernecking millionaires.

And then there was one very large ship that utterly dwarfed all the rest. The thing must have been five hundred feet long. A military vessel.

Some kind of destroyer.

It had obviously warned off the curiosity-seekers on its approach with the nautical equivalent of "get the fuck out of the way"—because they'd started scurrying out of its projected path well before it glided in. When it did, just fifteen minutes ago, it had left a wake that stretched all the way out of sight toward the northwest.

Bentley stood up. He'd been parked in his recliner in the living room, staring out the window, for hours. Straightening up was a gradual process. He pressed his fists into the small of his back, stretched and yawned.

The network affiliate's own boat was out there too. He could see them off to his left, just within sight. They'd circled around to the east, far enough away to avoid being paid any further notice by Big Brother while managing to stay close to the barrier. The sky was just showing the first pale horizontal smears of pink behind them.

Giving up on sleep entirely, Bentley walked up the short hallway to the conference room. He opened the door to find Hal and Dylan sitting at the table. From the looks of things, they'd been up all night too. Hal shook his head at Bentley.

"We've tried everything. Can't even get through overseas—"

"I know that." Bentley sat down.

"So we've been trying to get something to Five Seychelles. Can't even get through to them half the time. Started with full-color, full-frame thirty fps. No go."

"We took it back to the editing room," Dylan said. "Converted it to grayscale, small screen seventy-two dpi, compressed the hell out of it."

"And?"

"Still wouldn't go through," Hal said. "So Dylan had an idea to even more drastically—"

"We resampled everything," Dylan explained. "Cut the frame rate to three per second."

Bentley said, "Is this like 'amateur TV'? Like a webcast, or those fifty-something cable channels?"

"Way worse," Dylan said. He and Hal waited, expecting Bentley to explain—or complain about the sacrifice in quality—but he didn't. He just seemed thoughtful. Undecided.

So Dylan went on, "Kind of like jerky surveillance video. Convenience store holdups kind of shit. It has motion of a sort."

"It didn't work anyway," Hal said. "We finally just sent them a still. They got it, but they said they couldn't tell what it was."

Bentley nodded.

"If we had more power…" Dylan said.

They watched Bentley for some sign of acknowledgement. They'd done their best.

"Have you looked outside?" he asked conversationally.

"No," Hal said. "What's going on now?"

"There's a ship the size of Lake Tahoe out on the front lawn."

"What?" Dylan said. "You mean like a military ship?"

"That's exactly what I mean."

"How's that possible?" Hal said. "Seychelles doesn't have a military. They don't even have a Salvation Army."

"Well, it's there."

Hal went to the window and pulled the blinds. "Holy sea cow, Batman."

The sun had vaulted the horizon and in the gray light of daybreak they could make out the monster in detail.

To Bentley's untrained eye it was shaped like a canoe with all kinds of crap stacked into it. Near the front was a big, box-shaped affair that looked like a steel bunker with satellite dishes mounted on the roof. Behind it, radio towers rose up from the deck, with horizontal arms holding rows of antennas. And behind those was something that resembled a medium-sized PacifiCorp power plant.

Men moved around on deck. They looked like matchsticks.

And there were guns, Bentley noted. And missile launchers. Helicopters, even. Two of them.

"Where the hell did they come from?" Dylan said. "How could they get here so fast?"

He and Hal turned around to look at Bentley.

The phone rang.

Bentley lifted a finger for patience, then with his other hand picked up the receiver.

"Bentley."

It was someone from the ship. Calling to inform him, in English—with a midwestern accent—that their vessel was equipped with repeaters for cellular devices, and that the Navy would be happy to offer their assistance in establishing a more reliable communications link between the island and the outside world by re-routing Bentley's wireless signal through military channels.

The Navy? The *United States* Navy?

"Yes, sir. USS Frye, Guided Missile Cruiser, Ticonderoga Class, sir. We're assigned to ESG Thunderf—"

"ESG?"

"Expeditionary Strike Group, sir."

"I don't see any group. Just you."

"We were dispatched at all possible speed to the flashpoint, sir. We're the fastest ship in the unit," he added, *"thirty-si—uh, sorry sir, that's classified. But we're damn fast, sir. The rest of the group's on the way."*

Bentley said to Hal, "They're sending over the whole goddamn fleet." Then to the—"Who did you say you are?"

"Lieutenant Harrison, sir, Communications."

—lieutenant, he said, "How did you get here so fast, if that's not classified information?" Bentley put the call on speakerphone so Hal and Dylan could hear.

"We were en route to Indonesia from Mogadishu, sir, no sir, that's not classified. We were just three hundred miles away when the new orders came through. Just lucky, sir."

"Uh-huh."

The lieutenant explained that the Frye's close proximity to the island enabled them to pick up his signal at a much higher gain than the nearest repeater over on Ste. Catherine. Right now they were patched into the local GSM network. That would change as soon as the other ships arrived, but the improvement was already vast. *"Yes, sir, just like Verizon, sir. With fewer dropped calls,"* the young lieutenant said, somewhat ambiguously. *"Everything will be the same, but you'll be able to make calls to anywhere in the world."*

Only now, of course, he'd be going through their switchboard to place them.

Bentley was no fool, and he had to assume it meant all his calls would be monitored, but so what? They would be anyway, there wasn't much he could do to stop them. It just meant they'd be monitored at a higher level than they always had been. He could afford to feel flattered.

Bentley looked over at Hal and Dylan. They were ecstatic at what they'd heard.

With Bentley's permission, the lieutenant switched him over to a higher-ranking officer of some sort. After a brief exchange of pleasantries, the man notified him that the Secretary of Defense was urgently awaiting his call.

He hung up.

"Rob!"

Bentley again held up his hand for patience. He knew what Hal was about to say anyway. The footage was a go. Everything was set. And now they could send.

Bentley was the kind of man in whom a deep sense of loyalty and duty informed every decision. So—to the evident chagrin of the Frye's switchboard operator—his first call was to the Network. He was immediately put through via speakerphone in the middle of an emergency Board meeting presided over by the Chief Executive Officer, East Coast Division. The New York Office's highest-ranking executives were all present, including the Chief Operations Officer and Head of Programming, as well as a number of specialists in the more technical aspects of broadcasting and telecommunications. It was 8:30pm in New York—nine hours behind the Seychelles—and matters had already been thoroughly discussed before Bentley joined the conversation.

They listened breathlessly to his account of events following the barrier's appearance. After expressions of concern for the safety of the cast and crew and condolences for the casualties were gotten out of the way, the network executives were naturally curious about any footage that may have accrued during these trying and difficult hours.

Yes, there was footage (as they very well knew).

A generous application of censorship would be required in the case of the alligator—make that crocodile—attack, captured in all its startling detail by Hal's camera. The segment involving Jim's party and their mysterious encounter with some unknown beast, though less clear, was no less gripping and in its own way even more frightening.

All the major networks had spent the entire morning broadcasting and re-broadcasting the image of a giant mirror ball rising up out of the Indian Ocean. The public was enthralled. Any visuals—absolutely anything—from the other side of that smoked glass bubble would be pure gold. It was imperative that any available video evidence be gotten to the Network by whatever means possible, and quickly.

Watching Hal for confirmation as he spoke, Bentley told them he expected to have something coming their way shortly. Hal and Dylan nodded with bobble-headed vehemence, and Bentley went on to give the Network brass a quick summary of their method and explained that for the time being they'd all have to be satisfied with only a few shots in digested form.

They understood.

He warned them it would hardly be broadcast quality.

They assured him it would be broadcast nonetheless.

Bentley hung up the phone feeling his new position of prominence as something nearly tangible, and then picked it up again. In his exhilaration he'd almost forgotten to call the President. He glanced at the scrap of paper where he'd jotted down the call request. No, no, not the President—the Secretary of Defense.

He'd better find out the man's name first.

"Barry!" he yelled through the door.

Barry knew everything.

Dylan had left, and Barry and Grant had both joined Bentley and Hal by the time Bentley was ready to talk to the SecDef—who turned out to be a woman. He rushed her through the call, then got back to the Network.

The files had gotten through intact, but only the low res versions—the others would have to wait, in hope that the Verizon-like geometric increase in reliability offered by the coming fleet would suffice. The Network people confirmed that the video images were murky and lacked definition, but agreed that they did give a startling sense of what was taking place. The glowing ball of light bursting out of the swamp! Jim shouting, punters fleeing for their lives. The cast dormitory being ripped to shreds! Even though objectively it all looked like shit, it was awesome and riveting, especially with the accompanying audio, and they were going to run with it. They were in the process now of dropping it into the already taped and cut special report scheduled for broadcast at 9pm Central.

Bentley looked at his watch.

That would be 7am Seychelles time.

In about forty-five minutes.

The phone finally rang at five minutes after 8:00.

Certain of the details were lost to Bentley's ear because of the jubilant whooping in the background that cancelled out much of the speaker's words. The speaker was the Head of Programming. There'd been no official word yet of course, too soon, but unofficially, "Hunters & Gatherers – A Special Two-Hour Prime Time Report" was blowing the competition out of the water.

In a desperate bid to regain lost viewers, the other networks had responded immediately, cutting into their regularly scheduled broadcasts with their own hastily assembled Special Bulletins. The clueless handful still watching them were treated to stepped up and unprecedentedly graphic coverage of the Indonesia conflict, which was quickly escalating into a full-blown bloodbath replete with the slaughter of innocents and the first dark warnings of impending genocide.

Nobody cared.

The public was going wild over Hunters & Gatherers.

And the Network hadn't even dropped their biggest bombshell yet. They'd cunningly held back on the mother of all blockbusters, to be delivered as the coup de grâce after an hour's delay, in a repeat performance including what they described disingenuously as "just arrived" additional footage. And it would be an absolute stunner: Fred's take of the *thing*, tearing open the cast dormitory like a can of sardines—and Trask, the audience favorite, the pacifist, blasting away at it like a maniac with a shotgun.

Bentley hung up the phone. Barry and Grant and Hal were a single, gigantic, ear-to-ear grin.

"We've gone gold, people," Bentley announced.

A far-off gong sounded.

The grin stayed, but took on a shading of puzzlement.

The hollow clang modulated to a deep and sonorous, vibrato-steeped resonance.

They all moved to the window.

"I don't see anything," Hal said.

But they could still hear it, gathering layers of overtones, swelling to a roar of competing frequencies.

"Let's go," Bentley said.

Hal grabbed his camera and they hurried to the door.

By the time Barry stepped outside, holding a pair of binoculars, the roar had dwindled to a featureless wash of noise.

Another ship had arrived, similar to the first.

Hal went to full zoom. "It's a destroyer," he said.

Through his binoculars, Barry could make out a much smaller vessel in front of it, at the very foot of the barrier, with a group of sailors on deck.

"I don't believe it."

"What? What?" Bentley said.

"They're trying to break through. With a sledge hammer."

There was another deep clang. Barry saw the hammer head fly off and splash into the ocean. Another sailor stepped forward hefting a demolition hammer. Raising his voice over the crescendoing reverberations from the musical prelude, Barry said, "Cover your ears."

It sounded like a machine gun, only one that never ran out of bullets. The racket was unbelievable.

"God damn," Bentley said. He noticed Janet and her followers down the beach. They looked frightened. "Barry, go tell them what's going on and not to worry." To Hal and Grant he said, "Let's get back inside where it's quieter."

They fell in behind him. "This is a nasty turn of events," he complained.

There was an even nastier one waiting for him in the conference room—where the phone had been ringing non-stop for the past three minutes.

"What?" Bentley covered the mouthpiece and relayed the news to Hal and Grant.

This time it wasn't good.

Realizing any existing footage was likely to be sent over the GSM network, one of the rival stations had—against all international regulations, statutes and ethics—tapped into the signal and pirated it, legal consequences be damned. They'd intercepted it like a football thrown wide.

"Snatched it right out of the air," Bentley said.

Hal and Grant listened in horror.

"Bastards scooped us with our own footage."

Hal said "Oh no, not—"

"Oh yes, goddammit," Bentley said. "The big one, the one with Trask and the thing. The monster. *Our* monster!"

He listened some more, slammed his fist against the tabletop. "They're showing it over and over!" he raged. "Practically in a continuous loop. With all kinds of moronic commentary."

Hal began cursing in a continuous loop of his own until Bentley shushed him and sat down. The blue veins on the back of his hand gripping the receiver looked like they might burst.

Grant was already sitting. With an angry sigh, Hal sat down too.

The proprietary network was up in arms, filing complaints and cease-and-desists, at war with the FCC, the United States Government and whoever else they could think of. Bentley was forbidden to speak to anyone. They'd call him. That was fine with Bentley. His overlong and pointless conversation earlier with the SecDef had been a real time waster. Bentley was sure they both had more urgent matters to attend to. And anyway, he was having an idea.

When he got off the line his rage had been supplanted by a deep thoughtfulness.

Grant said, "What is it?" but Bentley needed more time. "We'll talk later," he said. Hal took it as a cue and nodded to Grant. The two of them got up and let themselves out, leaving Bentley to his thoughts.

The whine of power tools met their ears when they got outside, and this time it wasn't coming from beyond the barrier. The mess hall was undergoing major renovations.

The door slammed open and Vince and Tony hobbled down the steps lugging buckets of sandy dirt. They emptied them onto a growing mound, then paused when they saw Grant and Hal watching.

"What's going on?" Grant asked.

Vince said, "Secret escape hatch."

Hal was impressed. "Wow. Just like Stalag 17."

Vince and Tony looked at him blankly, then both said, "Yeah."

"Can we come see?"

Tony shrugged. "Knock yourself out."

Compared to the ruined dormitory, with its flimsy aluminum sheeting construction, the mess hall felt solid and secure. Like the bungalow next door, it was a pre-existing structure, sturdily built of lumber with a plaster-covered cement, stucco exterior. The two buildings were separated by a narrow breezeway, blocked at the inland-facing end by a generator room and the mess hall's kitchen, which protruded into the mess hall proper as an L-shaped extension.

But sturdy or not, the punters were using whatever materials they could lay their hands on to turn the mess hall into a fortified bunker. They'd already barricaded half the windows. Near the windowless back wall between the kitchen and bathroom, Brad stood waist deep in a circular hole in the floor, stomping a shovel into the sedimentary bedrock.

Fred filled Hal and Grant in on the details. After the windows, they'd block the door with Evans's oversize refrigerator. Barely movable empty, it would be weighted down even more at night with garbage bags packed with sand from the tunnel.

As usual, Trask and Lance had been at odds from the outset. Trask had been against barricading themselves inside the mess hall in the first place. Certain that Brad was right to the extent the things they'd encountered were computer-generated projections, he argued that it was a safe assumption they could materialize anywhere at will—bypassing such niceties as doors and barricaded windows. Those in the mess hall could find themselves trapped like rats with no way out.

Rashad had proposed the escape hatch as a solution, and Lance and the others had agreed it wasn't a bad idea.

The storage shed had provided the necessary tools, along with hardware and lumber. The dormitory's steel bunk frames made convenient reinforcing material with their pre-drilled holes. The punters had quickly developed an assembly-line routine for sealing the windows, and with a little practice it went pretty fast.

The tunnel was another matter. Vince had cut through the linoleum-covered planking with a circular saw. There was no crawlspace—the floor was only a few inches off the ground, so from that point on it was a matter of scraping and shoveling. Brad had done most of it so far, and if he had to, he'd do all of it. Brad was like a machine. He never paused in his work; he never took a break. But it was inherently a one-man job—at least until Jim got back with the other shovel—and one man could only go so fast. But they still had ten hours before sundown.

And Jim had just returned—with Evans at his side and the shovel slung over his shoulder.

They wouldn't be seeing any more of Nils.

"Morning, Hal," Jim said. "Grant." They returned the greeting and stepped aside to let him and Evans through.

"Where's everybody else?" Grant asked.

Lance said, "Janet and her pals keep disappearing for one reason or another."

"They want to leave everything in the Navy's hands," said Zach, "so they don't have to get their own all dirty and covered with blisters."

A few of the punters were sharpening machetes in the storage shed. Others scrounged around for more weapons material. It had been agreed that, before dark, they'd all take a break and see to the business of arming themselves.

Grant seemed to take personal pride in their efforts.

"This is what I like to see," he said.

Jim turned to Brad. "I'll start in from the outside and meet you half-way." He hefted his shovel. "Now that I'm warmed up."

"Keep up the good work," Grant said to the room at large before following Hal and Jim out the door.

Once asleep, Strindlak had an extraordinary ability to stay that way through almost anything, up to and including the aggregate din of an entire Flardnux 12000's complement of howling alarms.

Glumrok, being a light sleeper, awoke after the fifth or sixth siren joined the growing chorus to bolt upright, brow tendrils fluttering. After a moment of chest-constricting disorientation, she leapt from her pod and bounded over to Strindlak's. With a flurry of pummeling blows to the face she managed to slap him conscious.

Strindlak, fully awake and smarting, sensed immediate danger. Jumping up, he ordered Glumrok to assemble the halflings at the transporter room and without another word charged from the chamber to fly down the corridor toward the engine room, leaving her chittering in dismay.

CHAPTER TWELVE

BLINK

THE INCESSANT NOISE finally got to be more than Bentley could take. He stood up from the table, scattering pencils and notepads, and strode fuming to the front door. He paused to take a deep breath, then yanked it open and stepped out onto the sand.

The rest of the strike group had arrived. The air and sea were alive with aircraft and vessels. The three largest ships were each nearly twice the size of the one that had come in earlier, and they were loaded to the gills with fighter planes and helicopters. Their crews and complement of marines must have numbered in the thousands.

Barry saw him and headed over, ducking reflexively in mid-stride at another hollow boom.

Behind his lank form blossomed an orange glare.

Bentley covered his ears just in time. The ear-splitting crash followed an instant later when the exploding projectile—he had no idea what they were lobbing at the thing—burst against the barrier. Rebounding shrapnel caromed skyward in a tight cluster of fragments like a swarm of angry bees, trailing black smoke and fire.

Air molecules didn't penetrate the barrier, but sound waves vibrated it. So while the boom of the big guns' discharge was dampened to within tolerable levels, the shells the damn military was now tossing at it rattled the thing when they blew up, and the barrier responded like a giant omnidirectional microphone. The din was overwhelming.

"Why don't they give it a rest?" Bentley yelled over roaring echoes.

Barry couldn't possibly have heard what he said, but he shrugged as if he had. Apparently the Navy had heard Bentley though, because they took his suggestion and broke off the steady barrage.

Through his binoculars, Barry scanned the ocean, then turned to examine the jungle and the rising peaks beyond.

The beach grew quiet.

The day had an overcast look, but there wasn't a cloud in the sky. The barrier made everything a few shades darker, like you were wearing sunglasses. Shadows had a reddish tint. But that was all. You couldn't see it—there was no sense of the barrier's shape or how far away it was. From the outside they said it was like a two-way mirror.

Barry pointed over Bentley's shoulder at the sky and Bentley turned to look.

A big cargo helicopter, one of those double-rotor jobs, hovered over the barrier's apex, midway between the central peak and the camp. Indistinct shapes moved under its shadow.

"What the hell are they doing now? Let me see those."

Barry handed over the binoculars. It took Bentley a few seconds to find it, but then the helicopter jerked into view and he steadied on it. The indistinct shapes were men. They stood atop the barrier itself, positioning some large piece of equipment up top.

As Bentley watched, a skid piled high with sandbags was lowered from the helicopter's hatch. The men on the outside tugged them off the pile one by one and carefully laid them on top of the thing they'd planted.

Bentley lowered the binoculars and frowned.

"I'm guessing nitro," Barry offered.

"Well I hope it works. What'll they try next if it doesn't?" He glared at Barry, though of course Barry had had no say in the matter. "You think they've ruled out the nuclear option?"

Barry blinked, then responded with a weak laugh—apparently unsure how seriously the question was meant to be taken.

Bentley wasn't sure either, now that he'd said it.

He raised the binoculars again and swept his magnified gaze over the waves, searching.

For the most part, the rubberneckers had fled, but the Network still had its boat out there somewhere. They'd been ordered off just like everyone else, but were gamely putting up a fight, claiming to be journalists. As such, the Network's legal department was insisting, they couldn't be dismissed in quite so summary a fashion as the others. While the legal issues were being sorted out, the boat's crew had enough prudence to get themselves out of the line of fire and the boat was now loitering somewhere off the island's southeastern tip. That seemed to satisfy the assault group, and nobody paid them any more attention.

Bentley turned to his left. A short distance to the east, visible from the camp, a rocky outcropping stretched from the island's smaller southeastern peak toward the shore, forming a headland fronted by a narrow stretch of sandy beach. It came right up to within maybe two hundred yards of the barrier.

And there was the boat, just beyond it.

Bentley swung the binoculars around again and tilted upward. The helicopter was moving away, leaving its large pile of junk lying there like pigeon droppings on a penthouse skylight.

He lowered the binoculars and peered up at it, trying to get a sense of distance. He'd been told the barrier wasn't really a hemisphere. Its footprint made a perfect circle, but the dome itself was squashed down, flattened, so that it only went into a steep downward curve near the edge. He didn't know how tall it was, and hadn't thought to ask—but judging by the apparent size of the helicopter, he guessed it was somewhere around two thousand yards. Over a mile. Hal would be better at estimating the distance, but either way—pretty high up there.

It must really be dizzying being up on top, he thought. But then he remembered—from outside it wouldn't look like you were suspended in mid-air like it did from down below.

He lifted the binoculars again, and was looking through them when the sky brightened and he heard Barry say, "It's gone!"

Bentley glanced around, then quickly looked back up.

Somebody started cheering, and others joined in.

The barrier had disappeared.

The whole thing, without warning or fanfare had just vanished.

And then, just as suddenly, it reappeared.

With an angry crackle and flickering of blue fire that lasted only a split second, it was back.

The stuff the helicopter had dropped off, though, that had been piled on top of the barrier—it had vanished too, and it didn't come back.

Bentley angled the binoculars downward, just in time to catch a glimpse of it—a dark mass of materiel plummeting earthward.

It struck the southern flank of the southwestern hill.

Barry had been right. Like one of those sped-up nature films of a flower blooming, a ball of fire burst on the mountainside and swelled enormously. In a flash it was obscured by dark clouds of flying matter and roiling black smoke, and then the shockwave hit.

The blast pounded Bentley's ears. Chunks of dirt and rocks hurtled outward in all directions. Some flew straight up, to ram the barrier overhead and ricochet back toward earth. Others tumbled through the air, straight for the beach, all moving with alarming speed.

Someone yelled, "Hit the dirt!"—Hal, or Grant, Bentley wasn't sure, but he threw himself into the sand facing the shore and covered his head with both arms.

A loud whistling, rising in pitch and volume to a howling blast like an eighteen-wheeler bearing down at ninety miles an hour, made him lift his head against his will. It was coming from behind him, but he was afraid to turn around. Whatever it was, it crashed into the earth and kept coming. The ground shook the next time it hit, this time with a heart-stopping thud, and the back of Bentley's head was pelted with clods of wet sand. He saw Hal in front of him, with his camera aimed in his direction. For a brief instant he thought Hal was shooting him, lying prostrate in the sand, his face undoubtedly a contorted mask of pure terror. Then a boulder the size of a Humvee roared over Bentley's head, straight at the camera.

Hal took two steps backwards. The rock bounded past him with no more than three feet of clearance. Either intentionally, or compelled by the violence of the thing's backdraft, Hal whirled, still shooting, to catch it slamming into the beach on its final descent.

It gouged out a six-hundred-pound divot of sand and seaweed and flung it backwards, then bounced high into the air, came down with a mighty thump, and skipped and rolled over the sand like a gigantic lead beach ball, crushing flat whatever lay in its path.

Thank heavens, there was nothing in its path but a pair of unfortunate crabs, whose sideways skittering couldn't attain full acceleration in time to achieve escape velocity.

More sand and beach detritus rained down on Bentley. He closed his eyes and covered his head again until it stopped—a good fifteen seconds later.

"Rob, you okay?"

It was Barry. Bentley could hear Hal whooping, exulting over the shot they'd both almost lost their heads for.

Bentley had had enough.

He stood up, angrily swatting sand from his clothes like a loose-jointed hambone man. People around him were doing the same thing. At least nobody was hurt.

"I'll be in my office."

Upon reaching the engine room, Strindlak hurried to the control console and flicked on the diagnostic systems display. Behind him, the engine pulsed in the strobing glare of emergency lights like a living thing dragged from its mechanical slumber by the electrifying roar of sirens shaking the very walls around it.

The screen blazed to life. Strindlak's heart leapt into his throat. He swallowed hard, pushing it back down to clear his windpipe, and trumpeted in horror.

The life-sustaining plasma core was dying.

One by one, it had shut down system after system, working its way through the chain from superfluous subsystems to vital primary defense operations in a desperate bid for self-preservation. Basic life support was now one of the few left functioning.

But it wouldn't be for long. Even the diagnostics had been slashed to twenty percent. How would he even pinpoint the source of the problem? There was nothing to go by. He paged through menus. Screen after screen was blank.

His mind reeling, Strindlak returned to the main menu to scan the casualty list. The transporter was still functional. Of course—as the only means of escape, the transporter and the emergency hatch would be the last to go. The shield yet functioned, but its meter had plunged, and now palpitated feebly, deep within the critical zone.

How could such a thing be possible? The nursery was bursting with hatchlings. Enrichment was automatic.

And then it hit him. The rotor. It had torn through the nursery's far wall, just beyond the chute. It must have sliced through the wiring. Or worse, cut into the transmission housing and mangled the mechanism.

Cursing, he sprinted for the nursery.

Bentley hadn't been inside for more than two minutes when Grant and Hal burst in. They waited with jittery impatience for him to get off the phone.

"I don't care who's in charge, that thing came within an inch and a half of blowing me and my cast and crew right off the map! You do have a map, don't you?" He listened, grimacing at the others, then cut the speaker off. "You better believe I will. I'll call my congressman and the President and the goddamn Secretary of Defense—with whom I happen to be on speaking terms, for your information—and *they'll* listen to me, you can count on it."

He slammed down the receiver. "Except the goddamn call won't go through because the military and the twilight zone control the horizontal. And the vertical. And the—"

"Rob."

"What? What is it?"

"Rob, Hal just had a fantastic idea."

Bentley glared at Hal.

"Tell him, Hal."

"Rob, if the barrier disappears again—"

"It was gone for half a second."

"But that's all we'll need."

Bentley's interest was aroused just enough to at least hear them out.

"One of us can swim out with the footage on DVDs. It's only two hundred yards or so from the point up there. Stan could do it, he's a good swimmer. The boat's right there. If the barrier goes down again—"

"He tosses it through," Grant finished. "We can put them in one of Evans's watertight Rubbermaid containers."

Bentley was excited now. "Hal, you're a genius."

Hal nodded.

"Those things float, right?"

"Yep. It'll work, Rob."

"This is great. Could it happen? The barrier?"

"Worth a shot."

"I should say so." Bentley considered. "You two go get Stan and tell him the plan. I'll radio the boat."

Hal snapped his fingers. "You just gave me an idea. If we get Jim and what's his name to lend us their two-ways—"

"Then we can communicate with Stan. Good thinking."

Fifteen minutes later, Bentley and his colleagues, along with Jim and Roger, stood at the tip of the low headland that thrust its rocky spur toward the ocean, watching and waiting.

Stan had been skeptical, but he'd had no problem with his role in it. Bentley couldn't swim, and had brought along one of those styrofoam things you held on to while you paddled with your feet, the kind that's shaped like a headstone. Stan was using it, in case he had a long wait and got tired. He also had Jim's two-way radio, and Bentley had Roger's, in case they had to call him back. There was no way of knowing if there'd be a repeat performance, after all.

Hal had put the Rubbermaid container in a small parts bag with a belt clip that kept Stan's hands free. He'd unclip it when he got to the barrier.

Stan made exceptional speed—there was little current to contend with. The tides came in and out, though to a reduced degree, but the waves were only apparent along the water's edge, not noticeable at all away from shore.

The voice-activated radio chirped, and Stan's voice came in. *"I'm here. The network boat is like twenty feet away. I could probably toss the DVDs right onto the deck."*

"Perfect, Stan, nice job. They know approximately where you are. They'll be ready." Bentley pocketed the radio and swung Barry's binoculars toward the barrier's apex, where military activity had resumed. The helicopter was back, unloading more sandbags. It was unnerving, to say the least, considering what had happened last time.

"They don't care what happens to us," Barry observed.

"It's all bullshit, them telling us they were going to get us out of here," agreed Hal. "If they get through, it's going to be shoot first and ask questions later."

"Which one of you guys are alien monsters? Never mind! Blam, blam, blam—"

"What's the point doing it again anyway?" Bentley said. "Nothing can break through that thing."

"Maybe they think they did," suggested Barry. "They had all that weight piled up on top of it…"

"Is that what they're thinking? They think it collapsed under the weight of their sandbags?"

"I guess it's possible," Grant said.

Bentley was skeptical. But now, watching through the binoculars, it made sense to him. It didn't look like they'd planted any explosives this time, thank God. They were just lowering the whole skid, with only one guy beneath it to steady it. Some marine who'd forgotten to take a step back when they asked for volunteers. This time they'd taken the dubious precaution of outfitting the man with a fall-arrest harness.

"Look at that," Bentley said. "Are they crazy? What happens if—"

And then it did.

Without a sound or a flicker, the barrier winked out.

It wasn't the weight. The skid hadn't even set down yet.

The marine up top dropped like a stone. His six-foot lanyard was hooked to a length of rope, and when the rope went taut, the lanyard stretched like a bungie cord. The falling marine slowed, then stopped, dangling.

"You idiots," Bentley whispered.

Grant said, "What's happening?"

Bentley grabbed for his radio and turned toward the ocean.

"Stan! Throw the—*wait!*"

"Too late," came Stan's voice. *"Sorry, guys, I missed it."*

The barrier had only blinked, just like before. It had come back on almost instantly, with the same sparkling crackle.

Bentley whirled the binoculars back toward the marine in the fall-arrest harness, a sinking feeling in his gut.

The lanyard coiled upward to slap the helicopter's undercarriage.

It had been sliced in two.

The other half trailed from the harness strapped to the marine, who was now in free fall, plunging feet first toward the mountainside.

"I hope they gave him a parachute," Bentley said.

They watched for a few seconds.

The man fell out of sight behind the lower hills.

"I guess not," Barry said.

Bentley shook his head, disbelieving the stupidity of what he'd just witnessed. He turned toward the ocean again, speaking into the radio. "How do you mean, 'missed'?"

"Didn't see my opening in time."

"Still have it?"

"Yeah."

"Okay, Stan, don't worry. We'll get another chance. Sit tight."

They stood around with their heads bowed.

"I should have gotten that," Hal said. Unusually for Hal, he'd been caught napping. He hefted his Sony into shooting position.

Bentley nodded absently. He raised the binoculars.

"No."

"What is it?" Hal said.

Jim had already seen it. "Another boat."

It was some kind of patrol craft, making a beeline for the Network's vessel.

"No. Go away," Bentley said. "I don't believe it."

"Going to warn them off again?" Grant said.

"Warn them off nothing. They're after my footage! They hear everything I say." He brandished the two-way radio. "Hell, maybe they can even hear me over this."

"Probably," Jim said.

It was between the Network and the Navy. But neither of them knew the exact spot they'd find Stan. There was still a chance.

"Stan."

"Yeah, I see them."

"Okay, well, do the best you can."

The patrol boat was half a mile and closing when Bentley said, "It's coming. I can feel it."

At a disturbing thought, he lifted the radio again.

"Look, Stan. Whatever you do, don't try to get through when it goes down. If it comes back on…"

"Understood," Stan said.

"Be ready."

"Next time for real."

Bentley raised the binoculars again and quickly relocated Stan's head and shoulders bobbing on the surface.

And something else.

"Now what? What are those things?"

"Let me see," Barry said, and Bentley handed him the binoculars. Barry stared through them for a few seconds, then lowered them.

"Shit."

"What?"

"I think those are sharks."

Bentley's voice came over the radio.

"Stan. We have a problem." Something about Bentley's tone of voice made Stan's scalp tingle, and when Bentley said, *"Don't make any sudden moves,"* dread gripped him.

"What is it?"

"There's something in the water behind you."

Stan slowly turned to look back toward the shore.

"Barry thinks they're sharks."

Stan gasped. Seawater flooded his lungs. He coughed it up, trembling. His eyes teared.

Through blurred vision he saw three dark, sail-shaped fins skimming over the surface, just yards ahead of him.

Then three more.

He shook the water from his eyes, fighting rising panic.

They were all around him.

Why the hell did Barry always have to be right?

There must have been eight or nine of them. Their fins cut the water, gliding in slow back and forth patterns like weaving cobras. Stan very carefully stroked the water with his feet, turning the headstone-shaped board to face them. He was still holding the parts bag with the DVDs. He clipped it to his belt.

"Stan?"

"What the fuck do I do?"

"Just don't move. We'll think of something."

CHAPTER THIRTEEN

RELEASE

THE FAR WALL of the nursery's well was a disgusting mess of crushed and pulped hatchlings. Except for bits of teeth and claws sticking out here and there, the whole was an undifferentiated cake of throbbing flesh. Crowded toward the chute by the burgeoning throng of their stronger brethren, hundreds had been compressed into a compact mass overnight. Whether they yet lived in some way was a question Strindlak hadn't the time or the inclination to investigate. He leapt into the well.

Hatchlings lunged and snapped at him, but they were held at bay by the mound of protoplasm. The huge well narrowed at this end, tapering to a herding pen that led to the mouth of the chute, which was covered by a sliding plate. Strindlak kicked and scraped at the goop to clear a section of the plate and plunged his tentacle tips into the surrounding insulation. By wriggling them beneath the rubbery material, he managed to grasp the plate's leading edge. He strained and pulled, throwing all his might into it and breaking scores of tentacles, but the thing wouldn't yield.

Chest heaving from the exertion, he straightened and looked around, wild with desperation. Something this critical would surely have some sort of manual override in case of an emergency. There was no time to consult the ship's manual. He'd have to trust his instincts.

He got down on his knees and scraped along the wall, feeling his way beneath the dough of ruined hatchlings. Searching for any kind of—

A handle! With a release latch on its underside. There were instructions printed on the plate beside it. He didn't need to read them. Obviously there would be another handle at the other corner. Strindlak half stood to reach across, smeared away quivering glop, and found it. Right again. Wrapping his tentacles around both handles, he depressed the releases and pulled.

It took a tremendous effort, but little by little the plate began to slide away from the wall. A blast of exhaust, rising directly from the plasma core itself, singed his tendril tips with withering heat. He tugged and pulled until the chute stood half open. The pulp of flesh crowding his pods shuddered and shrank away from the gap, but the pressure from behind forced it back over the chute.

But it wouldn't go through. Compacted into a single, glutinous mass, it was too big.

Strindlak tore off a huge portion and rammed it through with his fist, then followed up with a dozen more, stuffing fistfuls into the chute one after another. It quickly clogged. He lifted a pod and stomped down on the obstructing mess, and felt it give. He stomped again, and with a crunch of splintering bone the plate snapped shut around his shin. Bellowing, Strindlak dropped to one knee and grabbed for the handles. As he worked to free his leg, his pain-widened gaze fell upon the instructions. He'd failed to engage the locks. Buttons at the end of each handle.

His leg made a tearing sound, and wrenched free of the trap, half roasted and skinned to the bone. Cursing with relief, he pressed the buttons and heard the plate click into a secure position.

He staggered up, and with his pod tentacles raked the residue of scrambled hatchlings into the now wide-open chute. The heat from below became a searing blast as the plasma core fed. Its depleted reserves were quickly replenished.

It would be a bit longer before all ship's systems were restored to reliable operational levels. They'd need careful monitoring for a time.

Bentley'd had about as much as he could take of life or death situations. He looked around at the others, at a complete loss.

Even Jim was grumbling. "Man, what is it with this place? If all of hell's devils don't get you, the locals'll step in and pick up the slack." He slipped out of his shoes and loosened his belt. "Hold this, would you?" he said to Grant. Handing Grant his high-powered rifle, he kicked off his pants and tugged his t-shirt over his head at the same time.

"What are you going to do?" Grant said.

"I'm gonna swim out to where I can get an angle on those things that doesn't include Stan."

Stripped down to his shorts, Jim took back his rifle.

"Thanks."

Grant just stared after him as he waded out into the water.

Bentley spoke into the radio.

"Okay, Stan, Jim's on the way."

Stan held the board before him like a shield. What the hell was Jim going to do?

The sharks drew steadily closer. They'd begun jostling each other for position.

One thought it saw an opening. It darted forward, covering half of the dozen feet between Stan and the pack in half a second. Just as quickly it slowed, and began moving back and forth in a figure eight, not five feet in front of him.

It was a lot bigger than the others, if fin size was any indication.

The fin tilted sideways and slapped beneath the surface.

Stan groaned and raised his knees as high as he could, leaning forward over the board, eyes wide, trying to pierce the depths for any sign of incoming teeth.

With a light splash the fin and a humped back broke the surface. Stan yelped and it swept past.

He could have reached out and touched it.

He was trembling violently now, and certain the thing could sense his fear. He glanced up at the shoreline and caught a glimpse of an arm sticking up out of the water off to his left. Holding a rifle.

"Jim," Stan whispered as if in prayer.

He stretched his legs out behind him, letting them drift to the surface, and the big shark dove again. He felt its head bump the underside of his board, lifting him partway out of the water, and something that felt like coarse sandpaper scraped against his thigh.

He kicked at it, but it was gone. Frantic, he scanned the water until he found it again, just below the surface a little ways off. Turning around to come back for him.

There was blood in the water.

The radio chattered. *"Stan?"*

The water swirled and swelled over the thing's humped back as it made for him, and Stan lifted his fist. Its jaws yawned open and he brought the radio down with all his might, right onto its snout. The impact sent a jolt of pain through his arm.

The shark veered away.

The radio gurgled. Stan jerked it up out of the water.

"Stan." The speaker crackled with static. It was shorting out.

"Not now," Stan hissed.

He shot a glance to his left. Where was Jim?

The other sharks smelled blood. They were closing in.

One of them thumped against the bottom of his board. He struck blindly with the radio and felt it connect with something hard, and then the big one rolled over again and went for his arm. Stan felt a tug and jerked his hand out of the water, his heart pounding in his chest.

It had bitten the radio off right up to his fist. Silencing Bentley.

Blood sprayed a few yards away and Stan heard the crack of Jim's rifle. The water heaved up and a shark splashed to the surface to writhe there, jaws snapping convulsively, tail fin slapping the water. The pair closest to the injured animal tore into it and the trio sank struggling beneath the surface.

The others still had their sights set on Stan.

In the short reprieve Jim's shot had given him, he'd managed to paddle backwards until now he was pressed up against the barrier. It was colder than the water.

He heard the bang of Jim's rifle, but couldn't tell if it hit anything, and then the big shark, flanked by two others, was plowing towards him again.

This time they meant business.

The fins dipped beneath the water and Stan gave himself up for dead. And at that moment he heard a crackle, and felt the barrier's resistance evaporate, and the sky went blue-white. He let go of the board and sank backwards as another shot rang out, and then he was swimming for the boat. There was a loud fluttering, like someone shaking a heavy rug, and he looked over his shoulder. The barrier was throwing off sparks and strobing furiously. Sharks caught in the middle burst at the seams, spraying blood and entrails.

The barrier was behind him. He'd made it.

And so had the big shark.

His last glimpse of it was of gaping jaws lined with steel-gray teeth, twisting toward his feet. He plunged forward, knowing he'd never make it, and then a volley of machinegun fire erupted in front of him. Bullets whistled in his ears and plunked into the water behind him like raindrops. Swimming with all his might, he looked up to see marines with automatic rifles firing down into the water. He lost sight of them when the boat's hull curved over him and the shooting stopped. A rope ladder pitched over the railing and he lunged for it.

Hands reached down and grabbed him by the wrists.

They hauled him up.

The watertight container holding the DVDs was a mangled wreck of impact-resistant polystyrene sporting a curving row of deep puncture marks.

The DVDs were still inside.

Crushed to jagged, worthless shards.

"Thank God for the military," Bentley said.

Only Barry and Hal heard him. Grant and Roger were wading out to meet Jim. When he reached him, Grant grabbed Jim's hand, shaking it without letting go, while loudly praising the big man's courage in sensational terms.

Jim seemed embarrassed by it. He told Grant he was glad Stan was all right too, and that it was a lucky thing those marines had showed up. Grant said it sure was, and reminded Jim that he'd been a marine lieutenant in the Gulf War. Jim nodded and mumbled something polite, handed his rifle to Roger, then picked up his t-shirt and pants and started out alone across the sand toward camp and the mess hall—telling them he supposed he'd better get back to work.

Roger stood undecided, holding Jim's rifle for a few seconds, then hurried after him.

Grant rejoined Bentley and the others to stand in silent elation, staring out toward sea, and the boats.

Bentley looked over at Grant and nodded to himself. That Jim was really something. And so was Stan. The DVDs had made it. The higher-ups would have to duke it out over ownership, but they'd made it.

Glumrok and the halflings were greatly relieved when Strindlak returned with the news that all was well.

He'd performed a complete inspection of the vicinity, alert for any signs of encroachment inside the shield's perimeters. He was well aware of the many vessels surrounding it, and could only assume hostile intent on their part. There were, however, no indications they'd been able to exploit the three short disruptions recorded in the log.

A while later Strindlak was able to report that the chute mechanism was undamaged. He'd had to tear apart the repaired section of wall, ripping out the patching material to get at the electronics buried inside. He hadn't noticed the sheath of bundled cables earlier. Evidently its own weight had caused it to retract into the hollow of the wall when it was severed by the rotor.

It was a relatively easy fix.

CHAPTER FOURTEEN

LABOR NEGOTIATIONS

BENTLEY WAS GAZING at the door when Barry opened it and came into the office, and now he was gazing at Barry, though he wasn't looking at him. He sat at the table, drawing little circles on its top with his index finger.

Barry knew Bentley, so he closed the door, sat down without talking, and waited.

Bentley lifted his finger, tapped lightly, and cleared his throat.

"The DVDs didn't make it," Barry guessed.

Bentley tapped some more, then looked at Barry.

"What? No," he said. "No."

"Hey, Rob, it was worth a shot."

Bentley gave him an absent nod.

"You know, Hal said he could see the camera crew on the Network boat. They got Stan coming through." Barry chuckled. "Can you imagine? The barrier disappears, and here comes Stan, swimming for his life!—this big monster shark snapping at his heels."

"Uh-huh."

"Machine guns blazing away. Brrrr-uh-uh-uh-uh—"

"Barry."

"God bless him. He made it out."

"Uh-huh. Listen. Barry. You remember the Viceroy's place? That shortwave kit?"

"You mean the ham radio set?"

"Yeah. With the computer, and the cameras?"

"Right. Amateur tele—" Barry blinked and his eyes opened wide. "Shit. You're right!"

"You think?"

Barry thought. Then nodded.

"Let's get Hal and Dylan in here," Bentley said.

Barry had already jumped up to reach for the intercom. "Hal, Dylan, Rob's office."

"I've been on the phone."

"They'll be here in a minute."

"With the NSA."

"Jesus, Rob. The NSA! Are they getting their fingers into this too?"

"I just stuck them in for them. Bunch of politicos."

"What's going on?"

"Well, Barry, if the Viceroy's television station works, I'm not going to just hand everything over to the military and let them fire it down a black hole after they get through debriefing it. I have an agreement."

"Okay. I'm listening."

"I understand a certain level of censorship, I told them that. But they have twelve hours to vet the footage before turning what passes security clearance over to the Network for immediate broadcast. And if they don't…"

"No more footage."

"Look at it from their point of view. Aside from the usual intelligence gathering—they're a little sensitive these days to accusations about going in half-cocked—there're public relations concerns. Congress is openly calling the administration a bunch of lying scoundrels over this business in Indonesia, and the public's getting a hazy suspicion that even Congress can sometimes be right.

"And now there's this. And what is this? Nobody knows, but it doesn't look good. The bloggers are screaming that the whole thing's some kind of sinister fraud. Trumped up as an excuse to invade Madagascar or who knows where."

"And who'd be surprised?" Barry said. "So they need evidence."

"Convincing evidence, and the more the better. And that's not all. They like the idea of the public seeing regular, ordinary Americans portrayed for all the world to see as heroes in an actual bona fide crisis. It's a big morale boost."

"The cast has been brilliant. Amazing," Barry agreed with unconcealed pride. He and Bentley had hand picked every one of them. The crew too. Beyond the call of duty. "How is he?" he asked.

"Stan? He's fine. Got a little roughed up. He's in the big ship's hospital.

USS Something-or-Other. The Network's leaving, now that they've got everything in writing."

"They get anything from Stan?"

"The ship brought the camera crew on board. Show of good faith, I guess. They'll be doing an interview with whatever's left of him after the feds get through with him. I'm going to see that he gets a medal."

"They have something for civilians?"

"They must have something. If they don't, they better come up with one because we're all going to get it."

"So we're still in rotation."

"Heavy rotation, Barry."

If they hadn't both quit smoking before they left LA, they would have lit cigars.

"Everything's falling into place. It's like it was meant to be. But of course we can't allow those things to wipe us out. The administration won't accept defeat. The President wouldn't like it."

"Neither would I."

"Won't happen. They're big and ferocious, but there's only a handful of them. Barry, I'm leaning toward Grant's idea. What do you think? Show 'em what we're made of. Show the whole world."

"Can Grant really pull it off?"

"You don't know Grant. Did you know he was a lieutenant in the first Gulf War?"

"No shit."

"He knows how to lead troops."

"Awesome," Barry said, envisioning the possibilities. "Hey, as long as I'm still around afterwards to pick up my medal in person."

Bentley smiled. "We'll slaughter them, just like we're going to slaughter those hot shot cable bastards that stole our footage."

Bentley looked up when the door opened.

Hal and Dylan came in, excited.

"Rob!" Hal said. "Dylan's theory was right. He picked up my wireless signal here from all the way out there on the point. That's way out of range. It's the barrier."

"It reflects back the signal somehow," Dylan said, "like a giant antenna. Same with the audio. You can monitor everything."

The news drew only an appreciative nod from Bentley.

Hal expected more. "Rob, do you get it? You can direct the action from right over in the control room. No matter where we are."

Barry said, "Oh, wow. You know what Grant's been talking about. It'll be perfect." He looked at Bentley. "If it gets the green light, I mean. We're still considering it."

"I like it," Bentley said. "And yes we are. But listen, we'll come back to that later."

Hal and Dylan pulled up chairs and Bentley told them about the Viceroy's rig.

"Amateur television," Hal said. "I don't know what that is."

Dylan did. "It's simple. Anyone with a ham radio can broadcast over shortwave. Just need the software and a computer. The ham radio's your station. If it's powerful enough to penetrate the barrier with enough gain—"

"Fifteen hundred watts," Barry remembered.

"That ought to do it," Dylan said. He looked Barry in the eye. "So who's this Viceroy dude?"

Barry glanced at Bentley and got the nod.

"Lives up at the other end of the island. He's kind of a hereditary overseer—he's like a baron or something—who spends half his time here and the rest of his time in the south of France. Descendant of some French knight. Nice guy, very well-mannered. Distinguished."

Dylan was non-committal. "That's pretty cool."

"His place is about eight miles to the west. Little house on the coast. Actually, it's a big mansion, but you can't tell that from the outside. They dug it right out of the rocks. There's a castle even."

"Interesting."

Bentley said, "Probably take a couple hours to get there. Door's never locked. Nobody comes here. Of course part of the agreement was that the Viceroy's house and belongings are strictly off limits."

"But these are extenuating circumstances."

"You better believe it."

Dylan fidgeted. "I don't want to go by myself."

Bentley was understanding. "There are risks involved."

"Uh-huh."

Bentley looked at Barry. Recognizing his cue, Barry thought fast.

"We were thinking maybe Howard."

"You'll have to cart all the equipment back here," Bentley said. "But I want you to do a trial run first, from there, make sure it works."

"We'll need one more. Howard can carry stuff, but he doesn't know anything about electronics or computers." Dylan seemed to consider. "What about Becky? She's a good second engineer. You could probably spare her for a few hours."

Bentley looked at Hal.

Hal nodded. "Done." He looked at his watch. It was a couple minutes before noon.

"Work out the details and get your team together," Bentley said. "Like to get this underway ASAP."

He stood up.

An hour later, Tony dropped in at the mess hall. Lance asked him if he'd come to help out, but Tony'd only come to use the bathroom, and afterwards hurried back outside, muttering something about leaving Janet alone with Jeremy. Tony seemed to assume everyone else would be as concerned about that as he was. It was too much for Lance. He put down his drill and went out after him. Pretty soon everyone in the mess hall heard him out on the beach yelling at all of them, Tony and Jeremy in particular—calling them self-absorbed jerks and overgrown junior high schoolers. But it was threatening to lock them out at nightfall and leave them to fend for themselves that got results. They stomped inside behind Lance, and grudgingly allowed him to assign them tasks, which they then carried out with an open display of resentment that was naturally insulting to everyone else.

Since they already had all the sandbags they needed, Lance put Janet, Gabrielle, Corey and Mei to work disposing of the rest of the dirt and rocks Brad's shovel tossed up onto the floor. The job was a simple matter of scooping everything into a bucket, then carrying the bucket outside and dumping it on the pile started earlier by Vince and Zach. But while simple, it still wasn't much to Janet's liking. Long after the others of her crew seemed to have resigned themselves to their fate, Janet herself went on fussing and pouting. It got on everyone's nerves. You could see Lance was really starting to regret having brought her in.

Even so, things were progressing. The windows were now close to being finished. And with Jim back, and tunneling in from the outside, the escape hatch was well ahead of schedule.

With the barricades almost completed, Evans took charge of a work detail that included him and Lance, along with Vince and Zach, to tackle the refrigerator. The fridge was heavy—even empty it must have weighed three hundred pounds. Under Evans's supervision, they rocked and swiveled it out of the kitchen and scuffed up the linoleum shoving it around the corner to its new station beside the door.

It was a good fit—about eight inches wider than the doorframe, and coming up to within a foot of the top. And with the sandbags for added ballast it would be unyielding.

By mid-afternoon, though, it finally got to be too much for Janet. She'd been hauling dirt and rocks all day without a break or a single word of praise or encouragement from anyone. After emptying her bucket for the millionth time, she staggered back into the mess hall, doubled over like she was about to collapse from exhaustion.

Stopping in the center of the room, Janet looked over at Tony. Tony didn't look up—he was helping Vince hold a wooden tabletop against the wall, while Rashad screwed it in place.

She looked at Jeremy. He was talking to Zach and hadn't noticed her coming in. He didn't look up either.

She dropped her bucket and her chin started to quiver.

Corey said, "Janet, are you okay?"

Janet saw Lance looking at her and started to cry.

She didn't answer Corey. She just kicked her bucket against the wall—that got people to look around—and threw herself into a chair and stayed there with her face buried in her hands.

"What's the matter, babe?" Tony asked, hurrying to her side.

In a break between silent sobs, Janet said, "I'm tired."

She said it with a tone of resentment that rankled Lance. "We're all tired, Janet," he said. It wasn't kindly or sympathetic, the way he said it.

"But I'm really, really tired," Janet said, angrily. She sniffed and wiped at her tears to make room for more. "I'm tired of carrying buckets and I'm tired of being dirty and I have bruises all over my legs and my fingers hurt. I don't want to do this anymore. I want to take a shower."

"Aww," Tony began, but Lance cut him off.

"Shut the fuck up." Then to Janet he said, "And you, give me a fucking break." He took a step toward them, and Tony put his arm around Janet like he thought Lance might hit her or something.

Lance stood glowering down at her. "You know what, Janet? I don't want to do this anymore either. I don't even want to be here. Much as I love being around you and Tony and Jeremy. And I bet nobody else does either. But you don't see them whining about it, do you?"

"Okay, Lance, take it easy, man," Fredo said.

"Yeah, come on, she's just tired," Jeremy said. He had edged closer to Tony and Janet and now stood right beside them. "This isn't easy for her, you know."

"Oh, shit. I didn't realize that," Lance said. "Damn, I'm sorry, Janet. Thanks for the heads up, Jeremy. I just naturally figured this was as much fun for her as it is for all the rest of us."

"I just want to take a break, that's all," Janet said, but she was still sniveling and it just made Lance angrier.

"So take a fucking break. Just quit acting like a big baby."

It was like he'd slapped her. Janet let out a shrill wail that made even Lance flinch, then buried her face in Tony's protective arms.

"That's enough, Lance," Tony warned him.

Janet raised her head again and lifted her gaze to meet Lance's. "I'm not acting like a baby. I just can't work all day like you. I'm doing the best I can, I'm just not as strong as you are. And you keep looking at me like I'm not doing anything."

Lance listened, his face impassive. Janet glared at him, gulped back another sob and said, "You're just picking on me because you wish it was me instead of Sondra."

Lance could only gape at her words.

"You all do," Janet said. "You all hate me."

"Don't talk about Sondra," Lance said quietly.

Now Jeremy was angry. "She can talk about whatever she wants," he said. "You keep forgetting, we saw that thing too, up close before anybody else. It could have killed her."

"Yeah," Tony said, "But it didn't, no thanks to you."

"Fuck you!" Jeremy shouted. With an effort, he kept his voice level. "You'd have run too," he said. "I didn't leave her behind like everybody thinks. We got separated and when I looked around I couldn't find her. I thought she was ahead of me."

Fredo said, "Okay, man. Forget about it, there's nothing to talk about. Let's just keep it together."

Janet was looking at Jeremy.

Tony said, "Is that what happened, Janet?"

She shook her head. "I don't know. I don't remember anymore."

"Case closed," Fredo said.

Tony's shirtfront was wet from Janet's tears. He'd been sitting on the arm of her chair. Now he eased himself up.

"Not quite. Maybe she doesn't remember, but I do." He jabbed a finger at Jeremy. "You're a fucking liar. She was about a mile behind you when you came out of the jungle."

"No she wasn't. You're the fucking liar."

They were standing inches apart, staring at each other with burning hatred.

"See?" Lance said. "Look at what she's doing to you two. Playing one against the other—"

"You stay out of it," Tony said. "This is between me and this piece of shit—" and Jeremy swung at him.

Tony jumped back. Jeremy clipped his jaw with his left fist and followed up with his right. Tony blocked backhanded with his right, got hold of Jeremy's wrist, and threw a hard left hook that caught Jeremy in the eye, staggering him.

They both went down. By the time the others could react, they were rolling around on the floor pounding at each other's faces and trying to knee each other in the groin.

Brad was the first to catch an opening, and he took a few stray punches trying to wedge them apart. Soon Trask and Rashad had dived in and between the three of them they managed to drag Jeremy and Tony off each other.

Brad held Tony, and Trask and Rashad held Jeremy. They all stood there panting for a few seconds before Tony said, "Okay," and shook off

Brad's iron grip—only because Brad let him. Jeremy and Tony glared at each other for another few seconds, then both looked away.

Tony went outside. That option taken, Jeremy had nowhere to go to be alone other than the bathroom, but he took it, storming through the door and slamming it shut behind him.

Everyone was shocked by what had happened.

Someone said, "This wouldn't have happened when Nils was here."

At that, Beverly started to cry.

"I'm sorry," Janet said, looking at the floor.

Even Lance was a little shaken. "Look, Janet," he said—and when she did, her eyes were pleading, and she looked so miserable he couldn't help feeling ashamed of his own part in what had happened. He walked over and sat where Tony had been, on the arm of her chair, and she hugged him.

Everyone else moved away, but kept casting sidelong glances at them while Lance tried to apologize.

"I didn't mean it. I'm sorry, okay?" He patted her arm awkwardly. "We don't hate you, Janet. Really."

Michelle said, "Speak for yourself," but only Rashad, standing right next to her, heard it.

"Come on, Michelle," he said. "Let's go outside." He headed for the door. When she followed, Trask and Paula glanced at each other in veiled surprise.

"I didn't mean to take it out on you," Lance was mumbling. "It's just—we're all—"

"Oh, Lance," Janet said. "I'm so scared."

Lance looked like he might cry now, but he just nodded.

Looking at them, Trask felt drained. He turned away and said to the others, "Okay, good idea. Let's take a break."

CHAPTER FIFTEEN

SECOND UNIT

HOWARD AND BECKY gazed open-mouthed at their surroundings, in a hushed state of grandeur overload—unlike Dylan, not bothering to hide their awe.

They stood just inside the Viceroy's triple-extra-wide front door in an entrance hall about the size of Howard's apartment back in LA. Ahead of them, from the right-hand wall, a wide staircase curved gracefully to the left on its way up to the second floor landing. The steps themselves were marble. The oak balustrade, hand carved in the rococo style, was replete with lion head banisters.

To their immediate right, a pair of oversize double doors, wide open, let into a dining room of appropriately regal proportions. A crystal chandelier that must have weighed two hundred pounds hung over the table, which seated twenty.

Howard had never seen anything like it, except in the movies.

According to Dylan, who claimed to have once been a guest of the Duke of Argyll, this was modest by aristocratic standards. Howard wasn't sure where Argyll was. Somewhere in England. And Dylan was talking about a castle. This was just a guy's house.

The hallway—properly, the "great hall", according to Dylan— stretched ahead of them, with doors set along the left-hand wall (and, one assumed, to the right, which was blocked by the stairs). Everything was trimmed with gold—the paneled doors, the upstairs balcony. Howard didn't have to wonder whether it was paint. There was no grout between the marble tiles inlaid with onyx. They fit together seamlessly.

And they were old. Everything was old. The tiles were worn beneath the tread of footsteps that must have numbered in the hundreds of thousands. The oak fixtures had the dark, rich patina of priceless antiques.

Of course they did. They were.

Howard tried to prolong and savor the experience, but Dylan's continual chattering kept bringing him back down to earth.

"Okay, Dylan," Howard said. "It's not a 'hall', it's a 'great hall'. Whatever. Where's the home entertainment center?"

"Well, let's see. This would have to be the drawing room," Dylan said, indicating the door opposite the dining room. "That's short for 'withdrawing room', in case you wondered. Where the Viceroy and the other barons withdraw after dinner for a smoke so they won't yellow the ladies' powdered hair."

He'd become their tour guide. He opened the door and ushered them through.

A herd of plush chairs with claw and ball feet grazed on an oriental rug before an immense fireplace. Multi-paned windows along one wall let in a cozy half-light through heavy drapes cinched with silver clasps.

"The drawing room," Dylan announced, flicking on the lights. His air had turned proprietary. Howard didn't mind anymore. It was fun really. Dylan was just being Dylan. It didn't come off as pretentious like it would with a lot of people.

"Thank you," Becky said.

Howard smiled. "Good of you to have us," he added.

"Not at all. Now if you'll follow me, the den is through the door down at the end." He pointed to the right.

They followed, gazing one after another at a row of gilt-framed portraits hung from ribbons along the fireplace wall. A couple of them, by the way they were dressed, made Howard think of Louis the Fourteenth. He and Becky stumbled after Dylan like sleepwalkers.

The adjoining room was indeed the den, and it did indeed house the entertainment center. It was done up as modern period, obviously so as not to clash with the sixty-inch display and 7.1 sound system surrounded by climate-controlled clear-front cabinets filled with state-of-the-art electronics.

Howard didn't even recognize the brands. He didn't say so, though, because he figured Dylan probably did.

"Dude," was all he said.

Dylan was running on zen. Without breaking stride, he crossed the room, opened another door and said, "Eureka."

Howard and Becky followed him inside. It was a miniature television studio equipped with high-end consumer version production facilities. A stationary camera was trained on a small set centered around a desk with a built-in microphone.

Apparently, the Viceroy had a hobby. Producing some kind of amateur news broadcast.

The camera was connected to an A/V mixing console on another desk that also held a couple of servers, a laptop, and the base station transmitter/receiver. A rack of audio processors—amplifier, patch bays, equalizers, effects units—stood beside the desk, with a 16-track mixing board mounted on a multi-positionable shelf.

Not bad.

Dylan grinned and set to work powering everything up in sequence. The laptop's screen lit up. He took the DVD case out of his pocket and unzipped it, then sat down in the operator's chair and watched the display. At the end of the startup routine the computer automatically launched the ATV application, opening on a fairly standard-looking group of A/V control windows. The main one showed the anchor's desk as depicted in the stationary camera's viewfinder.

"Beautiful," Dylan said, nodding to himself as he scanned the onscreen controls. "Nice, user-friendly interface. Even Hal could figure this out."

"Don't be so sure," Howard said. "We don't have a lot of time, either."

"Look at this," Dylan said. On a control panel beside a wall-mounted phone above the desk was a large rectangular button labeled "ANTENNE".

He pushed it. There was a faint, steady whine of hidden machinery. Howard grunted in surprise and Dylan laughed. Somewhere overhead an antenna was rising up out of its silo. After ten seconds, the whine cut off with a percussive thump.

"You want to know what I'm thinking?" Dylan gave them a crafty look. Especially Becky.

She laughed. "What's on your mind, Tiger?"

"What if—" Dylan began, but then changed his mind. "No, let's see how it goes. Let me get started." He ran the cursor over the application's main menu bar at the top of the display and started perusing drop-downs. "Later we'll talk."

Becky stood behind him, watching over his shoulder as Dylan slid the first DVD into the slot. Howard sat down on a stool off to the side and tried to follow the process, but it was all beyond him, and when Dylan opened some technical-looking plug-ins and then a secondary application directly from the DVD he soon became bored.

So did Becky.

Finally Howard said, "I mean, should we be doing something? Becky and me?"

"Nah, I'm cool, bro'." Dylan was still getting a basic overview of the unfamiliar application and wasn't yet completely engrossed in intuiting the functions he'd need to learn for their purposes. "How 'bout one of those sandwiches before I tackle this shit for real?"

"Good idea." Howard began rummaging in his knapsack.

"I've got a better one," Becky said.

The guys looked up at her.

"There's a well-stocked pantry back there in the kitchen on the other side of that dining room or I'm Old Mother Hubbard."

Howard jumped up, licking his lips at the thought. He looked at Dylan, eyes sparkling.

"Go, baby," Dylan said.

They must have spent half an hour raiding the fridge and the pantry. It was glorious.

When they came back, balancing silver platters overflowing with meat, cheese, bread and mountains of delicacies on their fingers like Russian Tea Room waiters, it looked like Dylan hadn't even gotten started.

Actually, he was finished.

"Finished? You haven't even done anything," Howard said, unbelieving. Dylan's eyes were still glued to the display. Howard moved into frame in the onscreen monitor window, and when he stepped away, two platters piled high with food covered His Excellency's anchor's desk. Dylan blinked, then the aroma must have hit him, because his jaw dropped. He spun his chair around.

"Good God."

Becky set hers down next.

"Hallelujah."

They dug in greedily. Laying a thick slab of meat onto a slice of sour-dough, Dylan explained, "Nothing to it. All that's left is a little programming."

He clicked another window to the front.

It was filled with lines of code.

"Shouldn't take more than fifteen or twenty minutes."

"Really?" Becky sounded disappointed.

Dylan's mouth was full of food. He nodded, gestured for patience, chewed and swallowed.

"What year?" he asked Howard.

"Huh?"

"The Bordeaux."

Becky read the label. "'35," she said. "It was a good year, I'm sure." She poured a glass, filling it to the brim. Howard waited for Dylan to say something about that, but he didn't. Even Howard knew you were only supposed to fill it up to the widest part. So it could breathe.

"I suppose it'll have to do."

"So that's it?" Howard said. "We transmit in thirty minutes? Then we just pack everything up and go?" Becky wasn't the only one who was disappointed. "How long's it gonna take?"

Dylan took a sip of Bordeaux after swirling it around in his glass for a while and savoring the bouquet. Then he said, "I've got an hour's worth of footage. That's about how long it'll take to send."

"An hour and a half," Becky said quietly.

"Hey," Dylan said, "Don't everybody look so glum. Didn't I tell you I had an idea?" Fixing his gaze on Becky, he said, "I like it here."

Then he picked up the phone and punched the keys.

"Mr Bentley? It's Dylan."

Howard couldn't make out the words, but he recognized Bentley's voice.

"Good, good. We're fine," Dylan said. "Yep, got here about twenty minutes ago."

Bentley's voice buzzed and Dylan said, "Yeah, I've been looking it over, mostly everything makes sense."

It sounded like Bentley said, "Mostly?"

Dylan didn't answer. Instead he said, "Is Hal there?"

Howard heard Bentley's voice phrasing a question. Dylan winked at them.

"No, that's okay, don't bother him. It's just that we've run into some unexpected technical issues."

Howard could imagine Bentley's eyes glazing over at the mere mention of anything technical.

"Yeah. There's a transfer problem with the non-native format. Looks like that's addressed by the manual but it's complicated. Not sure how long it'll take me to…

"Okay, we will, but—there's another thing. Seems like something's missing, some kind of hardware interface. I don't know if the Viceroy took it with him or what. I'll have to make something. Good thing I brought my parts bag and tools."

Dylan looked up toward the ceiling at nothing in particular, just gathering his thoughts, and then launched into a speech that was one of the most flagrant examples of pure bullshit Howard had ever heard.

"Well first of all it looks like I'll have to install a transmission gate to reverse the signal direction. And I'll need to jack in a multiplexer so I can select the laptop as an input source and ramp up my fan-out level. I can float most of the other inputs, and use a current sinker to keep both TTL transistors from coming on, which of course would cause a lot of transients."

Dylan shook his head and smiled at Becky as he spoke.

"Transients. Spikes." He paused, then sighed.

"Well, not quite. The big problem then will be clock skew." Dylan paused while Bentley apparently repeated the unfamiliar term, then continued with brazen nonchalance:

"Yeah, you know, too many asynchronous flip-flops in the path with skewed signals. Propagation delays. Because of the transmitter. One of those high-end systems with hybrid components. If I had a five-fifty-five or a couple of one-shots to replace the—"

He stopped, waited politely. Howard looked over at Becky. She was watching Dylan with a kind of breathless admiration. Here we go, thought Howard.

"One-shots," Dylan repeated. "No, not in the directorial sense. It's a logic circuit."

Bentley's voice made an inquisitive buzz.

"A monostable multivibrator," Dylan clarified. "Anyway, I don't have any. I'll have to make one."

Question.

Answer: "Probably an hour, hour and a half. And then I've got some programming to do, another couple hours or so… Yeah, probably around six or six-thirty. Yeah, I know. I guess it'll be starting to get dark by then. Probably oughta stay put here till morning if that's the case."

Dylan listened, then gave Howard and Becky the thumbs up.

"Yeah. No, not too bad. There's some food in the fridge. Okay… Yeah, it's a little tricky, but we'll get it. Thanks… I'll call you when we're ready to transmit. Okay, every hour. You got it."

Mission—

"So we'll just plan on camping out here till morning. Uh-huh. Call you in an hour. Four o'clock. Okay, talk to you then."

—accomplished.

Dylan disconnected and held up his hand for a high five. Howard grinned and slapped it, to Becky's giggling applause.

At four o'clock, when Dylan didn't call—and at Grant's insistent urging—Bentley called a "story" meeting to discuss Grant's proposal. After Grant outlined his plan, Bentley asked Barry and Hal for their comments.

Barry was enthusiastic. "I like it. It's got suspense, it's a great opportunity for character development. It could be a very exciting sequence, and in terms of story structure the timing couldn't be better. In fact, if we don't do it, we'll have to come up with something to keep from having second act problems. I mean, if nothing—extemporaneous—happens."

"I wasn't actually thinking of it in terms of story structure, Barry," Bentley said, sounding grumpy. "I do have other issues to consider. As producer, I'm responsible for the safety of the cast and crew."

What Grant proposed was laying an ambush. A trap.

A baited trap.

"Okay, Rob," Grant said, "point taken, but if you ask me, the best way to ensure the safety of the cast and crew is through a show of strength.

These things have had the advantage of surprise every time and so far they haven't seen any reason to back down. But when you look at the way they've behaved, you have to admit, it's underhanded and cowardly. They never show up where there's a large group, only when—"

"We can't predict their behavior based on what we've seen so far," Hal protested. "And what about the thing that tore open the cast dormitory? The room was full of people."

"And as soon as it saw it was outnumbered, it turned tail and ran."

"Yeah, well, Trask peppering its mug with hot lead might've had a little to do with it."

"Okay, but that just proves my point. And it was only Trask because he happened to be holding the shotgun," Grant added. "Anyone else would have done the same and probably with better aim."

"Hey, he didn't miss, just 'cause the thing didn't go down. And that ought to worry us some."

"We can bring it down. Or them, whichever it is. With concentrated fire, and the manpower and tactical sense to follow through."

"But will enough of them volunteer?" Bentley asked. "You've gotta have the numbers."

"Lance will," Grant said. "He's been talking revenge ever since what happened to Sondra."

"They didn't do that to Sondra," Bentley observed.

"That doesn't make any difference to Lance," Grant said. "And Lance being in guarantees most of the guys."

"Trask'll never go along with it," Hal said.

"That's true," Bentley said.

Grant sneered. "Good. I don't want him. I need troops that'll follow orders, and one guy questioning everything and making trouble is one guy we don't need."

"But Trask can be persuasive," Barry said. "He could talk the others out of it. Rashad won't do it if Trask won't, and neither will Paula, so we can count them out."

"Yeah—what about the women?" Hal said.

"Michelle. Erika. Those two for sure."

Bentley considered. "Okay, Grant. I want a minimum of twelve, counting you. Any less and it's a no go."

"You'll get them," Grant promised.

Bentley's gaze strayed to the phone and held there for a few seconds before he turned to convey his silent irritation to Barry with a glance.

Barry shrugged but didn't say anything.

CHAPTER SIXTEEN

CLOCK SKEW

IT WAS TIME TO KICK BACK. They'd had an early dinner under the chandelier in the dining hall—steak—and even Howard was feeling full.

They retired to the library, second door to the right off the great hall. Leather upholstered chairs, fur rugs, shelves of books lining one wall, some new, some ancient. Another fireplace, just like in the drawing room. The lamps had forest green shades with tassels. There was even an old-fashioned Victrola, the kind with the huge horn sticking up from the needle, and a bunch of records in the cabinet built into the stand.

Real elegant.

The other wall, the one not lined with bookshelves, was covered with a huge tapestry. Even Howard could tell it was old. Medieval. It showed a knight on horseback doing battle with a dragon, while other knights and noblewomen looked on. A blue forest covered the background, with the sky just visible at the top of the trees.

Howard was feeling a little tipsy from all the wine.

"Dude," Dylan said.

Howard grunted. "Uhh." He was settled deep into an unbelievably comfortable couch beside Becky.

"Break out the reefer."

Howard had forgotten he had it.

Becky punched his arm. "You've got pot? Howard, you're awesome."

Grinning, Howard laid out three fat joints on the coffee table. He selected one, fired it up and passed it to Becky.

Hal turned to Bentley. "How do you want to approach this, Rob?"

It was decided. "I want a stationary on the bait. You'll be in position with the ambush party. I'm keeping Fred out of it."

"We'll get some good storylines going back here too, in the camp," Barry assured him. "You'll see a lot of nail biting and soul searching after it sinks in to the stay-behinds that they've let the others go off to fight their battles for them."

Bentley nodded thoughtfully. "So tell me again how this wireless business works."

"It's perfect for this, Rob," Hal said. "There's something about the barrier. It reflects back and amplifies certain types of electromagnetic waves, but lets others pass through. Something to do with frequency. Dylan could explain it better if he were here. But for whatever reason, the wireless outfits work over way longer distances than normal. It means we can transmit live to the control room."

"You mean I can direct the action from here," Bentley said.

Hal shot a covert glance at Grant. Grant had been the picture of confident self-assurance talking about risking all the punters' necks in his offensive, but now his expression took on a worried tenseness.

"From a cinematic standpoint, yes," Hal said. "The action of course will be up to Grant. This is a semi-military operation."

"Of course." Bentley smiled and Grant beamed. "When do you want to talk to them?"

"After dinner," Grant said. "I'll ask Evans to make something special. The troops'll be more receptive on a full stomach when they're feeling brave and strong."

"They are brave and strong, Grant," Bentley said. "That's why we picked them."

Grant nodded, then turned to Hal and winked.

"Twelve minimum," Bentley reminded him.

"No sweat," Grant said. He stood up and gave the others a smart salute before striding crisply from the room.

Bentley sat for a minute biting his lip.

"Barry, what time is it now?" he asked.

"Four forty-five. You want to call them?" Barry had already stepped over to the telephone.

"Yeah, I guess I better."

Barry dialed and handed Bentley the receiver. Bentley frowned and listened. After the tenth ring, he dropped the receiver back into its cradle.

~~~~~~

"You're just feeling paranoid 'cause you're stoned," Dylan said. He was the one sitting next to Becky now. He patted her hand, which was resting on his knee, then casually draped his arm over the back of the couch above her shoulders.

Howard looked back down at the floor. He was pacing barefoot on the rug, just because of the feel of the fur under his toes. "I wouldn't call it paranoid necessarily," he said. "The one that went after Jim and the others wasn't fooling around. That guy Nils—I mean he was like—"

"We know, Howard," Dylan said.

"—like totally disemboweled," Howard finished.

He stopped pacing and looked up again in time to see Becky shiver. She took her hand off Dylan's knee and wrapped her arms around herself in a self-protective hug.

"Okay, Howard, we get it," Dylan said.

"You know what I think? I think it's aliens."

Becky shuddered. Dylan didn't say anything.

"There's no other way to explain it. The barrier."

"Yeah, I know," Dylan said. "Look, Howard, that thing didn't come after them. They surprised it. From what I heard, that's what happened every time. There's nothing to worry about. If we see one, which we won't, all we have to do is just leave it alone."

"But what are they doing here?"

"Howard," Dylan said. Howard had been watching Becky through most of the conversation and only now did he catch the exasperated look Dylan was trying to give him without Becky seeing it. "It doesn't matter, okay? Whatever it is, when they're finished, the barrier will go away and so will they. You'll see, they'll be gone in a couple of days. Tomorrow maybe."

There was no mistaking Dylan's "shut up" look, accompanied by a significant sidelong glance indicating Becky, curled up by herself in the corner of the couch.

Dylan may or may not have believed what he was saying. Howard realized he was just trying to reassure Becky, and regretted stupidly trying to continue the discussion. It wasn't cool, talking about this kind of stuff when you're stoned. Kind of an unwritten rule.
~~~~~~

"Yeah, I know. I just was, you know, wondering what they were doing here is all."

"Who knows, Howard? Some kind of scientific survey."

"I bet that's it."

"You guys really think that's all it is? That they're not here to—that they don't mean to…"

"Well, if they did, don't you think they'd have just wiped us out first thing as soon as they got here?" Dylan said.

She looked deep into his eyes, wanting to believe.

"Hey," Dylan said, and Becky gave him a half-smile. "Come here." He reached for her and she scooted over to snuggle under his arm.

Howard showed a sudden interest in the old Victrola.

He walked over to it, pulled a record out of the cabinet and laid it over the turntable's spindle.

He set the needle on the record, grabbed hold of the crank mounted on the Victrola's side and gave it a turn. There was a scratching sound, then a pop when the needle found the groove—and an instant later a bright fanfare of trumpets.

It was a lot louder than he expected, and Becky and Dylan both jumped.

Back at the mess hall, work continued on the tunnel. Brad and Jim knew they were close because they could hear each other's voices and the sounds of their shovels through the earth that separated them. Ten minutes later they broke through. Scraping with their shovels, they widened the initial hole until a final collapse of dirt and sand allowed Jim to clamber through, smiling, to the cheers of those inside.

They'd done it.

They'd had to dig deeper than they'd anticipated to get past a cinderblock foundation, but they'd widened the tunnel enough at the bottom to be able to turn around—which meant you could take your pick between going in head first or feet first, and still come out right-side up.

For the hatch itself they were using a steel worktable top scavenged from the storage shed. After positioning it over the tunnel entrance, which was about three feet around, they hammered three nails into the floor flush against each side to hold it in place. They used tree branches and shrubbery to conceal the exit outside.

Lance insisted that everyone try it. He even managed to persuade Janet to wriggle through. Tony and Jeremy were forbidden from helping her out on the other side, and Brad stood watch to make sure they didn't.

Most of them got through surprisingly fast. They guessed it would take maybe a minute for the whole group to get outside in an emergency.

Now equally and thoroughly caked with dirt, and satisfied that the tunnel would serve its purpose, their thoughts turned to the matter of weaponry.

Howard cranked faster, and the music sped up, rising in pitch, until Dylan, who'd been tapping his foot along with it, couldn't keep time anymore. He lurched up and started stomping, clapping his hands on the upbeats. Howard laughed and cranked faster. The big brass section sounded like a circus calliope on steroids. Dylan waved his arms like a conductor trying to stop an orchestra that had turned into a speeding locomotive, while Becky rolled on the sofa, holding her sides and laughing so hard she had to gasp for breath.

There was a zipping screech as the needle skidded out of control. It ripped across the grooves, flew from the turntable and bumped hard into the Victrola's raised sides.

Dylan dropped onto the couch, panting, lying half on top of Becky, both of them giggling and trying to catch their breath at the same time.

"Oops." Howard took off the record and put it aside, then pulled out another. "Let's try something else."

It was some kind of chamber music like Mozart. A waltz or something. Howard was glad to see Becky had seemed to have forgotten about the aliens. She got out from under Dylan and stood up. Swaying a little. Howard focused on turning the crank at a steady speed this time. He was pretty good at it when he paid attention and put his mind to it.

Dylan got up too. He and Becky started dancing. Not that either of them knew how to waltz.

Becky was still giggling. It was contagious.

It was really something, when you thought about it, being here in a place like this, living it up, dancing, drinking...

Drinking. Howard looked around for his glass.

He'd left it on a side table, out of reach. He didn't want to stop the music, so he switched hands and kept cranking with his left. Now, by turning his back to Dylan and Becky and bending at the waist, he could just reach his glass with his right hand.

He'd barely gotten his fingers around the stem and was straightening up when they plowed into him. The glass flew straight for the tapestry, splattering wine all over the bottom part right under the dragon.

Howard let go of the crank. The music slowed and pitched downward, then died.

Dylan and Becky stopped dancing. Howard felt his face flush, which it always did whenever he did something really stupid. Even though they were the ones who bumped into him.

Becky mock-cringed. "Whoops."

"Sorry, Howard," Dylan said.

Howard was already grabbing for the stack of paper napkins on the platter. He started daubing at the tapestry. It didn't do much. The material had sucked up the wine like Bounty. It must have been pretty dry after all those hundreds of years.

The disaster wasn't major enough to sustain Dylan and Becky's interest. They plopped back down on the sofa, not even bothering to help.

Howard wiped at the tapestry. Bits of napkin started coming loose, twisting up and getting tangled in the threads. The wine was coming off a little, but a lot of the threads were coming off with it.

Dylan laughed. Howard turned around.

"It's not working. What should I do?" Howard was kind of freaking out, but all he got from Dylan, who was obviously too stoned or drunk or both to care, was a dreamy smile. After a while, the absurdity of the whole thing made Howard feel a little better. He still couldn't help trying to clean it up, but now he was giggling along with Becky as he scrubbed.

He felt like if he scrubbed with a little more firmness, the wine might come out better, but the tapestry somehow didn't offer enough resistance for him to put any muscle into it. When he did, it just gave back under his hand, like there was nothing behind it.

Like there was…

A chill tickled the back of Howard's neck and he stopped what he was doing.

"Dylan."

"What is it, bro'?"

"There's nothing behind here. There's no wall."

For a second they all just stared at each other. Then Dylan got up. He walked over to the end of the tapestry and plucked the edge away from the wall. It was heavy, but he was able to pull it out far enough to see behind it.

"Howard, go get my flashlight, out of my toolbag," he said.

Howard ran for the den.

CHAPTER SEVENTEEN

WARDROBE

HOWARD STOOD RIGHT BEHIND DYLAN, peering over his shoulder down the length of the three-inch gap between wall and tapestry. In the flashlight's beam, he could clearly see the rectangular shadow of a recessed doorway in the middle of the stone wall. It was set about six inches above the floor, so the bottom of the tapestry covered it from the front. It was just blind luck that they'd found it.

"Follow me," Dylan said. He squeezed behind the tapestry and began inching his way along the wall. Howard slid in behind him, then Becky, holding his arm.

They reached the doorway and Howard put his weight into the tapestry, using his shoulders to lift it away from the wall so they could huddle before it. A dark oak door was set into the recess, its iron hinges mounted to the stone by large round-headed spikes. There was no handle. Sliding bolts at the top and bottom held it shut.

Dylan looked around at Howard, then turned back to the door and, without a word, reached up and threw the top bolt. Then he knelt and threw the bottom.

The door creaked inward.

A musty odor drifted to their nostrils. Dylan pushed the door open wider and played his flashlight over the dark interior.

Becky screamed. The flashlight beam darted back and focused on what it had passed over an instant before: Gleaming dully in Dylan's light, against the wall in a corner of the room stood a full suit of armor.

It looked just like the knight in the tapestry.

He must have been a big guy. As big as Howard himself.

Becky caught her breath and they stepped inside. The room was small, maybe ten feet to a side, and empty for the most part. Next to the armor, a long, horizontal display case stood about waist high on four legs. Dylan stepped over to it and shined the flashlight over its glass top.

Inside, on a long pillow covered with frayed velvet, lay a sword. A broadsword. It had a straight, double-edged blade and a heavy-pommeled hilt, long enough to grasp like a golf club, with both hands. The blade still looked sharp, but it was notched with dozens of nicks. Deep scratches where curving slivers of metal had been gouged out formed a dark tracery of tarnished steel up and down its five-foot length.

They gaped at it in silent wonder, then Dylan turned and his flashlight swept the walls again.

At the back of the room there was another door.

"Dylan," Becky said, "let's go back inside. We shouldn't be in here."

This one was fastened with a single bolt, much heavier than those on the outer door. Dylan struggled to raise the pin. It was frozen.

"Howard, give me a hand."

Howard put his thumbs under the pin and pushed, grunting. After several seconds of continuous exertion it snapped up with a squeak. Howard hammered at it sideways with the heel of his palm and it slipped by degrees into its runner. The door creaked when the bolt released it, and the hinges protested when Howard pulled it open.

A damp smell of mildew wafted out on a faint draft.

Dylan's flashlight swung up from behind him. On the other side of the door was a tunnel.

The stone walls and ceiling were covered with dark patches, slick and shiny with condensation. Shallow puddles here and there collected in the irregular shapes of the paving stones. From somewhere came the plunk of a drop of water. It reverberated away into the distance.

A few yards ahead, the stonework gave way to bare rock where the tunnel had been carved directly into the hillside. From there it stretched away with no visible breaks into a gloomy distance the flashlight beam couldn't penetrate.

"Howard, don't go in there. Let's not fool around, it's somebody else's place," Becky pleaded. "They'll be mad."

Dylan agreed. "Yeah, doesn't look like there's anything in here anyway." The tunnel was thrown into darkness as he aimed the flashlight back the way they'd come. "Let's blow it off. We already ruined the guy's tapestry."

Howard was a little surprised they thought they had to convince *him* not to go in there—like they thought he was the brave one, dying to explore the tunnel. So he acted like he was reluctant to turn back. "I don't know, could be pretty interesting."

"Nah, there's nothing in there."

"Please, Howard, let's forget about it."

Howard hesitated—stretching it out to a few seconds—then shrugged and closed the door.

Bentley sat at the conference table, alone with his thoughts. He didn't particularly want to be alone with them, but everyone else seemed to have other things to do. He thought hard, but couldn't think of anything he himself had to do. Hal was rigging the wireless equipment to the cameras and planning tomorrow's shoot. And giving the interns a quick course in live editing in the dismal event that Dylan, Becky and Howard didn't come back.

Goddammit, what the hell were they doing? He'd always known Dylan could be something of a flake, but he'd always been conscientious and reliable when it came to doing his job. At least with supervision. No, something had happened. Bentley could feel it in his bones.

The uncertainty, the endless setbacks and revisions, the coping, the gnawing fear—the weight of it all dragged at Bentley's shoulders and infected his thoughts, pulling him down like quicksand. It was unbelievable what was happening, especially after things had gotten off to such a promising start. Well, no, that wasn't true, actually. Things had gotten off to a miserable start. They hadn't turned promising until disaster struck, with the helicopter and the motorboat.

The truth was, the show was doing great because things were terrible. Was that it?—was that the secret that had always eluded him? He'd spent his entire career trying to keep things running smoothly, and the results had been for the most part undistinguished. Hal had once told him about the filming of Apocalypse Now, how it had been pure, utter chaos, with the director and stars out of their minds on drugs, the shoot plagued by calamity after horrific calamity, the crew's lives constantly at risk, imperiled in the most unthinkable ways.

And the goddamn thing was a masterpiece.

And this would be his. If he could just keep things together. No, if he could keep them falling apart.

Bentley found himself overwhelmed by the confusion of his own thinking. A bout of dizziness gripped him. His mind swam, like Stan, out in the ocean surrounded by sharks, alone, with only his thoughts, and sinking.

He jumped at the sound of the door opening. It was Barry, with Hal and Grant behind him.

"Any word?" Barry asked.

Bentley stared, uncomprehending for a few moments, until he realized Barry was asking about Dylan.

"No," he managed. His voice was hoarse. "No."

The sounds of Dylan and Becky's horseplay drifted to Howard's ears over the water. They were in a semi-secluded cove, surrounded on three sides by a steep, rocky incline, overgrown close to the banks with tangled shrubs and stunted trees. Higher overhead, the trees grew straighter and taller. A wide, beaten path wound upward through them from the cove to the Viceroy's house, and from there all the way up to the jungle that overhung the cliffsides—a feathery fringe of dark against a skyline only a few shades lighter.

Sandy beach extended partway into the cove's mouth, which opened onto a narrow view of the ocean beyond, deep blue now in the gathering twilight with purple and green clouds riding low in the sky between the steep-sloping sides of the ravine. It was an idyllic spot. It would have made a nice postcard. One of those humorous ones, with some kind of witty caption, Howard thought—since it was kind of hard to miss Dylan and Becky's clothes draped over a tree limb in the foreground.

Howard had moved a little ways off to smoke another joint, sitting on a tall boulder that stuck out over the water, listening to the others splashing around and laughing. Every once in a while Dylan had called out to him, "Come on in, Howard, it's really nice and warm." But Howard didn't want Becky to see him in his shorts.

She had even taken off her bra.

It was fun for the two of them, and Howard didn't resent it, he could see where it was going. They were both his friends, and that was the way it would stay. Of course Dylan got the girl, no big deal.

After a while they stopped yelling at him to come join them and Howard started feeling like three's a crowd. He climbed down from his perch and walked back up the path to the house without saying anything. They didn't notice anyway.

Back in the library, Howard suddenly got an idea. It was one of those ideas that at first just seems too audacious to even consider. But the more Howard considered it, the more he realized he had to go through with it, because if he didn't, he'd regret it for the rest of his life. After all, when would he ever get another chance?

And it was just the right size too, he was sure of it. That knight was a pretty big guy.

An evil grin crept over Howard's features. Hah! His old pal Dylan and Becky were about to get the scare of their lives. And just getting into it anyway—just to feel the vibe—would be awesome.

He looked around. Where was the flashlight? Yes!—there it was, wedged between the sofa cushions. He picked it up and slipped behind the tapestry.

The armor was on a kind of custom-made framework of metal rods. Holding the maglight in his teeth, Howard carefully lifted off the helmet and set it on the glass case. Now, with the helmet off, he could see there was another suit of chain mail underneath the plate armor.

He inspected the arm pieces. They were buckled on at the shoulder blades and over the chest of the main whatever they called it—breastplate, Howard guessed. He unbuckled the left arm and took it off, setting it down beside the helmet. There were elbow things that were separate pieces but also attached with buckles to the arms. He lifted the right arm off the stand and stuck his hand into it. With a little squirming he managed to get it all the way over his arm without having to take off the elbow thing. Good. But he'd have to put on the breastplate first. And before that, the chain mail. He wriggled out of the arm and set it on the case. The second he let go of it, there was a loud crack.

It startled him so badly he almost inhaled the maglight. He grabbed it out of his mouth and shone it over the case.

Shit! It was broken—the glass had fractured under all the weight and collapsed in shards.

All over the sword.

Howard reached in and picked it up.

Wow. It must have weighed like twenty pounds. It was almost as long as he was tall. There wasn't room to swing it—that'd have to wait till he got outside. He set it back down in its case for the time being.

Fifteen minutes later, Sir Howard stepped out from behind the tapestry, cradling his helmet in his left arm. The steel-clad fingers of his right hand curled around the hilt of the great sword. He held it upraised before him.

He felt awesome. Mighty. Lordly. It was totally worth it.

Damn, he wished he'd thought of finding a mirror before putting everything on—he couldn't very well hunt around for one now, in full medieval battle gear.

He'd get the others to help him when they got back. Maybe one of them had brought a camera.

Now that he was back in the library with a little room to maneuver, he put the helmet and Dylan's maglight down on the sofa and hefted the sword with both hands. He was just getting ready to swing it up and around in a circle over his head when the phone rang.

He froze, tensing as a heavy rush of paranoia washed over him. His sword arm drooped. The sword's tip made a dull clink against the carpet-covered marble tiles.

Dylan! He'd forgotten all about Bentley. He probably forgot to transmit the footage too! Shit, this was a real bummer. They'd all just totally forgotten. Should have waited to get stoned till they'd finished the job, big mistake. But it was Dylan's responsibility, Howard sure as hell wasn't going to pick up and let Bentley chew him out instead. And Bentley would be able to tell he was stoned too—there'd be no way he could hide it, he'd probably start giggling or something and then they'd be in real trouble. Anyway, the phone was back in the TV studio, and even if he made it there before it stopped ringing, how could he answer with these big gauntlets on? He could barely move his fingers. So there really wasn't much he could do anyway. He couldn't answer if he tried. It wasn't his fault.

The phone finally stopped ringing.

Like magic, all the tension Howard had felt only moments before evaporated. He let out a deep breath.

Okay. Now that that was over with, he could get on with the business at hand.

He propped the sword against the sofa back, picked up the helmet with both hands and eased it over his head. He could tell as soon as he got it on that it was going to take a little getting used to. It really cut down on the peripheral vision. There was nothing but a slit to see through. Could make maneuvering a little tricky.

He had to tilt his head forward and swivel it back and forth to find the sword. Chuckling, he picked it up and clanked out into the hall.

CHAPTER EIGHTEEN

COMMISSION

FOR MOST OF THE AFTERNOON, Bentley had been calling every fifteen minutes. Now he was calling every five.

He was no longer worried. He was alarmed.

He slapped the receiver back into its cradle.

Hal said, "Something's happened to them."

Barry heaved a sigh of resignation and Bentley shook his head. Not in denial. Just bewilderment and disbelief.

"Want me to go get him?" Hal asked.

Bentley nodded.

Hal got up and left the room, and a minute later they heard him outside yelling for Jim.

There wasn't much choice. It was Security's job, and Jim was Security. Roger was too, but Roger was only Roger—Jim was at a whole different level. Now Bentley'd have to worry about Jim too, and about who was going to take charge of the situation if anything happened here while he was gone.

Who could? Grant? Bentley grimaced.

The thought of a repeat of last night's performances sent a chill down his spine. It was accompanied by a faint twinge of guilt stemming from his awareness that he took a certain pleasure in the chill.

Well, it was hard. It was hard not to be torn. You couldn't suddenly shift gears just because the situation demanded it. Yes, he was the producer, but he was also human. There hadn't been time yet for the shock of their predicament to settle in. Everything was happening so fast. He hadn't internalized it in a way that made the new priorities—actual survival as opposed to a staged semblance of it—as real as they seemingly were, on the surface.

"Rob..."

Bentley jumped at the sound of his name. He closed his eyes to rearrange his thoughts and turned toward Jim, coming through the door with Hal behind him.

"Sorry if I gave you a start," Jim said.

Bentley waved the apology away. "Would you like a seat? There's some coffee over on the desk."

"Thanks." Jim walked over to help himself. "Hal tells me Dylan et al've turned up missing."

"Yes, Jim, that's right."

"Supposed to call you after he sent out some—'footage'?"

"He said he'd be ready to send by five or six. The network hasn't gotten it, and nobody's answering the phone over at the house. I know it's not six yet, but he promised to call every hour and I haven't heard from him since around three o'clock. Almost three hours."

"Nowadays that's a long time not to hear from somebody."

"Yep, it sure is." Bentley had never said "yep" before in his life. He wasn't even sure if Jim ever did—the big Texan's manner was that contagious.

"I imagine I better go see if I can find 'em."

"Do you think that's safe?"

"Not really." Jim smiled. "But isn't that what you called me in here to ask me to do?"

The man's straightforwardness caused Bentley a moment's confusion. Then he just said, "Yes. Thank you, Jim."

"Pleasure's all mine." Jim smiled at Bentley, and with a nod to Hal, ducked through the door, closing it behind him.

Bentley shook his head. "If I ever make another western…"

"He's a natural," Hal agreed as he opened the door.

"Where are you going?"

"Are you kidding? Gotta get my gear. I'm going with Jim."

Bentley considered, then said, "Fine. But no interiors at the Viceroy's. It's in the contract. Tell Jim to just be ready. I'll give the word if I don't hear from them in another twenty-five minutes. Six-thirty."

"Will do." Hal was disappointed, but still agreeable.

Grant came back a second after Hal left.

"What's going on?"

"Jim's going to find Dylan and the others," Barry said. "Hal's going along."

Grant shook his head in admiration. "I wish I could go with them. Could be dangerous. Even Jim might be able to use some backup."

"Why don't you?" Barry asked.

Grant shot him a look of suspicion. "What do you mean? How can I go, you know I've got to get ready for tomorrow. I was on my way over to the mess hall just now when I heard Hal calling Jim."

"Let's hold off on that," Bentley said.

Grant looked crestfallen. "Rob—"

"I'm not calling it off, just let's wait and see what happens. It's not late. If Jim ends up going, he'll be there by nine or ten. We'll wait till we hear from him."

Barry caught up with Hal in the hallway. Looking back over his shoulder to make sure he'd closed the conference room door, he muttered, "I can't believe he's changing his mind again."

"About Grant's thing you mean?" Hal said. "Rob's just being cautious. Anyone would be."

"I understand that, but Hal, Grant's the one with the experience to make the call. He's not exactly a rank amateur. You know, he was a Marine lieutenant in the Gulf War. He knows how to lead troops."

Hal stopped short of the control room to stare at Barry. "Who told you that?"

"What do you mean? I don't know, everybody's saying it."

"Grant." Hal shook his head. "Grant was a lieutenant all right. But he never led troops. He was a backline junior administrator in Requisitions. Strictly REMF. Probably never fired a weapon after basic."

Barry was dumbfounded. "You're kidding."

"How do you think I got this job? I've known Grant since he was ten years old. Got to be friends with his dad in Vietnam. Captain William Nolan. I tagged along with Bill's unit the month before Khe Sanh, shooting a piece for LOOK—wading through rice paddies, getting snakebit and shot at by Viet Cong for thirty days and thirty nights. Ten weeks later him and his radio operator were the only ones that were left."

Hal shrugged. "I always had the feeling it was Bill that was behind Grant never seeing anything but the inside of a desk drawer for his whole tour."

At a loss for words, Barry just said, "Wow…"

"Look," Hal said, "Let's not go spreading it around okay? I don't want to burst Grant's bubble."

Barry wasn't sure he wanted to share secrets with Hal, but he decided to go along.

"So what do you figure happened with Dylan and them?"

"I don't know," Hal said, "but I have my suspicions. And I hope they're right."

Halfway from the house to the cove, Howard had to stop to catch his breath. He didn't sit down, because he was afraid it could be tricky trying to get back up again. He pushed up the visor on his helmet and just stayed standing where he was.

He was still high up enough to see the wide expanse of ocean spread out beneath him, flat and smooth, the water stilled by the invisible dome. The sun, tinted a weird lavender by the barrier, was half-submerged and sinking fast—there was still enough light left in the sky for Howard to see where he was going, but there wouldn't be for long.

He realized he was staring directly into the sun and turned his head away. The sudden movement caused his visor to fall shut with a clang that startled him to action.

He lumbered forward.

There were two footpaths to the cove: One led more or less straight from the Viceroy's front door down to where Dylan and Becky were swimming (if that was what they were still doing); the other, the one he was on, started a little further around the mountainside and then cut back toward the cove along the shoreline.

He'd taken the longer route because it was more gradual and because it gave him a better chance of sneaking up on them. But it was kind of rough going.

It wasn't that he regretted his decision. The other route was probably way too steep. And for the first half of the trip, Howard had really been savoring the experience, grinning as he pictured himself—a knight in armor suddenly appearing out of nowhere, roaring a battle cry!—and the looks on Dylan and Becky's faces.

He was still savoring it—but at the same time he had to admit it was pretty uncomfortable. The chain mail chafed his skin through his clothes. Those knights probably wore a lot of padding underneath the stuff.

And it was heavy. He was already puffing from the exertion of carrying what felt like another hundred pounds on top of the more than two hundred he already carried.

But still—it was going to be worth it.

Even the sword was heavy. He had to bring it, though, it kind of made the whole thing. Hard to imagine swinging something like this at ogres and shit all day. He switched sword hands again for the fifth or sixth time. His left was starting to cramp now.

When he did it, something came loose. He heard it clink against the rocks. He stopped and tried to turn his head to look for it, but the helmet wouldn't let him.

He could barely look around. He tried to bend over to look down at the ground, but the visor fell shut. He was always pushing it back up and having it fall back down again. You could hardly see anything out of it.

He'd have to come back and look for it later.

He started forward again and the first step he took he heard a crunch. Something metal. Whatever it was he dropped, he'd just stepped on it and crushed it.

Great.

He shrugged—mentally, because the weight of the armor would have made physically doing it monumentally difficult—and kept moving.

He felt beads of sweat dripping down the back of his neck and soaking his t-shirt. It was stuffy inside too. But he gave up on the visor. He didn't want the clang it made when it fell shut to give him away. Not that it was even remotely possible to steal along quietly. The armor clanked and squeaked with every step he took. Probably hadn't been oiled in five hundred years.

Howard still relished the fright he was going to give old Dylan, though, and it kept him going. It was going to be worth it, it really, really was. And he was getting pretty close too—he couldn't see them yet, but he could hear them now, splashing around in the water.

Good. They wouldn't hear him coming, making all that noise themselves.

The sword was just too heavy. He finally had to drop it. He'd pick it up later, along with whatever it was he'd broken.

He remembered the glass case: Something else he'd broken. It was a pretty good bet the Viceroy was going to be pissed. Hopefully the three of them would be long gone before he got back and flipped out over all the damage.

Howard's foot slipped on some loose gravel and he almost went down. The sweat rolled down his back.

But he could see the shimmer of water ahead now, really close. Just a little bit further. Another few steps and he'd hit the banks—and the fun would begin.

But before he could take them, Becky screamed.

It startled Howard so bad he almost let out a yelp himself. Then he grinned. She'd seen him first.

He repressed a snicker. She sounded really terrified.

And then Becky screamed again—only this time it sounded for real. She screamed, "Dylaaaa-a-an" and her voice got higher and higher toward the end until it turned into a yodeling shriek that gave Howard chills.

Then Dylan screamed.

All of a sudden it wasn't funny anymore. Howard felt his face turn beet red like it always did when he realized he'd done something stupid.

He'd gone too far.

"Becky! It's me," he yelled. "It's Howard."

Becky wasn't screaming anymore. She and Dylan were both making these weird panicking sounds. Little cries and whimpering noises. And then there was a loud rustling and Howard heard Becky again, whooping in fear. He couldn't tell which direction their voices were coming from anymore. The helmet muffled everything so that it all sounded far away.

He tried to hurry, to get down to the banks so he could tell them he was sorry. He kept yelling, "It's me—Howard," even though you'd have thought they would've heard him the first time.

They were going to be really mad when they found out it was him.

His steel-clad feet sank into sand and the sudden drag threw him off balance, nearly toppling him.

He'd finally reached the bottom. He held the visor up, but he couldn't see them anywhere. Their clothes were still hanging on the branch, so they must still be around someplace. He looked up the ravine and then back toward the ocean. When he let go, the visor just fell down again.

He tried to take off the helmet. He jerked it and twisted it, but it didn't budge. It was stuck.

There must be some kind of latch. With his left hand he worked his right out of its gauntlet and felt around, but he couldn't find one, even with his bare fingers. He gave up and tried to raise the visor again. But now, somehow the visor was stuck too. Great.

"I'm sorry," he yelled again. It echoed a little in the cove. "It's just me," he said.

Nobody answered. It was eerily quiet.

Howard suddenly realized what was going on. They knew he couldn't see them. They were trying to turn the tables on him—getting back at him for scaring them.

That had to be it.

But for some reason he regretted dropping the sword.

Something moved.

He'd heard it. Somewhere off to the side. Quick footsteps in the sand. He saw a light—a glow, on the sand off to his left.

Dylan's maglight!

Without thinking, Howard jerked his head toward it and hurt his neck. The armor didn't allow that kind of movement.

"Dylan?"

It wasn't the maglight. The maglight was back at the house, Howard remembered. He'd left it on the sofa.

Something streaked past. It was bright. Howard was blinded by its afterimage.

Colors swam before his eyes.

It wasn't Dylan.

He could feel it now behind him. His vision gradually cleared. Everything was a deep red. The sand glowed, except where his shadow stretched out in front of him.

Fighting panic, Howard clawed at his visor, but it was really jammed shut now.

He turned around in awkward, shuffling steps. His shadow revolved right along with him. The red light was circling him, staying at his back.

Something pushed him hard from behind, throwing him face down onto the sand. He scrabbled helplessly, the armor weighing him down, and then another weight on his back pressed him down even harder. Terror seized him. He heard himself shouting, "No, no, no," until it became a howl, and then something rammed hard into his back. His armor cracked open like a lobster shell. A burning coldness slid through his chest and pierced his breastplate, pinning him to the ground. The armor filled with steaming liquid. Blood bubbled up into his throat, cutting off his screams. He choked and gurgled, writhing in agony. Something grabbed hold of the top of his helmet, jerked his head up and wrenched it back. The helmet creaked, then split and crumpled at the back of his neck, crushing his upper vertebrae with a sickening sputter of snapping bone. Blood gushed from his mouth in a dark flood, splashing against the inside of his helmet and into his eyes and nose. It cleared his esophagus, allowing one last burbling scream before something ripped upwards across his throat.

At six-thirty, Bentley called for Jim and Hal. The mission was a go.

They were ready. Barry and Jim talked through the directions on the way to the mess hall. Jim wanted to let the punters know he'd be away for a few hours—and he also wanted to leave his Winchester rifle with Trask. As he explained to Barry, he could have given it to Roger, but Roger still had his pistol. And he thought Trask had handled the shotgun pretty well the night before.

At the top of the steps, Jim turned the door handle and pushed. The door didn't budge.

"Dammit, I forgot. It's after sunset. We'll have to use the tunnel."

"Jim, is that you?" someone said from inside.

"And Barry and Hal," Jim answered.

"Hang on," came Lance's voice. A series of heavy thuds was followed by scuffing and scraping.

"I guess it'll make them feel safer, being armed," Barry commented while they waited. Jim gave him a wry look and the door opened just wide enough for them to squeeze through.

"Good timing," Lance said. "We were just starting to fill 'er up."

Though the cast had been decimated, there were still nineteen of them, all standing, with Lance at their head.

They bristled with weapons.

Machetes, sharpened and gleaming. Butcher knives. Carving knives, tie-wired to the threaded ends of broom and mop handles. Lance and Vince gripped the hafts of baseball bats. They'd driven four-inch nails into the ends, nipping off the heads with a spike cutter and flattening the shank tips with a hammer for maximum sharpness.

Brad held a four-foot length of case-hardened steel chain fitted with a wooden handle. The business end was a cluster of anchor shackles. It must have weighed thirty pounds.

Barry's jaw dropped. The punters looked like a band of murderous savages. And the paraphernalia of mayhem had transformed them psychologically as well. There was an indefinable, animalistic quality to them. Feral, and at the same time, hunted. The room was charged with it, as if drenched in testosterone. Even the girls seemed menacing.

"You look fantastic," Hal said, nodding his approval at Fred, whose camera was rolling. He hoisted his own. "I've got to get some of this too."

The punters posed self-consciously around Lance, pretending nothing was different.

"What up, Jim?" Fredo asked, trying to sound casual.

Suppressing a grin, Jim nodded, then looked at Trask.

"Some of the crew's got lost. Probably nothing."

Beverly sounded panicky. "Jim, you can't leave."

Trask said, "What happened, Jim?"

Jim looked around at Barry, and stepped aside.

"Well, Dylan and Howard, and Becky," Barry said, "we sent them over to the house to try to transmit last night's footage to the network." He paused. "And now we can't reach them," he finished.

There was a longer pause.

Then Michelle said, "The house?"

"Uh-huh."

"What house, Barry?"

"I thought the island was deserted," Brad rumbled.

"Well, it is. That is, it's not—uninhabited, of course—obviously there's the bungalow and everything—but, technically, the Viceroy's on the continent, as they say, so you know, right now, it's—his house is—at the present time—deserted."

"The Viceroy," Michelle said.

"The Viceroy's house," Rashad amended.

"Up by the castle," Barry clarified.

Lance exploded. "God damn it! Spit it out, Barry. The castle? You mean to tell us we've been breaking our backs building a house of twigs here when there's a goddamn—"

"No, no, no, no, no. It's just ruins, Lance. Only a little castle anyway. More of a tower. Heap of mortar now."

Lance set his jaw. "Tell us about the castle, Barry."

"And the Viceroy," Michelle said.

Barry chewed his lip, taking in the suspicion written all over the faces surrounding him, and decided to come clean. "Well, the Viceroy is—he's actually a baron. Or was. His great great great great grandfather's great great grandfather was this French knight back in like the fourteen-hundreds that got shipwrecked here with his men on the way to the crusades. Kind of got lost, I guess."

Rashad said, "You're not kidding."

"No, I'm not."

"So they built a castle," Michelle prompted.

"Actually, that was later. There's some legend about a dragon, up on the mountain. The knight killed it, and the king of France, Louis something or other, made him Viceroy of the island, and then he made him a baron so the title could be passed on in perpetuity to his ancestors."

The punters had forgotten their suspicions in fascination with Barry's story.

"Killed a dragon, huh?" Brad said.

"That's what they say. Or used to. So later one of the barons built the castle to protect his property, and then a lot later one of them built a house nearby. To use as a kind of getaway from—you know, court intrigue and what have you. It's not very well known. I saw a thing about it in National Geographic and got in touch with him. He's a sweet guy and loved the idea of the show. So Rob and I met with him and worked out a deal to shoot while he's away for the summer."

"So why don't we all go there?" Paula said. "If it's safer than where we are?"

"It might be safer, and if it is, you're right, maybe we should all move there. But right now there's some question…"

"So basically you sent three of your crew members off on a possible suicide mission, without any protection," Trask said, "in the interests of keeping the show on schedule."

"Well, Howard's a pretty big guy. It was still early. They would have gotten back while it was still daylight."

"If they hadn't not," Michelle said.

"Right," Barry was forced to admit.

Trask said, "So what do we know?"

Barry frowned. "Nothing. They were supposed to check in every hour, and they haven't. Only once, around three o'clock. Rob's—Mr Bentley's been calling pretty much continuously since then and nobody answers."

Jim put a hand on Barry's shoulder and stepped forward. "Thought I'd leave you with a little firepower just in case." He held the rifle upright. "Trask."

Trask didn't reach for it. He said, "You're going alone? You and Hal?"

There was no immediate reply.

"Give the rifle to Lance," Trask said. "I'm coming with you guys."

"It's not a big deal—" Jim protested, but Michelle cut him off.

"Yes it is. You can't go out there at night by yourselves, just the two of you. I'm coming too."

Jim glanced at the machete and the long carving knife tucked under Michelle's belt, then looked up again when Brad and Rashad stepped forward. And Paula and Vince.

"Trask," Lance said. "Take the rifle."

"You sure?"

Lance hefted his bat. "We've been getting mixed results with bullets. Maybe it's time to try something different."

CHAPTER NINETEEN

LOCATION SCOUTING

THE RESCUE PARTY set out in the deepening dusk, following the coastline northwest, with the ocean to their left. The moon and stars were out to help light their way, but there was something else too. A hazy glow that seemed to hover over everything. The barrier somehow amplified the ambient light. The effect was faint but unmistakable.

At the crest of a grassy ridge, Jim stopped and turned around to wait for the others to catch up. Behind him, blotting out the stars, loomed the three great rocks that guarded the island's northern coast. Following Barry's directions, once they'd regrouped the party headed west, leaving the ridge, and another hundred yards further on descended into a gap.

At the bottom, Jim called a halt. Brad had brought sandwiches, complements of Evans, and tossed them around after everyone found a log or a boulder to sit on.

They'd just unwrapped them and begun to eat. Trask heard Paula sigh and turned to her. She was smiling. Their eyes met and he smiled back at her. When he turned back to the others, Vince was standing, looking up the side of the ravine, and Jim had laid down his sandwich and was picking up his shotgun.

They were all on their feet in an instant—except for Brad, who took one more bite of his sandwich before stuffing it into his pants pocket and grabbing the lantern.

Something was tumbling down the slope. The lantern beam picked it up just as it dropped to the banks and splashed into a muddy puddle. It was only a rock, knocked loose from the steep incline. But there were more coming down after it.

Jim glanced over at Trask and nodded, and Trask realized he'd picked up and raised the Winchester without even thinking.

He took a step sideways for a better position and said, "Vince."

Vince turned.

"You're in the line of fire."

Vince ducked out of the way and stepped behind them as another rock skipped over the banks.

"It's coming," Jim said.

Trask expected the thing to come crashing down in an avalanche of rocks and breaking tree limbs. It didn't. This one was sure-footed and cautious.

Hal's beam joined the lantern's, and something froze when the lights passed over it. Trask's finger tightened on the trigger. Two pinpoints flashed and Paula said, "Don't shoot."

They were eyes. A pair of small, beady eyes, gleaming in the lantern light. And then their owner was trundling downhill at an angle, switching directions back and forth in a zigzag pattern to offset the steepness of the decline.

Jim lowered his shotgun.

It was a pig. At the bottom, it headed for Trask at an ungainly trot, its long snout snuffling over the ground.

"It's Trask's pig!" Brad said.

Trask was sure it was too, but it swerved around him, stopped to lift its snout and sniff the air, and walked right up to Brad, stopping just a few feet away.

Jim laughed. Brad pulled out what was left of his sandwich, and tearing off a piece, stooped and held it out in front of him.

"Don't hurt him," Paula said.

"What do you mean, I'm just giving him a treat." Brad sounded offended. "Here boy."

The pig got nervous when the others started to approach it too. It darted up to Brad, snatched the offering and gulped it down, allowing him to pet it on the head before dashing away and disappearing up the opposite slope.

"Can you believe that?" Brad sounded delighted—about as unlike Brad as any of them could have imagined.

Trask looked a little hurt. It hadn't paid any attention to him, and after him sparing its life the other day. Brad had thrown a goddamn spear at it.

Paula was watching him, smiling. "Fickle," she said.

Trask shook his head, grinning.

From there, their path carried them halfway down to the sea before it banked hard eastward, forcing them to travel in single file along the edge of what was now a sheer cliff overlooking a secluded cove.

Up ahead, the path wound around toward the west to join a narrow shelf in the cliffside on their right hand. Where the two met, the path leveled out, and the shelf widened to a broad ledge.

Brad grabbed Rashad's arm and pointed. "There it is."

It lay under the shelter of what at first appeared to be an upward-projecting spur of rock at the mountain's summit. Now, as they drew closer, they saw it was actually a tower—the ruins of the medieval stronghold Barry had called "the castle", but which was little more than a small fort.

They'd made it.

Under the cover of night, the two-story stone house built into the ledge ahead blended so completely with its surroundings that it was all but invisible. Only the lacquer-like finish of the terracotta roof tiles, incongruously lustrous in the starlight, gave it away.

That, and the even more incongruous warm glow of lamplight shining between the cracks of heavy curtains.

It was a welcome sight after their hard march. They hurried down the path toward it.

The doors were locked.

Jim tried ramming them with his shoulder, then turned and motioned Brad forward, and the two of them threw their combined weight at them. They rattled, but held.

Jim cupped his hands to his mouth.

"Dylan!"

"Howard, Becky!" Hal yelled. "It's Hal! Let us in!"

There was no answer.

"Break it down, Brad," Jim said, stepping back.

Brad lifted his mace, wound up and swung. The shackles ripped into the oak double doors, sending splinters flying. Another stroke flattened the door handles against their brass mountings, the next shattered the lock. The doors sagged open a crack. Brad wedged his fingers between them and gave them a jerk, and they heard the lock housing hit the floor inside with a clunk.

"Damn," Jim said.

Brad threw the doors wide and waited for the others to enter before stepping through himself.

They stood in the entrance hall. Jim appeared unmoved by the palatial splendor of the place. Maybe Texas oilmen had houses like this, and in his youth Jim had grown accustomed to being invited over to them for chicken-fried steak and curly fries. Or maybe he was just too intent on the job at hand to be distracted by what he considered irrelevant details, focusing his attention instead on those that mattered. Like the faint tracks leading up the marble-tiled hallway to disappear behind the staircase on the right.

The others followed his gaze. There wasn't much to see. Here and there a flake of dried mud, a bit of leaf or grass.

"Dylan!" Jim's voice rang off the marble tiles.

He stood for a few seconds watching a pair of half-open doors off the second floor landing. When nobody stuck their head out, he glanced through another open door to his left, then at the big double doors on his right, and his eyes narrowed.

He walked over to them and pushed them open. A heady aroma of cooked meat wafted out into the hall. And bread. And butter. Lots of butter.

"Looks like they've made themselves right at home."

"You can say that again," Hal said.

Brad shoved his way past the others into the dining hall behind Jim. At the kitchen end of the long table, three dinner plates lay amidst a scattering of serving platters, bowls, glasses and well-used napkins. One bowl still held a fluffy mound of mashed potatoes. Two empty wine bottles fleshed out the evidence.

Brad reached for a serving spoon, then hesitated, looking around at the others. "You guys mind?"

"Be my guest," Rashad said. "Or should I say, the Viceroy's. Looks like we're assuming he's a generous guy."

"Yeah," Brad said. "Thanks." Making short work of the potatoes, he reached for the heel of a baguette. While the others watched Brad eat, Jim and Hal went into the kitchen.

Rashad picked up and inspected a half-empty glass. Ginger ale. A layer of water—melted ice cubes—floated on top. At Trask's hopeful look, Rashad shook his head.

"Room temperature."

It might have told them something if it had still been cold. As it was, it didn't tell them much of anything.

A stick of butter on a saucer had turned shiny and bright yellow. Brad scooped it up with a crust of bread.

Jim and Hal came back from the kitchen.

"Anything?" Trask said.

Jim shook his head and said "no" and kept going. "Let's follow those tracks out in the hall."

He sounded more concerned than the others felt.

Back out in the entrance hall, everyone crowded behind Jim as he walked past the staircase with his head down, scanning the floor. A streak of dried mud marked the spot where one of the missing crew members must have slipped while turning to a door behind the staircase. Jim opened it and stepped into the room.

It was a library. Bookshelves lined two walls. A huge fireplace was set into a third, its wide hearth surrounded by leather-upholstered wingback chairs and sofas. Fur rugs covered the oaken floorboards. The fourth wall was hidden behind a single gigantic wall-to-wall tapestry.

But aside from the furnishings, the room was empty.

Trask walked toward the center of the room. He thought he detected a faint odor of wine in the air here too. He stared at the tapestry. It was medieval. The colors had faded, and what must have originally been green— the grass and the leaves of the trees—was now blue. It reminded him of the ones at the Metropolitan Museum, and one he'd seen once in a book. "The Lady and the Unicorn".

This one would be "The Knight and the Dragon". They were joined in battle, the knight on horseback, while ladies in conical hats and men in striped tights cowered in groups at each end. A dense blue forest covered the background, with the sky just visible at the top of the trees.

But it was the corner decorations that caught Trask's eye. In oval-shaped insets about two feet high, the top corners each showed a smaller version of the dragon. On fire.

But no—the one on the right was on fire, encircled by stylized tongues of bright red flame. The one on the left, though—that one looked more like it was surrounded by a halo.

Behind him, Michelle said, "Look, a flashlight. Must belong to one of them."

Rashad said, "Grab it, we might need it."

Another inset, centered below the main scene, showed the knight with a similar halo. That made more sense. He'd probably been beatified for slaying the dragon. He stood holding his sword, point down, with his left hand resting on the pommel, steadying it with the tip of his right index finger on the hilt. It was an odd pose, and probably meant something—Trask remembered reading once about all the symbolism behind things like hand positions and gestures in medieval art.

At the bottom right, in another oval was something that looked like a crystal ball, covered with cracks that made Trask think of Martian canals. Some kind of jewel. It was red too.

There was no fourth inset. Not anymore. The tapestry's lower left corner had been sheared off at a clean and deliberate forty-five degree angle.

Paula nudged him. The others were heading back out into the hall.

"Sorry," he said. He shook himself out of it. They were here to find missing crew members, not go sightseeing. And he was still carrying Jim's rifle, which meant he'd better pay attention and stay alert.

They returned to the front entrance and turned right into the room opposite the dining hall, making their way down its length beneath a row of framed portraits. Except for the lights being on in every room they'd visited so far, aside from what they'd seen at the dinner table there were few signs of recent occupancy.

But the next room—with a widescreen HDTV monitor as its center-piece—told the same story as the dining room. In a word, food. Piled high on two silver platters at a corner table, not even half eaten. Everyone's eyes widened.

"Might as well go ahead and dig in," Jim said. "I imagine Bentley's gonna have to foot the bill for this either way. Not to mention the front door."

Brad didn't wait to be invited twice. He picked up a knife and started sawing up a loaf of pumpernickel.

There was more wine here too. Or had been. Paula picked up an empty bottle and inspected the label.

"French. Bordeaux," she said. "1935."

Hal shook his head in irritation. "What the hell are they thinking?"

And—someone had, with impressive nonchalance, used a corner of one of the Viceroy's silver platters as an ashtray.

Rashad picked a resin-steeped roach out of the ashes, took a whiff, closed his eyes in brief contemplation, and announced, "Mexican. Acapulco Gold. 1969."

Paula laughed. "I think I'm beginning to understand."

But Hal was skeptical. "I can't believe they'd just forget the whole reason for their being here."

Vince was walking toward a door at the far end of the room. "The evidence is pretty conclusive if you ask me," he said over his shoulder. "They made themselves overly at home, got a little too comfortable—then *way* too comfortable."

"And now they're floating on a cloud somewhere over Never Never Land," Michelle said.

Jim agreed. "Maybe they're passed out in a bedroom upstairs. Brad, Vince—"

"We still need to find the television studio," Hal said.

"I think I just did," Vince said from across the room.

Hal hurried over and looked through the door Vince had just opened. "This would be it," he said.

Jim said, "Come on, Vince. Let's you and me and Brad go take a look upstairs." Brad downed the last bite of an oversize sandwich, grabbed a handful of macadamia nuts, and followed Jim and Vince back out through the drawing room, leaving Trask, Paula, Rashad and Michelle alone in the den.

They heard Hal's voice coming from the TV studio. He'd apparently found a phone and was calling Bentley. "No, not yet, but everything looks okay. They'll turn up. Jim's gone to look for them."

"Think they're really okay?" Paula asked Trask.

"It's obvious," Michelle said. "They got stoned and crashed out upstairs."

"They could have gone outside," Trask suggested.

Hal was still on the phone. "Everything's set. I don't know why he didn't send,"—trying hard to avoid busting them for getting stoned and flaking on their mission. He glanced up when Trask and the others crowded the door to stare at the racks of audio/video equipment. The Viceroy had quite a set up.

"Doing it now," Hal continued. "I'll call you soon as we find them." He ended the call and set down the phone.

Michelle said, "We're going outside to look around."

Hal nodded. "Okay, just check with Jim first. I'm about to transmit. After that I'll pack up the gear. We should plan on spending the night here, though. We'll talk about it when everybody's back."

When they got to the entrance hall, Rashad stopped before the ruined front doors to yell upstairs.

"Any luck?"

"Not yet," Brad yelled back.

"Brad, tell Jim we're going outside."

Jim appeared at a doorway with the 9-volt lantern. "You better take this," he said.

Michelle said, "It's okay, we have one." She held up the maglight she'd found in the library.

Jim nodded and looked at his watch.

"Be back here in thirty minutes. And be careful."

CHAPTER TWENTY

DEATH ROW

A LITTLE WAYS PAST THE HOUSE they found a rocky trail that sloped down toward the sea. Michelle led the way with the flashlight.

Trask guessed they were about halfway down when something caught his eye.

"What is it?" Paula said.

He picked it up. It was a small, metal oval with tiny, precision-engineered parts attached to it that looked like glass or ceramic. Some kind of electronics.

Trask called out to Michelle and Rashad to wait up. They stopped and turned. He handed Jim's rifle to Paula and got down on one knee to feel around in the dark with both hands. There were more pieces there.

"Could you shine that light up here?"

Michelle's flashlight beam moved over the ground at his feet, and Trask found the metal housing, broken in two. What must have been the front was bent, but intact. It had a single button in the middle, but no other controls or markings. Both sections had runnels and contours, with little slots covering their inner surfaces—for holding the parts strewn over the path behind.

"Some kind of remote control," Paula suggested.

"Yeah. Funny, though. All this stuff inside and just the one button." Weird that it was made of metal, too. This kind of stuff was always plastic. And what was it doing outside?

Whatever it was, it was broken. Trask put all the tiny parts he'd retrieved inside the bottom half, and with a little work managed to bend it back into shape enough to snap the two sections together.

The flashlight beam was whisked away. Michelle started forward again. Rashad waited for Trask and Paula.

"Find something?" he asked.

"Not really." Trask stood up.

"I just found something," Michelle said.

They looked around to see her bending over, struggling to lift something up off the ground with her free hand. Trask slipped the remote into his pocket and trotted after the others as Michelle turned to face them.

She was holding a sword.

Their search of the upstairs rooms had turned up nothing, and Jim was about to call it off. They'd reached the last bedchamber of the final suite of rooms in the house's north wing, and it was exactly like all the others they'd seen so far except for one thing: It had windows. Brad walked over to one, threw the latch and swung it open.

He stuck his head out, looked down and said, "What's this?" He turned toward Jim and Vince. "Another house."

They hurried over.

It was a rooftop, but probably too small for a house. Some kind of shelter at the edge of the shore.

"Jim." Vince sounded excited. "It's a boathouse."

Of course. The Viceroy would have to have some way to get to the inner islands now and then for supplies.

"If there's a boat, we can use it to get back to camp."

Jim nodded. A motorboat would cut their trip back to a fraction of the time it had taken them to get here. And it would be a hell of a lot safer. But they still hadn't found what they came there for.

"Let's take another look downstairs," he said.

Back on the first floor, Jim retraced their steps, this time stopping often to examine the tiles closely. Outside the library door, he knelt and studied the floor.

"What is it?" Brad finally asked.

"Toe prints," Jim said.

Brad and Vince looked at each other.

"Barefoot." Jim's voice had turned grim. "Dammit. Should have paid more attention when we first came in." He straightened up. "Blood too. Back there behind you."

Brad and Vince turned but couldn't distinguish anything from the dried mud.

"They were outside, and came back without their shoes. The littler ones. Dylan and Becky."

His expression was grim now too.

"They were running," he said.

Inside the library Jim paused to scan the floor, then walked to the center of the room—stooping on the way to pick up a leaf. He stood there for a long time, looking around. Spotting another leaf on the rug at his feet, he brushed his fingers through the fur, and shook his head. He walked over to the Victrola, stopping to lift the needle off an old 78 and replace it in its holder.

He turned toward the tapestry, and as he ran his gaze along its lower edge he noticed a dark spot near the middle.

Brad and Vince followed him over to it. The floorboards under it were sticky. Jim rubbed a finger over them and lifted it to his nose.

"Wine." He was just turning away when something else caught his eye.

It was a blade of grass, clinging to the bottom edge of the tapestry. It shouldn't have been there. They were in a hurry, maybe running from something. Why, instead of running straight through to the door at the other end of the room, would they come over here so close to the wall that they brushed up against the tapestry?

For a second he just stared. Then he grabbed the tapestry's tattered bottom edge with both hands and lifted it up.

"Holy shit," Brad said.

Behind the tapestry was a hidden door.

It was open.

They found Dylan and Becky's clothes hanging from a tree limb down by the water's edge.

Near the bottom, the trail had veered left, away from the beach to a greener and more secluded part of the small bay—a hidden cove overhung with tree branches and vines. Closer to its mouth, the banks were covered with sand, but here the ground was muddy and slippery.

At first, they were sure they'd found their missing persons. But after calling out to them for several minutes, it became clear that Dylan and

Becky were nowhere in the vicinity. And they'd left without taking their clothes.

It wasn't a good sign.

"Okay," Rashad said. "They went swimming, that much is obvious. Maybe they swam around to the ocean. Or for some reason they don't want to be found—or..."

Trask shook his head.

"Or what?" Michelle said.

"Or not," Rashad finished. He looked at Trask.

Trask knew what he was thinking: the sharks that had almost gotten Stan.

Michelle had switched off the flashlight when they'd reached the cove. Now she switched it back on and shined its light over the banks and out toward the ocean.

"We better go look," Trask said, though he didn't expect to find anything. If the sharks had gotten them, there wouldn't be much left to find.

But Michelle, moving along the shore ahead of them, had again uncovered something.

"Look." The flashlight's beam picked out a group of dark, roundish shapes half in and half out of the water near the cove's mouth—still fifteen or twenty yards away.

To Trask, they just looked like rocks, but then he saw how the light glinted off one of them when it hit it.

Michelle kept the light trained on the cluster of objects, and they crept towards it. As they got closer, the one that reflected the light took on a metallic sheen.

In a hidden antechamber behind the tapestry, Jim stood looking down into a broken, glass-topped case. Beneath the litter of broken glass, a deep depression worn into the velvet lining bore the unmistakable imprint of a sword.

"One of our missing trio must've taken it," he said.

Taking passing note of a metal framework beside the case—an ancient mannikin, topped with a wooden knob in place of a head—Jim stepped over to the inner door. Like the first, it was open, and also like the first, the bolt was on the outside. He aimed the lantern up the tunnel, playing its beam over the walls and floor.

"Like something out of one of those old Vincent Price movies," he muttered. Wisps of steam rose from the puddled flagstones ahead. Jim expected any second to hear the alarmed squeal and scrabbling flight of a startled rat, but there were no signs of life. A faint, foul odor emanated from somewhere deep within. He didn't recognize that, but it was tinged with something he thought he did, though he couldn't quite put his finger on it.

Vince said, "Over here."

An iron spike, bent into a hook, had been hammered into the stone wall just outside the door.

"Looks like they took the keys," Jim said. "That could mean they're in here somewhere."

"Who?" Brad asked. "You mean Dylan and the others?"

"That I couldn't tell you."

Brad hefted his mace and Vince drew his machete.

Jim said, "Be ready for anything," and stepped into the tunnel.

Still trailing behind Michelle, Trask could make out surface details on whatever it was she'd spotted. It was covered with intricate designs, shining like tarnished silver in the flashlight's beam.

He was close enough now for perspective to separate their object from the others around it. Those really *were* just rocks. As they got still closer, golden highlights flashed along raised edges around the thing's middle. It was half submerged in the mud along the banks.

Michelle said, "Omigod," and hurried forward. She was ten yards ahead of Trask when he realized what it was.

A helmet. A *knight's* helmet.

Michelle had stopped beside it and was reaching down. Without thinking, Trask said, "Michelle, wait." He ran towards her. "Don't pick it up." Rashad and Paula hurried after him.

Michelle tugged. It came free of the mud with a slurping sound, and her hand slipped inside.

"It's all full of mud."

Trask, Rashad and Paula had stopped in front of her.

"Michelle, just put it down."

She lifted it up. Something long and sinuous trailed from the flared collar. It coiled slickly around her arm.

She raised the flashlight and aimed its beam through the slit in the helmet's visor.

Howard's dead eyes gleamed dully back at her, staring unseeing into her own.

Michelle's scream sent ripples over the water and shook a pod loose from a nearby tree branch. She threw down the helmet. The thing tethered to her arm jerked tight and stretched. It was Howard's spinal cord. She clawed and scraped at it, shrieking. It snapped loose, hitting the ground with a wet smack.

Trask was closest. Michelle threw her arms around his neck and he just closed his eyes and held on until she realized it was him and let go. She backed away and Rashad caught her, and she grabbed and held him instead, while he murmured idiotically, "It's okay, it's okay."

Up ahead the tunnel turned a corner to the right. Jim switched his shotgun to his left hand.

He wiped his forehead and flicked the perspiration from his fingers. The bare rock walls here dripped with condensation.

Jim motioned to Brad to hand him the lantern. They stopped before the corner and huddled close together. With his back to the wall, Jim edged ahead, then swung the lantern up and out at arm's length, shining its light around the corner. When nothing happened, he pivoted on his right foot, taking a step around the corner as he leveled his shotgun over his right arm. He held the stance for a second, then swung the shotgun up and stepped back.

"All clear," he said.

They rounded the corner. The section of tunnel ahead was just like the section at their backs—except that the smell, while still faint, had acquired a new and unpleasant pungency here. It got worse the deeper they went.

Another right turn. Jim reprised his earlier maneuver—only this time after he stepped around the corner he didn't duck back. He stayed right where he was, shotgun leveled, with the lantern light flooding the tunnel ahead, and stared.

This stretch of tunnel was different. Doors ran along both sides, starting about halfway down. They weren't wood, and they weren't solid, like the first two. These ones were barred.

The rooms they opened into were cells.

Brad and Vince stepped out from behind the corner to stare along with Jim. Even from where they stood, they could see the rows of heavy iron uprights fitted into even heavier frames, with massive hinges at one end and thick, plate-metal enclosures for locks on the other. It was some kind of medieval dungeon.

Down at the end, steam fogged the tunnel.

It drifted out of the last cell on the right.

The smell had become a stench, and there was no longer any mystery about what it was.

Bile. Urine. Human excrement.

And blood.

They'd found the lost party.

Jim turned to Brad and Vince and said, "Just wait here," and they watched him walk slowly up the corridor, lantern in hand, to the last cell on the right where the steam floated out and hovered above the floor. At the end of the corridor, bent at the middle, with the crook propped up against the wall, was a human arm.

Jim recognized it for what it was without looking directly at it. He continued ahead. The puddles that reflected the lantern's light as it passed over the flagstones were filled with a darker liquid than water. Splattered clear across the floor outside the last cell, it ran in rivulets from inside to pool beneath the bars.

Jim stopped there, curling his fingers around the bars to steady himself. They were slick with blood.

As Brad and Vince drew nearer, one cautious step at a time, Jim looked up between the bars.

Right away he saw one of them was Dylan. The young electrician's head lay on its side in the corner. Its lower jaw was missing. Two teeth dangled by bloody strands from the crushed left cheek.

One naked torso was limbless. The other still had one of its legs. That one was the girl, Becky.

The leg was bent, with the knee resting on her head. Her face was hidden under the long hair that spiraled out in a circle around it like the train of a nightgown.

And everywhere, caked in all manner of gore, the trampled entrails that had sprayed their contents over the remains released a steamy fog into the stifling heat.

There was no denying it now. Whatever it was, it hadn't happened upon these two unawares and been startled into an unpremeditated and instinctual act of self-preservation. It had hunted them, come for them, to slaughter them here as they cowered in fear.

Standing behind Jim, Vince was saying, "Oh no, oh God," over and over in a hoarse half-whisper. Brad retched and moaned, and with a violent heave sprayed his pumpernickel sandwich over the walls.

But Jim couldn't tear his eyes off the cell's interior.

Near the barred door lay another arm. Just the forearm, the bones protruding from the ragged flesh where it had been torn off between wrist and elbow.

The hand still gripped the keys that had hung on the hook inside the tunnel door.

They'd locked themselves inside.

The bars were evenly spaced, four inches apart. Either the thing could squeeze like a rat through narrow openings a fraction of its size, or it had somehow materialized inside the cell itself.

Brad was on his knees, leaning forward with his hands on the floor. Jim went over to him and put a hand on his shoulder.

"Can you make it?" he asked gently. "Time to go."

Brad let out a long, shuddering breath and nodded.

Jim and Vince helped him to his feet.

There was no longer any need to discuss spending the night at the house. Especially now that they had a boat. Leaving Hal to phone in word of the loss of the first party to Bentley, Jim had gone down to the cove and around the beachfront with Vince to confirm that what they'd seen was indeed a boathouse, and there was indeed a motorboat inside, covered by a tarp. And it was big enough for all eight of them, along with the transmitter/receiver, the servers and laptop—and the deceased.

They couldn't just leave them there. Not like that.

In what had already become a grim routine, they carried the body parts down to the boat in four garbage bags from the Viceroy's kitchen. Fortunately, the luggage hatch was just big enough to hold them. Riding with the gruesome cargo would be disturbing enough without having to use it for seat cushions.

The loops of intestine covering the floor of the cell, and the ruptured organs that had slid from Dylan's limbless torso when they picked it up were collected in a plastic barrel and dumped, as respectfully as possible, in the ocean.

Howard's remains presented their own grisly challenge. They'd found his headless body lying face down—or at least chest down—a short distance from the footpath. His armor had been pierced straight through to the sand underneath, flooding the inside with blood. Trask and Rashad had removed it, piece by bloody piece.

Howard was too big for a 55-gallon bag. He was stowed away unpackaged across the others, and the helmet, with his head still inside, wedged in at his feet.

It was with a guilty but unavoidable sense of relief that they were able to close the lid on the compartment.

CHAPTER TWENTY-ONE

IDIOTS

SMOOTH AS A SHEET OF PLEXIGLAS outside the motorboat's wake, the ocean reflected the Milky Way overhead as an obsidian sheen sparkling over its surface.

According to Hal, who was at the wheel, they'd be back at the camp in twenty minutes tops. It seemed almost absurdly easy after all they'd been through.

Jim rode shotgun. Behind them, Brad, Vince and Michelle leaned forward to listen to Jim and Hal's conversation.

"Grant's calling up volunteers to go on an offensive against the things," Michelle told Trask and Paula, who were too far back to hear what was being said.

"Great," Trask said.

Before they'd gotten into the boat, Michelle had apologized to Trask for the way she'd grabbed him after the shock of finding Howard's head. Visibly disappointed by her apology, he'd told her, "I'm sorry you're sorry," and left it at that. But now Michelle seemed to be able to talk to him directly without loading her words with sarcasm.

Paula said, "Bentley's going along with it?"

Michelle asked Hal, then turned around again.

"He told Grant if he can get twelve volunteers, yes."

Realizing he was being paraphrased, Hal turned and raised his voice to add, "That was before I told him what happened here."

"So maybe now he'll call it off," Trask said.

"God, I hope so," Paula said.

Brad didn't. He was going through the same kind of transformation that had taken hold of Lance.

"Why? Kill them all, that's what I say."

"Don't be an idiot, Brad. You're not Arnold Schwarzenegger," Trask said. Brad craned his neck to glower back at him.

"You calling Governor Schwarzenegger an idiot?"

"Brad, there are way too many unknowns to go off half-cocked on some crazy raid. It's just going to get a lot of people killed for nothing."

Brad was in no mood for argument. He faced forward with his arms folded across his chest.

"What do you think of Grant's plan, Jim?" Trask said.

Jim shook his head. "I don't much like it either. It's hard to keep getting stomped all over and never get a chance to return the favor—with that I can sympathize. But till we figure out a better way to deal with these things, we're just gonna keep getting clobbered."

"But do we have time to figure it out before they kill all of us?" Vince asked.

"Yeah, right?" Brad seconded.

"I'm not necessarily agreeing with Grant," Vince said. "Just—whatever we come up with, we better do it soon."

"We need intelligence," Trask said.

Brad bristled. "Here we go with how much smarter you are than the rest of us."

"I didn't mean it that way, and I'm not, and I'm sorry I called you an idiot, Brad, because you're not. I mean, we need information. We need to find out where these things are coming from and what the hell is going on and why, and how to stop them, whether that means killing them or not. That's what I mean by intelligence."

"Okay. How we gonna get it?"

It was a reasonable question, but nobody ventured any suggestions. Trask just frowned and fell silent, and was soon lost in thought.

At a lull in the conversation, Paula asked Jim, "What do you think happened back there?"

"Yeah, I been thinking about that too," Jim said, pausing to collect his thoughts. "Something obviously scared Dylan and Becky down at the cove. They ran back up to the house and found Howard in the library. They already knew about the dungeon—there was wine spilled all over the tapestry, and pieces of paper napkin on the floor under it, so you have to figure they found the door when they were trying to clean up the mess they made.

"So Howard tells Dylan and Becky to go lock themselves in a cell where the thing can't get to them. But he—Howard—means to fight. He puts on the armor."

"But then why does he end up on the beach?" Michelle asked.

"Maybe after a while, when it doesn't show up, he goes out looking for it."

"And it attacks him from behind," Brad said.

"But the sword was up on the trail," Paula told him.

"So the thing threw it there," Brad was sure of himself. "Just like it threw his head into the cove after it killed him."

Nobody said anything. "God," Michelle said after a while. "I can't believe it. Killed trying to save his friends. Howard."

Jim nodded. "That's what it looks like."

When a few minutes later they passed the inlet to the lagoon that marked their trip's midpoint, everyone except Hal and Jim was nodding off. Few of them had had much sleep over the past twenty-four hours.

Trask tried to catch a little sleep too, but couldn't shut off the flow of disjointed and half-formed images chasing one another through his brain. He felt like if his thoughts would just slow down enough for him to be able to turn them over in his mind and see them all clearly, they'd turn out to all be pieces of the same puzzle.

He closed his eyes, but after a minute something forced them back open, and he found himself staring at the big broadsword. It lay across a blanket they'd packed around the Viceroy's equipment.

There'd been no question of their bringing it along. You didn't leave something like that behind, not when you were in their situation, even though only Brad and Jim were strong enough to wield it in the way it was designed for.

Trask gazed at it, wondering if it was the same one as in the tapestry. Maybe it *had* killed a dragon. He was ready to believe almost anything now.

From a distance he studied the blade, crisscrossed by scratches. The long hilt with its heavy pommel. He hadn't noticed the round indentation in the hilt before, just below the blade guard.

For some reason he wasn't immediately aware of—because his thoughts were moving too fast for him to follow—Trask suddenly wished he'd kept the broken remote control—which he knew it wasn't—and then a second later, as he leaned forward to stare hard at the indentation, and run his finger over its concave surface, which wasn't round, but oval-shaped, he remembered he *had* kept it, and his hand went to his pocket and he pulled it out.

With a chill running down the back of his neck, he set it into the indentation in the sword's hilt.

It fit perfectly, locking into place with a click.

He looked up at Paula. She was awake too, and staring at the perfect match in amazement, just like he must have been.

And then she looked up at him, and her lips formed a question:

Why?

Trask stared back at her.

Why would someone put electronics in a sword? But even weirder— when? The oval setting had the same worn look and dark patina as the rest of the sword hilt.

Fatigue caught up with him. His head spun. The tapestry seemed to swim up out of the darkness before his eyes. He saw the inset, with the knight resting his hand on the pommel, and he took hold of the hilt with his left hand. Closing his eyes, Trask concentrated on visualizing the inset. He laid his right hand on the hilt, placing his index finger by feel in the exact position as the knight's in the tapestry.

Then he opened his eyes and looked down.

His fingertip was on the remote. Right on top of the red button.

With a glance at Paula, he thumbed out the device and put it back in his pocket.

Lance stood up. "I don't know about the rest of you, but I'm with Grant."

Grant had counted on Lance. Now, with Roger already in, they were three. He needed nine more. The current pickings were pretty slim, but that could change with the return of Jim's party. Brad was a likely, Michelle a probable. And he hoped Jim would throw in his lot with them as well.

Grant had been hesitant to reveal what he'd learned from Bentley about the fate of Dylan's party, but in the end he'd played it as his trump card. Without it, as far as any of the punters knew, they'd made it through almost twenty-four hours without further incident, and while interested, most had remained unswayed by his impassioned call to action.

But it had done the trick.

Fredo stood up. "I'm down."

"Me too," Clayton said, rising to slap Fredo's palm.

Okay. That made five.

Beverly rapped the floor with the butt of her spear—a mop handle tipped with a ten-inch carving knife, decorated with a long lock of her own blonde hair. "I don't see why the boys should have all the fun," she said, standing.

Grant looked at her with admiration. "We're halfway there, people," he said.

"Okay, let's do it." Grant looked around. Erika.

And Heather. "If Beverly's in, so are we."

Grant rewarded the girls with a grin and turned his gaze on Jeremy and Tony. They stood at opposite sides of the room, while Janet sat near the middle, staring at the floor with her hands tucked between her knees.

There wasn't much chance of her participation, and it wouldn't be missed, but Grant had expected her two gallants to jump at the chance to reassert their individual claims to her affection with a show of valor.

Instead, they watched each other closely out of the corners of their eyes. It was like that old television show where the panel has to guess which of the three claimants is the real brain surgeon, or rocket scientist, or Royal Canadian Mountie—and which are the impostors. Jeremy shuffled his feet as if he were about to get up, then stopped when he saw Tony start to raise his hand. Tony's hand went to the corner of his lip to peel away a bit of dry skin he'd just discovered, and Jeremy sank back into his chair. Then Tony half-rose, but only to shift his weight from one buttock to the other. And then Jeremy cleared his throat and said, "Well,—" and Tony jumped up and shouted, "Count me in."

"Oh, Tony," Janet breathed, her eyes shining.

Tony smiled at her, then smirked at Jeremy. Careful not to let Janet see it, Jeremy smirked back.

Grant looked at him. "You were about to say…?"

"No, nothing," Jeremy said.

Grant extended his hand to Tony and Tony shook it.

"Welcome to the team, Tony."

Nine.

So Jeremy would be sitting this one out with Janet.

Mei and Gabrielle were doubtful. That left Corey and Zach. It was time to raise the stakes.

"For those of you still on the fence," Grant said, "let me remind you that our cause may be far greater than even we imagine." He let that sink in for a beat before continuing.

"We may never know—the world may never know," he said, "how sorely the earth itself stood today in need of champions. But in my heart I feel there is much, much more at stake here than the survival of our own small band of humanity, and in your hearts I believe you too sense the truth. Lance, Fredo, Clayton. Beverly, Erika. Heather. Tony—you've been guided by your hearts to stand up for what is right and good, whatever the cost. To make the ultimate choice. I won't minimize the risks involved. Not every one of us will return unhurt. But be assured your wounds will be tended and the world will repay your heroism many times over in gratitude."

The undecided punters had listened in rapt attention, but still appeared less than eager to accept the challenge. "The ultimate choice" may have been a less than ultimate choice of phrasing, and Grant was weighing the advisability of spelling out in more tangible terms the potential side benefits to participation—citations, awards, movie and publishing deals, in-store book signings, appearances on late night TV talk shows—when all of a sudden he had the rug pulled out from under him by the unmistakable sound of a fast approaching outboard motor.

Zach jumped up. "It's them!"

"Hold that thought, Grant," Beverly said.

It was after midnight—they'd blocked the door hours ago. Lance lifted the cover off the escape hatch and one after another everyone followed him through, leaving Grant staring after them, feeling deflated.

He'd already had to get down on his hands and knees and crawl through the muddy burrow to get inside, and was hoping they'd unblock the door to let him back out.

With a sigh and a grimace of distaste, he gave in to necessity and eased himself down into the hole.

Grant clambered to his feet just in time to see Hal run the boat up onto the beach. His volunteers rushed to greet them.

First out of the boat, Brad said to Lance, "Am I on time?"

"For what?"

"What do you mean, for what? The fight."

Lance looked around and caught Grant's eye.

Ten.

Grant came forward to slap Brad on the shoulder. Brad didn't like being slapped, and threw him a darkly menacing glance, but Grant had already moved on to Michelle.

"You've heard," he said.

He looked down at her scraped knees and torn clothes, befouled with dark stains and smears.

The party reeked of death.

"And so have we," Grant added gently. "I'm deeply sorry for what you've all been through."

"Not so bad compared to some," Michelle said.

Grant nodded.

Excitement at the rescue party's return began to dissipate in the face of uncomfortable reminders that it had ultimately failed in its objective. The subdued response to their welcome didn't help. Aside from Brad, Trask and his followers stared back at them with wariness and suspicion. And the gore-soaked clothing didn't help either. They looked like a band of leering cannibals just returned from some horrific blood feast.

Lance frowned. "Well—are you with us?" he demanded.

Grant put a hand on Michelle's shoulder.

"Michelle?"

She backed away from him, shaking her head, and said, "Fat chance, Grant." To the others gathered around she asked, "What the hell is going on, as if I didn't know?"

Lance said, "We're putting together a task force. We're going to hit back, hard. Take no prisoners, just like them."

"Really? What's the plan?"

"We attack in the morning," Grant said. "I've already scouted locations. There's a heavily-wooded hilltop just northeast of here with a clearing a hundred meters downhill. That's where we'll set our trap."

A few of the volunteers perked up at this.

"What trap?" Clayton said.

"We'll come to that. Right now we just need two more volunteers. I was counting on you, Michelle." He turned toward the motorboat. "And Jim."

Jim had unpacked the Viceroy's equipment and stood holding the transmitter/receiver under one arm, balancing the server on his shoulder with the other. He regarded Grant with disapproval.

"You can count me out too, Grant. I don't mind telling you I don't think much of your plan." He looked over the volunteers, who were clearly as crestfallen as Grant at his words. "And I don't much like it that those of you that are taking part in it are leaving the rest of the group at half strength. Has Roger had a say in all this?"

Grant said, "He's with us."

"Then even if I did approve, I wouldn't be coming along—since either me or Roger'd have to stay here with the others anyway."

"Jim, we can finish this—"

"That's just what I'm afraid of, Grant. If you all go and get yourselves killed, how many'll be left for the next time we get set on?"

"If we succeed, there won't be a next time."

"Grant, you won't even know if you've succeeded or not. You kill one or two of those things and then what? How many are left?"

"I still think there's only one. It's using all those special effects just to scare us."

"You're wrong, Grant. It's using them to kill us." Looking over the assembled punters again, he said, "It's not too late to change your minds."

All the talk of getting killed had taken some of the wind out of their sails, but nobody said anything one way or the other. Shifting his burden, Jim turned and walked up the beach toward the bungalow.

Trask said to Grant, "We've already talked about it. We can't stop Brad from going with you if that's what he wants to do, but the rest of us are out."

Lance turned on him. "What don't *you* like about it? Make up your mind. You were the one that didn't want to board up the mess hall 'cause you didn't think it'd be safe to be all cooped up. Well, now we're taking the fight to them—or it, if Grant's right—out in the open."

"This is different. It's too soon to go on the offensive. We don't have any idea what they can do or what kind of weapons they have at their disposal. For all you know they could wipe us all out with the press of a button."

"So why haven't they?"

"That's the right question," Trask said. "But the salient fact that prompts it to my mind is that they haven't, even though after what we've seen it makes sense to assume they could. As far as we know, Grant's plan could be the declaration of war that brings the real weapons of mass destruction down on our heads."

Grant looked at Trask with a feigned mixture of pity and commiseration.

"It sounds to me like you're afraid, Trask."

"Does it, Grant?" Trask seemed to consider the possibility. "Well, let's see. I mean, since until just thirty minutes ago some of us were part of a work detail that was about stuffing Dylan, Howard and Becky's arms, legs and heads into garbage bags and scraping their insides off the walls into a big plastic bucket and then feeding them to the sharks—it could be you're right. Yeah Grant. I am scared.

"But I'm mad too." He turned to Lance. "You're not the only one who'd like to get even with those pieces of shit, Lance, trust me. But in spite of that, I'd still rather try to stop this thing from turning into the interplanetary incident that sets off some kind of multiverse armageddon.

"Think about it. Yeah, they're killing us. But they don't seem particularly intent on it. More like they're just fooling around. Why?"

Lance said, "It's obvious. They're testing us. Gauging our strength. If we show weakness, they'll decide we're pushovers and walk in and take over. If we fight back, inflict some serious casualties in return, maybe they'll think twice about going through with it. Nobody's even tried yet."

"Are you kidding me?"

"Give me one example."

"I can give you more than one. What about Nils and Jim? And Howard—Howard, who put on a goddamn suit of armor to try to fight them. If you don't believe me, take a look in the trunk.

"And what the hell is it you think these things'll think twice about? And why the barrier, Lance? You think they don't know about all the military hardware outside? What could they hope to learn about strength or weakness from us? If beating the shit out of us is a test, what are the results going to prove to them? That they're ready to take on the whole fucking world? Will you try to remember for one second that you're just a contestant in a fucking television game show? And that Grant's just the fucking host? No offense, Grant."

"One question at a time, Trask, okay?" Lance said.

"Hey, man, Grant was a First Lieutenant in the Gulf War," Fredo said, offended on Grant's behalf.

"No, he was a *lieutenant* in the *First* Gulf War," Clayton corrected him. "Right, Grant?"

"What the fuck difference does it make?" Fredo yelled. He glowered at Trask. "Is that your final word, man?"

"Word, Fredo. Grant's plan stinks."

Lance snorted. "Look who's talking."

Grant said, "Fine, Trask. If you want to look like a coward on national—*international* television, you've made the right—"

"You asshole," Paula said. "Is that how you talked everyone into going along with your stupid plan? This isn't about all of your idiotic fake television personas anymore."

Trask didn't much care for being called a coward by Grant or anybody else. "Believe me, Grant, if and when it comes down to all-out war, I'll go down fighting along with you and everyone else, television or not. But I'm not about to waste my chance of getting even with those things by volunteering for a suicide mission for no other reason than to give the glory hounds a shot at looking like heroes in front of the fucking camera."

He turned his back on them and walked to the boat.

"What chance?" Grant said. "What chance, Trask?"

Trask didn't answer. Instead he said, "Who wants to help with the dead stuff?" He opened the hatch and hauled out a garbage bag. "Fredo?" The body parts inside shifted and tumbled gruesomely as he dragged it over the side and dropped it onto the sand. "Clayton?" he said, reaching for another.

~~~~~~~~~~~~~~~~~~~~~~~~~~~~~~~~~~

Trask did end up getting the help he needed, but most of it from the other members of the recovery team. Calling on them by name had shamed Fredo into assisting, but not Clayton. Clayton retired with the rest of Grant's pledges to the mess hall, along with the stubborn handful of uncommitted.

Using aggressive recruiting tactics, Grant managed to enlist one more: Zach. When he finally cracked, Zach was rewarded with a hearty pat on the back from Lance. Now desperate to secure the crucial twelfth on whom the entire operation hinged, Grant tried hard to enlist Jeremy. But Jeremy was adamant, insisting that Janet required his personal protection while "everyone else" was away. Even Tony's taunts failed to sway him, and in the end Janet had taken his hand and said—with a tear in her eye—"Thank you, Jeremy." Then, deciding that wasn't enough, she'd made a further display of her gratitude by treating him to a lingering hug. The betrayal was like a slap in the face to Tony, and he'd stalked off to throw himself upon his bunk, furious and resentful.

A little later, Trask, Fredo and the rest returned from their grisly chore, effectively breaking up the party. Trying to put a brave face on things, Grant told Lance to be prepared, promising the mission would be a go. He'd think of something. It was nearing 2AM when he left.

Trudging alone across the sand, Grant was for the first time in his life plagued by self-doubt. Hurt and embarrassed by Jim's disapproval, he even wondered about his own motives. Could it be true, what Trask implied, that his whole plan was just a reckless exercise in grandiosity?

Head bowed, lost in his own bleak thoughts, Grant never heard the swift footsteps padding across the sand, or saw the dark form approaching from behind until it was almost upon him. He jumped and whirled with a startled cry—to see Evans, his face contorted and ghastly pale in the starlight. In his hairy fist he gripped a huge cleaver.

Trembling with rage, the caterer shook the blade at Grant, and Grant backed away, confused and frightened—uncertain whether to stand his ground or turn and flee.
~~~~~~~~~~~~~~~~~~~~~~~~~~~~~~~~~~

Evans spoke. He was breathless from hurrying after Grant, and his words came in halting gasps.

"I saw—what those things did. I saw what they did to that—young girl, and—those other two."

Grant stood silent and uncomprehending.

"I know I'm only the caterer," Evans said. "But I've been in a fight or two in my day and I can dish it out as well as take it.

"I want to volunteer."

PART THREE: SUNDAY

CHAPTER TWENTY-TWO

GRANT'S OFFENSIVE

WEARING A FLOPPY-BRIMMED camouflage hat reminiscent of the Vietnam War era, Grant lay on his stomach, propped up on his elbows and peering through binoculars at the dale below. His silent company was arrayed in wings that spread across the tree-shrouded hilltop on both flanks.

Hal's camera panned over the group for a quick establishing shot—The Ambush Party, lying in wait—then tilted and swiveled to follow Grant's binoculared gaze. It came to rest on three lone figures in a small clearing at the bottom of the hill, a hundred meters away.

Zach, Fredo, Clayton. Standing back to back, casting fearful glances at the surrounding trees.

Hal zoomed on them. Zach, as if sensing the camera's eye upon him, looked uphill to squint directly into it.

Zach couldn't make out any sign of Grant's party up on the hilltop. That was the idea, of course. But now that they were in position and standing around with nothing to do but wait, that hilltop sure seemed far away.

"How long you think it'll take them to get down?" he said.

Fredo turned to look up toward the hilltop. "About ten seconds." He was doing a decent job of sounding unconcerned. "It's not far."

Zach had played college basketball. "A lot can happen in ten seconds."

Clayton said, "I don't know why we couldn't just tie a goat to a tree like they do in India."

"We don't have goats," Zach replied.

"We got pigs out the ass," Clayton said.

"They're not expendable. The others'll still need something to eat after we're dead."

Fredo broke ranks and stretched.

"Relax, son. It's Grant's show. You can be sure of one thing with Grant, it all about looking good."

"True," Zach said. "The cameras are rolling."

He looked over at the stationary camera they'd set up earlier according to Hal's instructions. The red light was on. They knew *it* was rolling at least. Zach flashed it a confident grin and gave it a thumbs up.

Back up on the hilltop, Hal framed a shot of Grant.

Grant was standing now, still peering through the binoculars. Only now they were directed at Hal's camera.

"Does it look okay, the hat?"

"Perfect. Lift your chin, I'm getting a little sag." Hal studied the image in the viewfinder. "How old are you, Grant?"

"These damn binoculars," Grant said. He jerked them away, swinging them over his head to free the strap, and handed them to Roger, who stood idle with his hands in his pockets and Jim's shotgun slung over his shoulder. "Here."

"What do you want me to do if I see anything?"

"I'll give the orders. You just let me know."

Roger got down on his stomach at the edge of the hillside to take up the watch. Grant's momentary irritation passed. He yawned and stretched. "Could be a while."

He re-composed himself, lifted his chin and nodded at Hal. Hal checked the image, then raised his hand and with a downward flick of his wrist, pointed at Grant.

Grant assumed an air of gravity.

"And so we wait," he intoned. "While out there, somewhere, something—some *thing*, lurks—ready to strike at the moment we least expect it. Our brave volunteers—Fredo, Zach, Clayton—wait below, ready to risk life and limb, to sacrifice their all in a valiant bid to lure the man-eater from hiding. Their courage and determination inspire in us a reverent awe. Their heroism…"

Back at the camp, in the bungalow's control room, Bentley caught Barry's eye and grimaced. Grant was at it again. "Fred, kill Grant please," he said. Fred was running the board in Becky's "absence", and using the opportunity to give an overview of the console's operation to the two interns.

"Just the mains," Barry emended. Fred pulled down the main faders and Grant's voice slid into silence. He handed Barry a headset, and Barry grinned at Bentley as he put it on.

Bentley was feeling grumpy. The enhanced wireless reception was a godsend, but he couldn't help being irked by the fact that the carefully positioned stereo microphone down in the dale was useless. Clayton had somehow screwed up the connection, and with none of the three wearing headphones Fred couldn't direct them to fix it.

Aside from that, though, everything was working even better than they'd hoped. It was a good thing Dylan had discovered the wireless business before going off and getting himself killed. Too bad they hadn't known sooner, they could have been doing it this way all along. Watching things in real time as they actually transpired.

Of course so far nothing actually was transpiring, and most of the drama appeared to be taking place MOS down at the bottom of the hill. They should have never trusted the nitwits to set things up on their own.

"I'm not sure if I like the hat either," Bentley remarked to Barry, who was following Grant's journalistic posturings with taut concentration. "Kinda dates him, somehow."

Trask and his fellow conscientious objectors awaited word in the nearby mess hall. They'd formed a circle of cots and chairs and sat talking in low voices.

"What are the chances they're going to stumble into the trap anyway?" Vince was saying. "I mean, it's a small island, but..."

"I don't know," Trask said. "They seem to be pretty good at finding us when they want to."

Paula agreed. "They didn't just stumble into Dylan and those guys. They have some way of tracking our movements."

"But," Trask pointed out, "since they must be doing it by remote, if they find the bait, they'd have to be pretty dumb to miss the main group up on the hilltop."

"So either way..." Rashad said.

"It's a stupid plan," Michelle finished. "About what you'd expect from Grant."

Trask sighed. "They'll give up after a few hours when nothing happens."

"Yeah," Michelle said, "and then what? Is Grant going to be calling the shots from now on? How does he talk people into this shit?"

No one had an answer for that. Trask suspected he knew the answer, he just couldn't bring himself to say it. Grant had charisma. He'd been an actor, after all, a working one, not an aspiring one like half the cast. Maybe that was why the thespian club had all thrown in with him. They looked up to him because of his dramatic abilities. He did have them, Trask was forced to admit. Listening to him talk, sometimes it felt like you were watching a movie. Definitely a "B" movie, but still. Grant could make the most insipid and contrived dialogue—either Barry's or his own—sound convincing just by speaking it aloud.

In the conversational void, Trask became aware of the rising voices of Janet's group, who'd assembled their own circle of cots across the room. Sounded like someone had touched an emotional chord.

He threw a covert glance in their direction.

Janet, Corey, Gabrielle and Mei slouched on their cots like neglected and disconsolate harem girls. Which would make Jeremy the palace eunuch, Trask guessed, and then immediately chastised himself for the thought. It was too unkindly appropriate. And besides, Janet must be worried sick about Tony, and it would be Jeremy's emotionally difficult job to console her.

"Janet, don't talk that way, you know it's not true."

"Jeremy's right, Janet. He's a guy—he knows," Corey said with conviction.

"You really think so?"

"Look," Jeremy said, his voice filled with authority, "It doesn't make any difference to us guys if you've brushed it in two days or two hours. It looks good all tangled up. Kind of wild. Sexy."

"Aww, Jeremy."

"See?" Corey said.

Swaddled in its harness like the mummified remains of some long dead giant, the ship's engine loomed behind Strindlak in gloom-shrouded slumber.

The giant would soon awaken.

Strindlak stooped to toss a fastener onto a pile of heavy tools under the console, where it joined its brethren with a dull clank of relief. Straightening up, he arched his spine, laid back his head and rolled it over his massive shoulders. Stiff neck muscles crackled like burning deadwood.

The better part of five cycles had seen him locked in a duel to wrest back control from the treacherous behemoth. But with the help of the ship's computer and the manual's detailed schematics, the stubborn engine and its controls had yielded their secrets and succumbed to his will.

He gazed up at it, sensing its latent power, eager to put his labors to the final test.

But Strindlak had acquired wisdom. He had learned to appreciate the value of diligence.

He'd give everything one more going over, paying meticulous attention to every detail. Only then, after he was certain beyond any shade of doubt that all was in order, would he approach the instrument panel and set the machinery of deliverance in motion.

Far down at the other end of the ship, through a hundred and eighty degrees of circular corridor, a small band of trespassers was gathered in another chamber, the thought of deliverance the furthest thing from their minds.

Churlo and Pirnod jostled each other for position at the transporter platform's railing. On the floor, with only her undulating tendril tips visible from the podium upon which Snorlok stood, little Zillior bounced up and down with the feverish excitement of a hatchling. Beside her, Ropsnag slavered and whickered in anticipation.

With practiced speed, Snorlok's tentacles skipped over the controls. He tapped in a command, then paused to peer over the edge of the console into the imager beyond.

Set in its own much larger elevated and railed-in platform, the great hemisphere pulsed with a pregnant translucency. Tracers of light swam through its murky depths like robotic fireflies.

Chafing with eagerness, the young ones hooted and chattered, and Snorlok was once again forced to command them to silence. There was little chance they'd be found out. But it wouldn't go well with them if they were.

A swirl of colors played over the imager's clouded surface as it neared transparency. Snorlok made a final adjustment, then stepped away from the console and regarded his siblings.

It was time to make his choice.

He looked from one to the other, considering.

Hopeful, Pirnod blinked back at him. Not counting Snorlok's initial reconnoitering expedition in the flesh, when he'd been caught off guard by the two howling natives—and before he'd hit on the idea for the game—Pirnod had gone first, and proven inept. For his turn, Ropsnag had played well, sowing terror in the soggy lowlands and inflicting heavy damage that had taken at least one opponent out of play. And last night Churlo had soundly defeated his lone foe at the foot of a mountain before Snorlok's own victory over two enemy combatants lurking in a cave.

The choice, then, must fall between Pirnod beginning the rotation anew, or Zillior—as yet untested.

Until now, Snorlok had ignored Zillior's entreaties, deeming her too young for such perilous amusements. But the peril had so far proven nonexistent, and his earlier fears unwarranted. And though Zillior was as yet a mere chrysalis, Snorlok noted a marked stiffness to Pirnod's movements, testimony to his having been sundered in two only the day before by the runaway rotor.

He turned again to Zillior. Her bright eyes, her soft, high-pitched keening, pleaded with irresistible urgency.

Snorlok relented.

He lifted Zillior up and plopped her down onto the platform. Pirnod sagged in disappointment, but soon chortled along with the others at the little one's joyful eagerness.

Snorlok picked up an Emergency Remote Retrieval Unit and pressed it against the tough dorsal hide of Zillior's forearm. Within moments, the unit's internal sensors latched onto a nearby ganglion. Despite their common designation as "retrieval units", the remotes relayed continuous status updates and other essential information between fielded drone, host and transporter, and were required for all transporter operations. After assuring himself that Zillior's was secure, Snorlok tapped the control panel display.

The siblings looked up to watch the harness descend. It enveloped Zillior's small frame, trembling along with her in anticipation. At the sound of a chime, all heads turned to the imager.

The veil of shifting colors had cleared. The siblings looked now upon a circular section of the world outside.

Depicted in full three-dimensional view, it was true to life in every detail. Beneath their own dense curtain of overhanging green foliage could be seen the tall supporting branches of the predominant native plant life, their epidermal layers dappled and striated in deep grays and umber; the ground below, visible through scattered breaks in the dusky canopy, dark and glistening with unabsorbed moisture, covered with detritus and creeping flora, dotted here and there with splashes of pink and pale blue. It was as if the whole melancholy scene had been lifted out of its bedrock with all its underpinnings intact and set down in the middle of the transporter chamber.

Keeping his gaze locked on the imager, Snorlok gave the positioning control a gentle sideways nudge. The scene's forward edge slipped out of sight beyond the hemisphere's confines while a hitherto unseen section moved into view from the other. He turned the knob, then pushed. The scene rotated, then blurred.

The siblings' heartbeats quickened. Watching the imager, they seemed to race over the ground, while the mantle of foliage whipped past in dazzling bursts of color.

Snorlok was already familiar with the natives' habit of periodically sending out small detachments to various locations in the general vicinity. With the imager set on wide-angle view they weren't difficult to locate.

The obstructing foliage now thinned to scattered patches as the terrain leveled off. Three short beeps sounded and Snorlok eased back on the controls. An instant later, three blinking cursors glided into view, then winked out to reveal three enemy combatants, huddled close together in a small clearing.

Snorlok steadied on them.

With a deft flick of his foretentacles, he dialed in a higher magnification, enlarging the scene until the overhanging foliage withdrew from the imager's sphere to give an unimpeded view of the clearing.

Zillior, prattling with delight, clamped her mouth shut at Snorlok's warning hiss. Even so, she was unable to contain herself completely, and small explosions of glee erupted in puffs from her puckered gill flaps. The siblings smothered their laughter as Snorlok turned to the control console's built-in display to browse through the selector index for a suitable utility drone.

Something not too complicated, with two arms and two legs, not so large that Zillior would be disoriented and overwhelmed by the unfamiliarity of its enhanced reflexes or the flood of incoming data from its bio-sensory simulators.

He quickly found an appropriate design.

Locking in the selection, he gave the transport settings a last check. The status bar, glowing emerald at the top of the imager, showed all systems primed and operable.

With a final glance at brave little Zillior, quivering in the harness, her round eyes looking into his own, Snorlok reached for the switch.

ACTIVATE

From tiny apertures in the platform's base, a swirl of electrons spiraled up and over Zillior's form, engulfing her in a halo of glittering particles. The harness snapped away, retracted upward toward the ceiling. The swirling electrons tightened to a slender beam, then collapsed back into the platform's base.

Zillior disappeared.

In her place stood a spectral figure that mimicked her body's basic outline. The insubstantial transporter "ghost" that would reflect her movements in the field.

The siblings turned to stare in tense excitement at the imager, where their younger sibling's forthcoming appearance was not to be missed.

CHAPTER TWENTY-THREE

DISASTER

DOWN IN THE DALE, Zach and Fredo sat watching Clayton trace intersecting lines and circles in the dirt with a stick. He might have been plotting battle diagrams or sketching out defensive deployment options for the anticipated attack based on a set of carefully formulated plans of engagement. But in actuality, he was doodling, randomly and absently, and the others watched not in keen interest, but in an advanced state of mental torpor.

Boredom had gotten the better of their fear.

Zach looked up at the sky to gauge the time by the position of the sun and estimated it had been over four hours.

Four hours…

He was just wondering how much longer before Grant called the whole thing off when he noticed Fredo and Clayton staring in mild surprise at the top of his head.

"Son, your hair's like sticking up all over the place."

Zach was suddenly aware of a tingling sensation crawling over his scalp. He lifted a hand to the top of his head and felt his hair standing upright like seaweed rising toward the surface of a pond.

"Something's going on," he said.

Clayton and Fredo scrambled up and eased away from him, and Zach got to his feet, carefully, as if any sudden move might be his last.

His throat went dry. His ears popped, and a whistling filled his head.

The air crinkled like aluminum foil.

At his chest, a flare burst, showering sparks. He jumped back as a swirl of motes coalesced out of nothingness, to hover, sparkling, in mid-air.

With a whump of depressurizing gases, it began to rotate.

The punters gaped at it, mesmerized.

It condensed into a whirling sphere, then abruptly elongated through its vertical axis, braked to a screeching halt and fused into a five-foot, electric blue monstrosity that swayed on spindly legs ending in a pair of over-sized toilet bowl plungers.

The earlier reports had been true.

Before them stood a hairless and tailless spider monkey, clothed in pixeline motes that rippled luminously over prehensile arms and legs, and crowned with the garish, haloed head of a Hindu devil.

At least, that was what it looked like from the back. The thing was facing the wrong way.

It teetered on trembling legs, ratcheting its head this way and that in seeming confusion. Two enormous, conical ears swiveled toward the punters, and the creature froze.

It had sensed their presence.

Zach and Clayton turned to run. They plowed into Fredo, who finally thought to raise the alarm.

"Mayday! Mayday!" he shouted.

At the sound, the creature jumped straight up and whirled, losing its already precarious balance.

There was no instinctual lunge for support or flinging out of its arms to cushion its fall. With a strangled gasp, it fell flat on its face, striking its head against a rock, and lay there thrashing at the ground.

"Come *in, Grant! Gra-a-a-ant!*" Fredo yelled.

The thing at last floundered upright, giving them a good look at its face. It was hideous. Nearly featureless but for two baleful round eyes. No nose. A small puckered orifice at the bottom of its chin that might be a mouth.

But the initial shock was wearing off. The thing didn't seem to have any definite plan of attack, and it wasn't big enough to be physically intimidating.

Fredo was the first to recover.

He leapt at it with a shout—it cowered at the noise—and swung his machete with all the brute force he could muster. This time the thing had the presence of mind to throw up an arm to protect its melon-shaped head.

Fredo felt the shock of impact as his blade sliced right through both arm and head. It caused no more than a slight ripple of distortion and light scattering of pixels.

He jumped back, cursing.

Unscathed, the creature blinked at him in perplexity.

It squawked when Zach and Clayton rushed in swinging.

Rashad and Michelle were starting to doze off. Paula was already asleep.

Trask looked up at the clock on the wall.

3:55. Almost four hours.

He'd just closed his eyes when he heard a foot thump onto the first wooden step outside and the door opened.

It was Chuck, one of the interns.

"It found them," he said.

It took a second for it to register.

Chuck was hurrying back to the bungalow when everyone ran outside to catch up with him. Unlike Janet and her crew, Trask and the others had brought their weapons.

"It's CGI all right, just like you said."

"Found who?" Trask said.

"The bait," Chuck said. "They're holding their own. It seems like it's just as scared as they are."

"What about Grant?"

"They ought to be there by now. It's not big. Barry thinks they can take it."

"Barry," Michelle sneered as they entered the bungalow through the back door and hurried down the short hallway.

"Shit." Chuck raised a handheld and started shooting. "Supposed to be getting this. Human interest. That's why Barry wants you guys here."

"Where's Jim?" Trask said.

"Kristine went to get him."

Bentley and Barry glanced around when they entered the control room, then quickly turned back to the monitors.

On the hilltop, Grant bowed his head and drank in a round of prolonged applause.

"Gosh, Grant, that was so beautiful," Heather said.

Roger stopped clapping to take a casual glance down below as Grant bestowed his winning smile on Heather.

"Heather, these kinds of situations bring out the best in all of us."

"I think something might be happening," Roger reported. He lifted the binoculars to his eyes.

Grant came dramatically alert. "What do you see?" he said. He cupped a hand to his ear. "Hear that?"

In the sudden tense silence, they all heard Fredo's voice drifting up from the dale.

"Grant, you fucking *asshole!* Where the hell are you?"

Grant winced, but shrugged it off. He steeled himself, cocked an eyebrow at Hal.

Hal was on him.

"Okay, this is it. It's *showtime*, people!"

Not great, but an adequate expression of determination and grit in the heat of imminent action.

Jim arrived from the other end of the hall just as Trask and the others squeezed into the control room.

They all took one look at the monitors and in an instant were oblivious to their surroundings.

Video Monitor 1 showed Grant's ambush party—inexplicably sitting around him clapping.

On VM-2, fed by the stationary camera down in the dale, a battle was in progress.

It was another version of CGI creature, every bit as bizarre as the one Trask's group had encountered, and behaving with the same erratic clumsiness. It flinched and stumbled, struggling to ward off the blows aimed at it by its human foes.

Zach swung wild, just missing Clayton. Fredo raised his machete, and as the creature scuttled away, Zach's body loomed into view, blocking the action.

"No!" Bentley said.

Zach backed toward the camera. The picture darkened, then pitched and keeled sideways, blurring, and went black.

"Shit!" Bentley yelled.

Like spectators at a tennis match, everyone angled in unison on VM-1—

where Roger, sitting behind Grant, turned as if on a sudden whim to look downhill through a pair of binoculars.

"What the fuck are they doing?" Trask said.

"I don't know," Bentley answered. He keyed the talkback button, connected wirelessly to Hal's headset, and put on his own.

"What the fuck are you doing?" Bentley demanded.

He listened briefly.

"They just heard. Jerkoff's been making speeches again. Goddammit, we're missing everything."

Grant felt heady with power.

His punters had hastened to their feet, prepared to charge on his word.

He had his command. A ragtag bunch, but he'd whip them into a fighting force to be reckoned with. The next few minutes or hours would tell.

"Let's *move!* Go! Go! *Go!*"

The company leapt forward to surge down the hill in a mad onslaught—but caught themselves at a frenzied shout from Hal.

"Wait!"

The foremost attackers stopped in their tracks and were bowled over by those behind them.

Hal ran around to the front to position himself a little ahead of the group for a better angle. He braced himself, then shouted, "Okay—Go!"

The now disorderly mob rolled helter-skelter downhill toward the dale, with Grant taking up the rear position.

He shot Hal an angry glance as he passed.

"I give the orders!"

"Sorry!" Hal said, falling in behind.

Bentley jerked off his headset. "Chuck, put it back on speakers," he said.

Chuck bumped up the stereo mains, and the larger-than-life sound of Hal's running feet thumped from the room monitors, overlaying a muffled jumble of voices. The scene on VM-1 whirled, blundered partway downhill, reversed, and focused on the confused ambushers, many of whom had apparently fallen, and were wiping dirt from scraped knees as they picked themselves up.

"*Okay—Go!*" came Hal's shout.

The punters streamed downhill into the camera.

"Finally," Bentley said.

He keyed the talkback button. "Okay, Hal, good thinking. Let's get some eye candy down there. We're rolling, folks!"

Watching over Bentley and Barry's shoulders, Trask felt himself drawn irresistibly into the action by Hal's expert camerawork.

The background became an emerald blur as the camera panned to follow the charging ambush party. The combatants down below came into view, then jerked away again when the lens jolted sideways.

A pandemonium of shouts and trampling feet blared from the audio monitors. The image skewed toward the ground in a kaleidoscopic swirl of greenery, then angled back up into the very midst of the melee.

The creature appeared dazed. Tripping over its own feet, it reeled under the blows of a half-dozen attackers.

"It's a newbie," Trask said.

"Like ours," Rashad agreed. "Bumping into trees like it didn't know how to walk."

"Meaning," Jim said, "whoever's at the controls—it's their first time?"

Trask nodded. Not that anyone was looking.

Onscreen, Fredo delivered what should have been a crippling blow to the creature's legs. The blade passed harmlessly through, streaming a comet-tail of pixels.

It was weakening, though. Its skin rippled, flickering back into alignment in faltering jerks. Apparently some kind of damage was being done.

"Look at Grant," Paula said.

Grant worked the fringes, keeping at a safe distance behind a wall of assailants, scrambling for safety when they surged outward to avoid the creature's long sweeping arms. However uncoordinated its defenses, it was still dangerous. There was blood on its heavy-taloned paws.

Trask cursed under his breath and Rashad looked over to see him flexing white-knuckled fingers in frustration.

Trask. The gamer.

All fired up, without a quarter in his pocket.

~~~~~~~~~~~~~~~~~~~~~~~~
~~~~~~~~~~~~~~~~~~~~~~~~

Watching Zillior's discomfort in the imager, Churlo and Pirnod chortled with cruel mirth. But Snorlok, casting frequent glances at the status readout hovering overhead, frowned.

A bloodthirsty mob of enemy combatants had the utility drone hemmed in. It squalled as the things hewed at it. And, Snorlok noted, Zillior's attempts at retaliation were growing increasingly feeble.

Zillior took another hit, eliciting a jeering bark from Ropsnag, and the status bar went from yellow to orange. It strobed briefly in warning.

Snorlok shook his head. Zillior had so far made no move to use her remote. Her courage was admirable, but if she failed to return before the status bar zeroed out, the transporter would reset and she'd incorporate in the midst of her assailants.

He grunted when Zillior stumbled. Flashing metal sheared through the drone's torso, ripping out a glittering stream of bright particles. Instead of merging to flow back into place, they dissipated, leaving beating waves of distortion chopping over the wound.

The status bar strobed again.

Ropsnag and the twins watched in silence. They'd noted their elder sibling's concern.

The drone's shoulders drooped. It lowered its arms.

Attackers moved in. Blades plunged into the wavering form from all sides.

The status bar blazed red for an instant—and blinked out. The twins gasped, and Snorlok whirled toward the transporter platform.

With a sizzling pop, Zillior's ghost burst into a cloud of sparks.

It was as Snorlok had feared.

Forcing himself to stay calm, along with his siblings he turned again to the imager in time to see the drone swallowed up in a fiery starburst that sent panicked foes scattering.

Zillior, heart of her mother's fiercely protective and vengeful heart, would at any moment stand incorporated, dazed and alone in the midst of her enemies.

They circled the whirling fireball, like cowardly scavengers. Keeping well back, no doubt stunned by the violence of Zillior's incipient transformation.

But they wouldn't be for long.

~~~~~~

The expanding fireball imploded with a thunderclap that sent booming echoes rolling over the hills. And now, a glowing nimbus settled over a fast congealing form, once-bright pixels dimmed to a hard corporeality—and the creature was made flesh.

It hissed in fear.

The punters stood paralyzed with astonishment. But despite the bared and gleaming incisors that gnashed and snapped, the monster standing before them was even smaller than its CGI incarnation, and they quickly recovered. Heartened by the thought that here was an enemy of flesh and blood like themselves, they renewed their attack with fresh vigor.

And they were right. Their blades and truncheons now met real substance, and inflicted real damage.

A blade flashed, biting into sinew and cartilage.

The monster bellowed.

He'd made a mistake. He'd have to bring her in.

She'd be disappointed, but they couldn't afford to take any risks. Even Snorlok himself had only faced a few of these creatures at a time. If something went wrong, and Father found out…

Snorlok turned away from the imager and started toward the platform and the control panel.

It was then, when his back was turned, that it happened.

Down in the dale, the thing broke away in a desperate attempt to flee.

Seeing his opening, Roger raised the shotgun and let fly.

The creature squalled as the buckshot tore into it. Its left arm, caught in the crossfire, exploded in a fog of vapor. A fireball erupted from its back, spraying gore.

Its shattered body slammed into the ground.

Churlo and Pirnod screeched.

A clanging like a firebell filled the chamber.

Snorlok dove, bleating, for the console, foretentacles straining.

He was already too late.
~~~~~~

Ropsnag and the twins stared in horror at the imager, then whirled to see Snorlok at the console, hammering the RETRIEVE button in half-crazed desperation.

The stunned siblings turned back to the imager.

Zillior still lay crumpled where she'd fallen, her body wracked by tremors.

Movement at the top of the imager caught their eyes.

Across the black bar of the status readout a message scrolled in blazing red letters:

WARNING: LOSS OF CONTACT REMOTE UNIT/HOST— EMERGENCY RETRIEVAL FUNCTION DISABLED—ADVISE IMMEDIATE RECONNECT—WARNING: LOSS OF CONTACT...

His features tight with dread, Snorlok stared at the mangled form of his youngest sibling.

The splintered tentacles of her right arm scratched at the ground. Her left, thrown back over her head as if in an attitude of repose, lay nerveless and inert, its ruined forearm nearly unrecognizable.

There was no sign of the remote.

Down in the dale, the punters stared in disbelief.

Incredibly, the thing was still alive and struggling to rise. After several abortive attempts, it succeeded, but reeled and staggered forward and back as if the ground underfoot were the deck of a small craft foundering in heavy seas.

No longer able to restrain himself to the sidelines from which he'd been directing the assault, Grant shoved his way to the front, eager to make his mark in battle.

He hurled himself at the enemy, laying about recklessly with his blade, forcing those near at hand to duck out of the way. They formed a widening ring around the combatants, with Hal charging this way and that around their perimeter, trying for a clear shot of Grant: A heroic, Thor-like figure, blade weaving a furious tapestry of vengeance as he pressed the attack home on his dazed and weakened foe. Backing away, it stumbled over a gnarled tree root and let down its guard. With the speed of a pouncing tiger, Grant struck its head from its shoulders. It landed with a dull thump at his feet.

But Grant continued his attack. As the company looked on in horror, he hacked the thing to pieces.

It was bloody work.

It wasn't red blood, bright and clean as the blood of a noble enemy would be. It was slimy—more like the viscous gunk you might pull out of a shower drain with a bent coathanger. But blood or not, it was still work, and Grant quickly tired of it.

A shocked silence had smothered the exultant clamoring of the assembled company.

They watched Grant uneasily as he straddled his handiwork with the complicated posture of a Victor Frankenstein gazing for the first time upon the thing his own hands have wrought. As the seconds passed, the arm holding the machete ratcheted downward like a chain hoist lowering a six-ton load. When the machete's tip touched the ground, Grant's shoulders slumped.

The steaming stew of monstrous body parts at his feet was an appalling mess that made even Grant's unsqueamish eyes squirm. He stared at one severed leg, sporting numerous deep gashes, oozing its obscene mucous. The knee-like joint flexed and contracted, stirring the pot with a grotesque mechanical rote.

Grant groped for the appropriate emotion.

His lips parted, quivered, tightened shut in a thin line. Then parted again.

"It's over," he said, but his voice squeaked like a rusty hinge and no one heard him.

He paused, cleared his throat. He lifted his gaze, drew himself up to his full height.

His voice rang out, strong and sure.

"Victory is ours."

A hesitant murmuring of semi-approval flowed through the ring of onlookers.

It was a good start.

Grant turned, and his gaze found the camera—without flashing it like an overawed extra—then swept over his troops. Shaking a stray lock of blond hair back into place with a flick of his head, he thrust his machete toward the heavens, pumped the blade, and shouted for all the world to hear:

"To Freedom!"

It was a bold flourish, but with the disturbing spectacle of his furious thrashing at an unresisting pile of meat still fresh in his audience's minds, Grant's jubilance came off as a bit overstated.

"Geez, Grant..." Fredo began.

Grant threw up his free hand, palm outward as if to ward off all doubt. He stared down at the gruesome remnants at his feet and found himself unperturbed by the sight.

Hal hurried over. "Grant, Rob says to bring back the remains. The Feds want to see anything we find."

Grant nodded. Fixing his steely gaze on Fredo, he said, "Somebody pick up this carrion and bring it back to camp."

Rooting through the butchered carcass was a disgusting business. Zach, Fredo and Clayton slipped out of their t-shirts to use them as make-shift body bags. Three weren't enough. Fredo called Brad over and persuaded him to contribute his own quadruple extra large.

Stooping to scoop a nameless organ onto his t-shirt, Zach noticed a glint of metal obscured by a thick glob of mucus. He poked at it. It was cold and hard. He picked it up, wiping away the sticky coating to examine it curiously.

"What have we here?" he said, then answered his own question with a grin. "Spoils!"

Grant heard him and hurried over. "No looting of prisoners," he said.

"What prisoner? It's dead."

"I'll take that," Grant said, snatching it away and pocketing it. Zach frowned, but declined to protest. After a moment's hesitation he turned away.

The trampled earth showed surprisingly few signs of the battle that had raged only minutes before. Aside from a few stray bits of flesh, the thing's remains had all been bagged.

Grant looked up to find everyone's eyes upon him.

The troops awaited orders.

He surveyed the now quiet battlefield with satisfaction. He had led his company bravely through a perilous encounter with an unknown enemy, and they'd emerged victorious, with barely a scratch.

It was one for the record books.

His clear voice resonated with the ringing authority acquired through his years of military training.

"Friends," he announced, "Our work here is—"

He was cut off by a piercing whine.

CHAPTER TWENTY-FOUR

GAME OVER

A LIGHTNING BOLT slammed into the earth at Grant's feet and exploded with a roar like a cannon, gouging out great chunks of earth and hurling them into the air.

Grant's stricken countenance was pelted with rocks. He yelped and stumbled backwards, to stare in stark, terrified amazement as the air itself ripped apart and reared up into a churning pillar of fire.

It towered over the company, whirling like the Tasmanian Devil, then abruptly ground to a halt with a braking squeal and fused into a snarling eight-foot nightmare straight out of hell.

The thing belted out a harrowing screech, then sprang with fearless recklessness into the very midst of the howling volunteers.

The awful fury of its assault knocked Grant clean off his feet, sending him scrabbling away between Zach and Clayton's quaking knees.

It swept its long arms like scythes through their stunned ranks and snatched up Fredo and Heather in great sawtoothed pincers.

Trask and Jim were on their feet in an instant.

Janet covered her eyes as screams of terror blared from the speakers.

Onscreen, The monster brandished Fredo and Heather over its head, shaking them like twin Oscars, then threw open its jaws and let out a nerve-shattering roar. Its pincers snapped shut like garden shears—severing their frail human bodies in two with a sickening crunch.

Covering her mouth with one hand and holding her stomach with the other, Janet lurched past the stupefied watchers in the back row, stumbled through the door and fled down the hall. Her shrieking admirers followed hot on her heels.

All except for Jeremy. The hideous spectacle held his feet impaled to the floorboards.

The image blurred and peeled away as Hal began to run, panning past Grant's upturned face just in time to catch it being splattered with gore.

Trask's horrified gaze met Jim's and the two of them bolted for the door.

"Wait! Trask!" Bentley yelled, but they were gone. The bungalow's back door slammed, and the thud of their footsteps pounded away over the sand toward the jungle.

Rashad looked at Paula, Paula looked at Michelle. Michelle looked at Vince—and all four of them jumped up and dashed through the door after the others.

Bentley turned back to the video monitor.

Hal must have been scrambling away backwards as he continued shooting. The image pitched and jolted through a widening long shot—centered on Roger, holding Jim's shotgun in one hand and tearing frantically at his pockets with the other.

The idiot hadn't even bothered to fill the magazine before setting out.

Bentley lunged for the talkback button.

"Hal, Trask and his gang are on the way, ETA three minutes. Tell Grant to finish that thing off now. And keep Trask and Paula out of trouble. That's an order."

The camera's backward flight slowed. Hal's voice quavered into the mic. *"Okay, okay."*

The picture steadied to re-focus on the action from a distance, then zoomed to pull the watchers in close to the melee.

Jeremy gazed at the monitor in a trance.

The thing loomed over Tony. Whether in panic or confusion, he'd dropped his machete, and now staggered backwards, covering his face with his arms as if there were some hope of fending off the coming blow.

Jeremy stared so hard his eyes hurt. His hands were balled into fists.

Tony broke and turned to run. The monster raised its gleaming pincers high above its head.

In his excitement, Jeremy half-rose from his chair.

But now Brad leapt into frame from camera right, twirling his mace over his head like a gaucho's boleros. Its steel shackles crashed into the descending pincers with an ear-splitting clang.

An instant later and Tony's head would have been pounded to splattering ruin. As it was, the deflected pincers grazed his shoulders, ripping his shirt from his back before slamming into the earth. Brad picked him up by his belt and heaved him to safety.

Cheated of its victim, the monster whirled, searching for a replacement.

Jeremy sank trembling back into his chair.

But now Bentley was on his feet, yelling at the talkback mic.

"Where the hell is Grant? Hal!"

On full optical zoom, the picture shook violently, exaggerating the fluttering tremor of Hal's usually steady hand.

"Hal!"

They could hear his voice now, from offscreen behind the camera, screaming at Grant.

"Grant! Kill it now!"

And they saw Grant yelling back. His words were drowned out by the din of battle.

"What's that? Say it again!" Grant mouthed.

"The thing! Rob says to kill it now!"

Grant cupped an ear toward the camera.

"Forget it," Bentley snapped at Hal.

Down in the dale, with blood flowing from a deep gash in her right leg, Beverly next captured the thing's attention by trying to limp to safety. Hoping to distract it, Lance, Erika and Evans hacked at its heels, ducking and skipping away when it twisted to aim vicious swipes at their faces.

Roger had finally located some shells. He tore them from his pocket and rammed them into the chamber.

"Get out of the way," he yelled.

Beverly and her protectors hit the dirt. The shotgun roared. The blast punched a bowling ball-sized hole in the monster's massive torso, staggering it.

But it didn't fall. Gleaming pixels crawled over its rippling form to fill the void.

With a pantherish bound, the thing was upon its assailant. Its red-rimmed eyes bored into Roger's as it arched over him, and for one heart-stopping instant it seemed to hesitate.

But only for an instant.

It struck like a steel cobra. Machinelike jaws clamped shut over Roger's head, shattering his skull.

The air seemed to fill with a red fog.

Grant felt himself falling.

Warm droplets sprinkled down over his shirtfront.

As his head hit the soft bed of ferns, dewy drops of crimson levitated upward from the fronds, like flakes in a snow globe.

They sparkled in the bright sunlight.

The siblings gazed into the imager in a state of rapture, overawed by Snorlok's prowess.

They chittered in wonder when the enemy fighter crumpled headless to the ground. And when the mighty drone that was Snorlok's terrifying counterpart reared up again to its full height, spraying dark liquid from its bared teeth and shaking its great head in triumph, Churlo and Pirnod whickered their tentacles in applause.

But cautious Ropsnag glanced up at the status bar.

It had crept unnoticed into the yellow.

Ropsnag's brow tendrils fluttered.

Bentley and Barry watched, spellbound, as Erika scooped up Roger's shotgun, pumped, and fired.

The blast blew MechaGodzilla's face right out the back of its head—but the stream of pixels quickly snapped back into place like a colossal rubber band. The creature whirled on her. Erika dropped the shotgun and ran.

Bentley grunted his encouragement at the screen, then tensed again when Clayton rushed into frame swinging a bat.

The monster stepped on Roger's shotgun, and with a wrenching of tentacles twisted it into a ball of mangled scrap—then turned to meet Clayton's screaming assault.

It hammered down with the broad side of one massive pincer, flattening him.

"Ouch," Barry said.

Bentley, his attention still riveted to the monitor, nodded as the remaining volunteers backed away. The events unfolding onscreen were without parallel in the history of television. The drama, the emotion. The spectacle.

The carnage.

"God," Bentley said, "this is horrible. Horrible!"

He looked about the room with a guilty expression.

Barry looked back at him tentatively.

"But—*damn!*"

Bentley half stood and leaned over Fred's shoulder into the talkback mic.

"Great shooting, Hal!"

In the semi-darkness of the transporter chamber, six warning beeps clucked, startling the grinning siblings out of their complacency.

Incoming. Six enemy combatants.

Ropsnag's eyes widened. He ran an apprehensive gaze around the imager's perimeter. Six flashing cursors swarmed in from the fringe, then blinked out. In their place, six baleful figures rushed toward the center—where Snorlok's utility drone battled against already unfair odds.

The twins babbled in alarm.

Lance shouted over the clamor of fighting and the monster's blood-chilling roars.

"Where's Grant?"

"I don't know," Brad shouted back.

"We've got to break off."

"Dude, I'm not turning my back on that thing!"

"Evans! The three of us are gonna have to hold it off till we can get everybody out of here."

Without a word, Evans stepped up and landed a stinging blow with a wrecking bar on the monster's unprotected flank. Pixels gushing from its side, it spun on him with a snarl.

"Retreat!" Lance yelled. Everyone back to camp!"

No one obeyed. After all this, they weren't going to leave Lance, Brad and Evans to face the thing alone.

"Go!" Lance screamed.

From the rear came a shout.

The beleaguered punters turned to see a squad of reinforcements cresting the hilltop with Jim at their head. A roar went up at the sight of them. They hurdled the hedge and swept down.

Jim hit the bottom at a run. "Clear out of the way!"

He leveled his Winchester thirty-aught-six and punters dove for cover. Erika tripped and went down. Cursing, Jim unleashed round after round into the creature as Trask made for her.

The monster howled, and Trask knew he wasn't going to make it. But Lance and Beverly had seen her.

They dove for Erika's outstretched hands.

The thing skewered her against the ground.

Lance and Beverly scrambled away. The monster ignored them. Screeching in triumph, it yanked out its pincer and charged its new opponents.

Trask snatched up Erika's machete without breaking stride and met his attacker head on with a blade in each hand.

The creature lunged, pincers snapping.

Trask sidestepped, swinging with both blades. They sliced into his foe's exposed abdomen, mincing pixels.

The monster bellowed in surprised rage. Its wounds chopped and blurred.

Trask rolled between its legs and in one smooth, continuous motion, aimed a whistling stroke at the back of its knees.

The monster stumbled, countered wildly and missed, and Trask's blades darted in and out, scattering pixels and hurling them from its glowing form in streaming arcs.

While he kept it busy, Jim fed five more cartridges into the magazine.

The punters were excited now, shouting, their voices filled with hope as Trask harried the thing. His fighting skills had taken them all by surprise. And this one too was finally wearing down. Every hit sapped its strength a little more. Even so, the thing's counterattacks never let up, and for all his speed and raw energy, Trask was tiring.

"Break off, Trask," Jim yelled.

Trask broke away, and Lance and Brad pulled him back into their ranks.

Down on one knee like a musketeer, Jim aimed his Winchester between the thing's eyes and pulled the trigger. The monster's face exploded into horizontal bands of distortion. It gibbered, its voice breaking up like an overloaded speaker.

Jim kept firing.

The thing stabbed at him with a gigantic pincer. It snipped through his rifle barrel like a power shear through quarter-inch hose.

Backing away, Jim saw Roger's body a few yards to his right, his pistol still in its holster.

He dove and rolled, and came up with the gun aimed at his opponent's jaws.

But the thing had finally had enough.

With a howl, it bounded backwards, scattering punters behind it. Its outlines fraying and crackling, streaming iridescent jets of pixels from scores of gaping disruptions, it snatched up one of the t-shirts holding its fellow's remains and clapped its pincers together.

With a flash and a boom, the thing blew apart in flying globules.

They drifted, wobbling like soap bubbles, then one by one burst in shimmering fountains of sparks that twinkled out as they floated lazily toward the ground.

Exhausted punters dropped to their knees.

They'd won.

The status bar strobed. Ropsnag dashed for the console. The alarm clanged once and cut off.

But Snorlok was already on the way in.

He'd activated his remote just in time.

His siblings heard Snorlok's enraged bellowing before he'd even completely materialized on the transporter platform. When the shimmerings ceased, he stood there trembling, pounding the console with one balled fist in a fit of savage fury that made even Ropsnag cower.

In his other fist, Snorlok clutched a white cloth bag stained with gore. He tore it to pieces and glowered at its contents. A single severed leg. All he'd managed to salvage of Zillior.

He hurled it to the floor. It struck the hard surface at Ropsnag's pods with a sickening splat.

Snorlok's siblings stared down in chagrin. Every hatchling knew tissue regeneration proceeded from the spinal cord. The sundered limb alone was useless.

On the platform, Snorlok had fallen grimly silent. With barely controlled wrath, he ran his tentacles over the console—keying in commands.

The siblings looked at each other, then back at the imager, where enemy combatants were gathering up the rest of Zillior's scattered pieces.

Within moments, they'd fled out of sight.

The status bar overhead elongated as the transporter recharged. As the siblings watched, it crept toward the orange. They gabbled in excitement and again turned towards Snorlok.

Still on the platform, he stood gazing up at the status bar with tooth-grinding impatience.

Far down the corridor at the other end of the ship, Strindlak stooped to peer one last time under the chassis for a final inspection of the brace covering the coolant system's lower seal. Satisfied, he drew himself erect and proceeded without haste to the waiting instrument panel—patting the engine's massive thruster shieldings as he passed by.

With a single tentacle tip, he depressed a round button, then stepped back to wait—his normally fierce features softened by a serene smile.

Nothing happened.

Out of the corner of his eye he saw the yellow flash of a READ ME notice, coming from the main control console against the wall. The ship's computer was apparently calling his attention to some overlooked detail.

It was no cause for concern. Some minor adjustments to the programming should be expected after such a thorough overhaul of the machinery. He crossed the room to the console and tapped the display.

The READ ME notice was whisked away. In its place appeared a bold-face legend:

MECHANICAL MODIFICATIONS DETECTED

Please Consult Screen 423.165-5 of Your

FLARDNUX 12000 Troubleshooting Guide and Repair Manual

With the barest hint of a frown, Strindlak complied.

At the sight of Screen 423.165-5, he suffered a sudden bout of vertigo.

Struggling against the returning fatigue seeping into his mind and body, he forced himself to read along with the chirping computer voice.

"Greetings, Strindlak Gratchnorr! Your FLARDNUX 12000's built-in self-diagnostic features have detected major modifications to the ship's mechanics. These modifications necessitate reprogramming of the system software."

The words filled him with dread. He clutched at his brow, yanking out a brace of tendrils in distraction. They shrilled feebly at him as the computer voice rattled on and he listened with eyes closed.

"Reprogramming is automatic thanks to the FLARDNUX 12000's advanced software engineering."

He nearly fainted with relief.

But there was more. Opening his eyes, Strindlak silenced the cloying voice to scan the page on his own.

> *However; subsequent to any such extensive repairs, a further built-in safety feature prevents initiation of the propulsion system's startup sequence until such time as the plasma core has been completely drained and refreshed.*
>
> *This time-intensive procedure requires close and continual monitoring and necessitates prior deactivation of all non-essential subsystems.*

'Time-intensive'? The phrase was unduly vague in Strindlak's opinion.

Reading on, he learned there was a sequence of simple operations that would need performing in a particular order. He'd be prompted at the end of each to begin the next and given a brief set of instructions for keying in the required commands.

Grudgingly, he keyed in the first set and hit *INITIATE*.

Again, the screen flashed a WARNING. Strindlak suppressed a growl.

The new warning read:

> *Your **FLARDNUX 12000's** sensors have detected a non-essential subsystem in operation. Deactivation of all non-essential routines is required before initiation of the selected sequence.*

QUIT ALL Non-Essential Routines?

YES

NO

SHOW ALL

Exactly which routines did the damned ship's computer deem to be non-essential, Strindlak wondered.

What was running other than basic life support?

Scowling, he selected *SHOW ALL*.

There was only one.

Back in the transporter chamber, Snorlok's tentacle tips hovered over the button, poised to activate the instant the status bar hit green.

The game wasn't over yet.

Down on the floor, Ropsnag's tentacles jerked tight around the imager railing.

The bar had gone from orange to yellow.

Churlo and Pirnod hooted in anticipation.

A musical ping from underneath the console startled them to silence. The instrument lights flickered and dimmed.

From the console, Snorlok stared at the imager in consternation as the scene within crumpled and dissolved. The status bar surged into the green, then blinked out.

He stabbed the *ACTIVATE* button.

The transporter failed to respond.

He hit it again, and again, trumpeting in despair. From beneath the podium came a metallic click, and now, over the soft thrum of systems electronics there rose a crescendoing whine. It sustained, then warbled and pitched downward to descend through the harmonics until it became a low flapping, and finally cut off altogether with a sharp crackle of electrical discharge. The hemisphere's gleaming surface dulled to a flat, opaque shell.

Snorlok pounded on the button.

The room lights died, plunging the chamber into semi-darkness, relieved only by the flickering instrument lights.

One by one, they blinked out.

Snorlok's mind raced. What were they going to do? If they didn't retrieve Zillior before their parents discovered her missing, they were dead. What could have caused such a massive, across-the-board malfunction?

There was only one possible answer.

Father.

Mother had told the twins that Strindlak was close to finishing the repairs. But now, as usual, something had gone wrong.

Or had it?

A dark foreboding crept into Snorlok's thoughts.

Strindlak's mishaps typically resulted in fiery explosions and flying debris. There'd been none of that. There'd been a click, that was all.

No—it wasn't. First there'd been that bell-like chime.

Terror slid through Snorlok's veins like tentacles of ice. No explosions. Not even a hiss of blown circuitry. The transporter's subsystems had deactivated one after another in what, now that he thought about it, looked like a standard powering-down sequence.

Had it malfunctioned? Or simply shut down?

Been shut down.

Stifling a yelp, Snorlok swung over the platform railing, landing with a chamber-jolting thump before his startled siblings. They stared at him in confusion and alarm, their underlit faces a ghastly red in the glow of the emergency panels.

Scattering them with a sweep of his long tentacles, he quickly found what he was looking for: Zillior's still-twitching leg. It had worked its way under the edge of the imager's raised dais. Seizing it, Snorlok dashed for the exit with a hoarse cry to the others to follow.

Without a clue as to what had brought on the sudden panic, but thoroughly frightened now, they hurried after him.

Not even looking to see if they'd followed, Snorlok punched the control panel.

He held his breath as the door slid open.

The siblings gasped.

A huge form blocked their way out into the corridor.

Strindlak.

Snorlok's face went numb as his brow tendrils shot toward the ceiling.

The twins wailed.

He loomed over them, speechless with fury, his red eyes blazing down at them in an apoplectic seizure of parental outrage.

Snorlok wrapped concealing tentacles around Zillior's spasming leg and hid it behind his broad back just in time.

CHAPTER TWENTY-FIVE

VICTORY

BENTLEY AND BARRY and the crew had hurried outside to await the victorious army's imminent return, and now stood staring at the wall of trees, fidgeting with impatience. At the sound of their excited voices, Janet and Jeremy and the others came out to ask what was going on.

"They won!" Bentley crowed. "You should've seen it. Jim drilled the thing full of lead, it started throwing off sparks like a bottle rocket, and WHAM!"

Janet let go of Jeremy's hand to ask meekly, "What about Tony? Is Tony okay?"

"He's fine!" Bentley said. "They're all—" he caught himself. Actually, not all of them, as Janet knew. He ran the footage back through his mind, tallying the casualties. Fredo, Heather, Roger. Dead for sure. Thought they might have lost Grant for a minute, but he turned up, only a little dazed. Clayton was a probable. Erika too.

It occurred to Bentley that the victory celebration he'd envisioned could be dampened somewhat by the heavy casualty rate. Might be best to keep the welcome muted until he had a chance to better gauge the returning punters' emotional state. He looked down at the six-packs of beer in his hands, suddenly self-conscious. Barry had a couple too. They had a limited stock, intended to reward the crew after particularly grueling shifts. Well, whatever their mood, they must be thirsty. Surely a cold beer's always welcome, whatever the occasion.

He heard the heavy tread of the group's footsteps trudging through the jungle undergrowth. It didn't sound like anybody was talking.

Flinging aside a knot of obstructing branches, Zach stumbled out of the trees.

Bentley paled at his appearance. What had come across on the studio monitors as just a naturalistic effect was shocking in real life. The blood splattered across Zach's face and bare chest gleamed in full living color, dark red against his skin, diluted and streaked pink where it merged with dust and sweat to run down under his belt.

Barry shouted.

"Hip hip!"

"Hooray!" the crew chorused.

Bentley cringed and shot a look at Barry, who'd obviously coached them. But Barry wasn't paying any attention to him, and at the next chorus Janet and her crew joined in.

Except, of course, for Jeremy.

Weighted down with fatigue, Zach gave the welcoming committee a half-hearted wave and headed straight for the mess hall.

And then came Tony.

Janet's squeal as she ran past was so shrill Bentley clapped his hands over his ears to protect them. She threw her arms around Tony's neck, pasting wet kisses all over his face in an almost sexual ecstasy of joy. Spent though he was, Tony ate it up. Bentley couldn't help casting a discreet glance at Jeremy to see how he was taking it.

Jeremy's face was beet red. He saw Bentley looking and turned away to stomp back inside.

Next came Beverly, hobbling on one leg and supported on either side by Trask and Evans. She grimaced in pain at every step. Paula hurried ahead—to prepare a cot and fresh bandages, Bentley guessed.

They didn't stop for congratulations.

"How is she?" Bentley asked Paula as she passed by.

Without stopping or turning, Paula said, "She'll make it."

Returning punters filed past on either side.

"Way to go, Rashad." Bentley was still too intimidated by Michelle to talk to her. He let her pass unaccosted.

"Give 'em hell, Jim."

No sign of Grant yet, but he was glad to see Hal for now, coming up behind Jim. Hal at least managed a tired smile. Bentley perked up and swatted his behind like a high school football coach.

"Beautiful job, Hal."

Hal nodded and reached for a beer. Bentley'd forgotten he had them, but now he was glad he did after all. He clapped Hal on the shoulder and handed him both six-packs.

"Pass 'em around. There's one for everybody."

But it wasn't as he'd imagined it. Somehow he'd pictured them all flushed with triumph, drunk with victory and boisterous rejoicing. Boasting, laughing—maybe even singing, like in all those old World War II movies he'd seen as a kid. He couldn't remember exactly which movies, but it must have been like that in some of them. Where else would he have gotten the idea? Wasn't that what people wanted?

He wondered if it might be worth doing the whole thing over. He was a director, after all. They could always stage a more compelling homecoming, have Barry script something. And Grant was a great extemporizer.

"Rob!"

Bentley'd been looking right at him, lost in thought.

He shook himself out of it. Here was Grant, at last, grinning broadly, with Lance and Vince by his side. And there was Brad. All four strode forward with heads held high, appearing fresh, projecting an aura of confidence and quiet exhilaration that Bentley found immensely gratifying. Fred moved up, camera in position, capturing the moment for posterity as he was paid to do. Now here was something. This was better. Sure, they'd suffered some losses. But they'd won, hadn't they?

Boy, they were a sight, though. Clothes torn and bloodied, their battle-hardened features exultant, bearing the fresh wounds of desperate combat now as marks of valor. And like Viking raiders returning in a ship laden with plunder, they carried the bundled t-shirts holding the grisly remains of their foe.

Gabrielle and Mei ran to meet them, and Lance, flushed with victory, dropped his burden and grabbed both by the waist, as if claiming them as his prize.

It was a thrilling moment.

"Grant! Fabulous! What leadership!"

Grants spirits seemed to soar even higher. Bentley put his arm around his shoulder and the two of them led the way to the mess hall.

"We did it, Rob! We beat them."

"Hey, but Grant—what happened? You were out cold."

"You didn't see?" Grant stopped walking and grabbed Bentley's arm. "Feel the bump on my head."

"I didn't see it," Brad put in.

"I did," Lance said.

Grant pressed Bentley's hand to the side of his head, near the back.

"Ow." Grant grinned sheepishly. "It's a little sore."

"Hmm." Bentley did feel something.

"I don't even remember it myself," Grant said. "Must have got me when my back was turned, when Hal was yelling. Can't wait to see the footage. Hah!"

"Close call, Grant," Bentley said.

"You're not kidding," Grant agreed.

They entered the mess hall looking like Grant's personal entourage, babbling in excitement, slapping high fives, pounding each other on the back. Their exuberance was brought up short by the distracted gloom of those bloodying the furniture inside.

The pall was short-lived, though. Grant and Lance couldn't contain their joy at having won, and Lance took it upon himself to personally congratulate and shake hands with every one of the participants. His private words to them seemed to lift their spirits. The mood remained far from celebratory, but his strength and resiliency had an effect.

The siblings conferred in their quarters in urgent, guttural murmurs.

They well understood the gravity of their situation. They'd lost Zillior. When Strindlak and Glumrok found out, things would turn grimly unpleasant, in ways too frightful to contemplate. Strindlak's wrath was fearful enough, but Glumrok's would be awful beyond words. There was no telling what she might do. Zillior was her most cherished offspring, and the only female to have survived the first mutation in untold ages.

Snorlok knew that when Zillior regained consciousness, she'd gather herself up and try to find her way back to the ship—if she were able to escape the enemy's clutches. But he had no way of knowing how long she'd remain narcotose. Complete dismemberment was a rare condition, one even Snorlok had no personal experience of. Pirnod had been cloven in two and hadn't stirred for close to an eighth of a cycle. Zillior was younger. In her case, it might be much longer. And even if she'd already escaped, it could take her forever, hobbled and disoriented, to find her way back to the ship.

There was no other option. They'd have to risk using the transporter again to effect a rescue.

It wouldn't be easy. Snorlok wasn't naïve enough to think they could just walk in and ask for Zillior's release. Their appearance would be seen as a resumption of play. There would be no way to communicate that they desired only to collect their sister and be on their way, would even be willing to call it a draw considering the urgency of their need.

They'd have to go in fighting and win Zillior's freedom through combat.

Churlo wailed at Snorlok's words. If Father caught them again, after he'd already caught them once...

Pirnod pleaded the case for making a full confession and throwing themselves on Strindlak's mercy. If they told Father what they'd done, he'd be able to bring Zillior back within minutes, and they could avoid further disobedience.

Snorlok silenced their whining protestations with a lashing tentacle across their startled faces.

Avoid further disobedience? Fools! It was Strindlak and Glumrok's wrath that needed avoiding at all costs. Would confessing their crime make the sting of punishment any less?

Ropsnag snarled his agreement. The twins whimpered.

Snorlok softened. They were closer to Zillior than he and Ropsnag, and were concerned for her safety, he realized. But, he explained, if they failed to recover Zillior themselves, chances were Father would still be able to bring her back. They wouldn't lose Zillior either way. But they would lose much if their reckless negligence were discovered.

They'd put Beverly in a chair against the long wall. Jim sat on a low stool in front of her, holding her foot like a shoe store salesman, supporting her injured leg over a mixing bowl. Trask and Rashad stood by. The field dressing had been removed, and as Bentley watched from behind Rashad's shoulder, Paula poured water from a pitcher over the long gaping wound, flushing out dirt and debris. Irrigating it. Paula worked in a hospital, Bentley remembered, so she must know what she was doing. Beverly gritted her teeth, groaning at the sting of cold water against her exposed flesh, and Jim leaned forward to mop her forehead with a wet rag, speaking to her in a low, soothing voice as he did.

Bentley shook his head. They really should have been better supplied in terms of first aid. He'd have to make sure there were no more foul-ups in that department next time.

Rashad, misinterpreting Bentley's unconscious gesture, turned and whispered, "Paula says she's going to be fine. It's not too serious. The biggest worry is risk of infection."

Bentley nodded. "Thank you, Rashad."

Beverly started to cry. Bentley thought it was from the pain until she said, "If Erika hadn't—", and then he remembered Erika—and Lance and Evans—distracting the thing so Beverly could escape. They were true heroes, all of them.

Beverly's words choked off into a sob.

"I know," Paula said. A tear rolled down her cheek. "Rashad, could you find us a clean sheet?" She wiped her eyes. "That duct tape would come in handy too, if anyone knows where it is."

Trask said, "I think it's in the toolbag." He glanced around as Rashad went off in search of a sheet.

Bentley reached out to pat Beverly's hand, then turned away. Beverly was fine. Now he could relax and see about getting the party into full swing. There was a hubbub of conversation now—people had started talking again. He even heard laughter. Lance, it sounded like. And Grant. Bentley headed over to join them.

The toolbag was on a table in the center of the room. Evans was helping Trask dig through it, and half its contents were now scattered over the table. Drills, screwdrivers. Pliers. A claw hammer. Boxes of nails. Trask finally found what they were looking for buried at the bottom. Bentley stopped in front of him and grinned at Evans when they both looked up.

"Is he something else, or what?" he said to Evans. "Trask! Where'd you get those moves?"

Trask just shrugged. The silence soon became awkward.

"Better get this to Paula," Trask muttered, and walked away.

Bentley snapped his fingers in sudden inspiration.

"Hal."

Hal, sitting in a corner nursing his beer, gazed up at Bentley without interest.

Right. Hal was probably a little burned out. Well, he'd earned his bit of rest. Fred was covering the scene, and doing a marvelous job. Recent experiences seemed to have transformed him. He got along well with the punters, too. He'd grabbed the beers that Hal had failed to hand out and was passing them around. And from Fred, they accepted them with gratitude.

"Fred, Barry. Quick interview." Bentley waved them over and threaded his way toward Grant.

Seeing them coming, Grant smiled eagerly.

Barry positioned himself beside Grant in front of Fred's camera. "I'm speaking with Grant Nolan, whose strong leadership proved vital to the success of today's action. So Grant," Barry said, turning to him, "tell us, how does it feel? Has it sunk in?"

"It feels good, Barry, I won't deny it. As you know, I owe it all to my men—and women!—and the character and fortitude we recognized in all of them months ago when they were chosen to compete on the show. Hunters and Gatherers! Who would have guessed where it would lead after only a single episode!"

"The show's popularity is really remarkable," Barry agreed. "So what do you think is behind today's win? Experience? Determination? Simple courage?"

"You know, Barry, I think it's all those things. My own experience as a platoon leader with the 7th Marines in the Persian Gulf stood me in good stead. But when it comes down to it, you know, you just go in there, and you give it your all. You give it a hundred and ten percent and…and…"

Grant frowned. He'd been absently fingering some large knob-shaped object in his pocket as he spoke and gotten distracted. He fished it out and smiled in recollection. The coating of gunk had dried and flaked off in his pocket, exposing the thing's ovoid shape.

"What have we here, Grant?" Barry asked on behalf of the hypothetical viewers at home.

Grant held it up and inspected it with curiosity.

"Some kind of—" Barry continued, "I don't know, are they aliens? Do we know? Some kind of alien artifact?"

Grant shook his head. "I'm not sure. Just a bauble, I guess. A charm worn into battle, perhaps." He raised it higher, displaying it to the room at large. "Let this trinket stand as a symbol of today's victory. Just as the power of good has vanquished the combined might of the forces of evil arrayed against us, so shall we—"

"Let's take a closer look at it," Barry interrupted. He waved Fred in and tugged Grant's arm back down. Fred's camera tilted to focus on the object.

It was a flattened oval of dark metal with a slight rim around the outer edge, devoid of decoration except for a smooth, red jewel-like stud mounted in a raised setting at the center.

"That jewel, if that's what it is," Barry said, "it looks like a button, doesn't it?"

"Well, yes, now that you mention it," Grant replied. "I wonder…" He put his finger on it.

"Grant!" It was Trask, hurrying over from across the room.

But he was too late. Grant pushed the button.

It gave under his touch, and engaged in the depressed position with a soft click.

Trask froze. Grant blinked. Barry held his breath. Beside Fred, Bentley tensed.

A few moments passed. Trask exhaled.

Grant pushed the button again. It snapped back out. He repeated the trial a few more times. Trask flinched each time he did. But nothing happened.

Grant shrugged. "Just a piece of junk, really."

"Grant," Trask said. "Can I see that for a second?"

Grant stared at him, then smiled. "A token for your aid, Trask!" He tossed him the trinket as he said it, chuckling when Trask caught it gingerly. "Not that we needed it!" he announced to the camera. "My volunteers had the situation well under control. Nevertheless, we're grateful for your assistance. Jim's in particular."

Trask turned away with a mumbled thanks. Paula and Rashad were watching him, but he avoided them and moved to an empty spot near the kitchen door.

Barry wrapped up Grant's interview and Bentley made the rounds, congratulating some and making socially awkward attempts at consoling others. There were few tears, though. Right now people were just glad to be alive.

He looked around for Hal, wanting to congratulate him again on his splendid camerawork, but it seemed he'd gone.

Beverly had been moved to a cot after having her leg bandaged up, and looked like she was resting. Paula, Jim and Rashad stood nearby.

Bentley walked over to them.

"Everything fine?"

"I think so," Paula said.

Bentley stood quietly for a few seconds, then said, "Where're the remains?"

Rashad's expression turned guilty.

"We had to leave them. We weren't sure if it was over."

Bentley frowned.

"We'll go back for them in the morning," Rashad said.

Bentley suddenly realized what he was talking about.

"No, no, no," he said. "The *thing!* The alien."

Trask was back. He said, "Evans put everything in a garbage bag. In the kitchen."

"Oh, um, Trask," Bentley said. "That thing that Grant found. I think it would be best if I hung on to that. For safekeeping."

Trask said, "Sure."

He opened his fist and Bentley took it, turning it over in his palm to examine it.

Trask watched intently. So did Paula. It looked like he'd cleaned all the remaining sludge off the "charm" and polished it up a little. It reflected the overhead fluorescents with a sparkling sheen.

Bentley pocketed it, then turned toward the kitchen.

"Fred."

Trask ducked Paula's steady gaze and wandered off again.

The garbage bag sat on the countertop beside the sink, bulging at its plastic seams. Fred braced himself with his hip against the counter and steadied on the subject. Even the bag was spackled with dried blood. Evans's, Bentley guessed—or at least it had rubbed off of him. Could've been anyone's originally.

Bentley undid the twis-tie and loosened the yellow drawstring. A glob of pink mucus slid out into the sink. He grunted and opened the bag wider.

Evans had transferred everything to it, t-shirts and all, all slick with gore. Bentley grabbed a hunk of blood-soaked white cotton and gave it a tug.

The head tumbled out.

It fell into the sink and bumped around in a circle, then rolled to the center, rocking from side to side before coming to rest over the drain.

The dull red eyes seemed to stare at the ceiling. A heavy, sharp-pointed tongue lolled from the dead lips. The thing's flowery crown of tendrils was pasted to its face by a coating of congealed slime.

As Bentley gaped, the lips smacked open and emitted a steaming gush of stinking liquid. He jumped back, startled. The greasy substance pooled in the sink in slimy strands, too thick to pass through the drain.

"God, it's ugly. Now that's a disgusting mess. Even in death, it's just…" He searched for a descriptive phrase and failed. "…indescribable."

Nostrils contracting, he stuck his hand in again and got hold of another t-shirt. He had to work it back and forth, but it at last came free, tangled around a severed extremity. A pinkish, gelatinous mass shot with a network of green veins extruded from the stump like the leg of an amoeba.

"Ugh." He let it drop onto the head and reached for a towel.

CHAPTER TWENTY-SIX

CHARACTER DEVELOPMENT

SOMEBODY GRABBED TRASK'S ARM from behind, and he didn't need three guesses to figure out it was Paula.

"Is that what that is?" she asked.

"Is what what what is?" Trask said, playing innocent.

Paula's expression hardened. "Don't give me that shit, Trask," she said. "You know what I'm talking about."

The room was crowded. Trask drew her over to the corner by the kitchen door where they could talk undisturbed.

"You mean Grant's thing?"

"I mean the thing that came off of the Viceroy's sword. You said it was some kind of remote control."

"That's what I thought it was."

"And you were right, weren't you? But not in the way you thought."

Trask looked away, pretending something had caught his attention and hoping she'd be distracted. His gaze landed on Jeremy and Tony. Janet's paramours were having words. Not too surprising. Janet had stepped between them and was trying to placate them with some drivel about how they were *both* her heroes.

Maybe he should go see if he could smoothe things over.

"I think maybe I better—"

"It *is* a remote control," Paula said. "One of *theirs.*"

Trask sighed. Lowering his voice, he said, "Maybe."

"Maybe? Trask, don't lie to me."

"I'm not, Paula. I don't know the truth any more than you do." He glanced around. Nobody was paying any attention to them, but he lowered his voice even further. "Let's just keep it to ourselves, okay? For now?"

She was whispering now too, but she wasn't giving up.

"They've been here before. That knight in the tapestry. The dragon."

"You're thinking too much."

"Not any more than you are."

Trask looked around again. Across the room, Jeremy said something to Tony that ended with, "asshole." A few other people were watching now too. Maybe he really *should* go and try to break them up. It was starting to sound ugly. Even Janet had retreated from them.

Paula said, "I wonder what the Viceroy knows."

"Bentley's tried to reach him. He's not answering."

"Who told you that?"

"Michelle. Hal told Jim about it last night, on the way back. He said they even tried the French embassy. They said it's what he does. Likes to get away from it all sometimes."

"This is the kind of place most people would consider 'away from it all'."

"Yeah, well, maybe not always."

"And by that you mean…?"

"I don't know. Maybe he does know certain things. Maybe he doesn't."

"You think he set us up?"

"Why would he do that?"

She had no idea.

"Don't think too hard. I didn't see any sign they've been here in the last five hundred years. Either way, he can't help us or hurt us now. We're going to have to figure our own way out of this shit."

"You think you already have."

Trask felt like a six-year-old caught lying.

"Okay, yeah, I thought about it. But Bentley has it now, so that pretty much settles it."

"Trask, you don't know what would happen."

But he did. He was sure of it now. When he'd fought the big alien, after it killed Erika, he'd seen it. Another remote, just like this one. The thing had it on its wrist. And after Jim reloaded, he'd watched the thing closely. Just as he'd expected, right before it disappeared, it clashed its pincers together. Pressing the button.

The remotes were homing devices. With only the one button, nothing else made sense.

They took you back to GO.

Paula was waiting for an answer. It was obvious she didn't believe him, but it was the worry in her eyes that really made him uncomfortable. She was afraid for him.

"Listen, Paula, like I said, Bentley's got it now. What am I going to do, steal it back?"

"You still have the Viceroy's."

"It's broken, remember?" Trask said.

The sound of scuffling brought both of them around.

Across the room, Jeremy and Tony's arguing had developed into a shoving match. They separated, but the second they did, Jeremy threw a punch. Tony blocked it with ease—and instead of returning Jeremy's punch, he slapped him.

Jeremy went ballistic. Screaming, he threw himself at Tony again, but Brad caught him by the arms and held him back, and Jeremy only struggled for a second. You didn't struggle with Brad.

It was like a bad episode of déjà vu. This time, Lance got behind Tony and stood ready to grab him if he made a move. Janet stayed back, not wanting to take sides, and wringing her hands at all the trouble she'd caused.

"Motherfucker!" Jeremy hissed. "I stay behind to protect Janet and you come back all full of shit like the big fucking hero—"

"Hey, pal, I never said I was a hero. Just that I'm not a chickenshit."

"Whoa, easy, guys," Lance said. "Let's not do name calling. No heroes, no chickenshits, okay?"

Jeremy's face was dark red. "Let's just see who fucking makes it out of here alive, asshole." He was panting.

"Maybe you will," Tony said. "But not because of anything you'll ever do."

"Okay, Tony," Lance warned him.

Tony threw a glance over at Janet. She avoided his eyes. "You shouldn't lead Jeremy on like this, Janet," he said, "he's starting to get delusional."

"That's your department, shit-for-brains," Jeremy said.

Tony didn't say anything and it seemed like that was the end of it.

Brad let go of Jeremy and shook his head.

"Maybe the beer wasn't such a great idea."

"Yeah, some people can't hold their liquor," Tony agreed.

"That's enough, Tony," Lance said.

But Tony had to get in one last dig. As he turned away from Jeremy, he muttered, "Twerp."

"What did you say?" Jeremy shrieked—and before anyone could stop him, he reached over and grabbed the claw hammer Trask had left on the table.

Jim said, "Jeremy!" But Brad already had him again. And now Lance was holding Tony.

The two rivals stood glowering at each other.

Then Tony laughed.

"You sure you know how to use that?"

"Put it down," Jim said.

Carefully, Jeremy laid down the hammer.

"Goddamn," Brad said, as he and Lance released their captives.

With a snort of disgust, Tony turned to walk away.

Jeremy snatched up the claw hammer with both hands, took two quick steps toward Tony and buried it in the back of his skull.

It sounded like a cleaver crunching through spareribs. Blood splashed across Lance's cheek. Tony's knees buckled and hit the floor with a crack when he dropped straight down onto them. He tottered, then fell on his face. His hands twitched and scrabbled, clattering his knuckles against the floor, then with a final tremor went dead.

Along with the rest of him.

The hammer's handle stood straight up, quivering. Its head was still embedded in Tony's skull.

Everyone turned to stare in horror at Jeremy.

Jim had put him in a headlock.

"You son of a bitch," Jim breathed. "You just murdered a human being in cold blood."

"So what?" Jeremy said. With Jim's arm around his throat, his words came out strangled. "Why should I let someone talk to me that way when we'll all probably be dead tomorrow?"

Jim dragged him to a cot and threw him onto it.

"I can't answer that," he said. Then, over his shoulder, "Somebody get some rope."

Bentley and Barry stared, unable to believe what they'd just witnessed. Beside them, Grant shook his head at Jeremy, uncomprehending. "We beat them. They won't be back. By tomorrow they'll be gone. We'll all be free."

Jeremy snarled, "We'll be free all right, jerkoff. One way or the other. You'll see."

"If Grant's wrong," Jim said, "we're two men short because of you. You just might get your wish."

"I can still fight," Jeremy said.

Jim had already recovered from his uncharacteristic flash of anger.

"Not after this, Jeremy," he said.

Evans handed him a coil of dragline, and Jim tied Jeremy to his cot.

Jeremy didn't even bother to resist.

Snorlok and the twins stood before the transporter chamber door, their rough hides gleaming a dull maroon in the red light of the lower fourth quadrant. Ropsnag, acting as lookout, was out of sight around the corridor's curve, checking to see that Strindlak was still occupied in the engine room.

Nerves jangling, Snorlok growled under his breath, foretentacles poised over the control panel in anticipation of Ropsnag's signal.

And here he came—whickering his tentacles as he rounded the bend.

All clear! Snorlok stabbed the control panel.

An angry beep startled him and the twins half out of their wits.

The door didn't budge.

Snorlok's gill flaps fluttered in confusion. Ropsnag approached. Snorlok glanced at him, then back at the panel as a message flashed across the display:

ENTER ACCESS CODE

Snorlok goggled at it.

Strindlak had locked the door!

He didn't trust them!

He stood immobilized by shock and uncertainty, shaking his head in numb despair. With little hope of success, he keyed in the ship's universal override sequence. The panel responded with the same angry beep and the message:

ENTRY DENIED

Failure. With a sinking feeling, Snorlok led the way in silence to the shaft.

Back in their quarters, Ropsnag and the twins sat on the edges of their sleeping pods while Snorlok paced back and forth before them like a caged animal. His siblings stole glances at him when his back was turned—fearful of the desperate turn his thoughts were evidently taking.

He at last stopped pacing and set his powerful jaw.

There was one other option.

His siblings knew what was coming. The transporter wasn't the only way out of the ship. They'd have to retrieve Zillior in person.

The door chimed. Snorlok bit his tongue and shushed the others as it slid open.

Strindlak had come.

The twins quailed and fell to their knees, groveling. Even Ropsnag flinched when their father stepped into the room.

With a bark, Strindlak ordered the twins to their feet. After fixing them all with a stern gaze for several long and uncomfortable moments, he cleared his throat and announced mildly that their punishment would be deferred until such time as they'd returned home.

Still too frightened to betray any sign of relief at the news, the siblings remained silent and attentive.

Strindlak continued.

He required assistance with the finalization of repairs. A simple matter of monitoring the progress of the programming update and following instructions at the prompts. Snorlok would take over these duties while Strindlak took some much-needed rest.

Concealing his chagrin as best he could, Snorlok bowed to his father's wishes. With a backward glance that reflected the dismay on his siblings' faces, he turned and followed Strindlak out into the corridor.

The door slid shut behind them.

At any party, people will begin to drift away once the beer runs out and the revelers start murdering each other. Knowing Hal, Grant guessed he'd be in the control room reviewing the day's footage. He got up and quietly let himself out, entered the bungalow through the back door and walked up the short hall to control room.

As he'd guessed, Hal was there.

Grant pulled up a chair. "There's been an incident."

Onscreen, they'd dispatched the first creature, and were gathering up the remains. It would be several minutes before the second appeared.

Hal nodded without taking his eyes off the screen. "Fred told me."

They watched a while longer. Grant sighed. "People are losing it."

Hal nodded again.

"I guess it helps to have something to do," Grant said.

"I don't even want to think about it," Hal agreed. "Have to get all this ready for the network anyway."

"I didn't know we were still editing," Grant said. "Thought we just bundled it off uncut."

"We do."

"God damn!" Grant said. The big thing had just appeared. He had to look away when it grabbed Heather and Fredo. It was different seeing it in playback. When you were there, in the middle of it, you were somehow immunized emotionally to what was happening. He supposed it was adrenaline. You'd never be able to act otherwise.

"I mean, we're supposed to," Hal corrected himself. "Rob promised the military raw footage. But I can't help it. I see something I don't like, I just can't let it go."

"You mean when it's too—shit!" Roger had just blown a gaping hole in the thing's chest.

"No," Hal said. "I mean, when it's not up to standard. Professional vanity, I guess."

"Oh." Grant was watching for the moment when the thing struck him down. It was coming. It had happened right after it got Roger.

"God!" The huge jaws clamped down on Roger's head and Grant looked away again. When he looked back he could see himself standing a little ways off in the background—almost, but not quite out of frame.

Any second now.

He saw himself stagger backwards. The monster wasn't anywhere near him. It wasn't even looking at him. It was facing the camera.

As Grant watched, mortified, he swooned and fell on his back into a clump of ferns. He'd fainted.

He felt his face burning.

"Shit!" Hal said, without looking around.

Grant's voice was tiny. "What?"

"Focus. Dammit."

"What do you mean?"

Hal rolled back. "Gotta fix it."

"Where?"

"Right after Roger. My hand must've slipped or something." He hit playback a few seconds before Grant fainted.

"See?"

Grant didn't say anything.

"There!—now it comes back in. Just a couple of seconds. See it?"

Hal turned around in his chair to look at him, and there was something strange in his expression. Grant kept his own carefully blank to hide his confusion. Hal had never lied to him, that he knew of.

"Okay, we're good. Nothing happening here anyway," Hal said. "Watch."

Grant held his breath and watched closely. Using the mouse, Hal selected start and end points for the edit. All the frames in between turned magenta.

"Say goodbye," Hal said. He pressed the keyboard's delete key.

The frames vanished.

Hal turned to Grant and winked. "All gone."

Grant was recovering. "Wow. But—I didn't really see anything wrong with it."

"Well, you're not a cinematographer, Grant. When your reputation's on the line, you notice things."

Hal hit the play button. The whole sequence was a lot shorter than it had felt when you were living through it. The cavalry arrived, and they watched as Jim plugged away at the thing.

Grant had to work hard not to feel some kind of admiration for Trask, watching him fight the monster. He hated him even more for it, and was glad to see that after Trask broke off he never appeared again on camera.

"Rest looks fine," Hal said.

The door opened and Barry popped his head in.

"How's it look?"

"Great," Hal said. "How's Rob?"

"Out cold."

Hal had gotten in the habit of sleeping in the control room. "I could use a short one myself," he said. "What time is it?"

"It's only seven-thirty. Hey, Hal, use my bunk. I'll be up another few hours."

"Okay, Barry, thanks. I'll have Chuck lock video and make the transfer."

Barry closed the door.

"I was hoping to take a look at last night's thing," Grant said. "The meeting."

"Be my guest." Hal got up. "Do me a favor, wake me up at nine. That'll give me time to set up the Viceroy's transmitter for the ten o'clock send."

"Will do."

"Just whatever you do don't touch the red button. That's the record button."

"I know what the red button is."

"Nine o'clock," Hal reminded him.

"You got it."

The door closed. Grant moved to the console and rolled back to Fred's "council of war" footage from the previous night. Watching playback, he nodded in approval. It was good stuff. Lot of heart.

Until Trask showed up and tried to sabotage the whole operation before it had even started.

By the time Trask got to his little speech about him being nothing but a "fucking game show host" Grant was scowling.

And then, right near the end—where Trask said, "Yeah Grant, I am scared—but I'm mad too,"—Grant suddenly had an idea. He checked the rest of the footage. Just as he'd remembered it, Trask dominated the entire discussion.

Grant had paid close attention to Hal's editing. He inserted his start point right after Trask said he was scared and deleted everything from there out.

Now he quickly located the spot where Trask made his onscreen appearance to fight the monster. Start point, a second earlier. Next, he rolled ahead to just past the spot where Trask broke off. End point. The frames turned magenta.

He hit the delete key.

No more Trask.

CHAPTER TWENTY-SEVEN

RELOCATING

STRINDLAK AWAKENED much refreshed. On his way to the engine room to relieve Snorlok, he stopped by the nursery to inform Glumrok that he expected to soon have news that would gladden her heart. Cheered by her quiet enthusiasm, he continued on to the engine room.

The computer's gabbling masked the sound of the door opening. Snorlok sat hunched over the console. Strindlak stepped up behind him to watch. Though not yet completed, it appeared the task was being performed with adequate diligence. He *hmmmed* in an unconscious expression of satisfaction. The sound gave Snorlok a bad start. He spun around in his chair, his expression upon seeing his father filled with apprehension. He was clearly fearful with regard to his forthcoming punishment—as well he should be.

Strindlak had already decided upon lenience. Taking into account the halflings' disappointment with their vacation's curtailment, it seemed a reasonable course.

But let them suffer a bit longer. They'd punish themselves in their own overactive imaginations with far more stringency than he'd contemplated.

Voicing grudging approval, Strindlak released the halfling from his bondage.

Barely able to restrain himself, with a muttered expression of gratitude Snorlok leapt up and bolted for the door. As it closed behind him, he lowered his head and loped away down the corridor, leaving Strindlak to gaze after him shaking his head in displeasure.

Bentley stopped scraping and took his little finger out of his ear.

Someone had once told him women looked at their fingernails by holding their hand palm down and straightening their fingers, nails up.

Men did the opposite, turning their hand upside down, palm up, fingers curled over. Well it was obvious, wasn't it? Women were just checking the condition of their nail polish, while men wanted to see what sort of substance had accumulated beneath their nails from whatever they'd been scratching. His had captured a few flakes of dead skin, mixed up with a yellowish crust. He'd had an outer ear infection for almost as long as the athlete's foot, and it continually drained pus that collected at the bottom of his ear and dried into a crystalline matter that irritated his skin.

He stopped pacing. Would the hot sand that had cured his athlete's foot do the same for his ears? And what side effects could result from filling your ears with hot sand? Probably not a good idea. Something bad. It sounded like some kind of medieval torture. Like being locked in a small cell and having rats gnaw at your extremities, until you slowly bled to death.

Kind of like what this island had become.

Bentley shoved the thought out of his mind. He'd seen men driving beside him on the freeway, actually sniffing their nails. God knows what they'd been scratching.

It had become extremely difficult to maintain focus. At times, he felt it was all a dream—sometimes so strongly that he wanted to treat the events that comprised the dream with a reckless contempt, prove to it that he knew it was a dream, so that it would give in and let him wake up.

Bentley thanked God he wasn't religious. If he had been, he would have cracked under the enormity of the challenge to his cherished beliefs, if he'd had them, that events on this earthly plane were guided by a benevolent hand.

His lack of any particular set of beliefs had kept him sane.

If he was.

Sometimes—a lot, lately—he wondered. He'd once heard that wondering if you were losing your mind was one of the major signs that you were indeed losing your mind. It was like one of those conundrums, though, like that Star Trek episode—from the original series, not that Star Trek Generation rubbish—where Spock said "I'm lying to you."

"I'm losing my mind." But if it's true, who am I to say so? It was one of the later signs, too, not one of the early ones that just signaled the onset.

Star Trek! What a wonderful show—terrific premise; fascinating, unforgettable characters; superb writers.

Bentley had a superb writer and some unforgettable characters of his own. And the premise was nothing short of spectacular: A production crew shooting a reality show on a deserted island suddenly find themselves and their cast sealed off from the rest of the world. One by one, they're stalked and killed, horribly, by monsters from another world, for their own unfathomable reasons. We'd probably learn those reasons in the end, in the dénouement following the climax, which hadn't been scripted yet, but Bentley had absolute confidence that when it was, it would be terrific.

He sat down on the bed, stuck his other little fingernail under the yellow flakes beneath the first, and flicked them to the floor. Wiping off whatever residue remained on the blanket as he climbed under it, he pulled it up—reaching out to turn off the bedside lamp before tucking it snugly under his chin.

Strindlak stared at the new message, uncomprehending.

PLASMA CORE REPLENISHED TO FULL CAPACITY

Was he reading it correctly? He'd expected some sort of countdown, or at least a progress report notifying him of the impending achievement of full refresh. The completion of the repairs process—if that was indeed what this signified—had come with such an absence of fanfare as to seem anticlimactic.

He read it again. Replenished. Could there be any mistaking its meaning?

Full capacity...

The screen dissolved to a readout consisting of a single pair of horizontal status bars. The top, labeled "PRIMARY SYSTEMS", was green, but that was to be expected.

They were all still alive, after all.

The bottom, "SECONDARY SYSTEMS", was at the moment a long and empty rectangular outline, with the word "Powering" blinking beneath it. But now, as Strindlak watched, a red bar crept from left to right until it had extended a third of the way across and turned orange. Accelerating, it stretched across another third. Now yellow, it sped toward the finish and flicked to green.

A cheerful ping sounded from somewhere overhead.

The word "Powering" was replaced by, "Secondary Systems Restored To Full Standby."

The status bars vanished.

A new legend appeared in bold letters:

CONGRATULATIONS, STRINDLAK GRATCHNORR!
YOUR FLARDNUX 12000 IS NOW SPACE/TIMEWORTHY

Strindlak blinked. There was nothing ambiguous about that! He bared his teeth in a wide-spreading grin and turned to behold the gigantic engine at his back.

Unable to contain himself, he rolled his tentacles into huge fists and leapt from his stool to shout with abandon and pummel the air with blows.

His triumphant roars rattled the walls of the cavernous engine room.

He'd done it!

The ship was fully repaired. One hundred percent operational.

They could leave this accursed place at last!

Paula came awake with a start. She stiffened, motionless and alert, eyes straining to pierce the room's dark corners. Rumbling echoes trailed off in the distance.

It was only thunder.

She lay beneath a boarded up window on a mattress damp with perspiration. She could smell the sleeping punters around her. Dirt and sweat, mixed with a hint of rotting vegetation. There was something else, too, less familiar, but still unmistakable. The sickly-sweet odor of putrefying flesh. She remembered the thing Grant had killed, and shivered. It was here. In the kitchen. It was the creature she smelled.

Her eyes were growing accustomed to the dark. Nearby, someone whimpered in their sleep—a high-pitched, childish pleading. Janet, lying on a bunk to Paula's left. Paula could make out other dark forms around her now, huddled close-packed like doomed poultry in the stillness.

Lightning flashed outside, rimming the gaps around the boarded-up windows with white. The thunderclap's bang rattled the bunk springs under Paula's back.

Trask had taken the spot between her and the window, sharing her bunk. He'd fallen asleep within minutes, with the back of his hand lightly touching her side. She didn't feel his hand now, and missed its touch. Her fingers fumbled over the damp mattress.

There was no one there.

With a clutching feeling in her chest she glanced over just as another lightning bolt threw a series of slender vertical rays sliding over the wall and across her bunk. The space next to her was empty.

She sat up, throwing off the blankets.

Stepping over sleeping figures spread across the floor, she crept toward the hatch.

Paula didn't think of herself as a fighter. She was one of the few who wasn't armed. Finding a long insulated screwdriver among the tools lying scattered about, she stuck it in her back pocket. She could use it like an ice pick if she needed to.

Standing on the sandy patch between the deserted cast quarters and the edge of the jungle, looking up at the sky, Trask sensed Paula's presence even with his back to her.

She took his hand, and they stood there for a long time, watching the fireworks.

"It's beautiful," she said, so softly he almost didn't hear her.

He nodded, staring upward in wonder. As they watched, a bolt of lightning pierced the invisible barrier, far overhead. At the point of contact, trembling fingers of blue radiated outward in a sunburst pattern over the surface of the dome. The lightning bolt passed through. It forked across the treetops to sink fiery tines into the dark earth at their hidden trunks. Above, the crackling sunburst spread over the electrified face of the barrier in rippling haloes of sparks. They twinkled like low-hanging stars, and blinked out.

Farther overhead, rain clouds rolled across the sky. Distant bursts of sheet lightning lit their undersides, and reflected down through curtains of rain that spilled over the face of the dome in waves, to cascade in out-ward-curving falls down to the sea.

And through it all ran the sound of raindrops on the rooftop high over-head.

Paula gave Trask's hand a squeeze.

"Come back to bed, Trask."

Trask suddenly felt like they'd been standing there together like this for a thousand lifetimes. It was such an ordinary, everyday thing to say, but the simple phrase, and the sound of her voice, filled him with a deep yearning he'd never imagined he could feel.

He'd probably never hear those words again.

"Don't drive yourself crazy wondering," she said.

He couldn't help smiling at that. He raised his left hand, with the re-mote attached to his wrist. It just adhered there, with nothing visible hold-ing it in place.

The red button glowed.

"It came on a half hour ago."

"You switched them," she said.

Trask nodded. Her hand was on his arm.

"Don't go, Trask."

"I can beat them."

"You don't know that. You don't even know how it works."

His muscles tensed under her grip. "Neither do they. They're amateurs."

"Trask. As a last resort. Not now."

"There's no way of knowing, Paula. Our last chance could come any-time. Before we knew it."

They were still holding hands. A few seconds passed in silence before she said, "I'm coming with you."

He laughed quietly, but shook his head.

"There's only one," he reminded her.

She didn't say anything for a long time after that, and Trask watched the play of emotions in her eyes as she struggled inwardly against stub-born reality. Fear, dread, followed by a sinking hopelessness. A flash of anger. Acceptance. And finally, hard determination.

"In case this is goodbye…" She put her hands around his waist, and said, "It's been nice knowing you, Trask."

"You too, Paula."

He put his arms around her, crossing them behind her back, hands on her shoulders, and drew her close. Her left hand came up to caress his cheek. She brushed his hair away from his face and kissed him.

"Goodbye, Trask." She kissed him again.

Her eyes were closed, her lips still pressed against his, when her hand strayed from his face, to reach back over her left shoulder, and before Trask realized what she was doing, she'd grabbed his wrist.

She jammed a finger down hard on the button.

Strindlak made his entrance from the vestibule through the grand portal, as befitted the auspiciousness of the occasion, and as was preferred by Glumrok in any event. He found her, ascendant upon her throne, gazing out over her chittering brood with a maternal attentiveness that sent a warm glow coursing through Strindlak's veins.

Sensing glad tidings, Glumrok rose slowly and with the greatest dignity to face her mate. They stood for a moment, gazing one upon the other. Then, all in a rush, Strindlak gave her the news. She listened patiently to his tale, beginning with initial advances and disappointments—glossing over certain details with respect to the latter—proceeding through his gradual mastery over the machine, and culminating at last in the day's triumphant success. She didn't interrupt even once to scold him or change the subject at the climactic moment as was her habit, disrupting his train of thought and leaving him flustered. And when Strindlak, his voice rising with emotion, declared the ship space/timeworthy and prepared to resume their voyage at Glumrok's earliest convenience, she whickered her tentacles in delight.

There was, of course, one other bit of business glossed over—in fact, left out altogether—relating to the clandestine activities of certain halflings. In the interests of familial harmony, Strindlak had deemed it expedient to shield the deceitful ones for now from their mother's disapproval.

Glumrok stepped down from the dais to embrace Strindlak and sent him away, after first making him promise to allow her the pleasure of bringing the joyful news herself to her beloved Zillior.

Strindlak inclined his great head, then turned and strode through the grand portal and out into the corridor, burbling happily to himself, as Glumrok busied herself with preparations for immediate departure.

Trask's vision clouded over in a shimmering aurora.

A final flickering lightning bolt fractured into slender filaments to race through the visible spectrum. A cold like the space between the stars wrapped him in icy coils and whipped away. His whirling body seemed to elongate. The rainbow filaments spiraled away beneath him. His feet, then his legs stretched like twisting strands of silly putty, and the rest of his body followed, spinning as he was pulled through a soundless void.

A light gust of warm air rustled the hairs on the back of his neck and he realized he was no longer falling, and that Paula's cheek was still pressed against the side of his face.

"You probably shouldn't have done that," he said.

"You're probably right."

"Are your eyes open or closed?"

"I'm not sure. Closed I think."

"We'll open them together. Okay?"

"Okay."

"Ready?" Trask felt Paula stiffen.

"Now," he said, and opened his eyes. Their jaws dropped simultaneously.

It was like the glitzy set of a television game show, all flashing lights and sleek hardware. And he and Paula stood at the control console on the railed-in contestants' podium, poised to answer the next multiple-choice question with a lightning fast press of a button.

The console was mounted at eye level on a cylindrical pedestal of dark metal—too high to allow easy access to the controls.

It was designed for someone taller.

A center panel held a rectangular screen remarkably like a standard LCD display. It glowed emerald, but aside from that it was blank.

Trask studied the controls, but soon gave it up as pointless and looked out over the top of the console into the chamber beyond.

The huge room was roughly triangular, with the platform on which they stood near its curved base. Vertical bands set into the walls at regular intervals emitted a soft fluorescence. The chamber itself was bathed in a muted blue light from an unseen source.

Even the walls were blanketed with instrument panels, and as he watched, the panel lights began to wink on in what looked like a powering-up sequence—flowing over the walls until the whole chamber twinkled with shifting patterns of stars in ruby, sapphire and gold.

They must have activated the transporter by beaming aboard.

It was aware of their presence.

At the center of the room, glowing like a dying sun, was an enormous hemisphere, featureless save for its own inner luminance. Only the top was visible above the collar of its circular base, but it must have been ten feet across.

Paula tugged at his sleeve.

On a shelf beneath the console rested six remotes just like the one on Trask's wrist.

"Seven," Paula whispered, looking at him.

He nodded. They turned toward the back of the chamber.

Behind the platform stood a semicircular array of tall enclosures. Near the floor, bundles of multicolored wires and flexible tubes connected to junctions at the foot of each tower. Others sprouted from wall jacks on all sides, to rise in convergent paths overhead. Paula and Trask looked up.

Far overhead, beneath a small dome set into the vaulted ceiling, a convex disc of some translucent material hovered, suspended by oiled metal rods that disappeared into shafts around the cupola's center. Delicate goosenecks ending in bulbous knobs dangled from the disc's curled edges. It was here that the multitude of tubes and cables merged—looping in thick, knotted clusters over the top of the disc into a jumble of lugs and connectors that studded its surface, trailing down and outward from them like ribbons around a maypole.

Head tilted back to stare upward, Paula clutched at the side of the console to steady herself.

There was a click as some mechanism engaged.

A light flashed. With a pneumatic whir, the console began to descend.

"What did you do?"

"I don't know," she whispered in alarm. "I grabbed the edge."

There were no buttons or other controls there. It had somehow responded to her touch.

The console stopped at a level just below their waists. Paula slumped in relief.

"It adjusts to the size of whoever's using it," Trask said. He shook his head, marveling, then went back to examining the controls. Now that the console was at a manageable height, he saw right off what he'd missed before.

"I don't believe it."

Right there in the middle of the central panel, below the LCD display. There was no mistaking it.

"It's a fucking rollerball."

Glumrok stepped up onto the dais and took her seat once again upon the throne, feeling well contented. The interminable waiting was over.

She raised the swivel arm mounted to the throne's side and punched in a command on the built-in instrument panel's keypad.

From the far end of the nursery came a deep thrumming as a chamber-wide horizontal panel glided forward. Transparent and flawless as the finest crystal, it slid over the bobbing field of hatchlings in tracks jutting from the chamber walls. Anxious infants turned inquisitive gazes upward to follow its approach and duck under its low ceiling. It rumbled right up to the foot of the dais and wedged smoothly under its front edge—sealing the chattering hatchlings in a vast airtight compartment.

At regular intervals beneath the glassy shield, hinged caps swung upward. Slender, tapered nozzles snaked out. Hidden valves opened with a rushing whump, and keening hatchlings scurried out of the way as the nozzles sprayed concentrated jets of white liquid. Fragile bodies caught in the crossfire were dismembered by the force of the spray. Those that survived the initial blast surged to and fro in a straining mass, then flattened themselves, cowering and nickering pitiably, against the floor.

Glumrok watched their struggles with an indulgent smile.

On contact with the air, the cold liquid converted to billowing gaseous clouds.

The compartment misted over, and the hatchlings began to freeze.

CHAPTER TWENTY-EIGHT

TRACKING

TRASK SWIVELED THE ROLLERBALL between his thumb and fingers.

Nothing happened.

There was no question he was right. What else could it be? Okay, so nothing had happened. But then, what did he expect? The LCD display was blank, there was no—

The display flickered. A series of regularly spaced, indecipherable squiggles appeared. Text.

As they watched, it scrolled up to disappear offscreen. It was replaced, with a crappy animated flourish, by something that could only be a corporate logo.

It was parallel evolution to a degree that was at once awesome in its immensity, and shocking in its paltriness. The entire universe, reduced to utter, prosaic triviality. It was beyond depressing. It was like everything *out there*—the stuff you thought of as being way beyond the crass concerns and stupid machinations of people—of humanity—was after all just more of the same.

But then, wasn't that what everyone had always suspected and feared? And now, the central, immutable, guiding principle of all existence: *Branding.*

The logo broke apart into spinning jagged shards that twirled brightly offscreen in all directions, leaving it an emerald green void as before.

"Trask."

Paula pointed. Out on the floor, the big sphere was waking up.

A hint of liquid motion rippled its surface, deepened to a delicate churning of vaporous clouds. They filled with swimming motes, then dissipated to a soft haze, suffusing the globe's interior with a pale light.

And like a crystal ball, it cleared.

The scene within wavered and blurred, but Trask recognized it the second it appeared—from having seen it on television only hours before. It was the dale below the hilltop, where Grant's ambush party had killed the thing. The image was about one-quarter life-size, giving it an apparent diameter of about forty feet. The ground bisected the sphere at the exact center. Beneath was impenetrable blackness.

It was night outside in the real world, Trask suddenly remembered. But here, in the globe, it was daylight. The device was adjusting automatically to the light level. A little toward the blue end of the spectrum, maybe. Other than that it had the look of a normal daytime scene.

At the far edge of the sphere, a stand of trees was visible. There was no fading away into the distance. The image simply cut off at the sphere's boundaries, and where it wasn't intersected by trees or other obstructions, the far side of the chamber showed through its now transparent surface.

With a sizzling pop, the image steadied, the mist was whisked away and the scene snapped into sharp focus—to the simultaneous accompaniment of a musical chime from somewhere overhead.

In the same instant, a light flashed below the LCD display, drawing Trask's attention back to the console.

The rollerball's rim had lit up.

Trask gave Paula's hand a light squeeze, and let go. They looked down through the tops of the trees.

He laid his index finger on the ball.

The trees jerked sideways. Then back again, a little beyond their original position—responding just as expected to Trask's first tentative movements.

He gave the ball a short, controlled spin. With dizzying speed, the image shifted then settled on a new scene.

Somewhere in the jungle. Here, dense foliage covered the sphere's surface, blocking their view except for small openings here and there between the leaves.

The image whirled and stopped again, a short distance further on.

Trask experimented, becoming acquainted with the device. Not much different from what he'd used a million times before. A simple ball in a socket. You moved in whichever direction you pushed the ball, and the further you pushed it, the faster you went.

"What do you say we take this baby for a little spin?" Trask said.

"Ride 'em, cowboy," Paula replied.

Strindlak gave the panel a jaunty slap. The door slid open and he gazed inside.

Along the far wall, four sleeping pods were arranged side-by-side. Electronic conveniences and assorted childish paraphernalia lay scattered across the floor. Strindlak rarely entered the halflings' quarters, and when he did, he rarely made it back out again unscathed. But he didn't need to enter to see there was no one at home.

His brows undulated in bemusement. After forestalling their fledgling attempts at mischief, Strindlak had assumed he'd find the youngsters in their quarters, idling away the dull hours of waiting by occupying themselves in the imaginative manner of youth, with whatever resources they had at their disposal. He had to admit there weren't many. He supposed he should have expected they might go looking for more adventurous forms of amusement. It probably wasn't fair to place too much blame on them.

But where were they?

He stood at the door, uncertain. He hadn't specifically ordered them to remain in their quarters. He shook his head at the realization he'd been over-tolerant of their curiosity, trusting they'd stay out of mischief and wouldn't harm themselves—though any harm they could bring on themselves would have to be pretty horrific to be irreparable. His kind were a hardy lot. The survival rate for halflings was greater than thirty-five percent—and if they survived to attain to their third mutation, after that it was even better, something like forty or fifty.

Strindlak considered going out into the corridor and calling out to them, but in all honesty he was a little hazy on their names. Glumrok was much better at such things. Of course he was certain of Glumrok's pet, Zillior, and the eldest, upon whom it was his habit to call when in need of assistance. Snorlok had reached that part of his development during which it was wisest to keep him occupied. The third mutation was proverbially a troublesome stage.

But there was no point roaming the ship shouting. The ship was large, and the corridors' dampening material prevented sound from traveling far.

If he'd thought ahead, he might have locked more than just the transporter chamber. But no matter. He'd find them soon enough.

Snorlok drove his siblings before him with snarled threats and lashing tentacles. The stinging blows served to spur them onward while distracting them from their own fear.

And well did they fear. The sky itself had gone mad. Roaring in fury, it spat great bolts of electromagnetic energy like javelins hurled from on high by howling demons. If not for the protective barrier overhead, they'd have been pierced in a thousand places by the swarms of projectiles battering the dome from above.

Yet still it was impossible, even under the living sky's awful clamor, not to be overawed by the strangeness of the alien landscape hemming them in on all sides. Transporting outside the ship as utility drones and experiencing this world filtered through their altered senses was one thing. Seeing it with one's own eyes, with the pungent mixture of gases that made up the planet's atmosphere circulating through one's veins, was another.

Snorlok himself had been outside in the flesh only once before. The experience had left him shaken. The overabundance of strange life forms was both staggering and terrifying. Giant, gnarled and weather-beaten organisms in a wild extravagance of varieties towered over them like vengeful shadows. From thick shafts clothed in tough hides, twisting tentacles branched out in all directions, and these separated still further into countless others in endless series of fractals. Minute tips lined every complex set, sprouting an inexhaustible profusion of blade-shaped platelets, all a startling green in color.

The spongy terrain exuded a heavy, penetrating clamminess and the very ground itself slithered and churned under their pods. Around their heads, tiny mobile forms buzzed continuously, so small they hadn't even registered in the imager.

Flogging his siblings without mercy, Snorlok drove them down the mountainside at a reckless pace, making for the soft land below the foothills of the lesser peak.

He knew from previous adventures that at some point they would emerge from the relentless crush of overhanging foliage upon the bare strip of ground at the edge of the sea. And that on that strip of ground huddled an assortment of small huts.

In one of these they would find their Zillior.

Trask was soon tracking through the jungle like a pro. It was exhilarating feeling the twirling rollerball beneath his fingers again. The old familiar rush was back—the jittery euphoria of all his senses on hyperalert. Every nerve and sinew keying up for the coming confrontation.

Jungle undergrowth blurred past, visible for fleeting instants through breaks in the foliage blanketing the globe's surface.

Four short beeps broke the silence. Paula grabbed his arm, startling him. "What was that? Oh, God."

"What, what?" He let go of the rollerball. It snapped back to the stationary position. The scene in the sphere jerked to a stop.

"Something moving. Between the trees. Go back."

She'd seen something all right, judging by the way her fingers were digging into his arm, but he'd been going pretty fast and left the spot far behind in the second it took him to react to her alarm. He backtracked, but there were no reference points. He was flying blind.

"Was it here?"

"I don't know. I don't recognize anything."

"What was it?"

"I don't know."

Her grip on his arm relaxed a little. It was probably nothing. He circled the area, but the search quickly lost steam. He was about to give up when another beep sounded, and he saw it.

He let up on the rollerball, reversed and eased backwards step by step. There!

A darting movement in the underbrush. Then the trees opened up, and through the gap they saw it—a low, ungainly shape trundling over the jungle floor.

A pig.

"It's him. It's the same one," Trask said, sure of himself. "Good eye, Paula." He glanced over at her with a reassuring smile, but she was still frowning into the sphere.

"Well, if it was something else, it's long gone by now."

She nodded distractedly. "Let's keep going," she said.

Trask rolled, and they were soon plowing through the jungle again at breakneck speed.

"So it beeps when something's moving. Interesting," he said, relishing the new discovery. It was pretty thrilling, barreling along at high speed through uncharted territory, and he began to recapture some of his earlier excitement. But at the same time, the lack of control was frustrating. He was accustomed to having a high level of expertise at this stuff, and he sure needed it now. They all needed it. He was going to have to know his shit if he was going to beat these things.

He backed off on the acceleration and scanned the controls again.

"What is it?" Paula asked. "Is everything okay?"

"Yeah, it's just—there's a lot I wish I could figure out." He increased his speed back up to full throttle. There was nothing to do but forge ahead. He'd find them soon enough.

But would he? The irony of his situation wasn't lost on him. He was an intruder on their own ship—which would also be the most likely place to hunt for them. But even though he was on it, he had no idea where the ship was! And with his limited grasp of the transporter's operation, he could only cover the island one forty-foot section at a time. What were the odds of finding anything?

It was time for a plan.

"I'm going to find the beach. Try to get my bearings."

You couldn't see where you were going anyway, and for this Trask didn't need to. As long as he traveled in a straight line, he'd reach the ocean. Then he could just coast along the beach until they found the camp.

"I mean, for example, there must be a way to change your point of view."

Scenery flew past. "It would normally be a keyboard thing." But there was no keyboard, and even if there had been, he couldn't just clatter away at random. Anything could happen.

The rollerball was floored. At full acceleration, the image in the sphere was just a horizontal blur of green and brown streaks tinged with red.

"You should be able to get an aerial perspective," he explained. "Or pull back. It's like we're looking through a camera lens at full zoom."

They broke from the trees so fast he overshot the beach and they were sailing over black, moonlit waves before he even had time to react.

Trask heard Paula's gasp at the sudden shock of being out in the open. It was so real. Like a 3D movie, where you duck every time something rips past.

He didn't even bother to return to shore. He veered hard around and sailed over the low waves, hugging the beach. Another problem: He couldn't look in one direction while traveling in another. The more advanced games could do that. This thing should be able to. On the other hand, maybe not. He kept forgetting, the trackball and sphere were mainly just a locating device.

He hadn't even begun to play yet.

His pulse quickened. Maybe it was time to quit fooling around and put the transporter to the test. He still had to figure that part out before he'd be ready to fight.

"Trask. I just thought of something."

He looked over at her. Her eyes were wide with hope. He stared at her, feeling dense.

"Maybe we can go outside the barrier."

It took a few seconds for him to grasp what she was saying. It hadn't occurred to him, but it made sense.

Now he was the one frowning.

"It can get us out of here," Paula said. "To one of the ships."

Trask balked bigtime.

"It might not work." He thought fast. "And even if we can navigate to the outside, it doesn't mean we can beam there. Doubtful."

"But we have to try," she insisted.

Trask rubbed his jaw between thumb and fingers, then stopped with his hand over his mouth.

"Trask." She said it sharply. "There are seven remotes. One of us can beam with them to the camp and bring in six at a time until they're all here. More if they do it in pairs like we did. And then beam everyone out to one of those ships."

"That could take a while," Trask said.

It sounded lame and he knew it.

"We have to try," she repeated.

She was starting to get annoyed at his reluctance. And what could he say? He couldn't think of a single argument that sounded convincing even to him. And this was no time to get into a big confrontation with Paula anyway. That was all they needed. A shouting match to wake up all the fucking morlocks and bring them running.

He'd have to go along with her. For now.

He shrugged. "Okay, why not? Let's at least try it."

He'd kept his finger on the ball the whole time. He rolled parallel to the shore, then swerved and accelerated.

They headed out to sea.

Beside him, he felt Paula relax. While he tried to concentrate on navigating, another part of his mind chewed on this new dilemma.

CHAPTER TWENTY-NINE

PASSAGES

THE OCEAN SAT IN THE BOWL of the sphere like the black sludge filled with glittering flakes of metal in a mechanic's oil pan. There was no horizon—as always, the image simply ended at the sphere's perimeter. Trask skimmed the dark surface, heading out to sea. He wondered if he'd recognize the barrier when they came to it. It was pretty hard to see anyway. Except when it was raining. And it was raining now, come to think of it.

And just as he did, something passed by, or they passed through. It engulfed them for an instant, like barreling down the highway and suddenly hitting a patch of fog. Blinded for a split second, and then the next thing you knew you'd plunged through.

And it was raining.

He braked and went into a curve, swinging around to face back toward the island.

When he did, instead of seeing the other end of the room beyond the far side of the sphere, he seemed to see within it an endless expanse of ocean. And there was no island.

For a second, Trask couldn't figure it out. Then it hit him. They were facing the barrier. Looking straight at it.

It rose up out of the ocean, smooth as glass, cutting right through the center of the sphere. Its mirrorlike surface reflected everything outside—the stars, the water, even the moon—so that at first it looked like there was nothing there. But there was no mistaking it. The white crests of the waves lapped up against its base, washing over their own reflections, and everywhere the water sparkled with countless tiny ripples.

Raindrops falling to the sea.

They'd made it through.

"Trask," Paula said in wonder. "It worked."

"Yeah." Trask felt a chill in spite of himself. "Still—we don't know if we can actually transport there."

"We can. It wouldn't let us go there if we couldn't."

She was probably right.

"We better make sure." He cracked his knuckles. It was an unconscious habit he'd gotten over a long time ago. "I'm beaming out."

"To the middle of the ocean?"

"I can swim. The sea looks pretty calm. And I have the remote." He smiled at her. Maybe it *was* better this way. Just get out of here and have it all be over.

"Why don't we find a ship?" she said. "They must be all around us."

Somewhere in Trask's mind, alarms sounded. Of course they'd eventually have to beam out to a ship. There was no real alternative.

He rotated the image until they were looking down the barrier's length. Even with their view cropped by the sphere's perimeter, the barrier's mirror finish gave them a workaround. If they wanted to find a ship, all they had to do was follow the barrier's circumference. If there was one anywhere in the neighborhood, they'd see its reflection.

But he still had a bad feeling about blundering unannounced aboard some random assault ship.

He shook his head. "Let's not get the military involved for now, okay? Not yet."

She looked at him for a long time before agreeing. "Okay, so let's do it," she said.

He let his relief show. But he still hesitated.

"Umm, okay—but. There is one other problem. I don't actually know how."

She stared at him with her mouth open. She must have forgotten that too.

"Sorry, Trask."

"No problem."

"Can you figure it out?"

"Of course."

Rashad opened his eyes, a tingling sensation crawling up his spine. He couldn't tell if he was awake—some unseen force held him in an iron grip, pinning him to the hard mattress. He couldn't move anything except for his eyes.

His gaze swept over the walls.

Around him, bone-weary punters slept fitfully through the continuous crackling boom of rainless thunder. Lightning strobed, outlining gaps around the boarded-up windows and flickering over the sleeping forms.

No one had expected the hastily-constructed barricades to fit together seamlessly. They weren't cabinetmakers. But it came as something of a shock to Rashad to see all the glaring cracks and holes exposed with every flash of lightning.

His feeling of dread deepened.

Another lightning bolt arced overhead, and in the brief instant before darkness returned, Rashad saw something moving along the top edge of a window. A tightening sense of impending horror washed over him. He willed himself to move, but couldn't even turn his head. He heard a brittle crunch and then a crash of thunder rattled the windowpanes, not quite drowning out another, softer crash.

An instant later a barrage of chain lightning flared across the gaps between boards like a rotating emergency beacon. Projected light sliced across the room in vertical sheets, glinting off a myriad of bright particles bursting overhead like an exploding mirror ball.

Gleaming, airborne shards of glass.

At the windows, silhouetted against the lightning's glare, writhing shapes poked and crawled, feeling their way around the protective boards like giant millipedes.

The paralysis drained from Rashad's limbs.

He clambered to his knees. The room was again plunged into darkness. All around him, oblivious punters slumbered on. He could make out Jim, asleep beneath the windows, and called out to him in a hoarse whisper.

Jim opened his eyes and twisted toward the sound of Rashad's voice. His right hand went to Roger's pistol on the floor at his side, and as he sat up he brushed at something on his shirtfront with his left.

He caught his breath and jerked his hand away.

"Jim. They're outside. At the windows."

Jim looked up. Another lightning bolt flashed.

Jim's fingers were flecked with blood. He glanced down at his hand, then back up at the window as he plucked a long, jagged sliver of glass from his palm.

"Where?"

A roll and bang of thunder machine-gunned across the sky, culminating in a deafening thunderclap that shook the building and finally roused a handful of sleepers.

Lance and Vince propped themselves up on their elbows, blinking and groggy.

Jim was standing now.

"They were there. I thought I was dreaming at first. I sat up and they were still there."

There was no sign of movement. Vince turned to Rashad.

"There's nothing."

Jim said, "Get your weapons."

The punters stared at him, then snatched up their arms and jumped up from the floor.

Strindlak struggled against a growing irritation. There was no real reason, now that he thought about it, that the halflings must be notified of the impending departure. They had a sentence over their heads anyway. Perhaps missing out on the excitement could serve as a preliminary to their forthcoming punishment. Some experts advocated that very technique—commencing disciplinary measures with some mild form of deprivation, then working one's way up through virulent stringency to a final act of barbaric savagery—as yielding positive results. It couldn't hurt to try it once.

An awareness that he'd just passed the door to Zillior's quarters brought Strindlak out of his musings.

He paused.

It was possible. The halflings were understandably fond of their younger sister. It wasn't inconceivable that they'd stopped by to relieve her in her solitude. Strindlak was mindful of his promise to Glumrok, but he wouldn't have to give away the surprise.

He stood outside the door, pondering.

Just dropping in to check on her well-being as any father might. Though until now he never had. But it was within the realm of plausibility.

He tapped the control panel.

The door opened and he took a quick glance around. Satisfied that the halflings weren't within, he turned to gaze for a long while at the little one's sleeping pod before continuing up the corridor.

If her siblings were yet to be found, at least young Zillior herself was safe and sound asleep in her pod.

When Jim told the punters to pick up their weapons, Fred reached for his camera and flicked on the bash light. Its wide beam threw everyone in its path into stark relief while plunging everything else into deeper obscurity. Pupils flashed as the light swooped over faces, freezing on each for a split second against a background of flapping shadows that loomed and wheeled over the walls.

The camera sought out the rattling windows across the room, but its aim was deflected by jostling collisions with scurrying punters. Jim pulled them to the center of the room, positioning them into a wedge with himself at the head. Grant's volunteers gripped their weapons, grim-faced, hardened veterans now. No more screaming, no more whimpering. The stay-at-homes were a different matter. They skittered around the perimeter like cockroaches trapped in the light.

"Janet, Corey, get back out of the way," Jim said.

Keeping one eye on the LCD and dragging a stool, Fred backed up with Janet to the corner by the bathroom. He pushed the stool into the corner and hopped up on it.

In Fred's viewfinder, Brad appeared beside Jim, armed with his mace and the sword they'd brought back with them. At a word from Brad, Jim nodded and shifted his pistol to his left hand, and Brad handed him the sword.

Trask stared at the incomprehensible controls, the blank screen, trying not to shake his head in bewilderment. His brain felt like a waterlogged hunk of clay. And it didn't help that he was acutely aware of Paula's lip-biting impatience as she waited for him to puzzle it out.

Dammit. Focus. It wasn't rocket science. It was a consumer product, the stupid logo proved that. The technology was intimidating, alien, but it was still controlled by a computer. And like all computer interfaces designed for the technologically impaired end user, it was user-friendly. Don't be distracted by the flashing lights, the strangeness.

"Goddammit!" he almost shouted. He swatted the face of the LCD display. "It's a goddamn touchscreen, you idiot."

Instantly, the screen wiped and a new one took its place.

Trask and Paula leaned in closer.

The new screen featured a pair of windows. The top one showed a stylized representation of one of the aliens—the authentic, flesh and blood item, a rough copy of the one that now lay in pieces in a Hefty bag in the mess hall kitchen. There were disturbing differences, but it had the same basic outlines.

The bottom window framed some kind of multi-limbed monstrosity that must be the CGI version. It was unlike any they'd seen so far.

"Transport mode. Normal versus CGI," Trask said. Paula pointed at the two buttons next to the CGI window. There were no buttons beside the other.

"Try it," Trask said.

She tapped one. A new version of CGI creature took the place of the first. They both recognized it as the thing that had nearly taken her arm off down by the stream.

They flicked through a few more variations. It soon became evident that most of the things were designed for work, not fighting. Hard labor. Drudgery. One had arms like twin steam shovels, for clearing debris. Another had piledrivers for fists. It might have been formidable in combat, but seeing it objectively, it looked like the designers had some more utilitarian purpose in mind. Next came the thing that had torn the wall off the dormitory. Looked dangerous, but seeing it in this new light it was more like a walking Swiss Army knife. A collection of handy, oversize tools.

There were exceptions, but overall the transporter seemed to be designed primarily for peaceful purposes.

And one thing was certain. It wasn't supposed to be a game.

But it wasn't hard to figure out. Professionals have to know their equipment. It's their job. Their "newbie" attackers didn't. They probably weren't even authorized to use the transporter in the first place. And who would be reckless and headstrong enough to go ahead and use it anyway?

Children.

Some little alien brats were commandeering the grownups' expensive—and dangerous—equipment, misusing it for the sake of the alien equivalent of tearing the wings off flies.

Little bastards.

"What's next?" Paula said.

"Next?" He blinked at the screen, then said, "Select."

"Normal, please, Trask."

Trask shrugged and tapped the "normal" alien window.

It expanded to fill the screen, and began to flash. Without hesitating, Trask tapped again.

From above their heads came a clank. The sound of a clutch engaging. A rustle and whir of mechanics springing into motion.

They looked up. The harness was descending.

The last window shattered. The barricade of boards and bedframes rattled like prison bars shaken by riotous inmates.

"Cut me loose!" Jeremy screamed, fighting like a maniac against the dragline binding him to his cot.

Wood splintered under a tremendous blow. Screws, ripped squealing from stripped anchors, clattered across the floor. A loose board bulged inward. Groping tentacles squeezed through the gap.

Jim hewed downward, shearing through their clawed tips. The stumps retracted with a jerk as the thing outside howled. Severed tentacle ends flopped over the floor like eels in boiling oil.

Janet screamed and Jim whirled at a heart-stopping bang.

The metal door had split at the center. The refrigerator blocking it jolted under a savage battering.

"Janet!" Jeremy pleaded.

Jim shouted. "Lance, Trask—hold the fridge!"

Lance and Evans dashed for the door.

"Where the hell is Trask?" Lance yelled, throwing his shoulder against the fridge along with Evans and Rashad.

"Gone," Michelle yelled back. "Paula too." She kicked aside the steel tabletop covering the escape hatch. "They went out the hatch."

Lance raged. "Unfuckingbelievable!"

"Michelle, keep away from there!" Jim shouted. "Rashad, screw down that hatch."

Rashad ran for the toolbag, tore it open and grabbed a screwgun and a handful of three-inch metal-drilling screws.

Michelle was on the verge of arguing with Jim when Corey shoved past her and dove head first through the hatch.

"Corey!" Jim yelled.

Zach and Mei disappeared into the tunnel right behind her. Lance raved at the precipitating betrayal. "Damn you, Trask! Corey! Mei! Get your asses back in here, now!"

Rashad stood holding the screwgun, gaping at Jim.

"Dammit!" Jim turned away to face the windows, the broadsword in one hand and his pistol in the other.

"Get off the platform," Trask said.

"I'm not staying here by myself!"

"I'll be right back."

"What if something goes wrong?"

"Nothing's going to go wrong."

The harness was coming down fast. Paula ducked under it and jumped to the floor.

Cables and flextubes draped themselves over Trask's shoulders. The transparent disk separated into two sections, and the smaller, bristling with antennae, settled over his head. Rubbery tendrils slid from the tubes to caress his limbs, searching out acupressure points and fastening their bulbous ends over them like sucking octopus tentacles. The air hummed with electrical currents, making Paula's hair stand on end. Seeing her look of dread, Trask said, "I'm okay." His voice sounded muffled.

In spite of Paula's fears, everything seemed to be working as it should. With the harness and its probing tendrils in place, the robotic murmurings ceased.

The chamber fell silent except for the sound of their breathing.

They waited, but nothing happened. There must be some final bit of business needed to activate the thing. Trask looked at the console. The rollerball's rim was flashing. And now beneath it a button flashed in unison.

"Of course," he said. "We didn't lock in the coordinates."

He paused. His next move could be his last.

He pressed the button.

A cloud of motes spiraled up and over him from the base of the platform, wrapping him in a rotating pillar of white light. The harness released him and snapped upward. He went semi-transparent. The pillar, now compressed into a slender beam, flared and collapsed in a shower of sparks and Trask was gone.

The skullcap quivered, rattling its cables, as the harness withdrew upwards, its dangling tendril-ends fluttering.

And then, just like that, he was back—and drenched from head to toe in seawater.

It poured off him in a small torrent, and Trask stood flicking spray from his hands and shaking his head, laughing in gasps from the shock of being dropped into the ocean.

Paula laughed along with him in relief. But they quickly got hold of themselves and shushed each other. Best not to draw the attention of their unsuspecting hosts.

It took Trask another minute to stop shivering and catch his breath.

The banging and rattling had stopped.

Lance looked around at Jim. Jim glanced back at him, then spun toward the escape hatch.

"Jim," Jeremy said. "Please."

Without turning, Jim said, "Vince, cut Jeremy loose."

In the eerie silence they heard Vince sawing at Jeremy's bonds.

Lance said, "Do you think—?"

A woman's scream reverberated through the tunnel.

Something chomped and snarled, and Zach clawed his way up out of the hole. Dropping the screwgun to help drag him clear, Rashad found Mei clinging to his legs, whooping in terror.

Jim started towards them, but stopped, cursing, when the pounding at the windows erupted again with renewed force.

"Lance, stay on the door," he yelled.

Corey's face shone from the darkness of the tunnel.

Her arms reached out.

"Help me."

Michelle and Rashad each grabbed an arm and tugged.

Something had her.

Corey's eyes bulged. She whispered, "Please." Then she screamed. Her body jerked and Rashad's grip on her arm slipped to her wrist.

It was like trying to free a doll from the jaws of a pit bull. Corey was flung from side to side, her head slamming against the tunnel walls. Rashad and Michelle's arms were flecked with blood. They held on to her wrists, but Corey's twisting and flailing at last tore them free and she was dragged screeching into the darkness. Her cries choked off in a horrible gurgle.

Michelle and Rashad stood gaping at each other.

From below came a wet crunching and shredding.

With a cry, Michelle lunged for the hatch cover. She slid it in place over the tunnel mouth, then staggered back against the wall, shaking uncontrollably.

"Seal it off, seal it off," she said. "It's coming."

Rashad grabbed up the screwgun and with trembling fingers shot a screw home through the cover into the floor.

"Get on top of it," he yelled, and Michelle, Mei and Zach jumped on, holding on to each other as Rashad shot another screw.

Something thudded hard against their feet, lifting the cover partway off the floor. It slammed back down under their weight. Mei looked down and moaned. A severed tentacle tip squirmed around her ankle. She kicked it away.

The screwgun whined. Rashad drove screws as fast as his shaking fingers could fit them while the thing down below rammed the cover. When he was finished, huge dents riddled the hard metal surface, but the screws held.

The battering stopped. They hurried back to join the defenders at the center of the room.

CHAPTER THIRTY

MONITORS

HAL SAT UP WITH A JERK. Someone had just called his name. "Hal. Tara. Wake up," the voice said.

Groggy with sleep, he looked around the darkened control room, then up at the monitors.

Blank. Sleep mode.

"I'm sorry," Chuck mumbled from the console. He tapped a key to wake the sleeping monitors. "Something's going on."

Somewhere, someone was yelling. It was Chuck's watch, Hal remembered.

On the mixing board a red light was flashing.

Awareness hit him in a series of jolts.

Fred's camera. Was transmitting. Hal got up from the sofa, a sickening fear dragging at his limbs.

"I fell asleep," Chuck was saying. Sleepers on the floor rolled toward his voice and blinked at the monitors.

They flickered on.

"Oh shit," Chuck said. "They're here."

"Wake up," Hal said to the others.

Tara and Kristine lurched to their feet. Hal grabbed for the intercom's receiver, but put it back down when the door banged open.

"What's happening?" Barry demanded. Grant was right behind him.

Speechless, Chuck pointed at the monitors.

The image skewed wildly through a tight knot of punters, raked across barricaded windows, then steadied and zoomed.

Straining tentacles pushed through the crevices between boards and windowframes.

The image locked onto Jim. He was shouting.

"Audio!" Hal said.

"Shit!" Chuck reached across the mixing desk and slapped up the master faders. Pandemonium blared from the speakers.

In three strides Hal was beside him. They pulled up chairs and Hal gouged the talkback button.

"Fred!"

There was no reply.

"He's off the headset," Hal said.

Grant assumed control. "Hal, take your camera and—"

"Are you fucking kidding me?"

Abashed, Grant shook his head.

"Of course not. Sorry, Hal."

Hal's flash of anger evaporated, replaced by his usual cool professionalism. "We'll have to trust him," he said.

Kristine tried without success to repress a moan of nausea as she sank into a chair behind him.

"Kristine, leave the room."

She jumped up and ran for the door.

Barry took her chair. "Don't worry. This shit's directing itself."

Trask wrung out his shirt and stepped up to the console. Now that that was out of the way it was time to get down to serious business.

He cracked his knuckles. "Let's go kick some ass," he said.

His hand was on the rollerball. Paula put her hand on top of his—and none too gently.

"Stop."

Keeping her hand on his, Paula came around the end of the railing and moved in close until she was right next to him. Almost in his face. Fixing him, Trask knew, with a hard look. He didn't need to meet her eyes, he could tell from her posture. He stared straight ahead, aware that he was blinking rapidly, but unable to control it and hating that she couldn't help but notice.

"You don't want to get out of here."

"What? Come on..."

"You don't think I can tell what's going on? Look at me."

God. He'd never seen this side of Paula before. He turned his head to stare back at her. Her expression was hard, he'd guessed that right. So Paula could be tough. You had to admire that. Even in an enemy.

"You don't care about getting out of here," she said. "You just want to *play*."

He blinked again.

"It's all just a game, isn't it? Only it's not *just* a game. It's the biggest, most bad-ass turbo-powered total-immersion multiplayer interactive game *ever*. The real deal. Future tech." She sounded like she was just getting warmed up. "It's got parental advisories and warning stickers plastered all over it in a dozen languages. Survival? That's just a potential side benefit of getting to type in your initials next to the all-time highest score."

He flinched.

"You want to go 'kick some ass.' You want your big shot at the championship. Make your big comeback. It's why you're here."

Trask closed his eyes. When he opened them, they burned with unconcealed rage.

"That's right," he said. "It *is* why I'm here." His voice was an ugly rasp. "I'm going to rip those little fuckers' lungs out and shove them down their fucking throats, and nobody, not you or anybody else is going to stop me. I'm going to kick the living shit out of them. I'm going to beat their asses at their own fucking game, only it's not a game anymore, Paula—it's *punishment*. Now it's our turn. They're going to pay for what they did to us. To Heather and Fredo, and Nils. And Erika. Oh, we could escape now, sure—maybe! But what if we can't?"

He stopped to catch a breath, but it didn't quell the unreasoning fury. "What if those things come in here before we get everyone out? I'll tell you what. They're going to waste us so fast you won't even have time to say 'cheese'. And where's our fucking escape then, Paula?" He was almost shouting. "We're dead meat. Unless I get them first. It's no fucking game."

"Oh yes it is," she said.

The unreasoning fury thing didn't intimidate her at all.

"Idiot rationalizations aren't going to cut it, Trask." She glowered at him, and Trask actually *was* a little intimidated. That fresh scar running down her cheek from her misadventure with the CGI-thing kind of added to the effect, too. It was turning blood red.

"You keep your damn voice down before you blow everything, and do what has to be done," she said. "And you know what it is as well as I do. We're going to get everyone off this fucking island and onto one of those fucking ships and we're going to fucking do it now before those fucking alien motherfuckers find us."

Trask had never even heard her use the F word before. Wasn't she from the Midwest? He was trembling. His fists clenched and unclenched.

"Do you hear me?" she said.

Every muscle in his body ached. He couldn't let go. He knew he was wrong. He couldn't help it. Goddammit.

"Goddammit, Paula. I just want to make things right."

"It won't make things right," she said. "It'll only make things worse."

"It would make some things right for me," he growled.

Paula's expression softened, her anger evaporated. She looked surprised. Trask suddenly knew there was more to this than he'd realized too.

Paula looked at him searchingly, and the last vestiges of his own anger melted away. It had almost gone too far and they both knew it.

"I'm sorry, Trask," she said. "You can't blame yourself for all of this no matter how badly you want to. It's just something that happened."

He slumped. He felt like the floor had just given way under his feet, but instead of falling he just floated there. The inner corners of his eyes felt wet, and he had to wipe them with the heels of his palms before enough moisture collected there to roll down his cheeks. Paula would think he was crying.

He let out a long, shuddering sigh and took a deep breath. He shook his head to clear it.

He looked down at the sphere for a few seconds, then put his hand on the rollerball again.

This time she didn't stop him.

"Let's go find the mess hall," he said.

The boards over the window in Fred's viewfinder creaked and groaned, but held. He whirled at a sharp crack of splitting lumber and caught a chunk of wood flying like a crossbow bolt from camera right straight into the punter's ranks.

Michelle ducked. The bolt plowed into Brad's forehead, lifting him off his feet and hurling him backwards into Rashad's arms. Offscreen punters screamed.

Rashad couldn't hold Brad, and Fred tilted to follow his slow drop to the floor, then angled back up. In three-quarters profile, Rashad stared ahead in horror. Careful not to jar the image, Fred got down from his stool and moved in close, swinging around for an over-the-shoulder POV shot that panned to follow Rashad's gaze.

One of the things was climbing in through the window.

It was flesh and blood. No more hiding behind the curtain. They were playing for keeps now.

Jim's pistol banged. Fred held on the leering face, its slitted eyes blinking, dazzled by the camera light. It flinched when the bullets punched into it, but kept coming.

From the back of the room, Janet shrilled. Jim shouted, "Janet, hit the lights," and as Fred panned toward the back wall, the refrigerator swung into frame. It shook like a tree in a gale. He held on Lance and Evans straining against it. Like trying to stop a bulldozer with your bare hands.

Fred continued right and found Janet, backed up against the windowless wall under the lightswitch. Jim yelled again, but Janet just shook her head in mute panic.

Beverly moved into frame, limping for the lightswitch. Fluorescent fill light flooded the room. Fred compensated with a few quick setting adjustments. At another shout he swung back toward the door and caught Rashad whirling as he moved back into frame. It was beautiful, like it had been choreographed—Fred sidestepped and locked back into Rashad's POV—panning to see Lance's detachment hurled against the wall by a tremendous heave that sent Evans's fridge jolting over the floor.

Fred tilted on its leading edge, plowing up sheets of linoleum, then swung back up on the open door.

Haloed by the exterior lights stood a gibbering giant.

It ducked its head and stepped into the room.

Jim fired again at two more clambering through the window to its right, shielding their faces with arms like segmented tree limbs. Bullets ripped into them, but they surged in.

Unintelligible amidst the tumult of combat, a frequency-modulated voice squawked. Grant, shouting orders over the intercom. Michelle crushed it in passing with the butt of her machete and hurried to join Lance and Evans on the door.

Trask rolled toward the beach and skimmed over it, skirting the shoreline until they shot past the camp's cluster of buildings. He went into a tight curve and pulled out of it heading for the bungalow.

They passed right through the walls as if they weren't there.

Trask released the rollerball. They were in a bedroom. The two beds were empty, the bedcovers turned down. Barry and Grant were roomies, so this would be theirs.

Must be working late.

The scale of things had changed, and Trask suddenly realized why. When they'd "entered" the enclosed space, the transporter had somehow sensed its dimensions and adjusted automatically, going to a higher magnification, leaving the walls and ceiling behind and unseen beyond its boundaries.

He moved toward the opposite wall at a walking pace. They passed through into the narrow hallway, crossed it, and cut through the next wall into another bedroom. The transporter let out a beep.

Bentley lay on the single bed.

The sheet was pulled up to his chin. He held it there with both fists. His eyes were open.

Fascinated, they watched him. Bentley was frowning. He swung his legs over the side of the bed and sat up. He sat motionless for a few seconds—he seemed to be listening—then threw off the sheet and stood.

"Oops," Trask said. He looked over at Paula, sheepish about invading the man's privacy. "Sorry you had to see that."

Bentley slept in the nude.

Paula paid no attention. Trask could see she was disturbed about something, though. And there *was* something troubling about it. Barry and Grant not being in their room. Bentley's expression as he stood there. He looked—angry.

What was going on?

Bentley pulled on a pair of pants, grabbed a shirt, and walked toward the door. Trask pushed up on the rollerball, and they glided past him, heading for the back wall.

"It's weird…" Paula began, but didn't finish.

"Yeah." They were outside again, in the breezeway behind the bungalow. The mess hall was right in front of them, six feet away.

"Duck," Trask said. He didn't even slow. They sank through the wall and were plunged into the mouth of hell before they knew what hit them.

A hail of beeps sounded and Trask's finger jerked away from the ball.

Paula covered her mouth to stifle a scream.

CHAPTER THIRTY-ONE

MESS HALL

NO ONE TURNED to acknowledge Bentley's arrival. All gazes were drilled deep into the monitors—where a battle was raging in the mess hall.

But it was no longer a battle. It was slaughter.

Onscreen, towering head and shoulders over the cringing defenders, the colossal alien reached into their midst and seized Evans by the neck. Coiling tentacles tightened in a stranglehold.

"Why wasn't I informed?" Bentley demanded.

Barry stammered. "I was about to come get you. We only…just now…"

His words trailed off as his attention was forced back to the monitor—in time to see Evans slam an iron skillet into the thing's face. It released him, yammering, but Evans wasn't finished. His other hand jabbed upward with a twelve-inch carving knife. It sank deep into the creature's neck.

"Never mind," Bentley snapped. He plopped down on the couch. "Next time, send someone, Barry."

"Sorry, Rob," Barry said without turning.

Bentley grumbled, but was soon drawn into the action along with everyone else.

Onscreen, Evans jumped back. But this time he wasn't fast enough. Sharp-taloned tentacles plunged into his eyes and mouth. Would-be rescuers rained blows on the monster, but it only tightened its grip. Crushing tentacles squeezed—then ripped free.

Blood fountained. Evans sagged, lifeless, to the floor.

There was no choice now. Their friends were being massacred before their eyes.

"Put on a remote. Get ready to beam somewhere safe if anything goes wrong," Trask said. "The bungalow, or the beach."

The touchscreen still showed the "normal" transport icon. He tapped it. It was replaced by a new screen of glowing text. He cursed.

"They can't hurt you, right?" Paula said. "It's not really you."

He poked the screen again, harder.

"The little one, that Grant killed. I think all the hits it took caused a system crash. That's why it all of a sudden became real. If that happens, I'll beam back before it's too late."

Indecipherable graphics filled the screen, accompanied by meaningless symbols. He gave it another vicious stab.

"If I can," he said.

"Oh, God."

The next screen was more of the same.

"Page back. Page back, dammit," He growled. He punched furiously. Screens flicked past. But not the one he wanted.

"This isn't going anywhere," he said.

"You can't physically beam in there, it'd be suicide."

"You're telling me!"

Trask glanced up, then quickly looked back down. The mess hall had become a grotesque circus of horrors—and in the center ring Michelle dangled upside-down, thrashing in the grip of a hulking alien monster.

"What the fuck do I do?"

Paula had seen it too. Her stomach churned.

"Try something. Try anything."

The thing lifted Michelle up by her legs until their eyes met. She spat at it in terrified fury. It licked her spit from its lips with a thick pointed tongue.

Slavering jaws twisted toward her neck and Michelle screamed.

A machete blow clove deep into the thing's arm, half severing it. Bellowing, it dropped Michelle to turn its murderous attention on its attacker. Vince.

Vince swung again with both hands, aiming for the thing's head. It caught the blade in its teeth. The iron jaws clamped down and wrenched Vince's machete from his grasp with a jerk so violent it dislocated his shoulder.

Vince screamed in agony. The thing rolled its tentacles into a huge fist as he turned to run and pummeled him to the floor.

Across the room, Janet huddled against the back wall, kicking at the linoleum in unreasoning animal terror. With the monster blocking the front door there was only one escape. The kitchen. She crawled towards it on her hands and knees.

At the windows, still half-dazed from the blow to his head, Brad staggered up. He grabbed Jim's sword arm to steady himself, and Jim heaved him to his feet as he pumped lead into a pair of grinning devils at point blank range. The bullets didn't even slow them. The nearest made a grab for Brad—and immediately regretted it.

Brad sidestepped and swung his mace up from over his shoulder. Steel shackles cracked into his attacker's skull. The thing's snapping jaws crunched against the floor and its head bounced back up like a basketball, red eyes goggling at Brad in shock.

Brad slammed it back down again.

The broadsword wasn't made for close-quarters fighting, but the pistol was next to useless. Jim emptied the clip and tossed it aside. Taking the sword in both hands, he chopped and jabbed at his own opponent. But every chopping stroke was deflected by clusters of tough tentacles, and his jabbing thrusts didn't even faze the thing.

The pounding Brad was giving its mate distracted it, though, and Jim saw his chance when his foe reached out a protective arm. He swung hard from the shoulder and sheared it off at the elbow joint.

That was enough for both of them. Gabbling, the injured alien scooped up its sundered forearm and the two of them turned tail and dove through adjacent windows.

A snarling horror had Mei cornered against the opposite wall. Beverly sunk a cleaver into the back of its neck. It spun on her. She ducked under its flailing tentacles and Mei scrambled around it on all fours.

At Beverly's shout, Jim and Brad whirled to see Mei clambering up and starting toward them.

The thing behind her was faster.

A pitchfork of rigid tentacles plunged into her back. The hooked talons burst from her stomach and caught, stopping her dead in her tracks.

Blood sprayed the kitchen door. Janet's hand slipped in the warm droplets, fingerpainting dark streaks across it as it swung open. She dragged herself inside, slammed it shut behind her and propped her back against it.

Onscreen, the claws jutting from Mei's abdomen withdrew with a jerk. She pitched forward and the picture skewed away.

Even Hal was overwhelmed by the sheer horror. Tara sat beside him staring blankly, no longer seeing. It couldn't be watched. Chuck muttered, eyes closed. He might have been praying.

Grant was still game. "Look out!" "Don't let it—" "Get another man on that door!" he shouted at the screen.

Sitting side by side on the couch, Bentley and Barry withstood the assault to the senses with all the tragic austerity of a pair of Carolingian wood carvings.

Fred's camera was back on the big one inside the door. The once-exposed sinews of the thing's half-severed arm had already pulled the wound closed. It still favored it, but there was no mistaking it was again functional.

The yelling and screaming was quieter from the kitchen. It was almost pitch black except for a thin white line under the door and the exterior lights coming through the cracks at the window. On the countertop over the sink, Janet could make out a shadowy bulk. The dead thing that Grant's men had brought back. Janet didn't want to look at it. She squeezed her eyes shut, covered her ears with her hands and waited to die.

A vertical series of toggle switches ran down the panel to the left of the screen. Trask reached for the top switch, hesitated, then swatted it down.

A howling siren blared. It was like a fleet of eighteen-wheelers all leaning on their horns at once—for half a second, before Trask slapped the switch back up. The cacophony died away in ringing echoes to a supercharged silence.

He was trembling. "Jesus!"

There'd be no more of that. Paula was really panicking now. But then so was he.

"What are we gonna do?" she said.

"I'm thinking."

The boom of distant thunder rolled away over the hills. In the darkened kitchen, something unfolded itself over the sink.

Janet's eyes were still closed, and with her hands still covering her ears she didn't hear the wet scrabbling along the countertop, or the fluttering plop when something landed on the floor beside her.

A final, silent burst of sheet lightning traced the gaps around the single boarded-up window. It lit up the white walls and steel countertop, and reflected redly through Janet's closed eyelids.

Instinctively, she opened her eyes.

Hot, rancid breath caressed her cheeks in the darkness. Her eyes adjusted on two gleaming rows of sharp teeth. She gasped and sat bolt upright.

Inches from her face floated a leering devil mask. Its head was cocked inquisitively. Slobber dribbled from the corner of its mouth. Over red, bulging eyes, tendrils bobbed and nittered from a knurled, reptilian crown.

They hissed at her.

Janet screeched like a banshee and flailed at the hideous features. Her hands slapped the thing's clammy hide, knocking it skittering toward the wall, and she scrambled to her feet, wheezing in fear and clawing at the doorknob behind her back as it lurched upright on one trembling leg and hopped toward her like a demented troll.

The mess hall walls ran with blood.

Lance was on the floor, tripped over Vince's corpse.

The giant alien pushed into the room, fighting Jim and Michelle for every inch.

Brad, Rashad and Gabrielle hewed at its comrade in the opposite corner.

Jeremy cringed by the bathroom door.

Zach threw aside a broken war club. Beverly shouted and tossed him a machete.

And all of them froze at a sudden shrill and terrifying yammering from the kitchen.

Janet.

The kitchen door slammed open and she came flying through it, ululating in terror. She rounded the corner at a run and made straight for the huge alien blocking the exit. It leapt back, striking its head against the doorframe. Ducking as she ran, Janet covered her head with her arms and dove between its legs.

The startled alien looked down, then whirled to watch her as she sprinted across the sand and into the trees.

A terrific blow to its backside brought it to its senses. It turned with a roar, a side of meat dangling from its left buttock by a strip of gristle.

Jim bared his teeth in a feral grin.

"No breaks, fuckface."

His sword plunged into its chest and the alien howled.

A growing fear for the success of their mission gnawed at Snorlok's heart. He'd expected resistance, but this was far beyond anything he and his siblings had hitherto seen. The faint-hearted twins had already fled, and there was a real danger now that either he or Ropsnag would be incapacitated before Zillior's rescue could be effected. The deranged creatures fought like demons, with a ferocity and recklessness that hinted at something far more sinister than simple competitiveness.

Some line had been crossed. It was no longer a game.

A chill ran down Snorlok's spine. And if that were true, then what of Zillior? What awful purpose lay behind their need of her? Did they require her young body for their sustenance? Had her butchered limbs already been spitted and roasted, or minced to—

But no. Zillior yet lived. Her scent remained fresh within these very walls.

They'd arrived in time to prevent that outrage.

~~~~~~~~~~~~~~~~~~~~~~~~~~~~~~~~~~~

Trask's brain buzzed. He looked around the room, at the floor below the platform, and turned. From the back wall, a thick bundle of cables ran across the floor to the base of the platform.

He vaulted the railing and Paula hurried around to where he knelt over the cables. They converged in a rectangular connector, plugged into a jack at the platform's base. Trask grabbed it and yanked.

"What are you doing?"

"Give me a hand!"

Paula wrapped her hands around his and together they strained and pulled, but it didn't budge.

Trask stood up and started kicking it.

"You'll break it. Wait."

She pulled the screwdriver out of her back pocket. "All I could scrounge up on such short notice."

"Perfect," Trask said.

Paula wedged the point in, working it from side to side. A gap appeared and widened, until the plug pried loose enough for Trask to jerk it free.

He took a quick step back and looked up. The console lights had gone off. The screen was blank. Dead.

"Yes!"

Trask picked up the plug and shoved it hard back into its jack and everything came on again.

He raced up the three steps to the platform and hit the screen twice. The corporate logo flashed.

Snorlok had fought his way far enough into the room to see the door from which the shrieking creature had just emerged.

Zillior's scent emanated from within.

His universe compressed to a single narrow corridor that held only himself and Zillior, separated by the doorway ahead.

With a tremendous effort, he hurled aside the attackers barring his path. They rushed back in—but not before he had won another step. And then Ropsnag shouted—and through the door, hopping on one leg, came Zillior.
~~~~~~~~~~~~~~~~~~~~~~~~~~~~~~~~~~~

Seeing her brothers, she threw back her head and screeched with gladness.

Snorlok flung his distracted assailants aside, and Zillior sprang into his arms. He whirled and heaved her to Ropsnag, roaring a command.

Ropsnag caught the flying halfling and pitched her head first through the nearest window.

A fierce joy flooded Snorlok's veins. They had won Zillior's freedom. Now it was needed but to hurry back to the ship before their absence was discovered or any further misfortunes befell.

But first, there were scores to settle.

"Bingo."

"Hurry."

Trask tapped the screen again.

Transport mode. CGI. The multi-armed Hindu demon.

Next.

Next.

Next. A thing with meat-cleaver arms and teeth jutting upward from its lower jaw like some Big Daddy Roth hot rodder. Trask's own jaw set in a hard line.

"I like this one."

Select. The image filled the screen, began blinking.

Lock in selection.

Clank hum. The harness descended. Paula jumped off the platform.

The muscles in Trask's arms stood out like coiled suspension cables. His eyes were wild.

The button under the rollerball flashed.

"Wish me luck."

"Luck, Trask."

He steeled himself.

ACTIVATE.

She could have sworn she saw him grinning just as he disappeared.

But this time, he didn't disappear completely. Where Trask had stood, an outline of his form in twinkling pixels hovered, sparkling.

It seemed to tense—ready to pounce.

~~~~~~~~~~~~~~~~~~~~~~~~~~~~~~~~~~~~

Creatures fled through the door to Snorlok's rear. The air outside resounded with their shouts to those still inside.

Ropsnag leapt into the breach, stemming the tide of freedom. Trembling with exultant fury, he looked over at Snorlok, bared his teeth and bayed like a crazed fiend. Snorlok lowered his massive head and snarled in reply.

There were only a handful of the odious creatures left inside. Now these would pay for their lack of compassion.

Snorlok threw back his head and opened his jaws wide to let out a roar—but he snapped them shut again when the air crackled around his head and a deafening whine assailed his ears.

A flash of white overloaded the monitors.

Hal jumped up. "Chuck, turn down the—" but his words were drowned out when a thundering sub-bass roar blew the speakers.

A red sunburst of video distortion flared and cleared on a showering column of sparks in the dead center of the killing floor. Punters and aliens alike leapt back.

A split second later, the rattling speaker cones shredded under a crunching howitzer blast and the whirling tornado coalesced into a glittering horror.

"Now what?" Bentley said.

Trask reared up. His huge head banged into the ceiling-mounted fluorescents, exploding a pair of tubes. Punters shielded their faces from the spray of glass as Trask whirled, the light from his glowing form kaleidoscoping over the walls.

His gaze found the alien blocking the door. The thing stood frozen in shock, its tentacles wound around Jim's neck. It reflexively tightened its grip.

Trask shouted "No!" but what came out was like the howling blast of a freight train whistle.

He threw up a massive cleaver. It ripped into the ceiling panels and came back down in a slashing stroke, trailing a jetstream of pulverized
~~~~~~~~~~~~~~~~~~~~~~~~~~~~~~~~~~~~

particleboard. The blade bit into the stunned alien's neck at the shoulder and sank through bone and sinew to shear clean through its abdomen, cutting it in two.

The thing's mouth gibbered as head and chest slid down over stumbling legs and both halves collapsed on top of Jim in a mess of limbs and throbbing organs. Lance and Brad punched and kicked at the disemboweled alien's head, trying to dig Jim out from under the thrashing heap, as its jaws snapped at their hands and feet.

Trask turned to face his remaining foe.

CHAPTER THIRTY-TWO

GAMER

SNORLOK'S FIRST THOUGHT was, "Father!" But even in the worst extremity of parental ire, this was beyond even Strindlak. And when the drone turned to face him, its eyes burning instead with grim eagerness, the full horror of what had transpired rammed home to his staggered brain with numbing certainty. The creatures had the transporter!

With a roar, the drone sprang and struck.

Snorlok threw himself to the side, feeling the wind in his tendrils as the cleaver sailed past his cheek. It tore into the wall and jammed, but the drone, unfazed, pivoted on the snarled cleaver, using its momentum to yank it free, and aimed another blow at Snorlok from behind.

The thing moved with a speed that Snorlok would never have imagined possible. He gyrated, just in time to avoid another slashing stroke by launching himself backwards, and plowed into the metal tower at the door.

The refrigerator trembled like a condemned building under the wrecking ball and tipped over. Lance and Brad just managed to pull Jim to safety before it toppled onto the dismembered alien's head. Gore splattered their feet.

There was only one left now, but it was the most dangerous, and howling mad. It screeched like a runaway paving saw and rushed its CGI tormentor, swinging its huge fists, talons jutting from them like giant stilettos. Its opponent dodged to the side and chopped as it skidded past, slicing off a clutch of spasming tentacles.

Cut off from the exit, it was all the remaining punters could do to keep from being crushed underfoot. Downgraded in an instant to mere spectator status, they fled to the perimeter, scuttling from one wall to the next when the battling titans pounded past like charging rhinos, trading ferocious blows that shook the building. Unlike all the others the punters had encountered, the new CGI thing's every move looked confident and well-honed, reflecting practiced skill. It was outmatched in speed by its rival's frenzied onslaughts, but more than made up for it in sheer brutal power.

When the alien's blows connected, they had little effect. But when the CGI thing's cleavers found their mark they inflicted appalling injuries.

Strindlak's irritation, further compounded every time he opened a door and found the halflings still missing, had now deepened to a scowling anger.

Continuing down the corridor, he passed the transporter chamber and stopped. It wasn't possible—but he could have sworn he'd heard the telltale hum of the transporter in operation as he'd passed by.

Would they dare?

Snorlok was a sly one, but it was doubtful he had the expertise to crack the access code. And even if he did, would they dare to commit the same misdeed behind his back after he'd already caught them at it once?

Convinced of its unlikeliness, but nevertheless fuming at the thought, Strindlak retraced his steps to stand outside the door. Cocking his head, he listened. He couldn't be sure, but—

He punched the panel button. To his relief, the unit responded with a beep and flashed the ENTER ACCESS CODE message.

Still, he did hear something. It wasn't his imagination.

He stood at the door, pondering.

He supposed it could be something along the lines of the idle needing adjusting. Something to do with the software update. It made a certain amount of sense.

He shrugged and turned to go, and then it hit him.

If they'd smuggled the Emergency Remote Retrieval Units out with them after he'd caught them, they could have bypassed the locked door by transporting back into the chamber as soon as the secondary systems were restored to standby!

Unforgivable!

With a low growl, he punched in the access code.

Trask had taken a few minor hits, but he'd dealt some stinging punishment in return. The invisible injuries sustained by his CGI counterpart were for the most part painless—Trask experienced them as an icy tingling, a pricking at his insides that was more ticklish than painful.

But when his cleavers bit into the alien's flesh, the thing suffered. Unfortunately, the suffering was short-lived. Wounds gaped open, exposing raw meat streaked with the pink gunk that passed for blood in these things—then just as quickly pulled shut again.

But it didn't matter. He'd fought plenty of monsters before, and this one was no different.

The alien threw a vicious swipe. Trask felt the slight sting of sharp talons tearing into his chest, and retaliated with a jab at the thing's face. He pressed his attack, fighting with deadly purpose, a killing machine bent with cold determination on his foe's utter annihilation. And after he finished this one he'd track down the others. He'd never played a game yet that you could win without first exterminating the enemy to the last man—or monster.

It was standard tactics.

But while the analytical part of Trask's mind mulled over tactics, his primitive instincts exulted in the savage thrill of battle. Fierce exhilaration lent an awful power to his attack. He brought all his skills into play—his fluid mastery of advanced gaming technique, combined with his intuitive approach to the interface, his martial arts training. All translated with smooth precision to the demands of the alien technology.

The cleavers became extensions of his own arms.

The CGI creature he'd chosen had its limitations. It was ungainly and took a lot of brute force to maneuver. But he'd faced these situations in games before and knew how to adapt.

The alien charged again and Trask raked his cleavers together like mammoth pruning shears.

Snorlok threw himself prone in an upward-flying leap, barely avoiding being sliced in half at the waist when the huge cleavers fanned apart.

The low clearance wasn't designed for such acrobatics. The ceiling canceled his flight and hurled him back down. He threw out his arms to break his fall, and with unbelievable good fortune, broadsided the cleavers, ramming them to the floor and dragging his attacker off balance.

He rolled, coming up in a defensive crouch.

Snorlok willed himself to master his emotions. Whether by choice or through ignorance, his opponent had chosen one of the larger worker drones. Workers weren't made for fighting. This one was designed for chopping—clearing vegetation, compacting garbage, and certain light demolition tasks. The scythelike blades were formidable, but no match for Snorlok's speed.

It was time for a change of strategy.

Snorlok could yet win this contest, but to do so he must give up the offensive and turn to harrying his opponent. Take every opportunity to provoke a futile assault. He would have to continue to evade the cleavers at all costs, but large worker drones sorely taxed their operator's strength, and the creature on the transporter platform would soon tire. Once the thing began to weaken, Snorlok could speed up the process with minimal risk, sapping its reserves through repeated disruptions of the energy field. And when soon it was reduced to helpless exhaustion he would tear it to ribbons.

Unless his enemy had grasped the full scope of the transporter's capabilities and operation—doubtful—and recalled the drone before it was too late, it would sooner or later incorporate and find itself at Snorlok's mercy.

And it was already showing signs of strain.

With grim relish, Snorlok took up the defensive.

Paula stared in the direction the beep had come from. There was a pair of panels in the wall over there that looked like it might be a door, and if that was where the beep had come from, it wasn't a good sign.

She'd already grabbed one of the remotes off the shelf under the console. Now, without thinking, she snatched up the others.

More beeps sounded, like numbers being punched into a cell phone, and they were definitely coming from the panels. It was good enough for Paula. She jumped off the platform—and tripped over the bundled cables plugged into its base. She had a few moments of heart-stopping panic before managing to disentangle herself and dive for the towers at the back wall. Squeezing behind the nearest, she peeked around the corner to watch the panels, then ducked back when they slid apart.

Footsteps. She backed deeper into the crawlspace behind the housing units, chest muscles tightening.

The steps came nearer.

She inched sideways until she reached a gap between two towers and found it gave her a constricted view of the transporter platform and the sphere beyond.

The footsteps stopped.

Paula still couldn't see anything, but she knew that whatever it was, it must be watching Trask. In the sphere, and right under its nose on the platform, in ghostly form. Dodging phantoms—oblivious to this new and far greater danger.

It took another step and she saw it.

She had to fight to keep from fainting. It was bigger than any she'd seen so far.

More than twice her height, it stood silhouetted against the sphere, peering into it. Paula expected an immediate reaction. A sudden Stanley Kowalski-type rampage of horrific destruction. After which, regaining its composure, the thing would retrieve Trask and peevishly tear him limb from limb. And she would die next—for trying like an idiot to save him.

But it just stood there. Watching the sphere.

Paula squirmed over to the next gap between towers. From there she could just see into the sphere around the alien's massive back.

They watched together.

Things weren't going well. Trask's attacks had grown clumsy. The monster kept moving, while keeping carefully out of reach of the heavy cleavers, avoiding every poorly-timed stroke with nimble ease. It was fast. Much faster than Trask now. And it looked confident, fresh, while Trask looked frustrated, his strength failing. He had no visible wounds, but he must have registered some serious damage by now. And if Trask was right, unless he managed to beat the thing soon, at some point the transporter would crash, and he'd incorporate on the platform, defenseless. And if he gave up and tried to beam back, it wouldn't make any difference. In fact, Paula realized with a sinking feeling, there was no way out. Even if he won, he'd still end up back on the platform.

Trask didn't know it, but he was doomed.

As she watched, his legs buckled, his shoulders hunched forward.

The huge head drooped.

He held the cleavers in front of him, shielding his body, but they sagged, their tips grazing the floor.

From across the room the alien watched. Alert, red eyes gleaming.

The predator had turned prey.

Trask must have sensed that the tides had turned. He bellowed and shook his head, like a boxer trying to pull himself together after a punishing round. He took a step forward and stumbled. His opponent's head darted from side to side, searching, ready to strike.

Trask's jaws opened in a silent roar. With effort, he raised both cleavers and shook them in a reckless, taunting challenge.

A foolish gesture. His strength failed him altogether. He dropped his arms. The cleavers thudded against the floor to either side—leaving him wide open.

Her own danger all but forgotten, Paula almost shouted. She caught herself—but not in time to suppress a gasp.

The alien heard her.

Before she could react and duck out of sight, it snapped its head around and trapped her in its gaze.

She stared up at it in mute terror.

Its face was like some insane deep sea fish. An elongated oblong box bristling with slender, erect tendrils. Low-set crimson eyes straddled a noseless muzzle. Long, needle-like teeth jutted upward at haphazard angles from the paddle-shaped lower jaw.

Its expression was unreadable, but its visage radiated menace and awful power. It held her the way a viper holds a terrified rat paralyzed in its gaze, for what felt like an eternity.

And then it turned its back on her.

She wasn't important. It was the contest in the sphere that held the thing's interest.

The monster took the bait. Winding up a spiked fist, it sprang. It was fast.

But this time Trask was faster.

The utility drone became a blur.

A cleaver sliced upward in a lightning stroke. There was a sickening crunch and the monster's head leapt from its shoulders. It whacked against the ceiling and ricocheted toward the back wall, sending punters scrambling out of its path.

The thing's body staggered but didn't fall.

Its head slammed into the wall and came flying back. It hit the floor, bounced up, and sailed, tumbling, straight at its owner's legs. The jaws snapped open and clamped onto a shin, and the headless body reached down with a cluster of tentacles and tore it loose, ripping its own flesh to the bone. Tucking the head under its arm like an NFL quarterback from Hell, it bounded through the door and fled across the sand straight for the jungle.

Glumrok stepped out of the shaft onto the first level, dropping to all fours beneath the corridor's low ceiling to lumber quadripedally the short distance to Zillior's quarters. Purring to herself in anticipation of the little one's joy at the glad tidings she brought, she pressed the control panel button and padded through the door.

At the sight of Zillior in her pod, sound asleep under the coverlets, Glumrok smiled with almost painful fondness. The tenderness of her own feelings sometimes overwhelmed her, and now she hesitated. Perhaps she should allow the little darling her rest. There was no real need for Zillior to be awakened—it was perfectly safe for her to sleep through the departure.

But then, she'd be disappointed to miss the excitement of leave-taking.

It wouldn't be fair to deprive her of the experience.

Glumrok stepped to Zillior's podside. Stooping further to peer beneath the canopy, she couldn't restrain a smile of amusement. Zillior lay completely bundled up under the coverlet, her head and entire body buried in its folds. Only her leg stuck out at the bottom, dangling over the floor.

With a chuckle, Glumrok set her tentacles upon the little one's forehead, intending to gently nudge her awake.

She withdrew them with a start.

Instead of the expected firm resistance of Zillior's bony brow beneath the material, Glumrok's tentacles had encountered only a soft mass. She reached out again and drew away the coverlet.

The soft mass was Zillior's foam-filled pillow, plumped up and carefully positioned underneath.

She drew it back further.

Zillior's entire bulk was a crude fake. The whole sleeping form composed of pillows and rolled up blankets.

But—

Glumrok's tendrils flexed in sudden alarm. She whipped away the coverlet.

The sight that met her eyes stunned her. With an anguished howl, she jumped to her feet, slamming her head into the ceiling. The shock of impact rattled the chamber, hurling knickknacks from nearby tables and dashing them to the floor in a fragile tinkling of destruction.

Dropping back to all fours, shaking with wrath, she stared at the hideous deceit.

Zillior's severed leg had been fastened to her pod's cradle in slapdash fashion with twisted lengths of electrical wire. It punctured the skin in a dozen places—piercing the extruding stump and crisscrossing the flesh in a welter of gruesome stitchery.

Some great mischief was afoot. And there was little room for wonderment as to whom would be responsible.

Snorlok!—and, by extension—Strindlak.

Inside the mess hall, all was quiet. Jim, Lance and Brad—and Fred, still armed only with his Sony handheld—stood with their backs against the wall, staring up at the glowing CGI creature. Waiting.

It just stared back. It seemed to be waiting, too.

Jim said, "Trask."

The creature nodded.

Lance looked at Jim, then back up at the thing and whistled. "Holy shit," he said.

The Trask-thing nodded again.

At the sound of their voices, those outside approached the doorway.

"It's Trask," Jim called out to them.

It took a few seconds to sink in. But when it did, it galvanized them.

Trask. All of a sudden everything made sense. They had a champion.

One who more than rivaled their enemy's own power and strength. And with whose help they just might have a chance of beating these things.

From inside came a loud whump.

Lance and Brad came flying out the door, dragging Fred, and Jim dove through the door after them, just as the mess hall's interior lit up like a Christmas tree.

Everyone hit the dirt. The blast shook the ground beneath them. What was left of the barricades blew through the shattered windows and door in a hailstorm of debris.

Brad was the first to scramble to his feet when the dust settled. He charged back inside—only to come out again a few seconds later, coughing and shaking his head.

A gloomy silence descended.

Then Zach said, "He's going after them."

A murmur swept through the punters' ranks.

"Right?" Brad said.

The murmur grew louder.

Someone shouted, and all at once a dozen machetes and war clubs spiked skyward in clenched fists—and the punters roared out Trask's name as a battle cry.

The blood-splattered walls fractured into rainbow-hued geometrics, then motion-blurred into vertical streaks, and Trask stretched simultaneously down into the earth and up through the clouds. The mess hall melted away and everything went white.

When the world faded back in, his eyes focused on what looked like a souped-up Camaro with an opalescent, deep metallic-green-sparkle paint job. Which, of course, could only mean he was gazing upon the gaily-colored abdomen of a huge alien monster.

He looked up and winced. The thing must have been twelve feet tall. It could kill him in an instant.

The simplicity of his situation brought Trask a strange feeling of serenity.

But instead of pounding him flat with a single hammerblow of its gigantic fist, the thing reached with exaggerated slowness for his arm. Careful, so as not to startle him. Following the tentacles' unwinding motion toward his wrist, Trask realized it was the remote the alien wanted. He obeyed by raising his forearm. A trio of tentacle tips tickled his wrist when they brushed against his skin and pressed the metal oval's edge. The remote released its grip, dropped into another waiting cluster of foretentacles and disappeared in their coils.

Again moving with the greatest care, the alien pressed a rectangular button on the console. It seemed to expect some concrete result, and when nothing happened, it repeated the action a few more times before giving up. It stood there, blinking, with a look of perplexity—like it was wondering just what the heck was going on, and what to do about this new development. Pretty much what Trask was doing too. And what Paula would be—

Paula… Where was she?—

Trask almost jumped out of his pants when the alien whirled at a short beep from across the room. When these things moved fast, they moved a lot of air.

Something was at the door. And it had scared this thing too.

What the hell could scare this thing?

With frantic haste, the alien ran its tentacles over the control panel, taloned tips clicking like mad. The console lights winked out. It twirled a knob, punched a button. The big sphere went dark.

The alien hurriedly positioned itself between Trask and the door and made a flicking motion behind its back with its foretentacles.

There was no mistaking the gesture. Unbelievable as it seemed, it was telling Trask to make himself scarce.

He hopped off the platform and slipped away toward the back wall, and there was Paula, waving him over from behind one of the big housing units.

After he'd squeezed in next to her, they both turned to watch the door. And all of a sudden their once-formidable twelve-footer didn't seem all that impressive.

The only way this new monstrosity could fit through the door was on all fours. When it cleared the doorway and stood up, you really noticed how perspective comes more strikingly into play over vast distances. Its head, high up near the ceiling, looked smaller than you knew it was. But even from a long way off, the suspicion betrayed by its features, however alien, was evident.

Its voice was strangely beautiful, in spite of the harsh note of accusation it carried.

CHAPTER THIRTY-THREE

MISDIRECTION

"LET'S GET THEM," Brad said.

Lance agreed. "Now, while they're hurting. Wipe them out once and for all."

"And anyway, we can't just leave Trask to fight them alone," Zach said. "Not after this."

They couldn't be certain what Trask was going to do next. But if he was going after them, Zach was right. CGI or not, Trask wasn't invulnerable.

Jim considered, then nodded.

"Is everybody in?" he said.

They were. All nine of them. That included Fred, who'd finally laid down his camera and picked up a weapon. Evan's knife. Evans didn't need it anymore. Vince was dead too. So was Mei. And Corey. Janet and Jeremy had disappeared.

"Rashad," Jim said, "go back inside and get yourself and Beverly something to fight with." Both of them had emerged from the mess hall weaponless. "Vince's machete's in there somewhere."

At that moment, Grant came tearing around the corner of the bungalow yelling like a madman, with Hal and his camera hurrying after him.

"To arms! We must strike swiftly while victory is within our grasp."

Jim was too busy conferring with Lance to pay Grant any attention. The others looked up without interest.

Seeing his exhortations met with what he took for slack-jawed obstinacy, Grant raised his voice.

"Listen to me," he shouted.

At that, Jim and Lance turned.

"This may be our only chance," Grant said. "We must not let it pass.

An opportunity like this may not present itself for, for…" His words trailed off under Jim's steady gaze.

"You're late," Jim said.

Grant blinked. Rashad came back outside with two machetes and a spike-tipped bat. He tossed a machete to Beverly.

"Let's go," Jim said. And as an afterthought, "Come on, Grant." He set off at a fast trot toward the jungle, and the party fell in behind him, leaving Grant staring after them.

"Grant."

Grant looked around. Rashad flipped him the bat, and he caught it clumsily.

Michelle was waiting for them.

"Last one in's a B-list TV star," Rashad said.

They hurried to catch up with the others.

Clearly suspicious of his presence in the transporter chamber, Glumrok ordered Strindlak to turn on the device at once, and he at once realized his mistake.

If he'd simply given the positioning control a good spin, when the transporter came back on she would see only an innocuous patch of native vegetation. As it was, the imager would clear on a scene of horrific devastation wrought by the halflings that was all but certain to pique her scowling curiosity.

Strindlak stepped around to the side of the platform as he spoke, pretending to examine the controls in puzzlement.

Unfortunately, the transporter doesn't seem to be responding, he lied. He'd been alerted to a hardware malfunction by the ship's computer and come to take a look at it. With practiced stealth, he uncurled his pod tentacles. They slid across the floor, groping toward the rear of the platform as he played for time by speculating aloud as to the most likely causative factors behind this latest malfunction. They soon found the bundled power cables, unplugged the connector with a deft jerk, and retracted back into his pod.

To prove the truth of his assertion, Strindlak engaged the power switch. Glumrok could now see for herself that the controls weren't responding.

She was far from satisfied.

Where were the halflings? she demanded.

Strindlak didn't know.

Where was Zillior?

Asleep in her pod—he assumed.

Did he? Then what, might she inquire, did Strindlak make of *this?*

Glumrok swung Zillior's leg out from behind her back, striking him across the forehead with it. When his head snapped back into position, she was shaking the limb in his face as she recounted the deception perpetrated by the innocent one's conniving siblings in all its colorful detail.

Strindlak stared at the leg, trying to hide his shock. His mind raced. He'd seen Snorlok, and what was left of the other halfling. He'd guessed the twins were with them, though he hadn't seen them. Now it turned out Zillior must be too.

Most of her.

Though Strindlak himself wasn't completely clear on what was happening, he did know that, whatever it was, if Glumrok found out, he'd never hear the end of it. The ship's manual had warned against the perils of reckless adventurism. And now the infernal halflings, through their bone-headed and wanton thrill-seeking, had exposed the cherished one to dire hazard and it was anyone's guess where she was or what kind of shape she was in.

But there was little question who would be held ultimately responsible for the halflings' misbehavior.

There was only one hope, however faint. He must keep Glumrok in the dark at all costs. Come up with some plausible story and then retrieve Zillior and the halflings as quickly as possible to put Glumrok's mind at rest before she ferreted out the true extent of their mischief.

Strindlak babbled, barely aware of what he was saying.

It was obvious what had happened. Zillior had suffered a bit of wear and tear, the result of excessive rowdiness, not an uncommon occurrence for a young female halfling with older male siblings. And now, overreacting out of fear of punishment, the lot of them were in hiding—hoping to give the leg time to regenerate before their carelessness could be discovered.

As their parents, it would be best for Glumrok and himself to avoid a similar overreaction, especially since it was evident there was no real cause for alarm.

Nevertheless!—he, Strindlak, would personally scour the entire ship from top to bottom until the miscreants were found. And rest assured they would be dealt with severely for the deception.

To Strindlak's vast relief, Glumrok was somewhat placated by his words.

Now his biggest worry—other than locating and rescuing the wretched halflings—was her seeing the creatures hiding behind the towers at his back. Their presence, if discovered, would suggest much, and set off a withering interrogation under which Strindlak would inevitably crack.

With a determined nod and purposeful stride, he made for the door, hoping and expecting Glumrok would follow.

She didn't.

He returned to her side and attempted to physically hustle her out, declaring that there was nothing more to be done here and that the best thing for her to do would be to await further word in the comfort of their quarters.

Glumrok threw him off with an angry flailing of tentacles. She would remain here, she told him, and see if there were anything she might do to restore functionality to the transporter.

The idea was absurd of course, since Glumrok's mechanical skills weren't even on a par with Strindlak's own. But she stood firm against all arguments, until it dawned on Strindlak that the true reason for her stubbornness was that she suspected there was more to this than he would have her believe, and that the transporter might hold the key to the truth. And that by over-remonstrating, he would only further implicate himself.

He'd have to let it go and hope for the best. With a covert glance at the towers—and seeing no sign of the two stowaways—he strode from the chamber.

The second the door closed behind him, he lit into a loping run down the corridor.

Hurrying to catch up, Grant felt his face burning with embarrassment. He must have looked like a complete fool to Jim, running outside yelling after sitting through the whole battle in the control room.

And now again it was Trask who'd saved the day.

He felt a sudden twinge of guilt for what he'd done the night before. Trask had surprised him. Maybe he wasn't as bad as Grant thought. A personality clash between natural leaders. Though it was an appalling thought that someone like Trask might harbor hidden leadership qualities.

And Trask had deserved it anyway. He'd done his best to sow discord and challenge Grant's competence from the very beginning.

And look where Trask's supposed leadership had gotten them. He certainly ought to have done something to make up for the trouble his dissension had brought about. So what if now he had? If Trask had gone along with him in the first place—instead of resorting to the strategem of rational argument to prevent Jim and the others from joining—they might have had a decisive victory over these things earlier, in the daylight. A sound thrashing then might have prevented this latest round of bloodshed.

His resurgent anger at Trask spurred Grant to greater speed. Winning through to the forward ranks, he took his place in the lead beside Jim.

Grant's admiration for the big man had never faltered. He couldn't blame Jim for being blind to Trask's machinations. On the contrary, he admired him all the more for it. Men like Jim were so far above deceit they couldn't imagine those their good nature led them to trust resorting to such scheming. His honor could not be tainted by the connivings of lesser men.

And now, again, Trask had fled.

This time, Jim would get a chance to see the stuff Grant was made of. He wouldn't be disappointed.

Glumrok lifted one gigantic leg over the platform railing, then the other. The metal dais creaked under her weight. Stooping over the control console, she threw a switch.

Nothing happened. She pressed a few buttons at random, then a few more. Still nothing.

In growing impatience she unsheathed a myriad of tentacle tips and pecked at the controls. The pecking accelerated to a blizzard of lightning strokes that clattered like a radiation sensor in a particle storm.

It was all for naught.

Giving in to frustration, she administered a sharp blow to the console's top—and was at once forced to rein in her anger when she saw she'd put a dent in its metal surface.

Glumrok knew little of electronics, but it was evident even to her that the mechanism wasn't drawing any power. She wouldn't know where to even begin to fix that. Without the proper documentation to refer to, she hadn't a clue how to proceed.

With some reluctance, she resolved to do after all as Strindlak had suggested and await the outcome of his search in their quarters.

She lifted one leg over the railing and eased it to the floor. In swinging her other leg up and over, she was thrown off balance by her pod grazing the topmost rail—and when she instinctively splayed her tentacles to prevent herself from stumbling, she felt something catch between them and nearly tripped.

Regaining her balance, she looked down.

A thick bundle of cables, ending in a rectangular-shaped connector had become entangled in her pod tentacles. Bending over to reach for it, she noticed the jack at the base of the platform.

She must have jerked the connector free by accident when she stepped on it. She pried the cables from between her tentacle tips and inserted the connector into the jack.

Careful not to bump the overhanging harness with her head, she stood up, and was just turning to leave the chamber when the glowing FLARDNUX CORPORATION logo caught her eye.

CHAPTER THIRTY-FOUR

EXPOSÉ

DAY HAD DAWNED. Strindlak's pods thudded over the hard-packed ground. A boulder dislodged by his passing tumbled down the mountain's steep face, frightening a gaggle of winged creatures to flight.

Strindlak barreled on.

Speed was of the essence. He'd succeeded so far in concealing the worst from Glumrok. All that was needed now was to bring back Zillior and the halflings intact before she noticed the unplugged connector or the stowaways. Once Glumrok had Zillior, the situation would become manageable.

It was unlikely she would discover the connector, given her general ignorance with regard to shipboard appliances. As for the stowaways, they appeared to have enough sense to keep out of sight. With the ship operational it would be a simple matter of surreptitiously transporting them to the planet's surface after takeoff. Or, if backup remotes couldn't be located, dropping them off at the lost and found department of the nearest transfer point.

If he could still find them, that is. If they left the transporter chamber they'd be doomed. Even if they survived the trip in hiding, the mandatory quarantine and fumigation procedures at customs following disembarkation would result in their certain death by asphyxiation. If he reported them, or if they were unlucky enough to be found aboard by the authorities before decontamination, Strindlak would claim they'd slipped in through the hatch unnoticed when he stepped out. He'd be slapped with a fine; the creatures would be examined—their intelligence evaluated, their physical characteristics and capabilities rigorously analyzed; their bodies probed and prodded—in the course of which they would most likely be reduced to a collection of carelessly labeled tissue samples—or destroyed altogether.

Unfortunate, but by that point probably for the best.

He hurdled a clump of greenery. Patches of tall plant forms dotted the slopes. Their slender tentacles seemed to reach for him as he sped past.

There was still the problem of concocting a believable story—and the halflings would have to be instructed to go along with it—but again, once Zillior was back, Glumrok would be mollified and ready to accept whatever version of events was handed to her. This was assuming, of course, that Zillior hadn't suffered any injury so horrendous that she was beyond… Strindlak's mind refused to pursue the thought further. If that had happened, there was no hope for it. Glumrok would flagellate him over the loss without mercy or letup until the end of his days.

But leaving that aside, there remained—what? The transporter, the creatures. The halflings… Yes, that was it, he'd almost forgotten. The damaged halfling in the natives' shelter. But it shouldn't be a problem salvaging a suitable section of spinal cord using only the one remote.

But that brought up another question: Where *were* the remotes? Would Glumrok notice them missing? And if she did, what then? She would assume the halflings had them. That was apparently not the case—when he'd tried to retrieve them, the screen had flashed an "UNATTACHED" error message—but it didn't matter. By extension she would conclude—correctly—that the halflings were outside the ship. And from there—

Strindlak's pod tentacles raked the ground, plowing up dirt as he threw himself backwards and plunged his talons into the solid rock at his back. Distracted by his growing concerns, he'd nearly sailed over the edge of a precipice. He would doubtless have survived the fall whatever its height, but it might have cost him precious time.

He swung himself up onto the ledge and, skirting the dropoff, resumed his headlong pace.

The piling up and infinite branching out of complications made his head spin. His story's cloth was unraveling before it was half woven. He'd already spotted a gaping hole and it was probably only his fast talking that had kept Glumrok from seeing it: Why had the halflings resorted to the ruse with Zillior's leg in the first place? It could only mean they'd lost the rest of her.

Damn the little ruffians and their disobedience! What were they think-ing? Had they brought the natives aboard the ship as playmates, naively unaware of the danger? Perhaps given their new friends the remotes to facilitate their coming and going? Would he return to find the ship inun-dated by a whole clan of unpredictable, thrill-crazy savages on top of the two already on board?

Strindlak was beginning to regret his rashness in trying to hide the facts from Glumrok. If he'd just admitted what he knew at the outset there would have been no need for the charade. As it was, he'd entrapped himself in an expanding web of deceit and compounded the practical difficulties immeas-urably. And the unnecessary delay could have grave consequences—in which case Glumrok's rage would be all the more intolerable.

The imager cleared. After a moment's confusion Glumrok realized the scene within must be of the interior of one of the native habitations. But why? Had Strindlak been spying on the things? To what purpose?

She recoiled in disgust at the scene. The place was an absolute hovel, worse than anything she'd ever seen among the worst of her own kind. That the natives of this dismal place lived out their pathetic lives in the most abject squalor was amply demonstrated by the appalling state of dis-repair of their rude dwelling. Gaping holes exposed the inhabitants to the elements. Ineffectual attempts at repair appeared to have been made with utter incompetence. Cheaply-constructed furnishings were scattered about, some overturned, many of them broken. What looked like soiled coverlets and other manner of feculent refuse was strewn everywhere in revoltingly unsanitary profusion. Even the walls were grimy, caked with unidentifiable filth.

And here, asleep in their own ordure upon the waste-befouled floor, lay the natives themselves. Two of them, in an apparent state of insensate inebriation.

The sight filled Glumrok with revulsion—and yet, she couldn't repress a certain fascination. Perhaps it was what had compelled Strindlak to visit the place.

Movement caught her eye.

Here was yet another of the besotted creatures, just regaining consciousness and attempting to rise. It was an ungainly thing, seemingly armless, with no discernible head. Nothing but a pair of legs and a… squat…

Glumrok's scalp tendrils lifted up from her skull to bob erect in taut alertness. She stared hard in dawning horror.

His head was squashed flat under a metal storage unit. But his mother didn't need to see his face to recognize her own offspring.

Ropsnag! Hideously, his lower half made another abortive attempt to stand upright, while the upper, glued to its ruined head by strands of mucus, twisted and scraped at the floor, trying to drag itself free by its talons.

Strindlak! He'd seen this already! It was he who had unplugged the transporter—to hide the evidence!

Howling and spitting with wrath, she reached again for the positioner. She'd get to the bottom of this one way or another. And if anything had happened to Zillior, Strindlak—and Snorlok—would pay dearly for their parts in the coverup.

The huge alien was terrible in its rage. It screeched at the sphere in near-mindless horror—as if, stripped of the capacity for rational thought, it hoped to force the awful sight out of existence through the sheer, overwhelming power of catastrophic volume.

Trask and Paula trembled like a pair of chihuahuas in an arctic blast. Edging deeper into the crawlspace, they found that the next gap between towers offered an unobstructed view of both the sphere and the console.

The bone-squeezing sound waves let up a notch. After several minutes the alien seemed to tire, and its screeching fell off to a more or less continuous snarling. Setting a single tentacle tip atop the rollerball, it experimented with a few tentative nudges.

It was obviously a novice. For Trask, time slowed to a crawl while it pondered its next move. Finally, it tapped the display. And then fell to studying the screen for what seemed like ages.

If there was anything that drove Trask up the wall it was the fastidious manual-readers with their endless looking-up and re-checking. Trask had no patience with manuals—"documentation" as their manufacturers and proponents pompously referred to them—and held those who did in low esteem.

Of course, he wasn't above sneaking a peek when they got around to applying what they'd learned.

Taking advantage of its irregular contouring, Trask scaled the tower for a better vantage point that brought the console's control surface into view.

The alien glanced between the controls and their onscreen representation. Seeming to find what it was looking for, it grasped a dial, checked the diagram once more, looked into the sphere, and turned the dial counterclockwise.

The image within the sphere shrank as its perimeter expanded.

They were zooming out. Going to wide angle—just what Trask would need to locate the others and beam them aboard.

The alien grunted, turned the dial a little more. The shift to wide angle sped up. Sure of itself now, the alien spun the dial all the way counterclockwise. The scene went momentarily white, then a split second later refocused in full wide angle view.

It was like looking down from an airplane. A quick search of the entire island had just become a realistic option.

Returning its attention to the rollerball, the alien gave it a minute sideways nudge. The trees flowed past from left to right in super slo-mo. They kept going, at an achingly slow pace, until the ocean pulled into view. The alien was adopting a methodical search pattern. And with each sweep, it gained the confidence to give the thing a little more gas.

The foothills of the central peak pulled into view. The terrain went into a steep ascent.

The alien jumped at a sudden flurry of beeps, and with a typical beginner's panicked reaction, it floored the accelerator. A tight cluster of blinking cursors sped inward from the sphere's leading edge. Coming quickly to its senses, the alien released the rollerball.

The image froze, centered on what appeared to be a ledge jutting from the mountain's steep western face.

The cursors had stopped blinking. At extreme wide angle, they obstructed any view of whatever they were meant to indicate.

After a brief pause to refer to the manual, the alien spun the zoom dial full clockwise.

The scene went white.

It came back into focus on—what? The side of the mountain? They'd apparently gone to MAX ZOOM, and whatever it was they were looking at took up all but the top quarter of the sphere. A solid wall of…some kind of iridescent…

Gaining familiarity with the controls, the alien pulled back. What had looked like a mountain of rock turned out to be a mountain of flesh: one of the alien children, on such high magnification that its abdomen filled the sphere. It seemed to be lying on its back. Its chest and arms gradually came into view. Something—it was just a dark blur—kept punching down at it from above, and the thing writhed and squirmed as the pullback continued.

Then a shadow loomed, and darted in, blocking their view. There was a whirl of color, a flash of reflected light—and as the pullback continued, Trask and Paula recognized Michelle, standing over the thing.

She had just struck off its head with her machete.

It rolled in the dirt, eyes swiveling convulsively.

She kicked it away.

Trask and Paula covered their ears. It didn't help. Their alien howled like a tornado. It whirled the dial and the entire ledge came into view.

It was the usual bloody mess. Gabrielle was dead. Zach was dead—if that was him. One alien was down, and the little one, unscathed save for its still-missing leg, was trying to scale the rock face to safety while Beverly and Fred tried to drag it back down. Jim, Grant, and the rest of the punters hewed and chopped at the one Trask had fought earlier. It had succeeded in re-planting its head, but was now missing an arm. And one lower leg, half-severed, dragged by a strip of sinew from its shattered knee, squirming and thrashing. It appeared to be straining to right itself and reattach to the oozing stump. But even missing an arm and a leg, the huge alien fought like a demon. Anchored to the ledge by talons plunged into the solid rock, swaying like a misshapen tree and spitting with rage, it lunged at its assailants.

As they watched, it knocked Brad off his feet. He tumbled from the ledge.

The base of the imager was ringed with built-in storage cabinets. Glumrok tore one open with such violence the door snapped off its hinges. Tossing it aside, she scooped its entire inventory out onto the floor, gave it a quick once over, then turned with a snarl to the next—looking up to cast a hurried glance into the imager as she did.

Zillior was as yet unharmed, save for her missing leg. For the moment, the bloodthirsty savages concentrated their attack upon her eldest sibling.

That could change in an instant.

She trembled at the thought. But somewhere, Glumrok knew, was an entire cache of spare remote units. And she only needed one.

Rashad let down his guard. A clutch of writhing tentacles flicked out, caught him around the neck and hoisted him into the air. He was thrust this way and that, clearing a path through his captor's ring of attackers— then flung away like a vole shot from under a power mower.

He flew screaming over the edge of the cliff, toward the rocks fifty feet below.

Shaken punters tried to scramble out of the thing's way as it bounded for the gap, as an afterthought snatching up Grant in its leap for freedom. Winning through unopposed to the cliff's edge, it whirled.

The exhausted punters, mauled and bleeding, could only stare, too weak to regroup and take back the offensive.

The loops of tentacles tightened around Grant's neck.

Jim lifted his sword. Beaten or not, he wouldn't stand by and watch Grant or anyone else killed in cold blood while he was still on his feet.

The monster gazed down at him. Then, seeming to sense the enemy's awareness of their own defeat, it shook its mane of tendrils in triumph, lifted its head and roared at the sky.

Its roar was met by another.

From below. Echoing off the cliff face beneath their feet and booming away over the hills, deep as rumbling thunder.

Spotting another long row of cabinets running along the wall high up near the ceiling, Glumrok rose up on her haunches—still well short of her full height—and began flinging them open one after another.

As she did, she glanced again down at the imager—and froze to stare in disbelief.

~~~~~~~~~~~~~~~~~~~~~~~~~~~
~~~~~~~~~~~~~~~~~~~~~~~~~~~

The combatants turned toward the cliffside to see Rashad levitating up over the edge—in the grip of a gargantuan fist. When they cleared the ledge, the enormous tentacles holding him unraveled, and Michelle pulled him to safety when he rolled free.

The tentacles groped over the ledge, breaking up and crushing great chunks of rock to powder as they strained to find a purchase that would support the unimaginable weight of their owner.

Punters and aliens alike trembled when another huge-taloned fist swung up and over, slamming into the rock like a mammoth grappling hook. The impact shook the ledge, throwing up clouds of pulverized basalt.

They settled over a monstrous head and shoulders.

Like a crested basilisk submerged in a pond up to its unblinking gaze, the new thing surveyed the scene through slitted eyes—then vaulted up onto the ledge, sending punters scrambling for the cliff face at their backs.

The ledge shook again under the punishing jolt of its landing. With a brittle crackling of ligaments, it straightened its broad back and stretched itself up to its full height. Somewhere between an eighth and a quarter of an inch shy of twelve feet.

Its weight would be measured in tons.

It was all over. Really.

From back in its throat, the giant alien growled. It was a soft sound. Grant's captor released him at once. He fell to the ledge, gasping but alive.

After a few uncertain seconds, the punters lowered their arms.

Under the giant's glare, the big alien reached for its lower leg, still hanging by fibrous strands from its mangled knee, and pulled it up. The stump thrust out a sticky protrusion that drew the limb tight against the joint. Soon, only a pale ridge showed where they'd once been cloven apart.

The operation completed, the giant turned its glare away and looked down.

An alien's severed head lay at its feet, eyes blinking up in apprehension. Tipping itself face up with the help of its crown of tendrils, it unclenched its teeth. A thick, blackened tongue poked out, licked dry lips, and silently retracted.

Ignoring it for now, the monster picked up a legless reptilian torso in one giant fist, a sundered leg in the other, and pressed them together. The parts bonded and set within seconds. Another leg, another arm, a head, and in no time at all, the punters' enemies stood resurrected before them.

The giant grunted in cold satisfaction.

It stooped again. This time, the body part it scooped up was human. Holding it gingerly, it cast its gaze over the bloody terrain.

Spared by the most recent violence, the smallest of the aliens—the punters had by now guessed they were the giant alien's own offspring—had clambered down from the cliff face at the cessation of hostilities. Now it pointed at Zach's torso and chirped. The monster took it up and connected the limb—an arm—to the torso's shoulder, applying firm, even pressure.

After a few moments, a look of confusion crossed its features. Muttering, it separated the two pieces and, holding them up to its face, studied them closely. It pressed them together again. And when again the operation failed, the thing stared at the bloody remains and huffed in bafflement.

Its bewildered expression slowly changed to one of dismay.

It looked down at the punters' faces, then half turned toward its offspring. Unable to meet its gaze, they studied the ground at their feet.

The giant stole another glance at the punters, then very slowly and gently laid down the lifeless body parts.

It whirled on its offspring.

Its contorted features and harsh snarls left no doubt it was giving them the bawling out of their lives. The tongue-lashing went on for minutes. It ended with a barked command.

After some hesitation, but in apparent obedience, the offspring approached the wary punters, stopping in a row facing them. With heads bowed, they mumbled a few words.

As if finding the exercise lacking in fervor, the parent snapped angrily, and the foursome repeated the phrase more earnestly. The intent was clear.

"They're apologizing," Michelle said in disbelief. She spat. Separating herself from the group, she stepped forward and hefted her machete. "They didn't know it was bad. And now they're sorry."

"Don't," Grant said. He reached for her but she knocked his hand away and advanced on the nearest alien. A foot taller than her, it flinched but held its ground.

"Let's make sure," she said. She looked up into the blood-smeared face. "I accept your apology."

As she said it, she wound up and swung her machete with every ounce of strength she had left.

It was still quite a bit.

The blade sheared through the tentacles the thing threw up to protect itself and ripped into the side of its face. Teeth and spittle flew from the dislocated jaw. Michelle wound up again and the thing gibbered and scurried away to hide behind its parent's tree-trunk legs.

The machete slammed into them and rebounded, blade wobbling. The giant thing looked down at her sadly. She swung again. The blade snapped off. She stabbed at it with the broken hilt, saying, "I accept your apology," over and over until she sunk to her knees and Rashad came forward and put a hand on her shoulder.

The huge alien stood staring for a long time, then growled softly and turned away.

With its offspring in tow, it scaled the sheer rock face to the overhang above and clambered up and over.

They quickly disappeared from sight.

PART FOUR: MONDAY

CHAPTER THIRTY-FIVE

STAGING

WITH A LONG, HARD MARCH still ahead, Strindlak's anger gave way to concern at the cherished one's struggling to keep up over the rugged terrain. Her siblings, perhaps fearing his disapproval, made no move to aid her, but they too watched her with worried frowns.

Strindlak gave her another appraising glance. The fresh extrusion had already taken on the semblance of a vestigial leg, probably an indication the time for reattachment was past. Strindlak was no expert on medical matters, but he knew from personal experience how long a full regeneration could take. Up to a certain point, an extrusion could be trimmed back to the stump, and the severed limb reattached with satisfactory results. But while Glumrok would likely be able to gauge whether that point had been reached, he would not.

Once again, Strindlak regretted disabling the transporter. If the machine were operational, he'd have been able to transport Zillior back with the single retrieval module he'd concealed from her mother. There'd be no—

Panic seized him. The module! Had he lost it in the—but no, here it was. He unraveled his tentacles—and stopped dead in his tracks.

The READY light was on.

Meaning the transporter was on standby.

His ruse was discovered.

And it didn't end there: Glumrok would by now have seen the missing sibling in the native encampment, and guessed that Strindlak knew everything all along.

There was no point in prolonging the charade. There would be no escaping Glumrok's wrath, but having Zillior back would soften its fury.

Zillior looked up at him innocently. Aside from the obvious differences in temperament, the little one was in many ways very much like her mother. She bore up under her hardships with admirable bravery.

How could he do otherwise?

Glumrok had begun to relax once Zillior and the halflings were safe with their father and on their way back to the ship. But lingering distrust compelled her to monitor their progress in the imager, using the navigation controls—she now considered herself something of an adept—to keep them in continuous view.

There was still the matter of Ropsnag lying senseless upon the floor of the native dwelling. But Strindlak should have no difficulty retrieving him once they'd located the missing modules or found the spares. Glumrok held all her offspring in the highest affection, and the loss of any one of them would of course be cause for the ritualistic display of grief required by revered tradition. But Ropsnag could wait.

Having apparently called a halt, Strindlak motioned Zillior forward. Perhaps it had finally occurred to him to carry the poor thing the rest of the way, as he ought to have done from the outset. But that was too unlike Strindlak—and when he wrapped his tentacles around her forearm and held them there, Glumrok's brow tendrils frilled with a sharpening suspicion that was justified the moment he withdrew them.

A retrieval module! He'd had it all the time.

But she reined in her anger. Zillior's return could only be occasion for joy and the greatest relief. For that, at least, Glumrok was grateful. Strindlak had, after all, come around to doing the right thing in the end.

In the imager, Zillior pressed the module's button and began to pixelate.

Her heart soaring, Glumrok turned to the platform.

Trask climbed down from his perch. Watching along with the giant alien, he and Paula had seen everything. Now they ducked back out of sight when it—she—the child's mother—turned in their direction, eyes shining.

The air above the platform came alive.

The little troll was returned to its mother's breast.

It was at first startled by its mother's closeness, but then squealed in delight when she swept it up in coils of tentacles and hugged it tight.

The sight was so impossible to reconcile with the carnage he'd witnessed over the last three days Trask wondered if he'd finally lost it.

It's all right now, it's all over, the child's mother seemed to be saying.

For them, maybe it was.

But not for him, or Paula, or anyone else on this side of the barrier. They were still hostages, at the mercy of these things' whims. And, thinking, feeling creatures though they might be, they were also warlike and cruel, and there was no predicting what fate held in store for his dwindling tribe of punters at their hands.

Big Mama Alien gently lifted her child off the platform, cooing something that sounded like, "Zillior, Zillior,"—and Trask realized that these things had names.

And with that, she carried her offspring from the chamber. As the door slid shut, she flicked a switch, throwing the chamber into semi-darkness.

Paula and Trask were alone.

It was time.

"You okay?"

She nodded. "I just wish she hadn't turned off the lights."

Trask walked over to the door, his way illuminated by the glowing sphere and a thousand multicolored panel lights, and turned them back on.

"I know how you feel," he said. He jumped up onto the platform. "Let's try and relocate the cliff."

They found Rashad and Michelle and the others just starting down the mountain. Trask beamed Paula right into their midst. There were some tense moments before they realized it was her, but once they did, their alarm gave way to excitement. As soon as he was sure everything was okay, Trask left them to go location scouting.

He quickly discovered there were limits to the transporter's range. When he exceeded a certain distance beyond the barrier, a buzzer would sound and the sphere would go white. That ruled out finding another island to hop to. The crash course in Transporter Navigation 101 had paid off, though. On full wide angle view, he'd have no trouble locating a ship—the ocean beyond the barrier teemed with them, and he had his pick.

Rolling over the waves like a pro, he considered. They needed medical facilities, so the bigger the better. Something with choppers. Medevac.

A ship slid into view. It looked like the one that had come in Saturday morning. Hal had called it a cruiser.

He zoomed on it.

There wasn't much going on. Some officers stood around on deck talking. Enlisted men went about their duties. Nobody paid any attention to the barrier. But then why should they? From their perspective, nothing had happened since they got here.

Were they ever in for a surprise.

He picked a vacant spot about ten yards forward of the group of officers and locked in the coordinates.

The others should have started coming in by now. Beaming in was fast. A few seconds. Beaming out was a different story, but still probably no more than thirty. Not too bad. Except none of them were here yet.

What was taking them so long?

And where were Jim and the others? They could have all come in on the six remotes by doubling up. But then, they couldn't double up on the beam out to the cruiser anyway. The transporter obviously wasn't designed for it, which made it a bad idea and not worth the risk except in a real emergency.

He checked and re-checked the settings, mentally rehearsing the beam. Everything was ready. He was just weighing the advisability of rolling back to the mountainside to see if something had gone wrong when the transporter started to hum.

It was Beverly. She materialized within seconds, glassy-eyed and disoriented.

"You're fine, just a little jet lag," he reassured her, guiding her down the steps at the side of the platform. He kept his voice down. "I've found a ship. You'll be out of here in a few minutes."

Lance was next. Trask winced at his injuries, but Lance didn't make a sound when Beverly helped him down. Fred followed, then Michelle. Everything was going smoothly so far.

"Where are the others?" he asked Michelle.

"The others?"

"Jim. And Grant. And—"

"And Hal?" Michelle said. "Oh. They went after the aliens."

~~~~~~~~~~~~~~~~~~~~~~~~~~~~~~

They'd gone half a mile when Grant got the shakes. Wobbling on legs that felt like they'd been de-boned, he had to grab Hal's arm to keep from falling.

Jim slowed the pace. "Don't worry, Grant—get the shit stomped out of you enough times, you'll start getting used to it."

Hal shook his head. "It's not just that. Battle fatigue. I've seen it before."

Jim looked at Hal, then said, "Let's pull over."

Grant tried to wave them on. He couldn't talk. There was a roaring in his ears. He saw Jim and Hal watching him, and wondered what Jim was thinking.

He didn't want to sit down. He just held on to Hal's shoulder and shook. It came in waves, each one building to a violent quaking during which he could barely breathe. Then it would release him for a few seconds until the next one hit. Hal glanced up the trail and Grant followed his gaze. The aliens were still in sight, but they hadn't slowed.

"We'll catch up with them," Jim said.

Grant closed his eyes. Just concentrate on breathing. But how? His lungs felt paralyzed, crushed under his chest. He bent over and gasped for air.

"Just put it behind you," Hal said.

The roaring in his head was finally dying down. It seemed to be made up of a thousand different sounds all jumbled together, and Grant suddenly realized what it was: He'd been replaying the battle over and over in his head. The sounds of scuffling, of machetes crunching into bone, feet thumping over the rocks. The wet splat of clubs pounding alien flesh, and the awful, indescribable sound of limbs wrenched from their sockets, the snapping of tendons as they were torn away. Jim shouting orders. Gabrielle's screams. The echo of every horrible sound, playing and replaying over and over until they all merged into a rumbling background wash of noise.

Grant turned away from his companions and hung his head. Tears welled up. He shut his eyes again, and at last a shuddering breath found its way into his lungs.

He took another. The constriction relaxed a little. Sweat mixed with
~~~~~~~~~~~~~~~~~~~~~~~~~~~~~~

the tears and stung his eyes when he opened them. He was drenched. He looked at Jim and shook his head. He was panting, but at least he wasn't trembling anymore.

Jim put a hand on his shoulder. "It isn't anything to be ashamed of, Grant."

Grant's legs were still wobbly, but he straightened up. "Let's keep going," he said.

They pressed on.

Grant's nausea and dizzy spells subsided and he'd managed to put the rest of it out of his mind by the time their path leveled out onto the high ridge connecting to the island's central cone. It was more determination not to fail Jim and Hal than anything else that allowed him to keep up.

After a while Jim said, "Grant."

Grant looked over at him, feeling himself somehow changed and not sure what it meant. He didn't try to hide the pain he felt anymore. He couldn't have anyway. His eyes would betray everything. And Jim was staring right into them.

Grant stared right back.

"Glad to have you around," Jim said.

Rashad had come in. The whirl of pixels taking shape on the platform now was Paula.

"He's trying to get them to let us go," Lance was saying. "While they're still feeling all guilty."

Trask shook his head. "It's a nice idea, but this way's faster." He looked at Paula, just materialized on the platform. "Talking about Jim and those guys. We have to find them."

"Okay, but right now there are too many of us here already," Paula said. "If something pops in to have a look around, we'll never be able to keep everyone quiet and out of sight."

"Agreed," Trask said. "We'll catch them on the next run."

"Find a ship?"

He indicated the sphere and Paula tapped the display and nodded. She hadn't left the platform.

"You're locked in," he said

"I'll be back for you, Trask."

"Thanks." He winked, and Paula hit the button and looked up to watch the harness. It rattled its cables, and began its descent.

"Rashad, come over here," Trask said. "Someone other than me needs to know how to work this thing."

While he went over the transporter's operation with Rashad, Trask kept one eye on the sphere to make sure nothing went wrong with Paula's beam to the cruiser.

She made a spectacular entrance, but the ship's crew recovered quickly enough. Lance was locked in and ready to go. Trask hit the button. Paula had been speaking to a group of officers, and when Lance arrived they had him carried belowdecks on a stretcher.

Good. It was all going better than he'd hoped.

Rashad was last. The instant he vanished from the platform, Trask spun the rollerball and headed back to the mountainside, in a hurry to find Jim and the others.

He heard the incoming before he'd even reached the foothills, and assumed it was Paula, coming back with the remotes according to plan.

It wasn't.

It was Rashad. "Trouble, Trask," he said, jumping off the platform. "The military's got the remotes. I barely got away with this one. Michelle warned me as I was coming in and I just pressed the button."

"Shit." It changed everything. And goddammit, he should have thought of it. Now what the hell were they—

"Did you find Jim?" Rashad said.

Trask shook his head and got up on the platform. "No. We'll have to hold off on that now." He reached for the rollerball. "See what's happening on the cruiser." Maybe they could somehow steal the remotes back.

"What do you think they'll do?" Rashad said.

"They'll screw everything up. Goddammit, the fighting's over. It's only a matter of time before the aliens leave."

"Think so? Then maybe we better let the military fend for themselves and get *our*selves off this ship before we end up somewhere in Alpha Centauri."

Trask frowned. "Yeah. But we can't let them beam in. We'll have to shut down the transporter. Find another way out."

Rashad blinked. "You mean—through the door? Go out into whatever maze of corridors is out there and get lost looking for the fire exit? Wouldn't that be, like—suicide?"

"Russian roulette maybe. We'd have a chance."

The ocean rushed in to fill the sphere and Trask changed his mind. He came about in a tight curve, heading back toward the island—and the camp.

"Think about it," he said. "They're not going to beam us out. Once they get here, they'll keep us for insurance."

The beach pulled into view. They hurtled over it.

"You wanna know what's suicide?—being in the line of fire between a bunch of kill-crazy marines and Big Mama Alien. You haven't seen her yet. She's like the Incredible Hulk meets the Attack of the 50-Foot Woman."

They slid through the bungalow wall into the conference room. And there, looking bored and clueless, sat Bentley and Barry. Barry was tapping the table with the eraser tip of a pencil. Bentley stared grumpily across the table at him. He crossed his arms over his chest, then uncrossed them. Then crossed them again.

"Don't those guys ever do anything?" Rashad said.

"It's sad," Trask agreed. "Anyway—"

"Anyway, we're screwed. What else is new?"

"No," Trask said. *"We're not. You're* beaming back to the camp. Then I'm going to unplug this thing and find a way out."

Nudging the rollerball, he crossed over into the control room. It was empty.

Rashad's bearing underwent a subtle change. He seemed to grow taller. He straightened his shoulders.

"Not," he said.

"No time to argue," Trask said, pushing him toward the platform.

"No way," Rashad said. "Fair's fair. You got to see the 50-Foot Woman."

"Really, man, there isn't time. Come on."

"I can't. Barry makes me really uncomfortable."

"Rashad, one of us has to stay to unplug the transporter. It's a necessary risk. Both of us staying is just stupid."

Rashad didn't budge. "Not going. All there is to it."

"Goddammit!" Trask said. His mind raced. "Okay!" He threw up his hands in exasperation. "But you know what? If you're staying, then I'm getting the hell out of here."

He locked in the coordinates, and turned to look Rashad in the eye. Rashad looked unsure of himself now, but didn't say anything.

"The cable's connected at the base of the platform." Trask pointed. "You'll have to pry it out. You have a knife, right?"

Looking really unhappy now, Rashad glanced at the connector and nodded.

"Give me the remote."

Without a word, Rashad removed it from his wrist and handed it over.

"You sure you don't want to go instead?" Trask said. "All the same to me."

Rashad shook his head.

Trask pressed the remote against his own wrist.

"'Cause I'm pretty sure I can find my way out. I know how all this stuff works now," he said. "You don't."

"Yes I do. You showed me."

"Okay, yeah, some of it. I didn't show you all of it." He slapped the touchscreen. From overhead came a clank and a whirr. The harness descending.

"I'll figure it out," Rashad mumbled.

"You might. If you're lucky."

The harness draped itself over Trask's shoulders. The helmet settled over his head. The button under the rollerball flashed.

"Last chance," Trask said. His voice sounded muffled even in his own ears.

Rashad didn't reply.

"I'm counting to three," Trask said. "One..."

He held the remote to his wrist. It latched on.

"Two..."

Rashad just watched him.

"You're sure," Trask said, putting his hand over the ACTIVATE button. "'Cause I'm really gonna—"

"No you're not," Rashad said.

"Oh yes I am."

"No, you're not," Rashad said again. And he reached out and slapped Trask's hand down on the button.

As he went transparent, Trask shouted, "You asshole! Why the fuck is everybody always—"

He was a fountain of sparks before he could finish his protest.

The dim light of the chamber brightened and fractured. Trask felt his body elongate. There was a buzzing sound. The cruiser's deck shimmered beneath his feet. There was a flash. An electric current surged through him, and he was dragged back through the rainbow-hued void to the platform. He heard Rashad yell, "Shit!" and the world disappeared, and again he was jerked back to the platform, like a drowned man being forced back to life.

Pixels slid down his legs and winked out around his ankles. The buzzer shut off. But the light kept flashing.

Rashad stared at him. "What's happening?" he said. "What'd I do?"

Trask jumped over the railing, and as soon as his feet left the platform, the flashing light went out. He hurried around to the back. "I'm not sure, but I have a sneaking suspicion," he said. He tugged at the connector. "Give me a hand."

There was a high-pitched whine. Then silence.

"Trask," Rashad said.

"Come on, help me."

"Too late."

Trask looked up.

Above him, a pair of marines in full battle gear stood back to back on the transporter platform.

CHAPTER THIRTY-SIX

PROFESSIONALS

THE MARINES SWEPT THE ROOM with weapons at waist level, then swung them around to cover Trask and Rashad.

"Stand back," one of them ordered, stepping down off the platform.

"Make me," Rashad said.

"They're clean, Sarge." the other said. The sergeant took note of the remote on Trask's wrist, then turned to face the platform. Another pair was beaming in. Both wore twin backpack tanks connected by hoses to large-bore firearms. Flamethrowers.

The last two—there were ten in all—came in front to back. Still clinging to the other's waist, the man behind grinned. "Hey, Vyskovsky, anybody ever tell you you have a really nice, firm ass?"

"—the fuck offa me," Vyskovsky said, throwing his rider with a rough shrug.

"Cut the horseplay, Krieger," the sergeant said. He turned to Trask and Rashad. "Sergeant Woods. Marines."

Krieger stepped down, smiling without friendliness at Trask. "Hey, looky who's here."

Sergeant Woods ignored him. "Whoever has remotes, keep 'em on."

"Those are ours," Trask said.

"Not anymore."

Trask took a step back, but someone behind him grabbed his wrist and twisted his arm behind his back. It was the one named Vys-something. He plucked off the remote and tossed it to Woods.

Rashad cursed and Trask rubbed his aching arm. "We need those," he said. "There are still people on the beach. Their lives are at—"

"The whole world is at stake, Mr Trask."

"No it isn't. This isn't a war. They—how do you know my name?"

"*Love* your show," Krieger sneered.

"We've been watching—'Mr' Trask," Vyskovsky said, his voice oozing sarcasm. "Or should I say, 'Ms'?"

"That'll be all, Vyskovsky. Mr Trask, we have a mission to accomplish." Woods looked around. "Is that a door? How's it open?"

"You have to shoot it," Rashad said.

Woods paid him no attention.

"Saving lives comes first," Trask said.

Krieger laughed. "Not in our business."

The marines trooped toward the door. Krieger gave the push-button controls a cursory examination. "Shit, even I can figure this out."

"We don't know what's going on," Trask said. "They might be friendly after all."

"Just a big misunderstanding, huh?"

Trask was grasping at straws. "Let me talk to your commanding officer."

"No radio transmissions from aboard the alien vessel."

Of course not. Out of ideas, Trask looked at Rashad. Rashad just shook his head.

"Batista, Omar, take point." Woods turned again to face Trask and Rashad. "You're going to have to come along with us."

"Nah, that's okay," Rashad said. "You guys have fun."

Trask had to disagree. "The first alien to see these guys is going to raise hell and set off every alarm on the ship. If we stay here, we'll be sitting ducks when they find us."

"Your friend's right," Woods said. He flicked his chin at Krieger. "Let's grease this junk heap."

Krieger frowned at the door, then reached out and pressed the biggest button. It slid open.

"Now, was that hard?" he said.

Back to back, he and Vyskovsky slipped out into the corridor, sweeping the opposite ends with their rifles.

"Clear, sir."

Woods snapped his fingers and pointed to the left.

"Go."

The corridor was about twelve feet wide. Inward-curving walls, made of the same dark polymer-like substance as those in the transporter chamber, converged in seamless barrel vaulting twenty feet overhead. Light strips set into ceiling and floor ran down the corridor's length, bathing everything in a deep red glow, which the walls' obsidian sheen reflected as a patch of twinkling stars. It followed them as they moved along.

The floor was layered with a soft-composition treading that gave traction while muting the sound of their footsteps.

Doorways set in the left-hand wall at irregular intervals were recognizable only by their outer control panels. The doors themselves fitted so perfectly into the wall they were invisible.

Thirty yards ahead, the unbroken curve of the outer, right-hand wall was interrupted by a large semi-circular niche that half enclosed a rimmed opening in the floor.

When they reached it, the marines gathered around to confer in hushed whispers. Craning his neck to look over their shoulders, Trask saw a deep well, almost as big around as the corridor.

"I'm with Sarge," a young-looking marine named Parker was saying. "My guess is engineering and navigation are gonna be on the same level with the transporter. No telling what's down there."

"Living quarters," Batista guessed. "Bad news."

Woods nodded. "We'll stay on course. One level at a time."

Omar and Batista still leading, they moved on up the corridor. Its curve limited their line of sight to seventy-five yards. Ahead, the lighting shifted toward a bright red-orange.

Vyskovsky turned to make sure Trask and Rashad were still following. Rashad threw him a mock salute and Vyskovsky returned it with a sneering grin.

The silence was eerie. There wasn't a hint of activity, mechanical or otherwise. No throbbing of engines or hum of electronics could be felt through the dampening treads underfoot.

Parker put out a hand and ran his fingers along the wall's surface as he walked. It was as smooth and uninterrupted as a pane of glass. He too glanced around at their captives, then turned to Krieger and whispered at his back.

"Hey, man, I missed the last episode. What happened? I thought Trask was cool."

Krieger half turned. "You didn't hear? Chickenshit hid under his bunk while my man Grant and his girls were out kicking alien butt."

Parker's disappointment showed. "Grant? Thought he was just a pretty boy."

The spookiness of their surroundings was wearing off.

"That's just his thing now. For the ladies," Krieger said. "Grant's a badass motherfucker. Lieutenant back in the First Gulf War."

Parker was impressed. "Huh. Marines?"

"You better believe it. Now, this Trask—"

"Bring him up on cowardly conduct if he was in my unit," Vyskovsky announced, loud enough for Trask to hear. "Asshole even admitted being afraid to fight."

"Really?" Omar said. "I don't remember—"

"Right before the commercial with the—"

"Clamp down on that shit, you goddamn couch potatoes," Woods hissed. "We're in hostile territory."

Omar stopped. He held up a hand, then advanced again cautiously.

They'd already passed two doors. Now they drew even with a third. Woods turned around and motioned for a halt.

"Let's try our luck." He put his ear to the door and listened, then straightened up. "It's not much, but there's something. Sounds like machinery."

"Let's hope it's the engine room," Parker said.

"You tell me how we're gonna tell the engine room from the fucking men's room in this shit," Krieger said.

Woods reached for the control panel. "You know what an engine looks like, don't you, Krieger? You see one, you're in the goddamn engine room."

He pressed the button. With a pneumatic whisper, the door slid open.

It was dark inside. But the darkness swam with a thousand multicolored fireflies.

Around the door, the marines tensed. A low, throbbing gurgle met their ears.

"What's that?" Vyskovsky whispered.

"Like Sarge said. Machinery," Batista whispered back.

"I can't see a fucking thing."

Trask pushed his way between the marines to the door and reached inside. He found the button and pressed it.

Dim light flooded the chamber. Batista cursed and jumped back as a jumble of boxy shapes leapt into dull relief. The marines threw up their weapons.

Trask stepped into the chamber. There was no one inside.

"I coulda done that," Krieger muttered. "If I was a fucking asshole."

Tall metal towers lined the walls in rows down the length of the chamber's center. Floor and ceiling-mounted junction boxes and relay housings filled every available space, their faces covered with blinking instrument panels. Cables draped from the ceiling. Bundled hoses pulsed and gurgled, alive with fluids.

The marines jumped again at a hiss when steam jetted from an overhead pressure valve.

It shut off with a click.

Omar leading the way, they crept up the wide center aisle between rows of towers, heads swiveling. At intervals, narrower aisles crossed the main thoroughfare at odd angles. The marines peered down these as they passed, still seeing no signs of life.

They reached the end and huddled.

"Where the fuck is everybody?" Krieger said. "Where's the fucking enemy? It's creeping me out."

"Yeah," Vyskovsky agreed. "A ship like this—you'd think it'd be swarming with crewmen. Or crewmonsters. Or at least a fucking janitor."

"Sarge," Parker said, "is this the engine room?"

Woods looked around, shaking his head. "I don't know..."

Krieger and Vyskovsky shared a wry grin. "Well, you know what an engine looks like, don't you, Sarge?" Krieger said.

Woods glared. "Okay, wise guy. Let's cover all our bets, why don't we."

Krieger squeezed between the wall and a large console and ducked his head under a tangle of hanging cables to disappear behind it.

The smallest of the marines rummaged in his jacket pockets.

Krieger's hand reached out. He snapped his fingers.

"Ante up, Natz," he said.

Natz and Krieger were the platoon's munitions experts, insofar as they'd had a crash course in their use by a real munitions expert on the cruiser right before beaming over. Normally Natz was the radio operator, but with the decree of radio silence he'd left his rig behind.

The crash course had lasted about a minute and a half, and culminated in Natz having a mess of charges and a detonator dumped in his lap. It was all state-of-the-art shit, the latest in plastic explosives technology, but you could have fooled him. It all seemed kind of primitive compared to, say, your standard mp3 player or iPhone.

They'd shown Krieger how to plant the charges. They were powerful. Their instructor claimed a single one would reduce a tank to a pile of unrecognizable scrap at the bottom of an eight-foot crater. Easy and simple to use. Self-adhesive. You peeled off the backing, stuck it in place and flipped the little standby switch to the "primed" position. Each came fully assembled and equipped with a built-in receiver. You didn't hard wire this shit like in the old days, the guy had said—making it sound like that had gone out with the Vietnam War. It was all wireless nowadays.

Fine. But the catch was that the transmitter had a range of only two hundred yards. So along with trying to keep track of what pockets he'd stuffed the charges into, Natz would have to try to keep track of the distance they covered as they moved through the ship. So far, taking the corridor's curve into account, he guessed maybe seventy-five. But that was irrelevant since this was their first charge.

This would be ground zero.

The transmitter was simplicity itself. A little palm-sized device with a single working part: the detonator button. Some considerate designer had added an impromptu trigger guard—a taped-on metal hood that projected up and over the button to protect against accidental self-obliteration. You had to slip your finger under it to press the button.

The plan, of course, included either finding a way out, or beaming back to the cruiser the same way they'd left. It wasn't a suicide mission. At least, not the way it was presented to them.

"Charge," Krieger said, impatient and uncomfortable in the cramped space behind the console.

Natz slapped something into his palm and Krieger withdrew his hand. After a moment's scraping and scuffling, Krieger struggled up from behind the console. He held up the object Natz had given him and fixed him with a look.

"It's a pack of gum, fucktard."

Vyskovsky snorted. The others snickered.

"Okay, sorry," Natz said, digging back into his pockets. "Dark in here."

"Keep it down," Woods warned. The marines smothered their mirth. "Natz, where are the charges?"

"I got 'em," Natz whispered back. "Couldn't fit 'em all in one pocket. Wait—" He pulled out his hand.

"Okay, here." He'd found a few inside his jacket.

"Just give me one," Krieger said.

Trask watched from a few yards off. Woods hadn't been kidding. They really were going to blow up the ship.

Back out in the corridor, he and Rashad hung back just far enough to be out of earshot of the prowling grunts.

"Is it true what you told Woods back there?" Rashad said. "One of them saw you?"

"The same one that caught you when you went over the cliff. The littler ones, they're like kids. They were playing with the transporter like it was a computer game. The big one that stopped the fight—he caught me and Paula in the transporter room, and let us go."

"He tried to put Zach back together."

"Yeah. Like maybe the little ones didn't really know what they were doing. Thought we just picked ourselves up and reassembled like they do."

"Even so. Malicious little brats."

"Yeah, but we can't let these guys start the War of the Worlds all over again. Not now."

Rashad lowered his voice still more. "The detonator."

They'd have to steal it. Catch Natz off guard, snatch and grab, run like hell and hope they can find a way off the ship.

Grant forced himself to keep up. They'd circled halfway around the mountain during their ascent, but were still far below the summit. The aliens lumbered along at a steady pace, the big one now and then slowing to let the others catch up. Despite their remarkable healing abilities, it was apparent the process taxed their strength.

Jim pointed. "Look."

All but hidden by dense woods ahead, a gleaming shape curved low over the ground, its mirrorlike finish dazzling even in the filtered sunlight. The alien ship.

"We better make our move," Jim said. "Come on."

Hurrying ahead to within shouting distance, he yelled, "Hey!"

The aliens whirled. They were startled, but made no move to approach or flee. The two groups stood regarding each other solemnly.

The big one said something to the others. With apparent reluctance, they turned away and plodded on toward the ship, leaving it to deal with the new situation alone.

Jim stooped and laid down his sword.

The big alien's gaze no longer appeared ferocious to Grant. Maybe it never was. It might be too much to expect of such a face that it could ever look benign—but there was no sign of malevolent intent.

The thing watched as Jim walked right up to it. It glanced at Hal when he raised his camera, but detecting no threat, returned its gaze to Jim.

It grunted—something between a huff and a snort.

"I guess we don't speak the same language," Jim said. "That makes things a little tricky."

The alien didn't respond, but it seemed to understand that Jim was trying to communicate with it.

Jim pointed to the sky with both hands, then swept them down and around to describe the curving dome of the barrier overhead. He watched the alien closely as he did. There was no change in its facial expression.

Now Jim pointed to himself, then to Grant and Hal, then back toward the camp. He brought both hands together in a thrusting movement—as if trying to pierce the barrier with the point formed by his fingers.

To Grant, Jim looked like some early American frontiersman, trying to communicate for the first time with the chief of an unknown tribe using sign language.

It was working. The chief understood.

It uncurled one tentacled fist and pointed at its own chest, in awkward imitation of Jim's gesture, then at the ship beyond the trees.

Then, as if hurling a stone, it swung its long arm upward. Its tentacles jabbed at the sky. It paused and looked at Jim.

Jim nodded. "You're leaving."

And then the alien lashed at the air—a demolishing gesture, like scattering a house of cards—and they knew. When the aliens left, the barrier would come down.

It was like an insupportable weight had been lifted from Grant's shoulders, and it was all he could do to keep from sinking to his knees in relief.

But there was one more thing. They couldn't just leave it like this. It was the first real meeting between humans and intelligent life from another world. The earlier meetings didn't count. For whatever reason, they had gone horribly wrong. But the bloodshed was over. It could no longer matter. There could be no thought of judgment or revenge. If the chance for peace, once presented, couldn't be secured, if friendship couldn't be established now that the opportunity presented itself, then they had failed. Not just they themselves, but all mankind.

Grant took a step forward, and Jim stepped back.

The alien's gaze swiveled to meet his, and Grant laid his left hand over his chest.

I/me.

He closed his fist and plucked it away. Holding it upright, he pointed with his right hand at the alien, and balled it into a fist as well, as if capturing within it the alien's essential being.

You.

He brought his fists close, then opened them and clasped them together before him, shaking them.

The alien stared.

Grant turned to Jim.

"I don't know if he understands," he said, feeling a little sheepish. It was kind of corny he guessed.

"I think he did, Grant."

Grant looked up at the alien. It pointed at them, then flicked its tentacles at its own chest. It turned and took two steps toward the ship, then stopped and looked back. It repeated the gesture, then pointed at the ship.

They approached it, and it walked ahead, leading the way.

Jim slapped Grant on the back. Hal called out from behind.

"Beautiful, Grant!"

In the next chamber a gigantic vat hung suspended over a cylindrical pool with a transparent cover. At regular intervals, a spout on the vat's underside disgorged a dung-like heap the approximate color and consistency of corn meal, that slowly settled into the darker liquid simmering below. It stank like rotten eggs.

Krieger hopped up on the lid and walked across it. Where the vat's lower housing tapered to pass through the lid, he found a hinged service entrance.

"Come on, Natz, gimme a fucking charge."

Natz pulled some wadded up pieces of paper and a candy bar out of a jacket pocket. A few loose coins bounced across the floor. Vyskovsky stooped to retrieve them.

"Here, hold this," Natz said. He handed Parker the detonator and rummaged through his pockets with both hands.

Trask shot Rashad a glance to make sure he'd noticed the detonator changing hands. He had.

"Jesus, Natz," Batista said.

The others grinned. It had become a running joke. But not to Woods. He glared at Natz.

"Here they are." He'd found two, in the side pocket of his fatigues. Along with another pack of gum and an iPod.

Like Woods, Corporal Omar was growing impatient. "Keep track of 'em, would you? Where're the rest of 'em?"

"I got 'em, I got 'em," Natz said. "Don't worry about it."

"Let me have both of those," Krieger said.

"How many did you have to start with?" Woods asked, as Natz handed them over.

"Around twenty," Natz said.

"*Around* twenty?"

"Twenty," Natz corrected.

"Count them," Woods ordered. "Parker—you hang on to the detonator."

"Natz, give me a couple of those charges too—in case we need 'em fast," Parker said.

Woods nodded. "Let's go."

Trask hung back, watching Krieger plant the charges while Rashad and the other marines started for the door after Omar and Batista. Krieger jumped down, slapping dust from his hands, and brushed roughly past Trask on his way to join his buddies.

"Krieger."

Krieger stopped, blinked a few times and turned.

"Why don't you call out how many are left?" Trask suggested. "Whenever you lay a charge?"

Krieger scowled. "Um, Mr Trask—sir—I'll take orders from you when you make lieutenant. Or suck my—"

Woods cut in. "Do it," he said.

Krieger's jaw dropped. "Sarge. Come on."

"He's right. You still taking *my* orders?" Woods said. "Give me the count."

Krieger suddenly realized he didn't want to get it wrong. He did a quick tally. "Eleven, sir." He tilted his head to look sidelong at Trask. And winked.

Trask winked back.

Before the last chamber, the corridor lights had gone from orange to yellow, and they'd passed another of the shafts leading down to the unexplored lower levels. Now, at the furthest reaches of their line of sight, the light became a rich emerald green.

They moved along in near silence, broken only by the shuffle of their boots over the treaded flooring.

Krieger fell in beside Vyskovsky. Ahead of them, Natz pulled a handful of junk out of another pocket, counted under his breath, and stuffed it all back.

Up ahead lay what at first looked like another shaft. But it seemed too soon, and as they drew nearer, a striking difference became evident.

CHAPTER THIRTY-SEVEN

HATCHLINGS

THE MARINES HAD LAID A DOZEN charges in half as many chambers, but so far, nothing that screamed "engine room" or struck them as particularly critical.

"This looks more promising," Krieger said.

Before them, the corridor bulged outward in a cylindrical antechamber crowned with a cupola, its gleaming dome worked with intricate patterns. A jewel-like lamp at its apex radiated a pulsing yellow light.

"This could be it," Woods said. "Don't wait for orders—if anything moves, waste it."

The men gripped their weapons tightly—eagerly. Ramos and Gurtman flicked on their pilots. A faint whiff of carbon monoxide accompanied the ignition.

Krieger reached for the control panel and turned to Woods. Woods nodded.

"Open sesame," Krieger said, and hit the button.

The door glided open. The marines poured in, fanning out in well-rehearsed fashion to the sides. Trask and Rashad slipped in after the last two—Natz and a silent marine whose name patch read "Chang".

The door closed automatically, leaving them in pitch darkness. They stood by the entrance, backs against the wall, eyes straining to pierce the darkness, their faces ghostly in the blue light of the flamethrowers' pilots.

"Somebody find the goddamn light switch."

Krieger and Parker fumbled at the doorframe.

A flamethrower was moving out across the floor.

"Ramos, get back here."

"I'm here, Sarge. It's Gurtman."

"There's something out here, Sarge."

"Gurtman! Get your ass back here, now."

Gurtman sounded like a man hypnotized. "It's the fucking floor…" His pilot flame dipped downward. Its reflection rose up to meet it, and Gurtman stooped, face almost touching the glassy surface under his feet.

Parker's groping hand found the control panel, just within reach. He hopped. His finger only grazed the button, and when he dropped back to the floor Gurtman said, "Holy fucking shit!" and let loose. A solid jet of flame thumped into the floor almost at his feet, splashing in an oval ring and ricocheting ceilingward in a spray of burning fuel. Gurtman jumped back, sweeping his weapon over the floor. Beneath its flame, writhing shapes flopped and heaved.

Parker jumped up again and swatted the panel. The lights came on.

"Jesus," Woods breathed.

Transparent as glass, the floor was a single gigantic plate laid across a shallow, chamber-wide cavity. And beneath it lay a squirming mass of fleshy shapes with bulging, heavy-lidded eyes and puckered mouths rimmed with needlelike teeth. Drumming their clawed fists against the soundproofing plate, they screeched in silent fury. Where Gurtman's flame had scorched its surface, the glass was mottled and blistered, and under those portions the creatures were cooked, the skin steamed from their bones. Forgetting their terror, others rushed over them to tear at their flesh with ravenous hunger.

The flamethrower cut off with a whump, and Gurtman stood staring down through the floor.

Trask looked like he was going to be sick. Krieger gave him a companionable slap on the back and sauntered past him into the center of the chamber. "Holy Hillary Clinton! What have we here?"

Natz breathed a sigh of relief, and the others took Krieger's cue, masking their awe with Marvel Comics banter.

"Looks like Creepy Crawler preschool."

"Hey, Gurtman, you woke 'em up," Krieger said, walking over to him. He stared at the things battering the plate beneath Gurtman's feet, scraping at it with their teeth and smearing its underside with thick saliva. "Boy, these things wake up grumpy."

"Look over here." It was Vyskovsky, his voice echoing from the edge of the chamber. Outside the circle made by Gurtman's flames, the creatures lay several thick, immobile, as if in an advanced state of rigor mortis. "Are they frozen?"

"Natz, toss me a charge," Krieger said. "Yeah, Vys, it's one of those microwaveable pouches." Natz came up beside him and slapped two charges into his palm. "Just heat 'n' serve."

Woods was staring hard at the things squirming beneath the plate and frowning. Trask could see he was pissed. Gurtman's impulsiveness had probably cost them whatever element of surprise they might've had.

But Trask didn't think that was all that was bothering Woods.

Krieger, meanwhile, had found the sweet spot: a big thronelike chair on a raised dais overlooking the nursery. He attached the charges to the thing's underside and trotted back.

"Whoopee cushion in position."

Woods stared at Krieger. "How many left?" he asked.

"Nine," Krieger said, sure of himself.

"Right," Natz confirmed.

Woods nodded slowly. "Okay."

"What is it?" Omar asked him.

Woods was looking at the spot Gurtman's flames had scorched—the squirming alien larva, silent beneath the sealing plate. "There's something…" He shook his head. "Well, lets—" he began, and stopped. And then it hit him.

"Dammit!" he shouted. "Weapons at the ready! Parker!"

The bewildered marines flinched and gripped their arms, then turned toward the door and braced themselves for attack. Woods leveled his own M27.

"Turn out the lights!"

Parker jumped and the chamber was plunged into darkness. When their eyes adjusted to the faint glow of the flamethrower pilots, Parker stood with a finger poised over the door's control panel, watching Woods.

"Now!" Woods yelled.

Parker hit the button and jumped back.

The door slid open onto a pulsating light show of flashing strobes and revolving beacons that would have rivaled Studio 54. Except there was no music. It was all utterly, eerily quiet.

"Silent alarms," Omar said.

Krieger gaped at him, then said, "Holy shit!" His words were drowned out by the roar of their own automatic weapons—which instantly set off a blare of clanging alarms echoing up and down the ship's corridors.

M27s rattled like jackhammers. The flamethrowers roared. The din was electrifying, drowning out the alarms.

And then Woods shouted, "Hold your fire!" and the clatter of automatic weapons died out as quickly as it had started.

The corridor was deserted.

But it wouldn't be for long. The jangling alarms reverberated over the walls, then switched to droning sirens. Woods had to scream to make himself heard.

"To the right! Go! Go! Go!"

The marines raced up the corridor, imagining all the demons of hell clawing at their necks. Woods shoved Trask and Rashad ahead of him, then sprinted after them, glancing over his shoulder as he ran.

There was still no one coming.

Behind him, Trask heard Woods cursing himself. They'd been outwitted by the ship's designers. Whoever set off the alarm would never know it—until they tried to escape into the corridor. While from the rest of the ship, the defenders would come running.

Which was exactly what they would be doing right now.

Glumrok looked up in annoyance at the warning light flashing over the door. She hadn't yet familiarized herself with all the ship's security functions, but the absence of sirens surely indicated a non-emergency alert status—no reason to alarm Zillior after the terrible ordeals she'd been through. The poor thing was just growing drowsy after the agonizing trauma of a late stage reimplantation. Excision of a developing limb and debridement of the tender stump from which it sprouted were not for the faint of heart.

Glumrok cooed over the youngster in an effort to placate whatever new fears the flashing light might arouse, and Zillior soon responded to her mother's assurances.

Her sleepy eyes drooped shut.

They flicked open again and goggled at a sudden blare of alarms. She hooted and buried her face in the coverlets of her sleeping pod.

Glumrok's brow tendrils chittered in distress. Strindlak! What calamity had his fumbling triggered this time, now that everything was finally in readiness for their departure from this awful place? At least she knew from the lights and fanfare of warning sirens that he'd returned. It would be fitting if all Strindlak's shipboard movements were accompanied by alarms, just so she'd know where next to expect trouble.

She reached down to soothe Zillior with a caressing tentacle and stepped over to the communications console.

The indicators told her at a glance that the site of the latest fiasco was the nursery. She navigated quickly to the desired page and swatted the onscreen RESET button.

The alarms died out.

Leaving Zillior with a promise to return soon, bringing news that all was well, Glumrok exited the chamber with an air of unconcern and proceeded to the nearest shaft.

Somebody cut the alarms.

In the sudden absence of their masking bellow, the pounding of the marines' boots over the dampening tread was like thunder.

They slammed on the brakes and stood still, listening.

Woods's face glittered with perspiration. He let out a slow, controlled breath to still his racing pulse, then nodded.

Closing ranks in a compact knot, they stole forward.

Subdued and ashamed following their father's chastisement, the siblings approached the ship in silence. The bright metallic sheen of its forward section curved away before them, a smooth, elliptical spheroid. The bulk of its mass lay beneath the rocks in the ancient and rarely-used underground docking facilities.

Snorlok touched a disk-shaped control panel. The hatch spun open and they straggled into the airlock.

Behind them, the hatch whirled shut. The small chamber depressurized with an audible sigh—a sepulchral sound that matched their mood. Moments later the airlock door opened.

With the twins in tow, Snorlok entered the corridor and turned right into the blue lower third quadrant, making for the violet sector and the nearest shaftway. Upon reaching the second level landing, they made their way toward the far end of the ship—following Strindlak's stern order that they take themselves straight to their quarters and wait there, doing nothing until further notice—by which time, he'd assured them, they'd be well on their way home.

This vacation was over.

The marines froze.

Somewhere up ahead a door had opened.

Footfalls. Omar's hand shot up for silence, but they'd all heard it. In the corridor ahead of them, something was moving. The steps were measured, even. Soft, but not stealthy like their own.

They faded away into the distance.

Omar gave the signal to advance. The marines crept forward, awash in the corridor's emerald light. A few yards further on, it changed to a muted aquamarine and they passed another shaft.

It occurred to Glumrok just before entering the nursery that a break in the wall between it and the engine room should have caused the system to signal a problem in both adjacent chambers, not just the nursery.

Perhaps it had. It was understandable if she'd missed it, naturally focusing on the possibility of an emergency here.

The door slid open and she turned on the lights.

Scanning the chamber on her way to the console beside her throne, she saw nothing unusual or out of place. The wall to her left, beyond which lay the engine room, showed no evidence of a rupture. She felt the first stirrings of concern.

Something must have happened here. And where was Strindlak? Could one of the halflings have been responsible? And if Strindlak were here, why hadn't *he* shut off the alarms, if everything was all right? Could something have happened to him? Could he be injured? Seriously enough to be in actual danger? Such things were not unheard of. What if he were lying crushed beneath some fallen generator or burned beyond recovery in some horrible accident?

With a sense of foreboding, she went back out into the corridor and headed for the engine room.

Again there was the sound of footfalls, and again the marines froze in their tracks. This time it came from behind. Krieger motioned for Trask and Rashad to move up out of the line of fire. They were quick to oblige. Under the tense stares of the marines they moved up to the front of the line past Woods. Imitating the marines' posture, they stood stock still, backs against the inner wall.

The unseen alien drew nearer. Its footfalls weren't loud, but had the massive thump of a ponderous weight—giving an ominous indication of the size of whatever made them.

Krieger's fingers tensed over the trigger of his M27.

The footsteps paused.

Everyone held their breath. There was the soft, gliding sound they now recognized as a door opening. A shuffle of footsteps, and the door closed.

The marines peeled away from the wall. At Woods's signal, they crept forward.

They hadn't gone another ten yards when the corridor bulged to twice its normal width—and in the middle of the widest section of the outer right-hand wall was a doorway.

"Whaddya think, Sarge?" Batista whispered. "Engine room?"

"Screw the engine room," Krieger whispered back. "Let's just find the goddamn exit."

The oval-shaped door's outline was delineated by a revolving series of glowing blue tracers, making it impossible to miss. For that reason alone, it seemed to offer at least the possibility of escape.

Batista tapped the control panel and stepped through without hesitation when the door opened. The others piled in after him and it zipped shut.

It was cramped inside.

The ten marines, along with Trask and Rashad, huddled up against each other like stowaways in a 747's wheel well. It was another ovoid antechamber, brightly lit, walls studded with instrument panels and humming with concealed electronics. Bracket-mounted cylinders fitted with gauges stood out from the wall.

In the forced perspective of the chamber's tight quarters it took a few seconds to recognize another doorway set in the opposite wall that mirrored the one through which they'd just entered.

"Sarge," Natz said. "I know what this is."

Glumrok completed her circuit of the vast engine room, peering into every nook and crevice. She'd found nothing untoward here either. And still no sign of Strindlak or the halflings. Trying to suppress a growing sense of alarm, she paused at the door. Could she have missed something? The indicator had pinpointed the nursery as the trouble spot. She'd have to go over it again.

Outside the engine room, she detected a faint aura of moisture, as if a pocket of humidified air were just now dissipating throughout the corridor. The main hatch was a short distance away. Someone had recently entered the ship. Or left it.

Strindlak?

She was tempted to call out to him, but a growing host of vague fears crowding her mind cautioned her against it.

This time, upon reaching the nursery, she noticed something she'd missed before—a slight discoloration of the corridor walls leading away from the vestibule. The spackling was clouded by a dull layer as if the surface had been abraded or annealed. Closer examination revealed little. The tough material was constructed to withstand rigorous abuse and betrayed little beyond the most superficial marring of its surface.

But something had happened. And Strindlak didn't appear to be anywhere in the vicinity.

She turned back toward the vestibule.

Natz chattered excitedly. "Look at the gauges. There's no other reason for a room like this, this small, with doors on both sides. It's an airlock, Sarge."

Parker found the control panel mounted seven feet up the wall and threw Woods a questioning glance.

Woods licked a bead of sweat from his upper lip.

"It's an airlock," Natz insisted.

Woods nodded.

Parker punched the panel button.

Like the shutter of a gigantic camera, the doorway spiraled open, widening in an instant to a fifteen-foot aperture. A bright glare flooded through.

Natz was right.

The sun, now high in the sky, blazed down.

Laughing, Natz sprang through the hatch, and Woods and Omar stepped outside behind him. Ramos and Gurtman followed, their boots sinking into the dewy grass. The air was misty and aromatic, filled with the pungent vapors trapped under the barrier.

They'd broken formation crowding into the airlock, and Parker, with the detonator in his hip pocket, now stood beside Trask.

Trask caught Rashad's eye.

Rashad tensed. He jostled Parker, then stumbled as he tried to shove past him, pushing him against Trask.

"Watch it," Trask said, pushing back with his right hand. His left dipped into Parker's pocket.

"Watch it yourself," Parker said. "Stop pushing."

Trask sidestepped around him and Rashad was poised to make a break for it—but Parker grabbed Trask by the wrist.

"Motherfucker!" he said.

Trask tried to twist away, but something slammed into his head. He turned to see Krieger swinging his rifle for a second time. It cracked into the side of his head and he slumped to the floor, out cold.

The quiet one, Chang, had Rashad in a headlock.

Krieger stared at him. "Whose side are you guys on?" he said.

Parker stooped to pick up the detonator. Chang released Rashad and shoved him toward Trask.

"What the hell's going on in there?" Woods said from outside.

"Parker's fooling around," Krieger said. He stepped over to join Rashad at Trask's side as Parker and the others jumped down out of the hatch.

"He'll come around in a sec, I didn't hit him that hard," Krieger said—then whirled to face the hatch.

From back in the trees had come a staccato burst of cracks—the sound of splitting greenwood.

Now came a steady crunching. The treetops billowed, as if their limbs were being shaken by giants. The disturbance advanced on the startled marines like a slow-moving tornado. They raised their weapons.

They caught glimpses of something huge approaching through the woods. Tree trunks creaked. With a screech of protesting fibers a half-dozen of the nearest bent toward the ground. Several, uprooted, were cast aside like twigs. And through the gap stepped a nightmarish shape that might have been the Devil himself.

CHAPTER THIRTY-EIGHT

THE DEVIL

IT HAD THE PHYSIQUE and posture of King Kong, but it was clothed in shimmering reptilian flesh that seemed to crawl over its brawny frame in the morning light.

The head was low slung and massive; the knuckles of its medicine-ball sized fists, made of rolled up octopus tentacles, were crowned with talons like railroad spikes.

The marines trembled before it like the Cowardly Lion before The Great and Powerful Oz.

The thing registered a hideous surprise on seeing them. It stopped in its tracks, letting out a howl that set thick membranes at its cheeks flapping like bellows and exposed gleaming, needlelike teeth the size of bayonets lining both jaws.

It was too much.

Woods let loose a chattering burst from his M27, and the others opened up. The pandemonium was instant and deafening. Bullets tore into the monster.

Ramos's flamethrower roared. The thing swatted it away and Natz howled.

"Ramos, Gurtman, hold your fire!" Woods yelled.

The thing's screams were almost human. It lunged at its attackers and latched onto Woods and Parker. Tentacles jerked tight around their middles, and Parker shrilled.

"Hold your fire!" Woods screamed.

Corporal Omar echoed the order, shouting at the top of his lungs, not even aware he was still blazing away himself until Vyskovsky slapped down his barrel. He looked around, face contorted with fear. The men had fanned out to both sides. Batista and Chang were still firing even as the thing swung Woods and Parker around to the front of its chest, trying to shield itself from the bullets tearing into it.

Krieger ducked deeper into the airlock as lead clanged over the hull.

"Lay off, you fucking maniacs!" Omar yelled.

The shooting died out.

Natz was screaming, holding up his hands. The skin hung from them in blackened strips.

Lying on his stomach in the tall grass, Grant realized the shooting had stopped and slowly raised his head.

After the initial relief of finding himself still alive, Grant's heart sank. He'd recognized the sound of M27s. The military had somehow broken through the barrier.

The cease fire could mean one of two things, neither of them good. Whoever'd been shooting had killed the big alien, or it had killed them.

He guessed it was the first when he heard voices drifting uphill. Human voices, one of them moaning in pain.

He rose to one knee and called out.

"Jim. Hal."

"Over here." Hal's head poked up from behind a clump of grass ten yards to Grant's right. Grant waved, and Hal scurried over.

"Where's Jim?" Grant said. He hadn't realized how far they'd scattered when the shooting started.

Hal shook his head.

Grant called out again, louder this time.

"Jim!"

There was no reply.

The alien was still on its feet. If its exploded torso held organs, they were pulped. Light shone through gaping puncture wounds around its leathery spine.

Woods and Parker still struggled in the alien's iron grip. By some miracle neither had been hit.

The thing's huge legs buckled. With a groan, it fell to its knees. By all natural standards, it should have been dead.

Krieger jumped out of the airlock and scrambled clear of the hatch just as the alien crumpled, twisting sideways to collapse against the hull. Woods grunted and Parker let out a yelp when the tentacled fists holding them hit the ground with a jolt.

"Natz," Woods said.

Natz had stopped screaming, but his hands were toast. Omar was with him.

"How bad?"

"Third degree. If we can get him to a medic in time…" Omar's words trailed off.

Woods's arms were free. He hammered at the thing's fists and strained to pry the tentacles apart. The alien didn't react. It seemed to be losing consciousness.

"Somebody get us out of here," Woods groaned.

Krieger approached warily. Vyskovsky slung his weapon over his shoulder and the marines came forward to add their strength to that of the struggling prisoners. They clawed and pounded, but the thing's grip was unyielding. Vyskovsky knelt beside Parker, shoulders heaving from exertion.

Rashad's voice came from inside the airlock. "Hey Krieger. Can somebody give me a hand? I can't get Trask out of here by myself."

"Shit," Krieger said, looking around.

The alien's upper body blocked the lower portion of the hatch. There was still plenty of clearance at the top, but it would mean climbing over the thing to get there.

"Help them," Woods said, grimacing.

Krieger's jaw tightened and he hesitated, then steeled himself. "Why me?" he said, but he clambered up. The alien flesh creaked under his boots. Its tentacles tightened reflexively, and Parker flinched.

Krieger jumped down into the airlock.

"What do we do, Sarge?" Vyskovsky said.

"See if you can cut through it."

Batista and Chang unsheathed long, serrated knives and began sawing at the ropey tentacles. Thick fluid gushed over their hands. The constricting loops tightened further and Parker gasped.

"Stop!" Woods said. "Shit!"

The marines stood looking at them, helpless.

Woods racked his brain for a solution, but none came. And then he had a disturbing thought. "Parker," he grunted. The alien's grip had tightened around his chest to the point that he was having difficulty breathing.

"Yeah," Parker answered, his voice weakening.

"Where's the detonator?"

Inside the airlock, Krieger shook Trask, but it was no use. "We'll have to pull him out. I'll climb up, you hand him to me."

They dragged Trask to the hatch and propped him up beside it.

"Hold him," Krieger said. He sunk his fingers into the wall of alien flesh bulging into the opening, trying to find a grip. He could hear Parker's voice outside as he climbed up.

The detonator was in Parker's hip pocket.

"Can you reach it?"

A thick knot of segmented tentacles like heavy communications cable was coiled around Parker's middle. He could feel the detonator in his pants, pressing painfully into his pelvic bone. He winced.

"No."

The tentacles tightened with a jerk. Parker moaned and his eyes filled with understanding—and horror. "The safety guard. It's going to flatten over the fucking button."

Gurtman backed away. "Who's carrying charges?" he said.

"Holy shit!" Vyskovsky swore.

Parker looked like a man in a rowboat drifting out to sea in a gale with no land in sight. "Me," he said.

The marines backed away further, sidling along the edge of the ship.

"Natz," Omar said. Everyone turned to look at their munitions expert.

With a curse, Krieger dropped back inside the airlock. Trask was coming to. Krieger grabbed him by a shoulder and dragged him with one hand toward the corridor, shoving Rashad ahead of him with the other.

"Get away from the hatch. Back into the corridor, now."

Glumrok's brow tendrils distended in horror. Beneath her feet squirmed a throng of roasted and half-eaten hatchlings. More swarmed over the injured, tearing into them, tugging the cooked limbs from still living bodies.

It wasn't the awful sight that filled Glumrok with dread—she'd witnessed such scenes many a time. It was the scorched seal, the ugly canker of hardened bubbles scarifying its translucent surface like a suppurating rash.

It was the work of some tool—or weapon.

Incredibly, the ship's security had been breached.

Natz slid his charred fingers into a pocket and moaned. He pulled out a charge and dropped it to the ground, trembling. Omar scooped it up and hurled it into the trees.

Natz reached into another pocket and howled. Biting his lip, he pulled out a candy bar.

"Fuck, Natz," Omar swore, "Take off your clothes." He tried to help him out of his jacket, but Natz screamed. "C'mon, man," Omar said. "It's the only way." Natz shook his head and backed away.

"Natz."

It was Parker, his voice little more than a gasp. "Two hundred yards."

Natz and Omar looked up at him, uncomprehending.

"Two hundred yards, Natz!" Parker said. "Run!"

Hope struck Natz like a slap in the face. He looked at Woods.

"Go!" Woods hissed.

Natz started to run.

Fired with hope, the others began cheering him on.

There was little hope for Parker. "You might make it, Sarge," he said. "Just hunker down."

"Don't give up, Park. It could still let go."

Parker's smile was painful. "It was nice knowing you, Sarge. All of you guys."

Woods closed his eyes and looked away. "You too, Park."

Glumrok hurried across the chamber to her throne, with its attached console. Shutting off the alarm had been a grave mistake. She must rectify that at once before taking further action.

〜〜〜〜〜〜〜〜〜〜〜〜〜〜〜

Natz ran for his life.

His buddies shouting encouragement over the increasing distance spurred him on, but he didn't look back.

At seventy-five yards he gave up on trying to find the rest of the charges. It was slowing him down, and speed was his only hope.

At a hundred yards, Natz gave himself over to pure reflex. His legs felt disconnected, spring-loaded, flying over the ground under their own control. His heart pounded in his chest.

He was halfway home.

Trask was leaning on Krieger's arm and Rashad was standing beside the airlock's inner hatch with his back up against the corridor wall when the alarms came back on.

The howl of sirens was deafening. Hands over his ears, Rashad turned to look outside.

The outer hatch was closing.

He sprang into the airlock and stabbed the button, but the door kept closing. He reached for one of the cylinders mounted on the wall, wrenched it from its mount, and rammed it into the narrowing opening, pressing it hard against the wall of alien flesh outside. The hatch closed around it like vise-grips. It burst with a squeal, spraying cold fluid. The hatch tightened around it in jerks, crumpling it, then jammed to a halt.

Krieger and Trask stared at him. Rashad was drenched from the tank's contents. But while frigid, the stuff didn't melt the skin from his bones.

"I'm okay," he shouted over the alarms, his teeth beginning to chatter. Krieger tore his gaze off Rashad and stuck his face close to the mangled tank. It had collapsed unevenly thanks to the bracket mount, leaving a gap of a couple inches.

The alien's body still blocked their view of the outside, but by pressing one ear to the gap and covering the other with his palm, Krieger could make out muffled voices.

His buddies outside were cheering.

CHAPTER THIRTY-NINE

200-YARD DASH

"RUN, MOTHERFUCKER!"

Natz stumbled, but regained his balance without slowing. Sweat streamed from his scalp. His temples ached. His legs were twin pistons.

He didn't know how long it took to run two hundred yards, and he wasn't sure he'd know when he did, so he just kept running.

At sixteen seconds he had forty yards to go.

Churlo and Pirnod lurched to their feet at the sudden clang of alarms. Snorlok, already standing, was riveted by the sound. Strindlak had never instructed them in emergency procedures, and not even Snorlok knew what action was called for. Growling, he cast his gaze about. A pulsing aura emanated from the communications display. With Churlo and Pirnod close behind him, he dashed to the console and stared.

The display spelled out its message in blazing red:

**INTRUDER ALERT…INTRUDER ALERT…LOCATION…NURSERY…
INTRUDER ALERT…**

The words knocked the wind out of Snorlok's chest.

The creatures had overrun the ship. Glumrok was under attack!

Grant and Hal found Jim lying on his back a dozen yards away. He was alive, but he'd been hit.

It was bad.

Grant knelt beside him.

"Jim," he said, afraid to say anything more.

"Grant." Jim could talk, but the effort was painful. He'd been hit across the gut and chewed open from right to left. Grant tore off his shirt and pressed it against Jim's torso. The blood seeped through instantly, pumping up through the loose weave in tiny red fountains and collecting there.

Grant looked up in desperation. Back in the trees, a group of human figures stood silhouetted against the bright hull of the alien ship. And something else flashed between the tree trunks off to the left.

Someone running.

"You men down there!" Grant yelled. "Give us a hand!"

They couldn't hear him. They were shouting.

He cupped his hands to his mouth and screamed.

"God damn you! Help!"

Jim gripped his arm and Grant looked down.

"I appreciate it, Grant," Jim said in a hoarse whisper, "but I don't think I'll be needing any."

Grant fumbled for Jim's hand, brought it to his chest and pressed it against his heart.

Jim said, "You look after those kids. If you can."

Grant nodded.

"Good luck, Grant. Hal." Jim's features went taut, then relaxed. His lips moved again, but nothing came out. Or if something did, Grant didn't hear it. He leaned closer and heard his name. Jim's lips barely moved.

In a voice that seemed to come from somewhere far away, Jim said, *"Saisir mon glaive."*

Grant closed his eyes and concentrated hard, willing Jim to come back. He was still holding Jim's hand when he felt it change. He opened his eyes, and Jim was gone.

He climbed slowly to his feet.

"I'm sorry, Grant," Hal said.

Grant shook his head. "I don't know what he said." He hadn't understood Jim's last words.

"I do," Hal said. "He said, *'Saisir mon glaive.'*"

Grant looked at Hal, uncomprehending. "It sounds like French."

"It is." Hal stooped and reached down, and when he stood up, he was holding the broadsword they'd taken from the Viceroy's house, that Jim had dropped by his side.

It means, "Take my sword."

~~~~~~~~~~~~~~~~~~~~~~~~~~~~~~~~

Twenty-five yards.

Natz was in the trees now, where layers of decomposing leaves muffled the sound of his boots racing over the soft ground.

Fifteen. His lungs were bursting. He was slowing. He was sure he'd made it by now, but he didn't stop. Sweat stung his eyes, blinding him. The trees blurred past.

Five.

He felt himself enveloped in a dense cloud of silence.

Time slowed.

Natz's hurtling flight braked to a crawl and he was left drifting, airborne, floating near-motionless in mid-stride, as if the air around him had solidified to a clear gelatinous mass through which his momentum carried him forward with infinitesimal slowness, and he realized with a sudden startling clarity and dreamlike impartiality that he was experiencing his own death.

Half hidden in the trees, Natz vanished in a burst of orange fire.

The marines hit the dirt.

From all sides came the roar of simultaneous explosions.

The alien's fist, and Parker in it, were blown to red mist. Hard gristle and claws like railroad spikes were transformed instantly into flying shrapnel, ripping into Woods in a blood-streaked barrage that tore him to pieces, and blowing the alien's upper body to fragments of throbbing tissue.

The throne blew apart in crystalline shards, hurling Glumrok from the dais and halfway across the chamber. She hit the floor, skidding across the transparent shield until her head slammed into the far wall.

A hail of spearlike projectiles sprayed from the exploded throne thumped into her, skewering her from head to foot. Her body jerked and twitched under the impacts until the last shard clattered to the floor.

She heaved once, gasped, and lay still.

Snorlok and the twins covered their heads as they ran. Explosions thundered through the ship behind and ahead of them. A ball of flame
~~~~~~~~~~~~~~~~~~~~~~~~~~~~~~~~

blew off the door of a utility chamber and roared across the corridor at Snorlok's knees. He threw himself to the floor and slid feet first on his back under the blast.

Churlo and Pirnod stopped dead in their tracks, clinging to each other, a thick fog of gases drifting around their ankles. Snorlok's footsteps echoed away up the corridor, and they dove into the choking blackness to follow with little but his voice to guide them.

Through the swirling smoke ahead, the corridor's yellow glow told them they were within a quarter-circuit of the nursery.

"Vys!"

Vyskovsky turned toward the hatch in a daze.

The alien had been blown nearly in two. What remained of it lay soaking in a stew of steaming gore. The hatch was closed, but a metal cylinder was sticking out of the center of it, and now something else poked through and wriggled.

"Vys! Open the hatch!"

It was Krieger's fingers, clearing bits of flesh from the opening. Vyskovsky stumbled toward it, like a man half-overcome with delirium, no longer able to distinguish between reality and the hallucinatory visions that still gripped him.

"Come on, man."

"Okay. Okay." He searched for a control panel. There was none. He ran his hands over the hatch.

"They turned the alarms back on and it closed," Krieger said.

The outer hatch was a complete blank. Vyskovsky returned to the gap. "There's no button," he said. "What about the one inside?"

"It's no good. Must be on emergency override or something."

"I can't open it, Krieg."

There was a heavy silence.

Finally Krieger just said, "Fuck"—as if the situation demanded it. The other marines gathered at the hatch.

"Who's alive?" Krieger said.

"Us," Omar said. "Woods is dead. Parker's dead. Natz is dead. The rest of us are okay. What are you gonna do?"

Trask answered for him. "Who's got remotes?"

"The remotes!" Krieger repeated. "Vys? You have ours?"

Vyskovsky pulled it out of his pocket. "Yeah." It was a tight squeeze, but he managed to push it through around the crumpled cylinder.

"Gimme two more," Krieger said. "Hurry."

Only Gurtman had another. As luck would have it, the three KIA had the others. Even if they could find them, chances were they'd be mangled junk.

Gurtman tossed his remote to Vyskovsky and Vyskovsky pushed it through—and then both jumped at the sound of a voice at their backs.

"Good Lord," it said.

The marines whirled.

A tall, blond, shirtless man approached. In his right hand he held a sword.

He looked at the alien's shattered remains, then at the marines, shaking his head.

"You stupid bastards…"

They recognized him right off. Another man trailed after him, carrying a camera. They didn't know him.

Omar saluted. "Lieutenant."

The marines gaped at Grant in awe. He stared at the carnage, still shaking his head, then looked back up at Omar. Grant's anger had left him. His eyes reflected only deep sadness.

"It was leading us to the ship. To take down the barrier."

He looked over the remains of Woods's platoon. Like his own party only yesterday, they'd fought and died for nothing. "They were leaving."

"Grant!"

Grant looked at the hatch in astonishment.

"Trask?"

"Grant. Hal. Glad to see you're okay. Rashad's here with me. Where's Jim?"

"Dead," Grant said.

He gave Trask a few moments to let it sink in.

"We were behind the alien when these men opened up."

"God, Grant. I'm sorry." It would hit Trask later, if there was a later. "Grant, we're trapped inside. We have to go. We're going to try to make the transporter room and beam out before it's too late."

The urgency of Trask's situation jolted Grant out of his stupor. "Go, Trask. Hurry," he said. "Good luck."

"Good luck, Grant," Trask said. And they were gone.

Grant listened to the sound of their footsteps fading away into the ship.

The man beside him spoke.

"I'm awful sorry, Lieutenant."

Grant turned and focused his gaze on the man. The poor grunt's expression was a mixture of fear, sorrow—and worshipful admiration.

From within the ship came a rattling boom. A puff of smoke blew through the hole in the center of the hatch in a delicate ring. A light breeze tore it apart. Grant watched it float away in tattered wisps.

"I take it your orders were to destroy the ship."

"Yes, sir," Omar said.

Another hollow boom. The fires spreading through the ship had begun setting off smaller, secondary explosions, in a chain reaction that would ultimately doom the entire craft and everyone inside it to fiery destruction.

"Then you've completed your mission." Grant looked over the decimated platoon, as if sizing them up. Then he nodded and said, "Let's get off this mountain."

He turned to lead the way. But Gurtman, following an overwhelming impulse, raised his flamethrower and gave the dead alien a prolonged blast.

The flames rose a dozen feet. The alien's thick skin sizzled and blackened.

The marines watched solemnly, as if witnessing such a spectacle were some required ritual.

Gurtman at last turned away from the alien's funeral pyre and looked at Omar. Omar gazed back at him with an uneasy frown, and Gurtman felt suddenly ashamed.

"You heard the lieutenant," Omar said. "Come on."

Shouldering their weapons, they struck out down the mountainside.

CHAPTER FORTY

SEPARATIONS

THE NURSERY DOOR OPENED just as the siblings reached it, and their mother tumbled out on all fours, trumpeting in pain and fury. They gasped at the sight of her. Spears of hard resin protruded from dozens of puncture wounds to her face and upper body. She plucked one from her throat and hurled it aside with a snarl. Behind her, the nursery was in flames. The twins ran to her, clutching at her legs. Snorlok wrapped his tentacles around a huge splinter embedded deep in her abdomen and pulled. He had to take three steps back to extract its full length. When he reached for another, Glumrok waved him away. Her wounds were a mere hindrance.

Trembling, she roared over the crackling flames.

Where was Strindlak?

The siblings didn't know. They'd left him outside.

Outside!

They jumped at another thunderous bang. Behind them, a spinning chamber door clanged against the wall and wheeled away down the corridor. Flames belched from the opening. Snorlok's rage was a match for Glumrok's.

What was happening?

The planet's vermin had broken into the ship. The destruction raging around them was doubtless their handiwork.

But where were they? The siblings had seen no sign of invaders.

Glumrok had no more time for questions. Zillior must be saved at all costs. The halflings must find Strindlak. Only he might be able to put a stop to the destruction before it was too late.

Find your father. Find Strindlak.

And with that, she left them, to disappear into the clouds of black smoke choking the ship, on her way to the lower levels—and Zillior.

Snarling at the twins to follow, Snorlok dashed up the corridor toward the main hatch.

"Which way do we go?" Krieger asked them.

"This way," Trask said. They ran up the corridor counterclockwise, from deep blue toward violet.

"What's this way?"

"The transporter room."

Krieger said, "Why can't we just beam there?"

"Too dangerous," Trask said.

Explosions wracked the ship almost continuously now. The treading moved under their feet. Clouds of thick, oily smoke rendered visibility to near zero.

"There's nothing subtle about beaming in," Trask explained. "If something's in there when you do, it'll notice."

Already, up ahead, they could see where the purple corridor lights began to shift toward a rosy pink.

"Anyway, it's not far," he added.

"Okay," Krieger said, after a pause. Then, to Rashad, "Take these things, I want to keep my hands free." Rashad took the remotes and pocketed them without breaking stride.

The corridor's curve was no longer smooth. The explosions were buckling the hidden supports. Patches of burning debris loomed and disappeared as they passed. Rashad kicked something and tripped. Krieger pulled him to his feet.

"I guess you guys were right about the aliens trying to make nice," Krieger said.

"Yeah, well," Rashad said. "Probably not anymore."

"Right," Krieger agreed.

Krieger's cocky, sardonic humor had left him. Rashad cast a sidelong glance at him as they ran. The skin was stretched tight over his angular features, his eyes hard with a fierce determination to survive.

"Sorry about your buddies back there," Rashad said.

"No time to think about that now," Krieger said.

"I know what you mean."

Krieger felt a flash of anger. "How the fuck would you—" The words died in his throat, and he instantly regretted what he'd been about to say. These reality show geeks had seen more of their friends die in the past two days than he had in three years of active combat.

They knew how he felt.

Up ahead, Trask yelled, and the direction of his voice changed from up ahead to ahead and down.

"Shit!" Krieger tackled Rashad by the legs. They hit the treading and their momentum carried them to the edge of a precipice. Rashad went over.

But Krieger held on to him, clawing for a handhold as his boots scraped over the treading. He came to a stop lying on his back, parallel to a yawning chasm, his left arm over the edge with his fingers around Rashad's ankle.

The floor had collapsed.

They were both screaming. "Climb up!" Krieger yelled.

Bending up from the waist, Rashad strained for Krieger's hand, missed and fell back with a jerk. They both screamed again. Rashad dangled upside-down in Krieger's grip.

"Never mind!" Krieger rasped. "Just hold still."

Still on his back, with his right hand and leg, he worked his way back from the edge, until Rashad's foot came up. He kept pulling. Rashad's knee bent over the edge and then his other leg swung up, and then a hand, clutching at the treading. His fingers caught hold and he dragged himself up and rolled onto the floor.

Without stopping to catch his breath, Krieger crept back to the edge.

"Trask!"

"I'm here!"

"Where's here?"

"Down here!"

Crawling, Rashad joined Krieger and looked down.

When the floor had collapsed, it had taken the lower ones along with it, and they'd given way as far down as they could see. There, far below, flickering bolts of energy arced and crackled through black clouds, to the sound of muffled bangs like depth charges catapulted from a submarine.

"Where?" Rashad said.

Krieger pointed.

Trask had sailed across and down and now hung by his fingers, one level below. Somehow, he'd managed to catch a loop of frayed treading that protruded over the lip, but now he dangled there, his weight dangerously stretching the fibers to their limit. Rashad and Krieger could hear his breath coming in panicky gasps.

"Trask," Krieger yelled.

Trask was making desperate lunges to reach the edge with one hand, but it was too far.

"Trask, listen to me," Krieger shouted.

Trask stopped struggling.

"The floor under you is only fifteen feet down. It's not far," Krieger said.

Trask was listening.

"You have to swing."

"No fucking way!"

"You can do it, it's not a big deal. Like on a trapeze. Let go and you'll sail right into the corridor."

Trask didn't move.

"Trust me," Krieger yelled.

Trask began to swing. His body arced forward, then back, then forward, gaining momentum as each swing carried him farther than the last.

"When you hit the floor, roll," Krieger said, and Trask let go, and was sailing through the air in a backwards somersault. He came out of it rolling, and the floor took him into its hard embrace.

"You did it," Rashad yelled, laughing with relief.

Krieger stared. "I didn't think he'd make it," he said.

Trask jumped to his feet and looked up.

Rashad shouted. "What do we do now?"

"We'll have to separate," Trask yelled back. "I'll find a way up—meet you at the transporter room."

"Trask," Krieger shouted. "I'm going to throw you my pistol." He waved it over the edge. "Can you see?"

"I see it."

Krieger tossed it underhand, nice and easy.

"Got it. Thanks, man."

"Trask, I'm throwing you a remote," Rashad said.

"No!" Trask yelled back. "I'll find one, don't worry. And anyway, I'll be there in a few minutes. It's not far, right?"

Rashad hesitated, then said, "Okay, right."

"But listen—" Trask shouted. "If you get there first, don't wait. Just beam out. Then—Krieger—after you've both beamed, give your remote to Rashad. And Rashad—when I get to the transporter room, if it's safe I'll beam you back. Then we can both get out of here."

When nobody replied, Trask said, "Krieger! Did you hear me?"

"Aye aye, Captain," Krieger said. "We read you." He rapped Rashad on the arm and said, "Come on."

Rashad yelled down to Trask, "See you in a few minutes."

"Go," Trask said.

He waved and turned away, disappearing into the smoke of the corridor two levels down.

Rashad trotted after Krieger. They'd practically been within sight of the transporter room. Now they'd have to go all the way back around.

"Krieger—" Rashad said.

Krieger looked around as they hurried up the corridor.

"Thanks."

"Nothin' to it," Krieger said.

They hadn't gone ten yards when Rashad came to a screeching halt and started frantically patting himself down.

"What? What the fuck is it?" Krieger hissed.

"The remotes! I can't find them. I have one, but I can't find the other."

"Are you shitting me? How the—"

"I must've dropped it when I went over the edge."

Krieger erupted with a stream of curses that would have made a midshipman cringe.

"What do we do?" Rashad said.

"Keep moving," Krieger said bitterly. "Put the fucking thing on so you don't lose it."

Rashad did as he was told. They hurried onward.

"I'm sorry, man."

"My fault. If I wouldn't have caught your ass, you'd be dead and I'd never know you fucking lost it."

"There'll be more. It'll be okay."

"Why can't we double up like we did beaming in?"

"We talked about that before. Trask doesn't think it's a good idea and neither do I. Remember *The Fly?*"

"The f… You mean the movie?"

"Yeah. Jeff what's-his-name? Sucking meat through a straw?"

"Right. I remember," Krieger said.

Finding no sign of Strindlak in the engine room, Snorlok and the twins hurried on to the main hatch. Gaining quick access to the airlock, they were met with a scene of horrific carnage. The walls ran with gore. The canister jammed into the hatch was caked with bits of purple-streaked flesh. They beat like rudimentary organs, clinging stubbornly to life.

His mind spinning terrible visions, Snorlok stepped up to the controls, while behind him, Churlo and Pirnod gibbered in terror.

With the ship on full emergency status, the normal push-button controls were disabled. Snorlok entered the universal override sequence. Beside the hatch a row of yellow panel lights flashed in series, then changed to green. The hatch spun open.

It was several trembling seconds before Snorlok realized what he was looking at. When he did, he fell to his knees in the charred heap that was all that remained of his father and howled.

Churlo and Pirnod's anguished cries soon joined his own. As the hatch closed behind them, Snorlok's rage and hatred toward this planet and all the foul things that dwelled upon it grew, filling his mind with a single thought whose weight crushed all others to flat insignificance.

Revenge.

There was only one course of action left to them at this, the final stage of the contest: Track down the cursed things that had ruined their vacation and destroy them, finally and beyond repair. Though they were mere halflings, he and the twins would scour the entire island until they'd exterminated every last one of them.

Back in the nursery, a scene of tragedy was fast developing into one of nightmare and horror. Panicked hatchlings, set aflame by the twin explosions that had blown Glumrok's throne to burning fragments and cracked open the seal at the foot of the dais, struggled toward the far end of the chamber, herding their terrified broodmates ahead of them toward the chute.

The same hard, resinous shards that had speared Glumrok had penetrated the shoddily patched rear wall housing the chute mechanism, once again severing the electrical cables.

This time, the chute had jammed in the open position.

Now, beneath the transparent seal, with the unquenchable thirst of a giant roundworm, the chute ingested all that fell within reach of its wide-open maw.

The heat blast from below soon reached withering levels. Squalling infants' flesh erupted in buboes that burst and sprayed boiling mucus over the herding trough as they neared the edge. Eyeballs popping from their heads, the hatchlings combusted as they toppled over to plunge into the chute as screeching fireballs.

And deep within the bowels of the ship, the plasma core fed.

CHAPTER FORTY-ONE

EXITS

AFTER WHAT HAPPENED BEFORE, Trask slowed his pace, feeling his way with care through patches where the smoke had become too thick to see.

Now the shaft was within sight, bathed in orange light less than twenty yards ahead. He hurried towards it. Visibility improved as the smoke, mixed with heavy gases, drifted to the floor and flowed toward the shaft's mouth. More poured down from the mouth above, forming a curving curtain around the shaftway's cylinder as it streamed down through the levels.

Trask stuck his head through the curtain. There was no ladder, just the ubiquitous treading, but its open webbing offered plenty of fingerholds. It was rough going nonetheless. The fingerholds were less than an inch deep. Tentacles would have worked a lot better.

He guessed he'd climbed about twenty feet when his hand sunk through the curtain of gases at the shaft's mouth where it opened into the next level. He pulled himself up and stepped out into the corridor to rest for a few seconds and catch a breath of oxygen.

One more to go and he'd be back at ground level.

He took a final deep breath and ducked back into the shaft.

"Are you sure this is the right door?" Krieger asked. His face, aglow in the crimson corridor lights, seemed to swim in the swirling smoke.

"Totally." Rashad pushed the button again. Nothing. The door didn't budge. Then it hit him. "Shit! The whole ship is in lockdown. Red alert," he said. "What the hell are we going to do?"

As if in answer, a labored lumbering sound rose above the rumble of distant explosions, and a monstrous shape rounded the corridor, heading straight towards them.

They slunk back out of sight against the curving wall. Rashad risked a quick glance. It was a huge alien, coming on all fours, with a smaller one riding piggyback, ducking its head to keep from banging it against the twenty-foot ceiling.

They stopped at the transporter room.

"Krieger," Rashad whispered.

Krieger slipped forward to peer around the curve. The alien was keying buttons in the control panel. Entering an access code.

"We'll go in behind it," Krieger said. "Before the door closes."

"We'll never get that close without it seeing us," Rashad said.

The gases swirling around their legs now reached to their knees. Pulling his sweat-soaked t-shirt up over his nose and mouth, Krieger said, "Can you swim?"

Rashad fished out the collar of his own t-shirt. "No."

The huge alien snarled at the panel while the little one high up on its shoulders made anxious chittering sounds.

"Just hold your breath," Krieger said.

He slipped under the fog.

Trask had no sooner made it out of the second shaft than he was forced to duck back into it.

The biggest alien of them all was standing in front of the transporter room door.

Lowering himself into the eye of the slow-moving hurricane of gases swirling around the mouth of the shaft, Trask watched. Except for a rippling effect surrounding each of the big alien's massive ankles, the surface of heavy fog covering the floor was unbroken. There was no sign of Rashad or Krieger.

They should have been here by now.

A bright vertical beam split the darkness and Rashad and Krieger froze. The transporter room door was sliding open, flooding the corridor with a widening wedge of white light. It splashed over the alien's splayed tentacles and trapped Rashad and Krieger in its rays like a pair of tadpoles in a flashlight beam.

But the alien never saw them. With its offspring still clinging to its back, it pushed inside with impatient haste. Rashad and Krieger slipped in after it as the door closed, scurrying like mice along the wall to the back of the chamber where they wedged themselves behind a tower.

Chests heaving from the adrenaline rush, they looked at each other.

They'd made it.

But there was little call for rejoicing. All was not well with the transporter.

From their hiding place, Rashad could see the console's panel display. He recognized the screen—the selection page Trask had told him he'd have to bypass. It was going haywire, blazing through CGI-creature icons in continuous shuffle mode faster than the eye could follow.

The big alien swatted at the touchscreen in vain. The escalating destruction throughout the ship was apparently playing havoc with the transporter's operating system.

Pausing to lower its offspring to the floor, the alien turned its attention to the navigational system, but here its luck was no better. It throttled the rollerball and tugged at the faders, but the image in the globe remained fixed on its last location—the location Trask had set it for before the marines interrupted his beam.

The bungalow control room.

Trask climbed up out of the shaft and stood in the corridor, undecided. The door had closed as soon as the alien passed through. He couldn't very well go in there now—not with her inside.

There was nothing to do but wait for Rashad and Krieger and come up with a new plan.

He knelt beside the shaft, keeping his head above the smog layer, listening to the rumbling explosions. Most of them now seemed to come from somewhere far away, deep within the ship's lower levels.

After several minutes passed with still no sign of the others, it occurred to Trask they might've already made it inside before he and the alien had gotten there. If they had, he hoped they'd heard her coming and managed to hide before it was too late.

More minutes passed. The stifling air seemed to vibrate to a shrill sound that Trask felt as much as heard, like the whine of a dentist's drill.

Something was coming. He could feel it. Somewhere below, powerful and unstable forces were converging toward some terrible rendezvous.

It was time to go.

The hatch was his last hope. He'd have to figure out a way to get it open.

Inside the transporter room, the huge female bellowed at the unresponsive controls. With one ferocious blow, she snapped the top rail off the platform. It spun away, clanging into the tower Rashad and Krieger cowered behind with their hands over their ears. But the damage caused by its own recklessness seemed to bring the alien to its senses.

It looked down at its frightened offspring as if all of a sudden remembering why it was here. Making a quick decision, it climbed off the platform, lifted the little one up and over the railing, and set it down in its place.

Seeming to only half-understand what was happening, the little alien watched its mother's face, flickering in the light of the strobing selection screen, and hooted in growing fear. Speaking in low and soothing tones now, its mother reaffixed the remote to its trembling forearm, closed her eyes and tapped the SELECT button.

The harness descended. The ACTIVATE button flashed.

This time, the little one closed its eyes.

Its mother pressed the button.

Krieger stared. The little alien vanished. Rashad pointed at the sphere. There, over the coffee table in the bungalow's control room, a shower of sparks coalesced into something resembling a giant albino tarantula. Snapping its blue-whiskered beak—at the end of a telescoping stalk attached to its abdomen—it crashed onto the tabletop in a tangle of limbs and splintering mahogany.

Rashad and Krieger turned back to the big alien to see it getting up off all fours to stand on two legs.

The transformation was breathtaking. The tops of their heads wouldn't even reach the thing's shins. Standing upright like the others of its kind, it could have looked down onto the rooftop of a four-story building without even standing on its gigantic tiptoes—which would have easily added another six or seven feet.

They watched it, awestruck.

~~~~~~

Again reduced to frantic rummaging for spare retrieval modules as her only means of saving herself, Glumrok reached for another of the cabinets up near the ceiling and flung it open.

Empty.

Down on the platform, Zillior's "ghost" was a blur of pumping limbs. In her panic, the little one had abandoned her beam coordinates. With the disabled locator unable to track her movements, Glumrok would have no way of knowing where to find her.

She trumpeted in frustration.

Confound Strindlak and his— A lump rose in her throat, choking off the thought. Strindlak! The unthinkable had happened. She could feel it. She knew.

Strindlak was dead.

Her jaw quivered. Forcing the thought away, she focused on her rage, cursing him, cursing the siblings, wherever they were, rushing headlong into destruction along with the hatchlings, the ship.

All because of the loathsome natives. Curse them all!

She ripped a cabinet door from its hinges and hurled it to the floor. A jumble of spare hardware tumbled down.

Snarling, she jerked open another.

From the well of the nursery, gibbering hatchlings continued their pell-mell plunge down the chute. Like a mosquito unable to extract its proboscis from a dilated vein, the fuel conduit became dangerously engorged.

Ambient temperatures throughout the ship began to rise.

Deep in the plasma core, far down in the inaccessible sublevels of the ship, the overload passed the critical stage. At the Sublevel Five main arterial juncture, a medium-duty duct seal burst open and a white-hot column of plasma roared through.

The next seal buckled but held when the plasma jet rammed into it. The plasma flared out along its underside, gathering its strength, and the seal began to rattle under the assault. With a percussive snap, a short length of its edge popped up out of its bushing, and a continuous, pencil-thin jet of plasma escaped. It streamed through, whistling.
~~~~~~

The seal creaked and strained.

The irresistible forces gathering beneath it pushed up on the ruptured edge, widening the break further. Strained beyond its limits, the seal blew. The plasma jet streaked upward like a missile, battering it through the ductwork until there was nothing left of it—then roared onward toward the next doomed seal.

Trask stood at the airlock, cursing.

Had he really thought he could get it open just by randomly punching buttons? Time was running out, and he was wasting the little that remained.

The shrill sound had taken on a darker character now, like the babbling of departed souls unleashed from some hellish underworld. Seeking escape toward the surface.

Trask wanted to scream, from frustration as much as fear. He should have never left the transporter room. He'd have to go back and take his chances that the aliens had left. It was his only hope.

The babbling was now a deep-throated roar. From somewhere came a series of muffled cracks, like someone smashing the windshields of parked cars with a baseball bat, and Trask realized he'd run out of time.

He got down on the floor, dug his fingers into the treading and held on.

The plasma jet roared through the ductwork.

It took its corners wide, puncturing weak spots around joints and losing huge quantities of energy to streaming ruptures with no slackening in its forward thrust.

Unheeded containment seals were shredded one after another in an accelerating series as it hammered its way to the surface—on a twisting path that led back to where it all began. The nursery.

It would reach its destination within moments. And there, sensing impending catastrophe, the hatchlings milled and nittered in terror.

With a low rumble, the broodchamber beneath their feet began to tremor, and the tremor intensified to a violent quaking.

When the shock of impact hit, the hatchlings went into seizure. The well of the nursery lit up under its sealing plate like a white dwarf trapped underneath an ice-skating rink.

The entire wall-to-wall seal lifted straight up out of its runners.

Released from the ductwork, the plasma stream exploded outward along the plate's underside. Like a semi-truck overturning in slow motion, the plate tilted and slipped off the wave of plasma, its leading edge crunching into the floor at a forty-five degree angle and skidding across it toward the engine room wall.

Shattering everything in its path, the plate crashed through the wall and burst against the engine in a hail of glass-sharp fragments.

Torn free of its moorings, the engine slammed to the floor, bounced and trundled toward the outer hull and crashed full length into it. The hull shrieked and tore open in a long, horizontal gash.

Rumbling and creaking, the leviathan wedged itself into the rupture, plugging it like a cork.

The treading bucked under Trask's fingers, hurling him ceilingward. He slammed into the wall and dropped back to the treading as it settled back onto the floor, cushioning his fall. He clung to it, half-dazed, until the ship stopped shaking. When it finally did, and he realized both he and the ship had survived, he got up and hurried down the corridor to investigate.

In the green section, a door he hadn't noticed before bulged outward. Further on, the corridor walls themselves were warped and split. Outside the throne room, the ruins of the cupola-crowned vestibule littered the corridor.

Trask stepped through the shattered doorway.

The transparent plate that once covered the pit was gone. Scattered fires cast an orange glow over patches of feeble movement. Beneath the crackling of flames, weak scraping and scrabbling sounds mixed with a pitiful keening. The thousands of alien larva were now a sickening mess of throbbing body parts. Many had been thrown from the pit and lay strewn across the floor, wriggling and convulsing like the tormented denizens of some medieval artist's vision of hell. Others hung from the ceiling, twitching at the ends of congealing strands of their own mucus.

Trask looked away, nauseated by the sight.

From off to his left came a light clinking of glass. Looking that way, his first thought was that the room was a lot bigger than he remembered it. But then he realized he was looking across it into a huge adjacent chamber.

The wall between the two had been demolished.

Exposed ceiling anchors dangled where it had stood, and beyond lay a junk heap of flattened polymer panels and shredded cables that must have been its mangled remains.

At the far wall of that other chamber, shafts of white light delineated a colossal machine. Trask recognized them at once for what they were.

Sunlight.

Feeling the hairs standing up at the back of his neck, he jumped down into the pit. Something popped under his boots, spraying warm fluid up his legs to his knees. Shuddering, he hurried across to the other side.

The plate had shattered into pieces that glittered like diamonds in the light. More dying larvae lay among them. It was their weak floundering that caused the clinking sound.

Trask approached the machine. There was no mistaking it. He'd found the engine room. The engine itself had been torn from its chassis and driven halfway through the ship's hull, and lodged there, wedged tight.

He hurried over, his heart pounding. He could see the world outside. But the gap between hull and engine, nowhere more than a few inches wide, followed the engine's outline as closely as a chalk line follows the shape of a corpse.

CHAPTER FORTY-TWO

STUNT DOUBLES

THE BLAST KNOCKED OVER the tower Rashad and Krieger were hiding behind and blew out the room lights. They sidled behind the one next to it, grateful for the cover of semi-darkness and hoping the big alien wouldn't come over to investigate.

It couldn't have cared less.

When they peeked out, it was glaring down at a pile of broken equipment and smoking rubble burying its feet. In the flicker of blinking panel lights, something had caught its eye. When it knelt to pick it up, they saw what it was.

A remote! They looked at each other with renewed hope, and when the alien rose back up to its full height, they looked back down at the pile of pulverized junk at its feet.

"There aren't any more," Krieger hissed.

"We'll find another," Rashad said. "After she's gone."

The chamber rumbled. The darkened sphere at its center groaned and filled with smoke. Flames licked the inner surface. With a sound like a rock hitting a windshield, cracks spiderwebbed over it.

Krieger's finger moved to the trigger of his M27.

The transporter platform creaked under Glumrok's weight. There was no disruption of Zillior's ghost—it retained her form without interference, even where it intersected Glumrok's legs.

Some danger could be involved in what she was about to attempt. While the big industrial model transporters could field multiple utility drones under the control of independent operators, most consumer models would accommodate two or three at most, and only while strongly advising against it.

But in this case the risk was far outweighed by the certain alternative. As far as Glumrok was aware, if the system crashed, the result would simply be incorporation in the field, which was inevitable anyway since it was clear the transporter was doomed beyond hope of recovery.

Onscreen, utility drone icons strobed past, obviating any hope of choice. It didn't matter. The choice of drone had become a non-issue.

Glumrok stabbed the SELECT button. It set off an angry warning buzzer, and the button flashed.

At least one of the transporter's built-in safety features was still functioning.

She stabbed the button again.

Zillior's ghost vanished, and the buzzer died away under the clank-whirr of the harness coming to life. At once, a shower of sparks erupted with a bang from a failed connector at the headset's rim. Molten wiring fountained over Glumrok's head. With a gnashing of gears the descending headset jammed.

Glumrok had no time for such nonsense. She snatched out the offending connector and tossed the three-inch cable aside. It coiled and skittered away across the floor, spitting sparks.

Peering down at the console, she guided the headset into place. Searching tendrils latched on.

The haze of smoke, shimmering orange in the light of fires breaking out up and down the chamber's length, was becoming a nuisance. Hardware and ceiling panels continued to rain down from the upper reaches of the chamber through a black cloud that hovered there like a pall.

With a sizzling crackle, a junction box exploded from the wall.

Finally, the button flashed.

Glumrok didn't hesitate.

ACTIVATE.

The glittering stream wound up her legs in shimmering coils.

Trask had searched the break around the engine on all sides from top to bottom and found it was nowhere wide enough for him to squeeze through.

Now, looking around, he saw a flattened cabinet lying half buried under the debris of the demolished wall. In falling, it had spilled out its contents: dozens of canisters like the one Rashad had used to jam the outer hatch. Many were damaged. But more significantly, some appeared to have exploded. Trask sprinted across the chamber and freed an undamaged pair from the rubble.

Hurrying back, he wedged them together into the gap between engine and hull, using a twisted hunk of metal he picked up off the floor to hammer them firmly into place.

He took ten steps back, pulled Krieger's pistol out of his pocket, took aim, and fired.

His first shot missed. He fired again and one of the tanks exploded with a bang and a flash.

Trask covered his head and ducked flying shrapnel as liquid fire splashed over the engine and across the floor. He looked up to see the unexploded tank bouncing and spinning straight towards him, propelled by a jet of expanding vapor streaming from a puncture. It leapt spinning past, and the spray hit him full in the face.

He staggered and fell to his knees, his whole body tingling. Through a multicolored haze of smoke and writhing flames, sunlight sparkled through the break in the hull. It had widened. Trask struggled up to reach for it. He couldn't feel his legs. He willed himself to float forward, and his awareness seemed to drift ahead of him, to the wedge of light that now beat and undulated like something alive. The soft shufflings of his movements set off streams of overlapping echoes. Jagged edges of hot metal vibrated past his fingertips. Half-blinded now by hallucinations, he wriggled over them and felt himself falling. He blacked out before he hit the ground, four feet below.

Krieger watched in grim-faced desperation.

He'd already thought about trying to waste the thing and take its remote, but after seeing what it took to bring down the one outside the hatch, he'd thought better of it.

That didn't leave many choices.

With just one remote left, only one of them was going to get out of there alive.

And the transporter might not even last long enough for that. It could crash any second. And then, even if the explosions ripping through the ship didn't blow them to pieces, they'd still be stuck here—in which case, sooner or later, they'd be wasted by one of the things.

It was all bad.

The alien looked like it was made of stars. It would be gone any second.

It was now or never.

Krieger turned to Rashad and lifted his M27.

"Remember what Trask said. Don't fucking wait, it'll only slow you down." He tossed the rifle at Rashad's chest.

Catching it reflexively, Rashad gaped at him. "What are you talking about?" he yelled, but Krieger had already made his move.

Darting out from behind the tower, he dove for the platform and threw his arms around a tree trunk-sized ankle.

Half-transported, the alien must have felt something. It reached down to scratch at its shin with an incorporeal tentacle. But there was nothing of substance left to scrape away—Krieger had become a swirl of motes embedded in the fabric of the alien leg.

On the floor of the bungalow control room, the coffee table's mahogany slivers stirred, then scattered outward around a whirlwind of glittering ions.

The whirlwind flattened like a boomerang and congealed with a bang into a tubular mass of muscular pixeline flesh, flopping and convulsing like a barracuda out of water.

A two-headed barracuda.

Delicate fins beat like hummingbird wings. The long jaws gnashed and snapped over four rows of serrated teeth.

Krieger was really out of his league.

He couldn't maneuver. How the hell could he? He had no arms or legs. He was a long, limbless hunk of meat with nothing familiar enough to take control of but a mouth that snapped and bit under its own volition anyway. And his field of vision was expanded in a really crazy way. He could see almost all the way around his head. If it weren't for the fact that he could see the tip of his nose about a foot and a half in front of him, he wouldn't know which way he was looking.

Not that it mattered. Because the alien was overwhelmingly in control of the situation. This thing must have had practice. He kept banging his chin against the floor as it dragged him along.

It worried at him now and then like a dog that's got a piece of crap stuck to its butt, and he kept having to duck to avoid the thing's slashing jaws.

Now they were outside. His unwilling host craned its neck, darting its head from side to side like a cobra, searching. Then he was spun around, bumping back up the steps and scraping over the floor. They were in some kind of electronics control room, full of computers and TV shit. A doorway flew past, and they floundered down a hallway.

Resistance was futile. There was nothing Krieger could do but go along for the ride and hope he got his money's worth.

Rashad stared at the glowing forms spasming over the transporter platform. It looked like The Fly might have actually happened. And Krieger's gambit was wasted if Rashad didn't do what he said.

But he wasn't ready to give up on Trask.

He hurried to the door and opened it, then jammed Krieger's rifle lengthwise into the opening, stomping on it to wedge it tight. After a few seconds, the door started rattling in protest, but the rifle held.

Now if he could just find another remote.

He'd barely begun sifting through the rubble when another jolt brought down half the ceiling and he had to dive behind the platform to keep from being buried alive.

Before the dust settled, he scrambled back out to survey the damage.

The mound of rubble had been buried under a mountain of rubble. If there'd been a remote under it, it was junk now.

He looked over at the console. Smoke was pouring out from underneath it.

It was going to be junk soon too.

Trying to ignore the glowing pixel thing lurching over it, he climbed onto the platform and tapped the touchscreen. The alarm buzzer sounded. He tapped again and it cut off. The alien/Krieger thing writhing at his feet disappeared and the harness began to descend.

Rashad grimaced as he waited for it to jam. It didn't.

Bless her heart, the Monstrous One had fixed it.

Writhing tendrils latched on. The button beneath the rollerball flashed.

Rashad looked over at the door. There was no sign of Trask.

From the sphere came a loud piping. Through its cracked surface he could still make out the bungalow control room. The piping ended with a muffled bang and the image went dark.

He looked back down at the console. The little transparent covers over the panel lights were melting.

He squeezed his eyes shut and swallowed hard.

"Good luck, Trask."

He pressed the ACTIVATE button. It burned his fingers.

Deep in the island's interior, lost and all but forgotten by others of her kind, Janet slogged through the lagoon. Turbid water sloshed up to her thighs.

A few yards behind her, the surface swelled and churned, spinning out eddies of frothy surface scum.

Alerted by some sixth sense, Janet stopped and turned, to stand motionless, watching the spot. Down around her shins, the water seemed to undulate. It surged up against her legs, and the surface swirled and parted over a long reptilian snout.

Janet threw herself forward and splashed into the water, yelping in terror. Looking back she saw the huge animal's jaws yawning open, muddy water washing over its rows of jagged teeth.

It lunged at her and she shrieked and pulled in her legs just as the jaws snapped shut with a wet crunch—missing her heel by inches.

Clambering on hands and knees up the muddy banks, she scrambled to her feet and ran. Straight into another, even larger reptilian shape.

This one stood on two legs.

It was the big alien from the mess hall. It loomed over her, its unblinking red eyes glazed with hatred.

Shrieking, she veered away just as fourteen feet of scaly horror splashed up out of the water behind her, stopped, and whirled in primitive surprise at the thing on the upper banks.

Janet skidded to a halt. Two more aliens blocked her path. She spun back around as the big alien stepped down onto the lower banks.

The crocodile's small brain grappled with the unexpected turn of events. Its hooded eyes blinked. Then it whirled again and darted for the water.

The alien stomped on its back, stopping it cold. The crocodile writhed and snapped as its captor pressed it deeper into the mud, then reached down with a clutch of tentacles. Taking hold of the whipping tail, it heaved it up from the muck and swung it head first against a tree trunk.

The crocodile's wide-open jaw cracked on impact. Its upper teeth, driven into the trunk like four-inch nails, caught and held. Leaving it to dangle gruesomely by its teeth, the alien turned to Janet. It seemed to consider as she sank to her knees.

But something else caused it to turn toward the jungle and listen.

The sound of running feet.

Janet's screams had attracted would-be rescuers.

The smaller aliens burst into excited hooting. The larger bared its teeth in a snarl. Lifting its muzzle, it roared out a challenge to the unseen enemy.

From the trees came an answering shout. It was joined by others.

The enemy had heard the challenge.

And now they came—to do battle.

Forgotten, Janet rose soundlessly to her feet.

The big alien, exulting at the promise of revenge, watched the trees in silent eagerness.

And then, remembering, it turned.

Janet froze. The alien stared at her without interest for several seconds, then turned back to face the trees.

As it did, it flicked out a single huge tentacle. The blow crushed Janet's skull, flinging her to the ground in a splatter of mud.

The alien cocked its head at a clatter of automatic weapons fire.

Bentley and Barry watched the fireworks from the bathroom window. The smoke drifting from the rumbling central peak called up images of an erupting Vesuvius in Bentley's mind.

"It doesn't look real. Like a postcard." He shook his head in awe.

"Should we leave?" Barry asked. "Are we safe in here?"

"Best to just wait here till it's over," Bentley said. "Someone'll come for us."

He suddenly jumped and let out a yelp. Looking down, he shrieked—

as much from the insanity of it as from the withering pain. A glowing sea snake had his lower leg in the vise-like jaws of one of its two heads—the other sprouting from its tail like a useless vestigial limb.

Barry screamed and jumped onto the toilet. Somebody'd left the seat up. His foot plunged into the water, wrenching his ankle. He crashed into Bentley, who was trying to kick the thing loose from his calf. It finally tore free, taking a hunk of flesh with it, and sailed through the door, smacking into the wall outside and skittering away.

Bentley grabbed his shin, hopping. Blood gushed from a bone-deep laceration.

Barry crawled to the door and slammed it shut, but Bentley yanked it back open.

"I see you!" he shouted. The thing had disappeared.

Bentley stormed out in pursuit. Casting fearful glances up and down the hall, Barry followed him into the conference room. At the table, Bentley fumbled with the lock on his leather attaché case.

"Rob, what are you doing?"

The latches sprung open. Inside were Bentley's matching pistols. He snatched them out.

"I'm going to get even with these things for making a mockery of my entire life's career if it's the last thing I do," Bentley said. Setting his jaw, he crept to the door and peered out.

The hall was empty.

"Come on."

They tiptoed into the living room. Putting a finger to his lips, Bentley stepped quietly over to a plush armchair in the corner of the room—his favorite. He lifted his wounded leg—wincing at the burning pain—and kicked the chair away.

The glowing monstrosity reared up like a cobra and struck at his chest, hissing and spitting.

Bentley jumped out of the way. The thing's jaws darted past him, snapping, then jerked back like a rubber band, coiling to spring again.

Bentley fired.

The bullet slammed the thing's head against the wall. It rolled over and slithered away, the eyes in its vestigial head goggling as it was dragged along behind.

Bentley was disgusted by the sight. He strode after it, almost calmly, blazing away with both pistols like Chow Yun-fat. The creature jerked and squirmed as bullets ripped into it.

"Die! Vanish!" Bentley roared. "Goddammit, you can't kill these things!"

A thunderous blast shook the rafters. "Krakatoa!" Bentley hollered, staggering.

The snake-thing skittered over the jolting floorboards. As the shaking subsided, it began to coil and twitch in mute agony.

CHAPTER FORTY-THREE

GHOSTS

THE ALIENS MELTED into the trees when Grant's marines stormed the clearing, rattling off bursts from their M27s, then rushed them at close quarters, charging into the hail of lead like it was raindrops.

The biggest alien leapt screeching at Grant. He met its attack head on, shearing through a half dozen tentacles with the first stroke of Jim's sword.

Around him the fighting quickly descended into chaos. The clatter of automatic weapons fire, mixed with the screams of Grant's men and the aliens' roars, echoed off the water in pounding sheets. Within seconds the lagoon's banks were transformed into a flaming arena where the combatants on both sides stumbled over weaving shadows through a world of nightmare and terror, glazed a hellish orange in the glare of burning trees set fire by the flamethrowers.

Then the crocodiles attacked.

Swarming over the banks in a blood-maddened panic, they tore into human and alien alike, lunging and snapping at anything that moved. Marines were dragged screaming into the lagoon. The battle became a melee. And the tide shifted.

The tough-skinned aliens used their tentacled feet to hold the snapping jaws at bay even as they lashed out at marines tripping over the crocodiles' ridged backs. The marines' initial advantage of heavy firepower evaporated.

One by one, they went down.

And through it all, one man drifted, untouched, invisible—a silent spectator at the end of the world.

Hal.

At a shout from Grant, two marines dashed off-camera to Hal's right, pumping rounds into some unseen assailant. Leading them in his viewfinder, Hal found his subject—one of the smaller aliens—stomping its victim into a patch of bloody ground. It looked up to meet its new opponents, and its teeth exploded through shredding cheeks.

Hal zoomed out, pulling all the action into frame.

Grant yelled, "Gurtman, hose down those crocs!" and a flamethrower whumped. Liquid fire blasted a leathery hide and glanced off to roar skyward. Hal angled up on the jungle canopy. Branches overhanging the water burst into flame.

Grant was shouting, "Hal, get out of here!" Hal panned toward him. Grant had been knocked down when he'd turned to yell, and now one of the men opened up to cover him. The big alien dove for its attacker and cut him in two.

"Hal!" Grant screamed again. But Hal was like a man in a trance, under a spell that he didn't dare break.

Gurtman had turned his weapon on the two smaller aliens. One dove screeching into the water. The other staggered towards its tormenter with outstretched arms, but collapsed under the withering fire and curled up on the ground, crackling and popping like bacon in a hot skillet.

Hal panned left. Standing over Grant, the tall marine, Vyskovsky, was tossing off bursts at the giant alien at point blank range when a huge crocodile's jaws clamped onto his foot. With both hands, Grant stabbed downward, ramming the broadsword's tip through the croc's neck and into the ground beneath. The jaws snapped open.

As the marine scrambled to safety, Grant jerked out his sword and whirled to aim a stinging blow at the alien.

Maneuvering for a better shooting position, Hal took a step sideways and tripped. Heart pounding, he looked down.

"Shit!" It was only a knobbed tree root, but the jolt had spoiled his shot. He locked back onto the viewfinder and angled up on the alien. Grant was gone.

The alien, frantic to save its brothers from Gurtman's flames, lifted Vyskovsky up by the neck and hurled him across the clearing. The marine crumpled against a tree and lay still.

The alien's huge form blurred, and Hal followed.

Gurtman never knew what hit him. The thing picked him up from behind and tore him apart.

Only Grant was left now.

On full zoom, the big alien turned toward the camera.

Grant yelled, "Run, Hal!" and Hal zoomed out, pulling him in from frame right. Grant was rising up out of the mud at the water's edge, swinging the broadsword up over his head.

Behind him, an enormous crocodile leapt onto the banks.

The thing was a monster. It shook its jaws open, and Hal yelled, "Grant, behind you!"

Sensing the threat, the alien too whirled.

The croc's jaws snapped shut on Grant's leg, and the sword flew from his grasp as he pitched forward on his face, clawing at the banks as the huge animal dragged him to the lagoon.

The alien took a step toward him—then changed its mind and turned instead toward the camera.

Hal held steady on both of them. Grant, in the background, now up to his chest in the muddy water, caught hold of a tree root. The crocodile shook him loose.

The alien was coming for Hal.

Grant's elbow bumped over a weapon dropped by one of the men. He snatched it up, and Hal's camera caught the glow of a blue pilot just before Grant's image was lost, blotted out by a clutch of writhing tentacles, reaching for the camera. Hal's viewfinder went white—and the world outside of it bright orange. Grant had fired the flamethrower, scorching the alien's hide with a searing blast. Screeching, it whirled on him just as his head disappeared beneath the surface.

But it wasn't over. The alien leapt in after him, spearing the water with its tentacles. Snarling, it waded deeper, following a trail of turbulence. The flamethrower's muzzle broke the surface, thrashed and went back under. The alien pounced and stabbed. Its tentacles came up empty.

The thing hunched forward, searching, its iridescent skin glowing orange in the firelight of burning branches crackling overhead. It lowered its head to the water's surface, trying to peer beyond.

A waterspout exploded in its face.

Only it wasn't water. It was kerosene.

The alien jumped back, bellowing.

Grant, as he was dragged to his doom, had seen his enemy looming over him and fired.

But the flamethrower's pilot had been snuffed out. Unignited fuel sprayed harmlessly against the alien's chest, deflecting outward and upward toward the tree branches over its head.

The flaming branches.

With a whump, the fuel ignited. Fire raced down the stream and roared back up.

The alien's kerosene-soaked body burst into flames. It bolted screeching for the shore and charged up the banks.

Too late, Hal tried to dive out of its path. When the bellowing bonfire plowed into him, the camera flew from his grasp. An instant later he was crushed under a thrashing mountain of burning limbs.

Hal's camera arced out over the water, and down.

Plunging through the surface, it splashed up a crown of droplets that sparkled orange in the firelight, and sank like a stone to the bottom of the lagoon.

Trask lay on his back, breathing in the fresh air, feeling the moist grass beneath him, the sun warming his closed eyelids—wondering what he'd see when he opened them, and fearing the answer might be nothing.

He'd dreamed Rashad was there, shining the sunlight in his eyes to make him wake up. Paula had been there too, made up as always of bright colors and sparkling stars.

He was awake now, watching a stream of extraordinarily vivid and impossible figures float across his field of vision like Cambodian temple dancers. They scattered when he opened his eyes.

Just a crack at first, but it was enough.

His head was still spinning. His vision was blurry.

But he could see.

He squinted at the sky, then his eyes opened a little wider, to gaze up in wonder.

He'd been in the dark behind his closed eyelids for so long, the sky seemed unnaturally bright.

He saw the tops of trees not far away, moving in slow, geometric patterns, the leaves all changing directions together like schools of fish. He watched them for awhile, letting his eyes adjust until, with a dipping motion, the white shapes of the clouds overhead separated themselves from the pale, bright blue of the sky and hung there, gently rocking.

Trask marveled at the sight. He hadn't seen the sky that blue since...

Since...

Oh shit.

The barrier. It all came back in a rush.

Blinking, Trask scrambled to his feet.

The barrier was down.

He looked down the mountainside, out over the jungle and toward the beach, and out across the beach to the ocean, and the cordon of ships surrounding it.

And as he watched, from one of the ships, and then another, something arced into the sky, until the sky teemed with them—all accelerating as they climbed skyward above the horizon toward the island's central peak.

Straight at him.

He was already running, faster than he'd ever run in his life, in long, leaping strides straight down the mountainside.

Bentley and Barry stared in amazement. The snake thing seemed to be in the throes of its final torment.

But there was more to come.

A white halo enveloped the writhing form. Its edges blurred toward transparency, then burst apart in tatters like a child's balloon, exposing a core of glittering luminescence. It bulged, then roared upward.

"Now comes the dénouement, eh, Barry?" Bentley said.

Their eyes couldn't follow it. The blistering speed of the transformation sent them reeling backwards.

Something reared up and the bungalow walls blew out. Sheetrock and powdered mortar poured down on their heads.

The floorboards creaked beneath their feet and sank, as if a great weight pressed down at the room's center. With a crack they sprang back up like a diving board, and Bentley and Barry bounced straight up in the air, just managing to land on their feet when they thumped back down.

Through breaks in the dust clouds, they caught glimpses of a pair of giant sequoias, sprouted fully matured from the linoleum. Their goose-fleshed bark rippled with an iridescent copper sheen.

The still-settling dust revealed a system of well-differentiated roots, each as big around as a python with a young bullock in its craw. The crack had been the sound of the floorboards splitting and giving way beneath them.

The root tips were presumably sunk into the sand beneath the building's foundation.

An eerie silence descended. Sunlight shone down on them from all sides, and indirectly from above.

Indirectly, because they were standing in the shadow of the giant sequoias.

But of course, they weren't really giant sequoias, Barry and Bentley both knew.

Standing side by side, the producer and his writer looked up, their gazes slowly scaling the colossal trunks to the place where they merged into a single great trunk high overhead. Tilting their heads still further back, their gazes climbed up the broad abdomen until they were looking almost straight up. And there it was: the gargantuan head and its demonic face, its features distorted in a mask of pure ferocity, looking straight down at them—its blazing red eyes boring into theirs with a burning rage beyond human imagining.

From her full bipedal height of nearly forty feet, Glumrok threw back her head and roared.

It wasn't possible to look away. The sight of Glumrok in all her glory was too awfully magnificent.

Bentley nudged Barry's ribs.

"Goddamn, Barry! Have you ever seen anything like it?"

Barry's mind, enshrouded in a pall of terror and sunk in deep despair, swam toward the light. Bentley's unexpected jubilance electrified him.

Bentley threw his arm around Barry's shoulder, and together they gazed serenely upward. Overhead, missiles dopplered past, heading for the mountain.

The colossal alien roared again. The sound rattled the planks under their feet like the elevated F train to Coney Island, and Bentley cackled with wild glee.

His enthusiasm was so contagious Barry couldn't help grinning.

The monster's head seemed to pierce the clouds—although it actually wasn't clouds, but the smoke from all the explosions, rolling down the mountainside.

Bentley tensed, and Barry braced himself for the plunge.

The slavering jaws opened wide.

Bentley squealed in childlike delight.

The alien screeched. Its head darted down with the stunning speed of a striking cobra.

It was like going over the big one, over the edge of the first big breathtaking drop on the Coney Island Cyclone.

With the cool wind rushing in their ears, Barry and Bentley opened their mouths wide and shrieked in delicious terror as the mammoth jaws rushed downward.

In the perpetual dusk beneath the rainforest's canopy, the eight-legged utility drone struggled over the crest of a low ridge. Its movements were ungainly, a haphazard progression of spastic leaps and bounds.

Zillior had never gained the experience necessary to control even the least challenging drones.

Leaves overhead seemed to flutter in the thing's glow and shiver with the blue light of its passing. The trees thinned abruptly, and before Zillior could react, her drone teetered at the edge of a sharp drop, then toppled over.

Clutching in vain for anything that might halt its plunge, the thing tumbled down, landing at last with a splat in soggy ground. Lying on its back, half submerged in dark muck, it turned its head this way and that, beady eyes surveying the terrain.

All around it rose the steep rock walls of the dell.

Zillior winced at an eerie cackling that blurted from her drone's beak. It was caused by her own panicked chittering as its body began to vibrate. It struggled up, took a step through the thick slush and exploded in a burst of white light.

Blinded, Zillior felt herself flying apart. The unfamiliar form enveloping her limbs was ripped away in tatters. Sparkling motes cascaded down her legs, winking out with a sizzle when they touched the bogwater around her knees.

She had incorporated.

It could only mean one thing. The transporter had failed.

Holding very still, Zillior turned to face back the way she had come, and listened.

From far away came the sounds of awful destruction. And above the din rose a bellowing roar, choking with fury.

Her mother's voice.

With trembling hope, Zillior rose higher on quivering legs. Glumrok yet lived.

But Zillior's hopes were soon betrayed.

Amidst a clatter of explosions, her mother's roars turned to snarls of pain and fear. And then all was drowned out by a drumming of hollow booms. They were followed by a volley of terrific blasts, building to a single sustained roar that shook the walls of the dell. Zillior arched her tentacles over her head to cover her ears and shield herself.

It ended almost as suddenly as it had begun.

The rolling echoes faded into the distance.

Leaves fluttered down over Zillior's intertwined tentacles. She lowered her arms when the last echoes trailed away, and the world around her fell silent.

Her mother's voice was stilled.

CHAPTER FORTY-FOUR

DÉNOUEMENT

WHEN THE BARRIER CAME DOWN, it didn't blink out like the other times. It melted.

With a crackle and a flicker, the mirrorlike finish turned the color of molten lead and began to flow, running down its own curving sides and dissolving them like acid, until the whole once-impenetrable barrier poured into the ocean, boiling the water in its passage before disappearing forever beneath the waves.

And there was the island.

Thirty seconds later, the sea had overflowed with landing craft speeding toward the shore. In less than a minute they'd begun hitting the beach.

Hovercraft belched armored assault vehicles. Marines swarmed over the sand.

And overhead, missiles climbed toward the mountains.

They'd watched it all from the cruiser's deck. Paula, with Michelle beside her, and Fred and Beverly behind, taking turns with a spare set of binoculars brought up by one of the crew.

Only Lance had remained belowdecks, and only because he'd been unconscious, under heavy sedation in the ship's infirmary.

After the ship's crew took possession of the remotes by force, they'd put the punters in "protective custody". But once the marines had beamed out, there'd been no reason to continue holding them. There was nothing the punters could do without the remotes.

Paula had expected Trask and Rashad to be beamed aboard as soon as the marines made it to the alien ship. But they hadn't, and there'd been no word. Her questions had all been answered with a pronouncement about radio silence that was obviously scripted.

After that, amongst the punters there'd been no need for talk. Each of them knew what the others were thinking.

When the first marines piled out of their landing craft, Hal's interns had stepped out from behind the mess hall with their arms crossed over their heads like surrendering militia fighters.

In the distance, the missiles had begun to strike the eastern face of the central peak, sending up plumes of black smoke mixed with powdered basalt and disintegrated trees.

From behind Paula, an excited sailor yelled, "I see one!" and to everyone's surprise, both on the cruiser deck and down on the beach, here came one of the alien CGI things. Right out of the bungalow, using the front door.

Marines swerved en masse from all sides to make straight for it, firing as they ran, but it made no move to flee. It broke up under the hail of bullets in horizontal interference patterns like an old TV picture tube.

They must have thought it had seen the interns surrendering, because—apparently in imitation—it raised its hands.

Of course they weren't hands, exactly.

And then it had started throwing off sparks like those things always got around to doing sooner or later, and everyone stood back. It expanded to twice its size and exploded in a cloud of motes.

And there was Rashad.

Michelle had screamed with joy.

A half second later the bungalow blew apart.

When the mother alien rose up in the middle of all the flying debris, Paula had to look away.

It was horrible. She'd seen Bentley and Barry in her mouth, and they were moving.

But it was no less horrible when the machine guns opened up, and the rocket-propelled grenades slammed into her—and then the big artillery shells that finally finished her. When the explosions stopped and Paula opened her eyes, all she could see through the tears was a blur that looked like a house on fire.

And behind the burning house, the missiles still streamed overhead. They'd pounded the mountaintop until all you could see was the mushrooming fireball, with more and more missiles burying themselves in it, feeding it to such a frenzy of violence that Paula had been afraid the whole island was going to break apart and sink into the ocean.

And on the beach, everything that still stood was razed to the ground and burned to cinders.

After an hour or so, when things had started to quiet down, one of the officers had handed Michelle a cell phone.

Rashad was on the other end.

The first thing she'd asked him was if he knew where Trask was.

He didn't. He was afraid he might have still been on the alien ship.

It had started to get dark, and Fred and Beverly had gone below when Paula and Michelle saw the pig.

It scampered out of the jungle like a lost dog that had just found its way home, then turned and ran back in, and then ran right back out again.

Then it sat down and waited.

And there he was. Crawling out of the jungle on his hands and knees, caked with dirt and dried blood. Brad.

He'd somehow survived his fall from the cliff. And the pig had led him back to the beach.

He reached for it and it came to him.

Paula and Michelle watched the soldiers help him to the shore. A boat came to take him away.

The pig went with him. Brad wouldn't let anyone else near it.

And there was still no sign of Trask.

It would be another six hours before a pair of sentries sent word through Group Command that he'd been found.

CHAPTER FORTY-FIVE

TROLL

ZILLIOR DIDN'T KNOW how long she'd wandered, trying to find her way back to the ship. The terrible sounds hadn't stopped when they'd killed her mother. They'd only paused, to start up again from another direction—the direction in which Zillior feared the ship lay.

Somehow, she'd made it out of the steep-walled valley. By then, the awful sounds had finally stopped for good—and in their absence she had lost all sense of direction.

She'd stumbled at last upon a sluggish stream that she seemed to remember, and followed it.

Several times, overcome with terror and exhaustion, Zillior had collapsed and lain in some nook or hollow by the stream, trembling and unable to move.

Now it was growing dark.

Staring straight ahead as she crawled on all fours along the muddy banks, her gaze fell upon a group of dark shapes huddled along the banks further upstream.

There was something both horrible and familiar about the still forms. Standing, she tottered toward them—and even before she was close enough to be sure, in her heart she knew.

Her kind didn't cry. Standing over her brother Snorlok's charred remains, Zillior wailed. Not even a full halfling, barely into her first mutation, she could but dimly comprehend the horror of her circumstances. But she wasn't too young to understand she had lost everything.

Her mother, her siblings, her father. Gone. The ship that might have taken her home. All dead or gone.

She was alone.

She bowed her head. Her shoulders sagged. She slumped and sank to her knees.

Behind her stood Trask.

Face covered with soot, tangled hair sticking out in all directions, his eyes burned with the crazed stare of an acid head on a dangerously bad trip.

His fingers were wrapped around the hilt of Jim's sword, raised aloft over his right shoulder.

He brought it down in a slashing arc.

The sword bit through flesh and cartilage, severing Zillior's right leg at the thigh. She screeched and pitched face forward into the mud.

Trask raised the sword again as she rolled over, eyes wide with fright. Seeing her attacker, she yammered and skittered backwards.

The sword flashed again.

The blade hewed through the terrified halfling's arm, taking it off at the neck.

Trask's face was grim.

"I'm sorry," he said through gritting teeth. His dilated pupils flashed. "There's no other way."

He swung again.

Hot fluids splattered Zillior's face. Her left arm flew from the shoulder and plowed into the muddy banks below.

She collapsed onto her back.

Trask stepped forward to stand over her. The sword came up again, and she nittered pitiably, eyes beseeching.

He struck off her head.

It tumbled toward the stream, collided with a boulder, bounced away and mired in the muck. The mouth sagged open.

The eyes dimmed and closed.

EPILOGUE

CHAPTER FORTY-SIX

THE VICEROY

"BARON" ROBERT DE MÉZÈRES, Viceroy de La Naufragée, didn't waste any time petitioning for his right to return to the island. There'd been a great deal of government red tape to cut through, with hurried and often heated diplomatic negotiations held on his behalf, but it was all settled quickly enough.

The United States had been inclined to look upon his hereditary home as a kind of protectorate by virtue of their having considered wiping it off the face of the earth and then deciding against it. It was understandable. The perceived threat was dire, and the Americans had got in the habit lately of making things up as they went along whenever they felt their hegemony was at stake.

But the threat had vanished with the destruction of the alien ship, and the Baron supposed he should be grateful that cooler heads were in control of the American military than had been in the relatively recent past.

The French had made something of a national hero of the Viceroy for asserting his legal rights and standing up to the Americans, which His Excellency found both amusing and quaint. But he appreciated the outpouring of support, based as much as anything else on a patriotically anti-American sentiment, and it had certainly helped to expedite his return to the land that was, after all, rightfully his.

The United States of course refused to be persuaded to give up all claims on the island—apart from its ownership and jurisdiction—and their agents would have to be tolerated for many months to come. In the interests of all mankind, it was argued, little Naufragée was declared of vital scientific and military importance, and much of it was now off-limits even to the Viceroy himself. Instead of television crews (though there were frequent visits from the various news agencies), the island was now populated with crews of physicists and astrophysicists, geologists, biolo-gists—even archaeologists, for their experience in recovering and catalog-ing the ruined, dead and buried. There were armies of governmental administrators and military attachés—the list was endless.

The Président himself, however, had insisted that the Viceroy's hered-itary rights be honored and that all provisions for international teams of investigators be subject to His Excellency's approval. He had approved them all, with the stipulation that his ancestral home, dating to the latter part of the seventeenth century, and the castle ruins, dating back several centuries more, remain inviolable.

Disembarking at the mouth of the inlet, accompanied by a retinue of two, consisting of his manservant and personal chef, carrying his own bags, de Mézères strode across the narrow strip of beach in a pair of dual-tasseled wingtips that filled quickly with sand.

The party climbed the steep footpath up the rock face to the house. Glancing about, the Viceroy saw few signs here of the violence that had overtaken much of the island. Though damaged and sagging on its hinges, his front door was closed, an encouraging sign.

Opening it, he found the great hall to be in relatively good order. He'd already been told that the "punters"—as they were called the world over by legions of admirers both young and old—had availed themselves of certain amenities. He appreciated that they hadn't ransacked the place. He knew about the armor. And the helmet, which had been carefully un-earthed, packed up—human remains and all—and shipped to a forensics laboratory in South Africa.

His chef begged leave to tidy up and prepare him a light lunch, and left for the kitchens through the modest dining room that opened off the right from the grand entry hall. His servant proceeded up the wide stone stair-case to see that all was well in the upstairs bedchambers.

The Viceroy opened the double oaken doors on the left and entered the drawing room, closing the doors behind him.

It was dark inside. He went at once to the far wall and pulled open the heavy drapes to let in the sun. Its light fell upon the marble tiles and over the great hearth, and there his eyes caught the glint of steel.

It was Chevalier Geoffroy's broadsword, propped up against the man-telpiece.

He stepped over to it, noting the dark stains that covered much of the blade. Taking it up, he saw at once that the oval casing with the "jewel" set in its center had been removed.

He laid it back down and walked through the den to the studio to check his email.

A tongue-tied and visibly overawed nurse ushered the patient's visitors into the private room, discreetly closing the door behind them.

"So you assholes finally decided to come pay your respects," Krieger said. "How long's it been, a fucking month?" He wasn't fooling anybody. He was smiling like it was his birthday.

"Ten days, Krieg," Trask said. "Tried to come sooner but they wouldn't let us anywhere near you. 'Fraid you might be radioactive."

"I am radioactive, man. Always have been."

"You haven't had a single visitor?" Paula hadn't met Krieger, but she was already concerned. Michelle was behind her, with Rashad.

Krieger stared at the girls like he'd never seen one before and said, "Just some idiot stopping by every ten minutes to stick a medal in me."

"Yeah?" Rashad said. "Where are they?"

"I got 'em, don't worry about it. I got drawers full of that shit."

Rashad and Trask shook Krieger's hand and introduced him—not that introductions were needed on either side.

They asked him what had happened. No one had seen him. They'd only found out where he was two days ago and come down as soon as they could get clearance. They were all in DC. They'd been flown straight from La Naufragée to Quantico for three days of grueling debriefings and only been let go the day before.

Krieger himself wasn't sure what happened. Apparently when he and his alien Siamese twin incorporated, he'd been thrown clear—far enough away to survive the bungalow's destruction.

But nobody'd known who he was. They'd just loaded him on a stretcher like any other casualty and choppered him to a shipboard infirmary. It wasn't until the Navy surgeons there got a good look at his legs that they'd shipped him stateside in a hurry via UPS Next Day Air, attention Bethesda Naval Medical Center.

"Want to see?" he invited.

His injuries—though not severe, as far as anyone could tell, were—unusual. A continuous stream of doctors came in to take a gander, along with samples and MRIs and ECGs—with a couple of endoscopies thrown in just for the heck of it. Everyone wanted to put a piece of Krieger's strangely altered physiology under the microscope.

He pulled his sheets aside to reveal a patch of green and scaly flesh with an iridescent copper sheen. It was like no rash any of them had ever seen.

"Freaky, huh?" Krieger said.

Everyone just stared. Rashad finally answered him. "Yeah…kind of."

"Kind of?"

Trask said, "We're hard to impress."

Krieger said, "That's cool." Obviously hurt, he covered his leg back up.

Paula looked at Rashad, then at Michelle.

"Well I think it's awesome. Right?"

"You bet," Michelle said.

Somebody's phone rang. Trask pulled his out of his pocket and said, "Oops, 'scuse me, better find out who this is." He moved away to a corner of the room, leaving the others to get acquainted.

"Hello?" he said.

"Monsieur. It is an honor to speak with you. You are well I hope?"

It was the Viceroy.

Trying not to stutter, Trask said, "Yes, I'm well. We're all fine. Is everything okay? Are you back home?"

"Yes, thank you. I have your note that you left in my studio. I must tell you I am most grateful for your service to me. Everything is as it should be."

"Please don't regret the loss," the Baron said. "It's only a trifle." His computer had finished booting up. He opened the mail application as he spoke. "Does anyone else know the secret? Of the tapestry?"

He nodded, listening, then said, "Yes, it's been in my family for many years—since it was made, in fact. By Nicolas Bataille of Paris," he added proudly.

"The other secret? Ah…" He smiled. "Yes, it's time the tapestry was restored to its original condition."

A thought occurred to him. "You are somewhere where you may receive email?"

~~~~~~~~~~~~~~~~~~~~~~~~~~~~

Paula's laptop was open on Krieger's tray table.

"What's your email address?"

"Trask at armbreaker dot com. All one word," Trask said.

He spoke into the phone. "We're checking it now." He lowered his voice. "So you already knew."

The Viceroy said, "In my family, we always knew this day would come. I will tell you the story when we have a chance to meet in person. I hope you will all accept my invitation to be my guests one day soon, when all of this is settled."

"We'd—" Trask began, then looked up. Paula was waving at him. "Excuse me," he said and covered the phone.

Paula said, "Trask, what's your password?"

Trask walked over to Krieger's bedside and she spun the laptop towards him. He keyed in his password and walked back to the corner.

This time Paula followed him.

"Mr—Your Excellency…"

"Please call me Robert." He pronounced it, "Ro-bair".

"Robert—there's something else you should know."

"Indeed?"

"Yes, indeed."

The Viceroy was stunned. "But is it possible? Where did you say?" He stood up from his chair. "Yes, yes, the underground passageway, of course. It leads under the castle ruins."

Taking the phone with him, he hurried out through the den to the library, where he paused to listen into his phone, looking at the tapestry— then walked over to it.

"I am going there now."

He slipped behind it to the hidden door. Once in the antechamber he flicked a concealed switch. A low-watt lamp came on in the lid of the broken case. He heard Trask speaking and raised the phone back to his ear.

"There's a flashlight beside the…all right, I have it. I'm going inside."

Pushing open the heavy door, he entered the passageway, walking quickly, keeping the flashlight trained on the floor just ahead.
~~~~~~~~~~~~~~~~~~~~~~~~~~~~

He turned the first corner. The hollow sound of his footsteps ringing off the stonework prompted him to lighten his pace, but he soon came to the next. Taking it, he said to Trask, "I've nearly reached the third bend. The last."

A minute later, he said, "I'm approaching the cells."

The flashlight beam played over the bare rock walls. They were slick with condensation.

"But do you really think—?"

From somewhere came a steady drip, water droplets falling into shallow puddles in the cracks between paving stones.

And something else.

It was quiet again now, but he'd heard something. A light scraping over stone.

The Baron felt the hairs tingling at the back of his scalp. Slow and cautious, he pushed ahead, shining the flashlight to peer into the cells as he passed, until there was only one left. At the very end, on the right.

Dimming the light with his hand, he crept towards it.

And froze.

"Yes! I see something," he whispered. He uncovered the light.

It squawked, and he jumped in spite of himself when a pair of red eyes flashed.

"Yes. Yes! It's here!"

The Viceroy struggled to remain calm. The thing stood up and backed away into a corner, trembling. It was almost as tall as he was, but it mewled like a frightened kitten.

"It's not dangerous?"

Trask exhaled. "I don't think so."

He turned to Paula.

"She's alive." Then, to the Viceroy, he said, "We think it's a girl. Her name is Zillior."

He ended the call.

Paula was smiling. He smiled back and she hugged him. Looking over her shoulder, he saw everyone at Krieger's bedside gathered around the laptop. Staring.

"Paula," he said, and she let go of him and turned to watch with him as Rashad swung the tray table around so they could see the laptop's display.

The Viceroy's email had come through. A JPEG of the tapestry's missing lower left corner filled the browser's window.

Trask couldn't say he was surprised, but his mouth still fell open.

Hand-woven six hundred years ago by Nicolas Bataille, tapestry maker in fourteenth century Paris, was a picture of the Earth. Seen from space.

Clouds and all.

ABOUT THE AUTHOR

Rock Savage is best known as the drummer for 90s noise rock group Barkmarket, who, when not on tour, could be heard regularly at such legendary New York City clubs as CBGBs.

Savage led a restless early life. Before being sent away to boarding school in Austin Texas, he spent his late childhood in Mexico, way down in Veracruz, where the jungle was the equivalent of a few blocks away down a dirt road. This reportedly explains why the jungle scenes in the book are so strikingly realistic (if indeed they are).

He moved to NYC in 1988 with industrial rock trio Miracle Room, whose shows at the original Knitting Factory on Houston St. regularly sold out.

Hunters & Gatherers is his first book.

Savage still lives in New York City's East Village with his partner, abstract painter Juri Morioka, and their cat. And yes, it's changed a lot, but what are you gonna do? You can never go back—

www.ingramcontent.com/pod-product-compliance
Lightning Source LLC
Chambersburg PA
CBHW031155310726
48969CB00001B/91